TOO HARD WRONG SPOT

3
8
5

Too Hard
Wrong Spot

MARTY SHEVELOVE

Published by
Forty South Publishing Pty Ltd
Hobart, Tasmania
www.fortysouth.com.au

Printed by
IngramSpark

Cover and title page images
YAY Media AS / Alamy Stock Vectors

About the author

A long-time racing fan with enough losing tickets to wallpaper a barn, *Too Hard Wrong Spot* is Marty Shevelove's first novel. If enough copies are purchased, the former journalist and his better half plan to set fire to their long underwear and leave Melbourne for the warm sunshine of Far North Queensland. He does not have an online betting account and can be found at his local TAB most Saturday mornings putting on a quaddie.

The author can be reached via email: Martymelbourne@gmail.com

GARY DELANEY HAD BEEN TO MORE FOOTBALL AND basketball games, covered more race meetings, enjoyed more than his share of food and drink from sandbelt golf course hospitality tents, and fallen asleep at more track and field meets than any of the younger sport reporters he shared the second floor of a suburban office building with combined.

Luckily the noise from the starter's gun at Melbourne's Lakeside Stadium a few years ago roused him just in time to see some lad from Tassie set a new Australian Under 18 record in the 100m.

Delaney had frozen his arse off at a VFL game last July, nearly been trampled by a runaway horse at Warrnambool's jumps carnival in 2009, been pissed on by a drunken biker who mistook him for a urinal during a boxing card at an out in the boondocks basketball stadium, tripped on the ice and broken his wrist after dropping a ceremonial puck at an Australian Ice Hockey League game and was once chased to his car by a pack of fans at a National Premier League soccer match which accused him of trying to pilfer the home side's star striker when all he did was ask for the goal scorer's first name so he could it write down in his notebook.

Delaney was on the wrong side of fifty and very happy to chase down stories from his desk when it was not being overrun by ants. On some days the ants came by the thousands, drawn out into the open by remnants of breakfasts and lunches eaten by his colleagues. If a single crumb fell onto the cheap carpeting, the ants were on the scene like first responders. They scurried up the legs of desks and chairs in search of more food. Battalions of their mates marched over old newspapers gathering dust on window sills to join in the feeding frenzy. Foul smelling bug spray could not stop them. Neither could ant traps. But one Friday afternoon Delaney stopped the invading horde and drove them back by using grit, determination and fistfuls of wet 3-ply, extra-strength paper towels.

"I will decide who comes to my desk and the circumstances in which they come," Delaney yelled at the others who had thoughts of attempting the journey.

During a conference call one Monday afternoon, Delaney and the other sport reporters were asked by their likeable chief of staff to go to a suburban footy or soccer game and report on the mood of the crowd for an upcoming group-wide piece on the behaviour of local fans who stirred up trouble every once in a while, usually at end-of-the-season footy finals series.

He picked a soccer match since the venue was close to home, accessible by train and would be over in less than two hours. In retrospect he would have been safer covering a V8 supercar race from pit lane. Initially, the gods were on his side. For the first week of August the temperature was mild, the wind light, and the sun was shining.

The first half saw the underdog home side stick right with the division's first-placed team. It ended—like most soccer matches—without a goal being scored. But it featured several good saves by each keeper which drew scattered applause from the well-behaved crowd of about 200.

The bar was doing a brisk business and not one coarse word was heard until half time when Delaney let loose with a few expletives while watching a horse he had a small wager on lose by a nose in the seventh race at Caulfield which was airing on a huge TV in the clubrooms.

He returned to his spot at the fence just in time to be approached by two lads. The elder of the two, perhaps twelve, wore a Melbourne Victory shirt and held a clipboard. He asked Delaney to give a donation to benefit his school. There was no mention of which school, just a sheet with about fifty names scribbled on it and the amount each had contributed. The younger lad held a clear money bag which was full of $5 and $10 notes. Having deftly avoided the woman manning the entrance gate and the $5 admission fee seventy-five minutes earlier, Delaney handed over a $5 note.

Not even ten minutes later, Delaney's day took an unexpected turn.

As two players gave chase to a loose ball near the fence, the home side's midfielder tried to kick the ball down the sideline. But the ball struck the foot of an opposing player and ricocheted right where Delaney was standing.

He was a bit slow to duck out of the way and the ball caught him flush in the face. The blow broke Delaney's glasses, a new pair he had picked up just a week earlier, and his nose. Play continued, but without the blood-stained ball that lay beside him.

Delaney was flat on his back. Stunned, he tried to get up, but once he spotted all the blood and realised it was his, he fainted. When he came to several minutes later, the home side's trainer was holding an ice pack to his nose and cradling his head. A siren sounded in the distance and Delaney knew it was an ambulance—for *him*.

He heard several people in the crowd ask, "Anyone know who that is?"

"Never seen him before," someone said.

Delaney was discharged from the local hospital more than three hours later after being treated for a non-displaced fracture of his nose. He was sporting two black eyes and his right eye was nearly swollen shut. He lied to the doctor treating him when asked if there was someone who would look after him during the night. "My wife will," he said even though he and his better half had been living apart for several years. In truth, the only one waiting for Delaney back home was his dog.

His good mate, Chris Simmons, who was surprised to get a call from an emergency room nurse an hour earlier, was at his side when he was discharged. Chris gently eased Delaney into the passenger seat of his dark blue Kia.

"Take me home please," Delaney said.

"Right after I stop for a coffee," Chris replied.

Delaney looked at him in disbelief, reached into his pocket and tossed four Vicodin he got from the hospital pharmacist down his throat. He had another eight tablets in the box, to be used only if they were needed. "They'll be needed," Delaney told the pharmacist. "I look and feel as if I just went ten rounds with Mike Tyson, the Tyson of old, not the one who got his arse kicked by Buster Douglas."

Before Chris returned to the car, which was parked in a disabled spot, he vowed never to attend another sporting event in his life and drifted off to sleep.

Chris was a counsellor with his own practice and a part-time football coach at a secondary school in the south-eastern suburbs and had his hand in more pies than Little Jack Horner.

Delaney passed a beautiful century-old church every day on his way to and from the office and one afternoon a bloke on a step ladder wearing a bright yellow shirt was changing the lettering on the church's message board while Delaney was stopped at a red light. Sunday service at 10am with Pastor Chris was the new message. Delaney looked at it and nodded. "Yup. I could see Chris preaching to the flock every Sunday morning." So, from that day onward, Chris, who as far as he knew hadn't been to a church, synagogue, temple or mosque in at least twenty years, became Pastor Chris.

Delaney woke up in his own bed early on Sunday morning with a massive headache and a deep cut on the bridge of his red nose where his glasses were usually perched.

He was having trouble breathing through his nose. It had two strips of bandages across it and pieces of gauze stuffed in it.

He trudged to the bathroom and reeled back in shock when he looked in the mirror and saw his black eyes and swollen nose. "Part raccoon, part sportswriter," he said.

He was able to see a little bit out of the badly swollen right one and figured it would be weeks until it was back to normal. The emergency room doctor who treated him the previous afternoon said no permanent damage had been done to either eye. Delaney tried to focus on an after-care sheet a nurse had given him. With the use of just half of an eye and a doctor's sloppy handwriting to decipher, it wasn't easy.

"If the bleeding has subsided overnight, carefully remove the gauze pads." Delaney did not see any fresh blood on the pads or any dripping from his honker, so he carefully removed the pads from each nostril with tweezers. He tried to take a small breath through his nose and was relieved that he could. "That's one obstacle overcome," he said.

Even though everyone he worked with knew he would be out of action for a few days—thanks to a tweeted photo of him lying on the ground with the hashtag #ballbuster—Delaney called the office to officially let them know he would not be in until the end of the week.

The sound of scratching at his unit's back door got Delaney's attention. In all the commotion of the last 18 hours, he had forgotten about his dog. "Be right there Cheyenne," he yelled.

The pooch had been on her own and not eaten since the previous afternoon. He turned the handle on the creaky back door and then opened the screen door which had a long tear in the centre held together by duct tape. Six weeks ago his landlord had promised to put in a new screen but hadn't. The rent had to be paid on time though. Delaney was told when he signed the lease that there would be no grace period. Pay on time or you're out. A new tenant would move in before he even got his bond back.

Delaney took a seat on the step and played with the bubbly golden lab for a few minutes. When she licked her empty food bowl Delaney went inside and opened a fresh can of food which seemed to increase in price on a monthly basis. He mixed two tablespoons of meat with a big scoop of dried food that some young vet had recommended at her last check-up. It was supposed to keep her coat looking healthy and keep her weight down. To Delaney's eye Cheyenne's coat looked the same. Her weight might have gone up by a kilogram but that was probably the result of their shorter and less frequent walks during the cold Melbourne winter.

Cheyenne polished off her breakfast within a minute, took a large drink of water, laid down on her favourite mat, which had been vacuumed a few days earlier, and closed her eyes.

Delaney had a cup of coffee and some toast, the first food he had eaten in nearly twenty hours, and then showered. That turned out be a mistake since each drop of water that landed on his swollen nose and eyes felt like a bee sting. He dried himself off with a fresh towel and went to his bedroom where he put on a pair of jeans and a long-sleeved shirt. He dug around for the spare pairs of glasses he kept in the back of the messy top drawer of his bedside table, grabbed his jacket from the couch and walked three blocks to the shops to get a few essentials; his eyes hidden behind a pair of sunnies on what was a cloudy and dreary day.

On the way back, just when he wondered what else could go wrong, he put his right foot in a pile of dog shit which one of his neighbour's dogs had deposited on the footpath. Rather than clean the shoe, he took it off and tossed it and the other one in a bin on the nature strip and walked the remaining block home in his socks.

"This," he said, "is not going to be my weekend."

As he got closer to his front door and took out his keys, his neighbour, Susan, a happily married mother of two who was stunning even in a baseball cap, hoodie and no make-up, waved hello.

"What happened to you?" she asked. "I saw your mate drop you off yesterday and he basically had to carry you inside."

"Just a little accident," Delaney said. "I'll be okay, really."

She saw the nasty gash on the bridge of his nose and gently ran her finger over it. Suddenly he felt much better.

"Were you in a fight?"

"No," he said as he lowered his head. In fact, the last fight he had been involved in was a draw, with no bruises or breaks. He and a seventh-grade schoolmate, Bruce something or other, threw punches at each other one afternoon, none of which landed, before they tumbled into the gutter and were pried apart. For the life of him he could not remember what it was about, probably something to do with footy trading cards.

"I was at a soccer game yesterday afternoon and got hit in the face with a ball. It broke my nose and,"—he took his sunnies off—"did this to my eyes."

Susan gasped, took the sunnies from his hand and put them back on his face. "Much better like this," she said. "Let me know if you need anything," she offered as she trotted off for her morning run.

Inside his flat, Delaney put some ice cubes in a wash cloth, walked to his recliner, the one he bought for himself on his last birthday—no one else was going to—leaned back and put the cold cloth on his eyes and nose. "Much better," he said.

2

DELANEY WAS FILLING CHEYENNE'S WATER BOWL outside when he heard his phone ring—his land line—the first time it had rung in weeks. He hoped it was Pastor Chris telling him he had his mobile phone.

It was. They agreed to meet over lunch at the local sporting club. Delaney did not feel like driving so he hopped on the train for all of one stop. He got to the club early and decided to put a few dollars on the first two races at Cranbourne.

Being an early Sunday afternoon, there were just a handful of punters present. Several others were tucking into the lunchtime specials. Waiting for his chicken parma, Delaney placed a couple of bets. He watched his $6.50 chance in the first take a decent-sized lead into the stretch only for it to be collared at the 100m mark. He backed the $4 favourite in the second and it got up, putting him ahead $15, the same price as his parma and pot. He saw Pastor Chris wander in and gave him a wave. Chris was an outgoing fellow and wherever he went he seemed to know at least a handful of people. Today was no different. Delaney watched him shake a few hands and say hello to a gorgeous young woman behind the bar before he sat down.

"I've seen you look better pal. How's that nose of yours?" Chris asked.

"Sore, Pastor, sore."

"Here's your mobile. You're about as popular as I am."

Delaney looked at his phone which badly needed recharging. "One message? That's it?"

A moment later his phone pinged with the sound of an incoming message.

"That's more like it," Delaney said. He looked down at his phone and shook his head.

"Who's it from? One of your co-workers?" Chris asked.

"It's an email from the hospital. It's not a follow-up to see how I'm doing, it's a bloody marketing survey asking how my hospital experience was. Can you believe it? 'Ranging from one, which is poor, to ten which is excellent, how would you rate the care you received?'"

Delaney turned the phone off and stuffed it in his pants pocket.

Delaney's first day back on the job was the following Saturday. His nose was healing nicely and the swelling around his eyes had noticeably decreased. But he kept his prescription sunnies on anyway as he made his way from his dependable Honda to a local footy club's function room for a luncheon he'd agreed to attend months ago.

The tucker was good, and he had a good yack with Pastor Chris, who was the compere of the event.

Chris helped put the names to the faces of an endless stream of club officials and former players to whom he was introduced. Soon after, as he made his way down to the fence to watch the game, Delaney started feeling uncomfortable.

He traced the pain in his stomach to the two servings of lasagne he had consumed. "Have another portion," someone said as he noticed Delaney's empty plate. He did and downed it with two beers. It would have been impolite to say no. Plus, it was free.

He regretted it as he inched his way along Nepean Highway after ducking from the ground at quarter-time. The local side was six goals down despite having the breeze at their backs and had little hope of turning things around.

Meanwhile Delaney was going against the breeze. Only this breeze had turned into a gale; in his gut. He would never make it home before the old trapdoor opened, so he pulled into the massive Southland shopping centre. Amazingly, he found an empty parking spot close to the entrance and made a run to the toilets.

The closer he got, the more the need to go increased. Running down the mall corridor he found his path partially blocked by a large woman pushing a pram the size of a tram. He dodged the obstacle like Joel Selwood evading a tackler, looked up and saw the toilet entrance less than twenty metres away.

As he got to the door of the men's room it was blocked by a cart along with a sign that read 'cleaning in process'.

"The one time of the week they clean the thing and it's now?"

He turned and saw he had two options; the ladies' or the disabled toilet.

He'd have a lot more explaining to do if was found in the women's toilet, so he burst through the door marked 'disabled'. He saw two cubicles. One was occupied, the other, luckily, was empty. With a major disposal just seconds away Delaney lined the public toilet seat with ten layers of toilet roll instead of the usual twenty, sat down and breathed a sigh of relief.

A small smile came across his face. But there was nothing to smile about for the man in the other cubicle who had to hold his nose as he finished his business.

Delaney heard the toilet flush and then a flurry of expletives as the fellow unlocked the cubicle and made his way to the door without even stopping to wash his hands. "You're disabled in more ways than one mate," he barked as he left.

Delaney laughed, hiked up his trousers, flushed, unlocked the cubicle and walked to the sink. Feeling like a new man, he washed his hands, put them under a hand dryer that was as loud as a footy siren and opened the door only to come face-to-face with an old-timer in a wheelchair.

"You don't look disabled to me," the elderly man said.

"Maybe not now, but five minutes ago I was," Delaney said as he walked off.

JOHNNY PASTRAMI AND FRANKIE 'FINGERS' TANNEN-baum had a look around the members' area at Flemington. It was a late winter Saturday afternoon at headquarters and plenty of cashed-up men and women from the top end of town were sheltered from the cold wind blowing in off the Maribyrnong River, enjoying a drink in the members' area's numerous bars and sitting down to sumptuous lunches in the dining areas.

Each was proud of the fact that they never had done an honest day's work in their lives. Pastrami, the more dapper of the two with his thick, dark, slicked-back hair and his expensive suits and jewellery, met the more unassuming Tannenbaum in a low security prison for blue collar thieves in Northern Victoria two years earlier. Pastrami was serving sixteen months for his part in a real estate Ponzi scheme while Fingers, one of the best pickpockets in the business, and an astute numbers man, had taken the fall for an organised crime ring's illegal bookmaking racket which the cops got wind of a day before Hawthorn's third straight AFL grand final victory.

"If you take the rap for us on this one Frankie you can walk away from us scot-free if you want," explained Tony 'Breadsticks' Battaglia, the man in charge of the elaborate bookmaking operation for which Tannenbaum set the lines and prices. The cops want us to give someone up, ya know, to parade in front of the media to show everyone they're cracking down on organised crime. I'm getting some heat from my boss. We'll make a deal and the most you'll have to serve is eighteen months tops at one of those country clubs up north. And when you get out, we'll set you up with an apartment for as long as you want and give you ten grand. Waddya say? You in?"

Tannenbaum was in his late thirties and had never served any time in his life. He'd been fined and placed on probation for a few 'minor indiscretions' as his lawyer called them and was not happy about the prospect of serving real time. But to say no to Breadsticks would mean retribution in the unkindest of ways. He gazed down at his fingers which had made him a very comfortable living since high school. The thought of losing one or two was most unpleasant. He took a sip of his latte and looked across the table of the Carlton café to which Breadsticks had summoned him. The bookmaker adjusted his gold cufflinks and redid a button on the vest he wore over a navy-blue shirt.

"All right. I'll do it, but then I'm out. We have a deal?"

"We do," Battaglia said as he extended his hand to seal the arrangement.

"All the particulars have been sorted," he told Tannenbaum. "The cops will come to your apartment on Thursday morning, take you into custody and escort you to police headquarters on St Kilda Rd where the media will be waiting. Those guys are ruthless. They'll stick cameras in your face and pepper you with questions but do not say a word. Not one word. Do not even nod. Our lawyers will take it from there. You'll be well looked after. It's part of the deal we made with the cops."

Tannenbaum nodded.

Two days later at around noon, just as Battaglia said, there was a loud knock on the door of Tannenbaum's rented one-bedroom Carlton apartment. Four cops, two of them detectives in plain clothes, opened the door which Tannenbaum had left unlocked.

"Frank Tannenbaum, you are under arrest," the larger of the two detectives said.

One uniformed officer put him in handcuffs as the detective read him his rights.

"I put a few things in a bag; medicine, toothbrush. Is it okay if I take it along?" Tannenbaum asked.

"You're not going on holiday mate. You're going to jail," the detective doing the talking said. "The bag stays here. You'll be provided with whatever you need down at the station. Let's go."

The officers marched him down one flight of stairs and tossed him into the back of a waiting sedan which pulled away from the kerb. It travelled all of fifty metres before it came to a stop, a victim of Carlton's lunchtime traffic.

"I knew we should have done this earlier," the copper doing the driving said.

Two weeks later, after a plea bargain in front of a usually tough judge who was aware of the deal with the police, Tannenbaum was shipped off to a minimum-security prison called Dhurringile in Murchison, 150 kilometres north of Melbourne, which housed just over 200 prisoners.

He met thirty-six-year-old Pastrami in the prison mess hall the first week he was there. They shared the same cottage with four others. Each prisoner had his own bedroom and there was a main lounge with a television. There were no cooking facilities in the cottage but since neither could cook it didn't matter much.

Tannenbaum and Pastrami could barely stomach the food in the mess hall and had to make do without many of their Lygon Street favourites; Veal Verde, Saltimbocca Alla Romana, Polo Parmigiana, and Gnocchi Sorrentina. There was no tiramisu on the dessert menu, only tasteless jelly, and the coffee was barely drinkable. The first Friday Tannenbaum spent in stir, the prison chef, his title was clearly not deserved, served up his version of lasagne. Pastrami quipped that the person in the kitchen should be serving time for impersonating a chef. Tannenbaum missed Italian cooking so much he even asked for an extra serving which was given to him.

Pastrami, which Tannenbaum later found out was his real name, had a love of mayonnaise which he put on everything. After about a week of watching him slather mayonnaise on every sandwich he ate, Tannenbaum started calling his fellow prisoner 'Mayo'.

The pair, who had never crossed paths on the outside, each liked to have a punt on the horses and kept track of the happenings around the racetracks through the two daily Melbourne papers, which were available every day, and the free over-the-air racing channel. Pastrami was the bigger gambler of the two, often putting on bets of $200 and $300, while Tannenbaum was content to wager $5 and $10 a race. Amazingly, each won more than they lost as a result of hours of form work which included going to trials and jump-outs prior to their being locked up. Their side jobs in real estate and pickpocketing allowed them to afford the finer things in life. Pastrami was the flashier of the two when it came to clothes, cars, women, apartments and furnishings.

Pastrami had thousands stashed away waiting for him in secret bank accounts and investments in other people's names. He convinced prosecutors at his trial that he had gambled away much of what he made through his dodgy real estate scheme which fleeced dozens of people of their life savings. He didn't feel anything towards the victims.

"If they are greedy enough to think they can get fourteen per cent on a real estate investment they deserve to be taken advantage of," Pastrami told Tannenbaum one afternoon while they were 'working' in the prison garden which supplied much of the produce to the prison's kitchen. If only the chef knew what to do with it all.

Tannenbaum also had no qualms stealing from the well to do which is why he put his fingers to work in the members' area of racetracks and not in the pockets of racegoers on the lawn and in the public areas. He was also a fan of the opera and the arts. He did not particularly enjoy modern music or stage performances or openings at the National Gallery, but that was where the money was. People did carry less cash than they did ten years ago but the advent of debit cards, where one could just tap a card if the amount of the purchase was less than $100, kept Tannenbaum's fridge full, put petrol in his car and paid for numerous meals and gifts for the women he dated.

Tannenbaum and Pastrami had to watch the 2015 Flemington spring carnival on a prison TV set in the main common area along with the other inmates. They were given soft drinks, chips and chicken sandwiches on Cup Day, a far cry from what they usually consumed in the members' area or one of the marquees they managed to finagle their way into.

"Everything always tastes better when it's free, especially when those multi-million-dollar companies are paying for it," Pastrami said.

Tannenbaum nodded in agreement and chuckled to himself when Pastrami asked one of the guards if some mayonnaise could be put on the table. "For the sandwiches. They're a little dry," he noted.

Pastrami was able to get a few bets down on the outside on 101-1 shot Prince of Penzance and won close to $100,000. His mates thought he was nuts to be backing a 100-1 shot ridden by a woman, but they also knew he was the best form man going around so they backed it as well and also cleaned up. The person he trusted most of all, Bobby Robertson, was keeping the money in a safe place for him until he got out.

Tannenbaum set up a book among the prisoners and even some of the guards. The bets were mostly $5 and $10. Winners would be paid the official tote odds. Not one punter backed Prince of Penzance and Tannenbaum cleared close to $2500. Since word had got around about Tannenbaum's connection to the mob, nobody tried to relieve him of his windfall. Most of his fellow prisoners in the minimum-security prison were not known for being tough guys.

His company on the inside consisted of shady bookkeepers, dishonest stockbrokers, con men and real estate agents and developers who promised clients the moon with slick presentations and the lure of saving thousands by getting in early on new apartments. The apartments were never built, and the smooth-talking developers and realtors skipped off with the deposits.

"It's a victimless crime," developer Stan Harrison told the judge who sentenced him to four years in Dhurringile Prison. "If anyone is the victim, it's me. I'm being taken away from my wife and kids. I ..."

"All right, that's enough out of you," the judge interrupted as he banged his gavel, ordering a courtroom guard to get the forty-three-year-old Harrison out of his sight.

Time passed slowly for Tannenbaum and Pastrami, but they did their best to fight off the daily boredom by working in the garden, reading books from the prison library and playing basketball and tennis in the recreation area. Pastrami got the better of the smaller Tannenbaum on the basketball court, muscling his way inside for easy baskets while Tannenbaum used his superior speed, court coverage and a cracking serve to prevail on the clay courts.

Prisoners were allowed one conjugal visit a month. In his eighteen months at Murchison, Pastrami was visited by eighteen different women. Tannenbaum's steady, who was shocked by his imprisonment, visited him the first month he was away and never returned.

"C'mon, let me set you up with someone," Pastrami told Tannenbaum. "You can't spend the next seventeen months whacking off."

He took his mate up on his offer once, going to bed with a long-legged brunette from St Kilda. But he was left a bit cold by the experience, hopping into bed with her just five minutes after they had exchanged hellos.

"I've gone twelve months without before. I can do it again," Tannenbaum told Pastrami after the leggy brunette and the blonde Pastrami had spent his two hours with left to head back to Melbourne.

"To each his own," Pastrami said.

4

DELANEY WAS UNHAPPILY SINGLE AFTER THE BREAK-UP of his marriage several years earlier. He and Linda married while they were both in their forties. It was his first marriage and her second. They were too old to have children and frankly, after raising two children with her first husband, Linda had had enough. So, about a year after their nuptials they decided to get a dog instead.

The eight-week-old Labrador pup completed their family. Instead of taking a toddler to the park on weekends to go on the swings they took the dog to a beach not too far from their home for walks. Occasionally she got her feet wet in the surf and on one occasion, snow at Lake Mountain.

As Cheyenne grew into an adult dog, Delaney celebrated his fiftieth birthday and continued to clock up the years with the global media empire of Consume and Devour.

Despite being fifty-three, Delaney was in pretty good shape. He was about 183cm or 5-foot-11 on the old scale. His hair was thinning, and his waistline was slowly expanding due to a few too many pizzas and parmas. But he walked a lot and it kept his weight at a steady 79 kilos. He took a pill each morning for his slightly elevated blood pressure and another few pills here and there for a couple of minor ailments.

He had been a journo since he left uni and was approaching his twenty-year milestone with Consume and Devour.

However, he could see the writing on the wall, and it was not good. The downward trend of newspaper advertising showed no signs of reversing or even slowing as readers went online to get their news. Even if it was fake, they gobbled it up with relish, not even taking the time to have a think about what they had read; the Pope endorsing Donald

Trump for president? Please. He wouldn't even endorse a campaign for eating fish on Friday.

Delaney was flabbergasted one Saturday morning to read in a financial paper—a printed financial paper—that advertisers were spending eight out of every ten of their online advertising dollars with Facebook and Google.

And that number was growing. Advertisers were changing the way they did business and that business model was to go where the eyeballs were. And no matter how hard the printed and online media giants tried to counter the two behemoths—which were just thirteen and twenty years-old respectively—with their own advertising plans, they had missed the boat. It had sailed without them and there was no way to get back on it.

Delaney had a chat two days later with one of Consume and Devour's top advertising men, Dean Hobson, who had been in the racket when the money was coming it so fast there was barely enough time to count it all.

The two occasionally had a coffee together on Mondays when they checked where they stood in the floor's Footy Tipping Contest. It was usually towards the bottom.

"Is it true what I read over the weekend Dean, that nearly eighty per cent of all online advertising revenue is being spent with Facebook and Google? If that's the case, then our online division doesn't have a chance of making money."

Hobson looked down at his desk and shuffled a few papers around. He was in his early fifties but looked ten years older, no doubt due to all the stress he was under to reach targets and build and find new streams of revenue.

"It's true, Gary. We're fucked. But keep it between us, okay. The others will find out soon enough. We're basically treading water. No matter what we do; cutting rates, bundling packages between print and online, advertisers don't want a bar of us. And you know what? I can't blame them. I'd go where they eyeballs are too, and that's with Facebook and Google. We simply can't compete with them."

"How much longer do you think we can stay afloat? And I'm asking that as a friend."

Hobson leaned back in his black leather chair and let out a deep breath.

"On the print side, two or three years, tops. And unless the suits come up with something new to combat Facebook and Google, I reckon that within five years there will barely be enough advertising revenue coming in to keep the online division in the black and that's even with a bunch of twenty-two-year-olds doing all the work. Our only chance lies in subscriptions. But getting people to pay for something they are used to getting for free will take some doing."

Delaney uttered just one word. "Jesus."

"Even he can't save us, mate."

"Thanks for being so candid, Dean. I'll keep it between us. And, by the way, how many winners did you get in the footy tipping?"

"Just five. Who the heck could see Sydney starting off 0-6? Shit, they're going even worse than we are." Delaney laughed. "I also had five. See you later," he said, leaving Hobson to go over last week's numbers.

Papers were getting smaller or disappearing altogether, advertorials of all things were making frequent appearances, and mistakes were becoming more and more noticeable due to a lack of staff. Check subs? They went out the door ten years ago leaving the task of proofreading and fact-checking to the same reporters who had written the stories.

Management said it was not cost effective to have a new set of eyeballs look over the completed yarns and pages before they went to print. So out the pages went, with spelling mistakes, stories which were continued on the wrong page or not continued at all, and Wednesday's weather page being printed again in its entirety on Thursday. It was enough to make a seasoned journalist cry. Plus, the morale of those who remained was at rock bottom.

"It's death by a thousand cuts," one of the long-time female editors was fond of saying as she shook her head, pondering her future which was directly tied to the paper's fortunes. "How am I going to pay my mortgage?" she asked. No one had an answer.

Delaney's pay cheques kept coming but after speaking with Hobson he wondered for how much longer. Perhaps by the end of the financial year, some eight months away, they too would stop if more staff cuts were made or the men upstairs decided to pull the pin on more than a hundred years of print history.

Several months earlier Delaney realised just how dire things were for newspapers as he waited for a flight at Tullamarine Airport in Melbourne for a week of warmth in sunny north Queensland. There were approximately 500 people sitting in the departure area and just about all of them had their heads buried in their smartphones; checking their Facebook pages, emails, texts and playing mind-numbing video games.

He took a quick walk around and counted the number of people reading the daily left leaning former broadsheet turned tabloid which he subscribed to, the Consume and Devour right-wing tabloid or the same company's national daily newspaper.

There were five. Five, at 10.30 in the morning. And, they were all over the age of 50. Twenty years earlier at least half of those 500 people would have been reading a newspaper. The rest would have been reading a book or a magazine. However, bickering with check-in staff over the length of a flight's delay remained a constant.

"We'll make an announcement as soon as we have more information," a female clerk told a man about sixty-five dressed in shorts, slip-on sneakers and a T-shirt sporting the words 'I love Cairns'.

"That's the last time I fly this bloody airline," he yelled as he walked back to take a seat next to his wife in the departure area. She rolled her eyes when he told her about the delay.

"We'll get there when we get there. It's not that important," she said as she went back to her book.

"The damn thing should leave on time," her husband grumbled. "We got here on time."

Delaney wondered how long the woman had put up with her husband's constant complaining; thirty years, forty? *If it was me, I would let him go by himself and enjoy a week's peace at home—alone.*

Put it online, put it online, was the catchcry in the newsroom these days. When the axe fell on staff whose sole responsibility was to put stories and photos online, the task fell to the reporters. They now had to put their own stories online which took about twenty minutes per yarn. Delaney had a checklist to go through that was longer than the one Armstrong and Aldrin used to land safely on the moon nearly fifty years earlier.

Plus, there were constant emails from the small digital team to wade through. "Don't forget to capitalise the first word in the standfirsts, no more than four words in the main headline, remember to get the photos in the correct order otherwise they won't show up on a mobile, get it up on Facebook ASAP, remember to copy and paste the URL when you tweet it."

Tweeting, Twerking, Facebooking. It was enough to drive a sane man over the edge. But Delaney ploughed on, doing what he was required to do—even if he had to occasionally ask some kid half his age for some help to stay afloat in the new digital age.

Delaney was old school and proud of it. He had saved historic issues of the former broadsheet for years; the Apollo 11 moon landing, Prime Minister Holt's mysterious disappearance in the Portsea surf, Nixon's resignation, Australia's America's Cup win in 1983 and Makybe Diva's third straight Melbourne Cup triumph in 2005 just to name a few.

Somewhere in Melbourne's southeast the papers were yellowing in a box tucked into the corner of a mate's garage. He couldn't take them with him when he moved into a small flat with no storage space after uni so he asked his mate Carl Higson to keep them. And there they stayed for years. But seeing how he hadn't talked to his uni chum in more than fifteen years—since he backed Kim Beazley and 'Higgy' went for John Howard in the 2001 federal election—they were more likely buried under a decade and a half worth of filth at the Ravenhall rubbish tip.

Even these days when something notable occurred, like the Western Bulldogs winning the 2016 AFL premiership, people bought newspapers as souvenirs. No one printed out the front page of the Consume and Devour tabloid or the former broadsheet on an A4 piece of paper to hold up to the television cameras at Whitten Oval the day afterwards. Newspapers were a living record of events, good and bad, but selling an extra 50,000 copies of a paper one day a year was merely a drop in a bucket that was nearly dry.

Delaney knew good journalism. But what filled print and web pages these days could not even be described as journalism. It was garbage aimed at the lowest common denominator.

But Delaney kept at it, day after day, year after year, still taking pride in the pages he produced and the yarns he wrote. He wasn't covering the AFL and VFL anymore. That gig went to kids who spent more time on their phones and laptops, blogging and tweeting, than watching the games they were sent to cover.

Delaney's beat included racing, golf, a bit of tennis, athletics, baseball—yes, baseball is played in Australia, and the quality is surprisingly good—and basketball.

The food and refreshments were always top notch at the tennis and at golf's major events while most racing clubs made sure the media was fed and watered.

He couldn't stand going to the basketball anymore, whether it was the NBL or the WNBL, where court announcers were constantly screaming—LET'S MAKE SOME NOISE OR DEFENCE, DEFENCE. It was excruciating to listen to. A close game was even worse. The last three minutes of a tight game could drag on for more than fifteen thanks to constant fouls and timeouts. And it was accompanied by a blaring sound-track. After watching Melbourne United down Adelaide one night at Hisense Arena, he brought earplugs to any basketball game he was sent to cover.

The women's games were not any better. With crowds dwindling, club officials turned to the young girls in their junior programs to fill the seats, girls who screamed so loudly when they were asked to MAKE SOME NOISE that Delaney felt he was at a One Direction concert. On a positive note, the players from the home side, win or lose, hung around after games to pose for pictures, sign autographs and conduct mini-clinics.

Later that week, when Delaney's hearing returned to normal, he was sitting at his desk when an email arrived from one of his colleagues. 'Take a look at the radar,' it read.

There were no intercontinental ballistic missiles headed to Melbourne, but a band of rain—heavy rain—was closing in on the city. Delaney felt it in his bones, which at times made him feel like a league player with fifteen years and dozens of brutal state of origin games under his belt instead of a reporter whose arse occasionally fell asleep due to long periods of sitting in front of a computer screen. A gag award from several years back for 'Biggest Waste of a Work Station' was perched just to the left of the screen.

Rain was on the way and it looked as if it would hit around lunchtime. It was right there in greens and yellows on the 256 km Melbourne Radar Loop; one of the few websites he visited every day. "I like to be prepared," he said when one of the young general assignment reporters came by and glanced at his computer screen. "Go on, shake your head. But you'll be the one soaking wet later without an umbrella," he squawked.

It reminded him of the time one of his older male colleagues—yes, there was someone older than him in the building—stepped out to get his lunch and came back fifteen minutes later as the winner of a wet T-shirt contest. He wasn't quick enough to dodge the raindrops but turned in copy cleaner than any of the young kids he worked alongside.

5

IT WAS PASTOR CHRIS WHO ALERTED DELANEY TO A job ad—seen online of course—that piqued Delaney's interest. "Experienced sports journalist with sub-editing and marketing experience wanted for racing publication."

Delaney had the experience and could sell elephant shit to a circus if he had to, so the marketing aspect of the job was well within his reach.

The ad asked for a resume, along with a cover letter, to be sent to an email address—did postal addresses even exist anymore?—by the 22nd of the month, ten days away. Delaney gave it some thought. *They're probably looking for someone twenty-five years younger, who will work for peanuts.* He didn't even know where the job was based, but ...

So he put together a resume for the first time in twenty years, fudging some of the dates because he simply couldn't remember them and could not be bothered looking them up, wrote a kiss-arse cover letter complete with referees—Pastor Chris featured prominently—typed in the email address, attached said resume and cover letter and off it went. He was coming up on two decades at his current job, which meant he was either dependable and damn good at what he did, or the company couldn't find anyone else to spend two hours each Monday morning typing up lawn bowls results which were part of the gig.

A copytaker used to have that unenviable task, but she was told in a phone call one Monday that she was no longer needed due to cost-cutting measures, so the results landed on Delaney's desk and in his inbox. But at least the lawn bowls crowd was appreciative of his efforts. And, they began sending in more and more news from their respective clubs— pairs winners, club champions, new life members and a note on a rare occurrence at a pennant match called a "resting toucher in the ditch" which sounded as if it would be of more interest to someone doing the police rounds. Delaney was more than happy to get the yarns and photos in the paper since the demographics of the bowls community, in the fifty-five and over range, was the only group publishers could count on to read their newspapers on a regular basis.

Delaney wasn't expecting to hear anything back from the racing publication. That's the way companies worked these days. They did not even have the courtesy to send back a reply—an email reply—saying they had received what was sent. He was shocked a week later to receive an email from the editor's assistant, asking him to come into the office first thing Friday morning for an interview. He sent back a reply and said he would be there—in the city—at 9am.

Delaney called his office in the morning from the train on the way into the city, said he had a doctor's appointment and would be in around lunchtime. It was plausible. Delaney was at the age where doctor's appointments were becoming a monthly event. He remembered the days when he walked into a doctor's surgery and the receptionist behind the counter asked if he had been there before. Now he was greeted by, "Hi Gary, please take a seat and the doctor will be right with you."

Delaney was wearing one of his better sports jackets under his coat, a collared shirt, slacks but no tie; his usual office attire. He never wore a tie unless it was necessary. He hated the feeling of being choked. His new shoes were a tad uncomfortable. They'd need at least a week to be broken in. It was a crisp morning, but the sun was shining and there was just a light breeze as he made his way to Mentone train station in Melbourne's southeast.

He weaved his way through the hundreds of teenagers who flooded the footpaths on their way to the private schools their parents were shelling out a fortune for when there were plenty of perfectly good state schools just minutes away. They were in groups of three or four, cackling like chooks. He picked up bits and pieces of the conversations. The guys were talking about footy and girls, and the girls were gossiping. Some were even carrying coffees with them. Coffees? What kid is drinking a latte at the age of fifteen? But, Delaney figured, it was better to be drinking a latte at that age than smoking a ciggie in a bid to look cool.

Delaney waited to cross the last street standing between himself and the station. The council had still not put a bulb into the broken red light in one of the most heavily traversed intersections in town. A couple of months ago when the street lights were out altogether, causing chaos for pedestrians and motorists alike, Delaney had called an 1800 number listed by the light to call in traffic faults. His reward? A bill of $4.85 for the call.

"Someone else can do it this time," he muttered as he crossed the street.

He took out his myki card—the $1.5 billion disaster needed to travel on Melbourne's network of buses, trains and trams—and touched on. He walked to the front of the platform where it was less crowded and before he could even open his paper to have a glance at the morning headlines, a train arrived.

Delaney was lucky to get a seat. He used an inside run to out-hustle some hipster carrying his coffee in one hand and an expensive briefcase in the other.

The trip into town took just thirty minutes.

He had his paper with him, the former broadsheet of course, which again looked like it had been in a bar brawl the night before. Half of the paper, starting with the sport on the back page inward, was ripped, more than likely by the paper wrapping machine used by newsagents to protect papers from the elements. He thought of taking the paper into the newsagent one morning and presenting it to whomever was in charge but decided against it since his paper would likely wind up on the roof the next morning. Most mornings the paper was out of his reach, tossed under his neighbour's truck. His neighbour kept a canoe paddle outside—there was no sign of a canoe of course—which Delaney used to nudge the paper from under the truck to a spot where he could grab it. And on mornings it did rain, the paper was never under the truck out of the rain, but right on the footpath where despite the plastic wrapping, it got soaked. About once or twice a month he needed to iron the paper to render it readable.

But since so few people read a newspaper there was never any danger of anyone stealing it no matter how late he went out to fetch it on his days off. One Saturday more than a decade ago, before the rivers of gold— the classifieds—dried up and moved online, when the broadsheet and the Consume and Devour tabloid were both massive, Delaney went out to get his paper only to discover that someone had removed the plastic covering, taken just the employment section and left the rest of it in a perfectly stacked pile.

"That is a man I would hire," Delaney said as he walked back inside.

Delaney found a seat and had a look around at the people in the carriage with him. His heart sank. He was the only one with a newspaper. Just as it was at the airport, everyone else had their head down and was glued to a phone; earbuds in place, totally cut off from the world. To his surprise, a couple of women were reading books. He tried to make out the titles but couldn't. About four rows in front of him, facing him, a very attractive woman, who looked to be in her mid-thirties, was applying her make-up. She studied her handiwork in a small mirror, gave it the tick of approval, put her make-up back in her bag and reached for her phone.

As the train made its way to the city, the carriages deposited their cargo of noisy schoolkids which were replaced by office workers and university students. It was a potpourri of the old and young, the well-heeled and those struggling to get by. Delaney wondered if he was the only one going to a job interview. By the time the train got to Malvern station twenty minutes later, the train was packed thanks to Metro's bright idea a few years ago of removing seats to accommodate even more passengers. Every carriage carried more people than it should have which meant even more sneezing, coughing and loud phone conversations. "I don't care if you have just thrown up, get out of bed and get to school!"

Delaney had another fifteen minutes until he arrived at Flinders Street Station, so he buried his head in the paper. He checked the entries; there was a good card at Caulfield on Saturday. If it was a nice day, he might even go. But it was Melbourne and the beginning of September so what would pass for a nice day—sunny with temps in the high teens—was iffy at best. He didn't want to sit in the glass-enclosed grandstand or the press room for three or four hours as rain pelted down. Delaney liked the excitement of the mounting yard and hanging out at the stalls at the back of the course having a chat to the strappers, trainers and owners. That's where the stories were.

The train limped into Flinders Street Station about 8.30. The doors opened and like horses breaking from the gate, the passengers spilled out onto the platform in a mad rush to the escalators. Delaney was not in that much of a hurry. He had three blocks to walk and half an hour to get there. Southbank was one of the better places to work in Melbourne. Good people, good restaurants. *I could get used to this.*

He passed a vendor selling the *Big Issue* and was all set to buy one until he saw the cover which featured Harry Potter. "Next time," he told the vendor who kept smiling despite the lack of a sale. He pushed on and spotted a near-catatonic homeless man seated on the cold cement, leaning back against the railing which protected him from back-flipping into the muddy Yarra River 10 metres below. He was dressed in clothing that needed a washing machine more than peanut butter needs jam. He appeared to be about fifty-five but was probably closer to forty. Time on the streets ages one quickly. He had a weathered face and every line had a sad story to tell. When he had worked, most of it had probably been done outside under a hot sun; construction perhaps or some sort of farm work. His beard had bits of grey in it, and the glasses perched on his nose needed a run through a car wash.

A faded baseball cap was tucked tightly over the fellow's head. He stared at the pavement, fingering a scarf around his neck which pooled in his lap, not making eye contact with any of the hundreds of people walking by. A few looked at him but never broke stride. Delaney stopped for a moment and read the words on an old piece of cardboard that was tucked up against his knees. "Homeless and hungry. Please help. God Bless You."

Delaney put his hand into his pocket, pulled out a two-dollar coin and gently placed it into the plastic container at the man's feet. It was the only coin in it. "Thank you," the fellow muttered.

"Best of luck to you," Delaney said as he walked off. *The most liveable city in the world and this poor guy is reduced to sitting on a cold piece of pavement. It's not right*, Delaney thought.

Delaney walked over to a nearby kiosk at Flinders Street Station and bought a simple cup of coffee and a donut. He walked back to the homeless man, bent over and said, "Here, take this please. It will at least warm you up."

The fellow looked up, made eye contact with Delaney for the first time, and slowly took the coffee and donut. He took a sip of the coffee and grinned. "That's pretty good, thank you."

"Will you be able to get anything to eat later on?"

"A food van comes around about 6 o'clock. Volunteers they are. They might even be able to find a room for me for the night."

"And if not?"

"I'll go sleep by the aquarium. There's some shelter there if it rains."

"Doesn't the council offer to help?"

"They don't care about people like me. If it wasn't for the volunteers, I reckon I'd be dead by now."

Delaney shook his head in disbelief. He knew that spot by the aquarium. He had seen homeless people gathered there before. It was about two-hundred metres from the Crown Casino, if that, just a short walk over a bridge which spanned the Yarra. People would be getting ready to leave their $300 a night hotel rooms about now, slipping into their $1000 suits and fastening their $50 ties. Others would be throwing thousands of dollars away on the casino floor playing blackjack, craps, Baccarat and feeding the slots. And coming from overseas no less to do it. One large bet from one of those tourists would be enough to feed a homeless man or woman for a month. Delaney took a $10 note out of his pocket and tucked it into the man's hands.

"Just in case you get hungry later on, okay?"

The fellow put the note into his jacket pocket. "Thank you," he said. "Thank you."

"It's the least I can do. I've got to get going. Take care of yourself."

"I'll do my best."

"What's your name, mate?"

"Fitzy, that's what everyone calls me."

The fellow extended his hand. Delaney shook it. "Stay safe Fitzy."

Delaney walked off to his appointment. A couple of young women headed to their offices were beside him. The taller of the two looked at him. "You know he's just going to buy drugs or grog with what you gave him," she said.

"Well at least I'm doing something," Delaney snapped as he sped up.

As a uni student in Melbourne more than thirty years ago, Delaney once had no place to go after a lease on an apartment he shared with two others ran out. One fellow decided to move back home and the other moved in with his girlfriend. There was no way Delaney could pay the rent by himself and after scouring the apartments for rent section of the local paper and asking his friends and fellow students if they knew of anything available, Delaney packed his things in his barely roadworthy Torana and checked into a local motel for a week. It was a dive and ate up a good part of his savings but at least he had a roof over his head. There were knocks on the door at night from pros asking him if he wanted a good time and he could see drug deals going on in the parking lot. But he kept to himself and nobody bothered him.

A day before he had to pony up another week's rent at the motel, Delaney saw an ad for a room about ten minutes from campus. It was an old two-storey house with seven separate rooms and one common bathroom. Had the board of health or a building inspector come by, it would have been shut in five minutes. But with nowhere else to go and his cash reserves dwindling, Delaney took one of the two rooms upstairs. There was enough room for a bed, a chest of drawers, a table, his TV and a portable fridge which a mate gave him. It was far from ideal, but it was warm, safe and cost $35 a week, a third less than the motel. With no cooking facilities, Delaney had to bring his own food in or dine out. He wound up staying at the dump for a year, saving what he could from his part-time job at a call centre for an apartment of his own. But the year wasn't a total loss. For a few months, he dated a waitress named Gina who worked at a pizza place where he ate a couple of times a week. Eventually, she got so discouraged with uni, her roommates and her job that she went back home to the tiny town of Ouyen which on most summer days recorded the highest temperature in Victoria. They exchanged a few letters and phone calls and never saw each other again.

Delaney made his way to Southbank, walking along the Yarra. He seemed to be going against the flow. People were in a mad dash to get to their offices by 9am while a handful of others were trying to stick notices in their hands for lunchtime specials, after-work drink specials and massages. The much slicker pamphlets were reserved for the apartments in all the high-rise apartment buildings going up around him. Delaney took one; $499,000 for a one-bedroom apartment the size of a large dog kennel. He tossed it in an overflowing garbage bin.

Before he reached his destination two Jehovah's Witnesses—one has to admire their tenacity—wished him a good morning and extended one of their pamphlets for him to take.

"No thank you," Delaney said.

As he kept walking Delaney remembered an encounter with a group of Jehovah's Witnesses which knocked on his front door one Saturday morning several years before.

After putting Cheyenne in the backyard, a half-dressed Delaney opened the front door to see two gorgeous women in front of him. Behind them were three young men dressed in jackets and ties. They were all holding copies of *The Watchtower*, their pamphlet which he found out later was published monthly in 294 languages. *Two-hundred and ninety-four*? Off the top of his head Delaney was able to come up with ten. He could speak and write only one fluently, barely.

One of the women, who looked to be about twenty-five, said good morning with a set of gleaming white teeth you could read by. "Would you be interested in hearing about—"

Delaney put his hand up and stopped her right there.

"I'm sorry," he said. "But I am really not interested."

"Don't you believe in God?" she asked.

"Well, I did about four years ago."

"Why then?"

"Because I was sleeping with a twenty-seven-year-old."

The girls looked at one another, searching for a comeback. When none was forthcoming, Delaney wished them a good day and slowly closed the door.

Four years earlier Delaney, then forty-nine, was in fact sleeping with a twenty-seven-year-old. Six months after he and Linda parted company—to make a long story short there were irreconcilable differences—he signed up for one of those online dating sites and put his profile out there. While the presence of Cheyenne helped ease his loneliness, Delaney was eager to have some female companionship; someone to talk to, go to a movie with, go out to dinner with.

What did he have to lose? He filled out the forms truthfully, trying to add some humour in his answers. A month went by, and then another. Finally, he had a few positive responses. He had three dates; none of them memorable, all of them awkward. Dating was not as easy as it had been. Everything was now being done online and while it was fun perusing the ads put up by women it was also a chore. Delaney put a line through anyone who had kids living at home or who had kids bedded down at a correctional facility.

Once, with a schoolteacher named Leanne, who lived just ten minutes away, he got lucky. She was a few years older than Delaney, very pretty, petite and very sharp. Leanne had been divorced for several years and had two children living interstate. They met for dinner at a small Chinese place in Bentleigh, a well to do suburb in Melbourne's southeast, which had surprisingly good food. Dinner turned into a drink at her house, one she got in her divorce settlement, and after some good-natured banter and a bit of flirting they decided to call it a night. They shared a kiss at the door and Delaney said good night.

He drove home feeling pretty good about himself. Things had gone better than expected and with another date set for Friday night, just two days away, he slept well.

Leanne sent him a text around lunchtime on Friday asking what he would like for dinner. She was cooking at her place and Delaney, who was not all that picky, said anything was fine unless it was Indian food which was just too spicy for his troubled stomach. She ended up making lasagne. Delaney arrived a few minutes after 7pm with a bottle of red after first driving down the wrong street.

Leanne greeted him wearing an apron and kissed him on the cheek as he entered. "Thanks for coming. Please, sit down. I'll be right with you."

Smooth 91.5 was playing in the background and Delaney took a seat on the couch as *The Carpenters* sang about being on top of the world, looking down on creation. *Ugh. Well, at least she hasn't put on rap music*, Delaney thought.

"Brings back memories, doesn't it?" Leanne said as she bounced into the living room with two glasses of the wine he brought.

"It sure does," Delaney replied, making a note to himself to look at her CD collection at the first available moment.

Please let there be some Zeppelin, Pink Floyd, INXS or even the Eagles mixed in it.

The night went well. Dinner was terrific and the conversation was just as good since they were each on the same wave length politically and followed the footy. "You must really enjoy your job," Leanne said.

"It beats digging ditches."

After dessert Delaney helped clear the table and wash the dishes. They washed them instead of shoving them into a dishwasher which could drone on and on for up to ninety minutes and still not get everything clean.

The two cuddled up on the coach together after everything was put away and polished off what little was left of the wine.

"Maybe you should spend the night here, since you've probably had a bit too much to drink," Leanne said.

"That's wise thinking," Delaney replied.

And later, for the first time in a very long time, Delaney made love to someone other than his wife. At first, he was so nervous he thought he wouldn't be able to perform. But Leanne had a terrific body for a woman over fifty and was quite keen. Delaney finished strongly after missing the start by a couple of lengths and got up to score.

"I never go to bed with someone so soon after meeting them," Leanne said as a ceiling fan whirred above them. "But I like you, Gary. We may have something here."

"I like you too and for the record you are the first woman I have slept with since my wife and I separated."

"How do I compare with your wife?"

"Let's just say that you ticked all the boxes."

"And more?"

"And more," Delaney said.

Delaney got up before Leanne the next morning, took a quick shower and made some coffee which he brought to her.

She rubbed the sleep out of her eyes and Delaney was surprised by how good she looked first thing in the morning. She needed very little help from a make-up box.

Leanne took a shower as Delaney glanced at the sport section of the former broadsheet which was delivered right on the front step of Leanne's home. "Go online for all the news on last night's Saints v Pies clash," a pointer cried out. "Oh, for goodness sake. Can't they send the paper to bed after the game?" Delaney cried out. "And the executives sit and wonder why circulation and ad revenue is down."

Later in the day Delaney had a look at the Consume and Devour tabloid at Woolies. It had photos on the back page and a match report inside on St Kilda's narrow win.

Delaney had a VFL game to cover that afternoon in Sandringham where the wind whipping in off the bay always made for a cold afternoon if the sun decided to take a holiday. Around eleven he left Leanne's place with an invitation to return for dinner on Monday night.

Several text messages bounced back and forth between the two over the next couple of days.

Delaney picked up some takeaway from the same Chinese place where they had eaten a week ago.

They washed down dinner with a couple of cans of diet coke and made their way to the couch in the living room. All was going well until Leanne turned on the TV and put on the *X Factor*, another scripted reality TV talent show where every audience member is bathed in spotlights and screaming as if they've just won Tattslotto while the worst music imaginable blares from a PA system.

"You're not going to watch this, are you?" Delaney asked.

"Sure I am, it's fun."

"Fun? This is shit," Delaney said. "How can you watch this shit?"

And with the words having barely left his mouth, Leanne wheeled around and delivered a stinging rebuttal. "Fuck off and get out of my house."

"You can't be serious?"

"I am. Now fuck off."

Delaney scratched his head for a moment, grabbed his coat and left. And that was the end of Delaney and Leanne.

Delaney met the twenty-seven-year-old through an online dating site and once they moved from emails to texting to the phone, they talked for a couple of hours a night until they met a week later at Federation Square.

A drink led to dinner and dinner led to a roll in the hay back at her apartment. He and the very attractive paralegal saw each other two or three nights a week for nearly four months. Movies, book launches and an occasional night at the theatre were vast improvements over Delaney's usual night-time fare of take-away food and bad television.

After Cindy's sister-in-law gave birth to her second child, Delaney noticed a difference in his young lover. They each celebrated a birthday—he turned fifty and she twenty-eight—and even though they never talked about it he could sense that she wanted a child of her own. And having a baby with a fifty-year-old man was not part of her plan. Delaney didn't have any children. The responsibility would be just too much for him, or so he said. He got along well with the children of friends and colleagues but that was for an hour or two at a time. He didn't think he could handle being on call 24/7. It wasn't due to selfishness, he just didn't think he could be a good parent without worrying himself into an old-age home well before he received the pension.

So, when Cindy told him one afternoon after lunch that she was also seeing someone else, someone just five years older than she was, Delaney knew things were all but over between them. They had one final phone conversation before she said goodbye—forever.

He should have bowed out gracefully but regrettably hounded her for a couple of weeks with texts and calls—all of which went unanswered—asking her to change her mind.

She had *moved on* and Delaney had to do the same, which he eventually did.

6

DELANEY TURNED RIGHT AND HEADED TO SOUTHBANK. He found the office building he was looking for and made his way to the front desk. "I have a 9 o'clock appointment with Bob Nicholls of *Turf News*," he told the Kardashian clone manning the desk. She glanced at her computer screen for a moment and then reached into a box on her desk for a building pass.

"They're on the fifth floor. You'll need to swipe this when you get into the lift otherwise it won't go anywhere," she said. "Okay, fifth floor. Wish me luck," he said.

"Luck?"

"I'm here for a job interview."

"Whatever," the barely out of Year Ten receptionist said.

And on that note, Delaney slowly walked to the lift.

He pressed the up button and was the only one waiting when the doors opened, and two men exited. He got in, pressed floor number five and then looked around for the spot to swipe his card. The doors closed but the lift stayed put. Delaney ran the card over the top of the buttons, then to the left of the door and then to the right of it. The lift did not budge. He glanced at his watch; five minutes to nine. At this point he would have swiped the card between the crack in his arse if it would get the lift to move.

"Oh, come on already, move!" Delaney shouted.

Just as he finished his rant, the lift door opened and a young woman stood in front of him holding a briefcase and a coffee.

"Not sure if you're going up or down?"

"I'm going to the fifth floor but can't figure out where to swipe this card I got from the reception desk."

She took a card hanging from a lanyard around her neck, gently touched it against a small lit circle underneath the buttons and pressed seven.

"You have to touch the card before you indicate what floor you want," she said.

"Ahhhh, would have been nice to have been told that a few minutes ago but never mind, five please," he said, and up they went.

"Thanks," Delaney said. "I don't think I could have walked up five flights of stairs."

The lift door opened on the fifth floor and Delaney got out.

"You don't have to touch the card on your way down, just on the way up. A security measure," she said.

Delaney smiled. "Thanks again, have yourself a good day."

The *Turf News* office was to the left. As he neared the door, he got nervous. And when Delaney got nervous, he had to pee.

"Damn, where are the bloody toilets?

He found the men's toilet and pushed the door, but it didn't budge. He tried the handle. The damn thing was locked. Suddenly the door opened. Some bloke was coming out and Delaney managed to sneak in before the door closed behind him.

He headed straight to one of five urinals, stuck his newspaper under his arm, opened his fly and took care of business.

He glanced around. To his left were about six or seven cubicles. Halfway through, Delaney heard a lot of grunting and groaning coming from one of the stalls and then a loud, long fart.

What the hell is going on in there? Delaney thought.

After a few more grunts Delaney heard the rip, rip, rip of toilet paper coming off a roll and the stall toilet flushing.

Delaney zipped up and headed to a row of sinks to wash his hands. A cubical door opened and a slightly overweight man about fifty years of age in a shirt and tie and black trousers emerged. He was still fiddling with his belt. Delaney nodded as he washed his hands while the man made his way to the sinks.

"Was it a boy or a girl?" Delaney asked.

"What?"

"That was quite a performance you gave over there. Sounded like the 1812 overture; badda, badda, badda, bum bum bum. Badda, badda, badda bum, bum, bum. Very stirring."

The guy stormed out of the toilets, muttering something under his breath while Delaney washed his face, adjusted his glasses and walked to the office for his 9 o'clock appointment.

He opened the *Turf News* door and was greeted by a young, dark-haired receptionist who was so well dressed—on what was supposed to be casual Friday—that she could have been a Derby Day Fashions on the Field winner.

"Hi, my name is Gary Delaney. I have an appointment with Bob Nicholls."

"Good morning Gary. I'm Lisa. Please take a seat and I'll tell Mr Nicholls you're here."

Delaney sat down on one of several couches available for visitors. He fidgeted with his newspaper as he had a look around. There were racing photos everywhere; Makybe Diva, Black Caviar, Lohnro, So You Think, Northerly, Bonecrusher. And plenty of signed photos of jockeys and trainers too. He felt at home.

'Mr Nicholls will see you now," Lisa said. "He's in the big office on the far left."

Delaney walked across the newsroom floor where a handful of reporters were busy at their desks. Not one of them looked over thirty. Probably why an experienced sub-editor was needed.

They all took notice of him but not one said hello.

The door to Mr Nicholls' office was open. Delaney knocked and stepped inside. To his shock the man rising from a large desk to shake his hand was the one he had spoken to in the toilet.

"Well this is slightly awkward," Delaney said. "But I thoroughly enjoyed your performance."

Nicholls took his time responding. "My wife insisted on going to this new Mexican place last night. First and last time," he said. "Sit down, sit down."

"With all the people our age being given redundancies we've had quite a few applicants. You're one of four on our short list and the first I've seen. We need someone here with a sense of humour. The kids out there think bloody cat videos on YouTube are funny. But they love their racing and that's what we're all about.

"You're familiar with us?"

Delaney picked up a copy of *Turf News* occasionally. He felt that the writing was a bit subpar. There was no flow, no narrative and a lack of creativity. Racing was the best beat to be on. There were rags to riches and riches to rags stories everywhere. But one had to stop tweeting, get off Facebook and go to the stables and the public trials to find them. Delaney had gone to a picnic race meeting just four days earlier and had come back with a yarn about a major metropolitan trainer who was acting as a strapper for a young trainer on the peninsula. "She asked so I said why not," the Blue Diamond winning trainer said. "It's my first time at a picnic meeting. It's a fantastic atmosphere here. It's what's missing at the city meetings."

Picnic meetings were the exact opposite of city meetings. Run by volunteers, they charged just $10 admission, or $15 on their cup days, to get in. Racegoers were able to bring their own grog through the gates as opposed to paying $8 for a can of VB in town and the lawns were plastered with people sitting in chairs brought from home around tables stacked with snacks. Go to Derby Day or Melbourne Cup Day and your $79 ticket won't even get you a seat.

"I am," Delaney told Nicholls.

"And ...?"

"The writing and stories could be a bit better. We all know who won. The lads need to be telling us what we don't know."

"Exactly," Nicholls said.

"The form guide though is top of the line," Delaney continued. "Much better than what the dailies give us, and I like to form my own opinion rather than listen to some expert who is more often wrong than right."

Nicholls nodded in agreement. "And the marketing side of things?"

"I have a few ideas," Delaney said without giving anything away. *Keep them guessing.*

"The start of the spring carnival is just a few weeks away. If I were to offer you the job, when could you start?"

"Well, depending on what sort of money you're talking about, maybe in two or three weeks. I'd have to have a yack with the HR people at Consume and Devour and get back to you".

Delaney had a feeling his mob wouldn't mind seeing him go and replacing him with someone in his twenties on a lower salary and with fewer benefits.

"I'll be frank with you, Gary. The job pays $85,000 a year with all the usual benefits plus super. And if some of those marketing ideas of yours pay off there could be more. We're holding our own circulation wise and our online numbers are good. We just need an experienced hand around here. I'm too busy going to bloody sales pitches and presentations. The kids will handle the social media side of things. You tell them what to put up and they'll do it. I just need to ask you a few questions, unnecessary really, but HR insists. They need to be asked to all potential employees, even if I was interviewing my own mother."

"Shoot," Delaney said.

"What are your strengths?"

"I'm the ultimate team player," Delaney answered. "Good at nurturing young talent and a damn good reporter, sub-editor and lay-out man. An all-rounder."

"And your weaknesses?"

Delaney kept it brief. "Kryptonite."

Nicholls let out a hearty laugh. "Love it."

Nicholls put down his notepad and looked Delaney right in the eye.

"What do you say? Are you in?"

"Let me discuss it with my partner and I'll get back to you later this afternoon."

"Deal," Nicholls said as he shook Delaney's hand.

Nicholls walked Delaney back to the front of the office. "Lisa will give you my office number and mobile number."

Lisa gave Delaney a card with Nicholls' numbers and told him to enjoy the rest of his day.

And with that Delaney glided to the lift. He hit the ground floor button and within seconds the doors opened in the building lobby. He tossed his pass to the Kardashian at the front desk and walked out of the building with a new lease of life.

7

AFTER LEAVING THE OFFICE OF *TURF NEWS*, DELANEY rang Michelle, his girlfriend of eight weeks, at her office at the National Gallery in the city where she handled the admin side of things for upcoming exhibits. She was an artist herself, with a few shows under her belt. However, despite lots of interest, she hadn't sold a painting in the last six months. So, when she heard about the job at the National Gallery she applied and got it. She was in an environment that she loved, got a first-hand look at the new shows before the general public and her 20 per cent discount at the gift shop came in handy for birthday presents and at Christmas time. Plus, she got a chance to mingle and do some networking which she was hoping would lead to some of her work being shown at some of the more prestigious galleries in town.

"Hi baby, I can only talk for a minute. How'd the interview go?"

"Very well, they offered me the job. Twenty thousand more than I'm making now plus all the usual benefits."

"Fantastic, are you going to take it?"

"Do you think I should?"

"Absolutely, you've said you don't want to continue working for Consume and Devour. This is the perfect opportunity for a new start, and you'd be writing about what you enjoy the most."

"Just wanted to get your thoughts. I'll ring them back this afternoon to tell them I'm in. See you tonight. I have a busy day ahead of me."

"We'll celebrate later, okay?"

"You bet, bye."

Delaney and Michelle, 50, had moved in together just six weeks earlier, settling on a rental in a small complex of units on a quiet street on the beach side of Mentone.

The unit did not allow pets, so reluctantly, Delaney gave Cheyenne away to a mate who was married with two young girls. Greg Audette's family home in Beaumaris had a big fenced backyard and there would be someone home most days which was better than leaving Cheyenne on her own for 10 hours on work days. "You're welcome to come by and see her anytime you like," Greg told Delaney when he dropped Cheyenne off.

Michelle was a stunner; tall, blonde and shapely with a lovely smile. She was also a fantastic cook, a fine conversationalist, had a wonderful sense of humour, magnificent legs and looked ten years younger than any 50-year-old woman Delaney had ever seen.

She was also a leftie, hated what passed for television these days and read books—printed books—and did not mind the sport of kings. She had one grown son who was so busy trying to keep his unbelievably gorgeous girlfriend/housemate happy that he rarely even rang his mum let alone came around uninvited.

Was girlfriend even the right term for a fifty-three-year-old man to use when describing the woman three years his junior he was living with? Partner? People could get the wrong idea and assume that Delaney had switched sides. Not that there was anything wrong with that. So instead of using the words partner or girlfriend, Delaney simply called Michelle his better half to people he knew or his wife to those who were merely acquaintances.

"Hey mate, I was speaking to your wife the other day, and I won't keep you, but she said you followed the races," a neighbour told Delaney one morning. "Now I've got this system ..."

Why bother correcting him and getting into the whole *she's not my wife, she's my girlfriend* discussion? Delaney simply said he followed the races since he wrote about them and then excused himself by saying the bath was about to run over. There was no bathtub of course but he couldn't think of anything else to say. With Delaney's luck the fellow would show up in his robe and slippers a week later asking if he could take a nice warm bath to ease the pain in his troublesome back.

Delaney fell for Michelle as soon as they met, and she must have felt the same way since they found themselves in bed together on their third date. Drinks, dinner, dessert, a walk and a hotel room for the night in that order. A rendezvous at *The Rendezvous*. He was embarrassed to tell people they met on *Tinder* so he merely said they met online.

A week after their rendezvous Michelle even went with him to see the Saints lose to Hawthorn at the MCG and enjoyed it. He in turn went to an exhibition at the National Gallery and had to admit he would go back for the next.

Delaney got back to his desk at Consume and Devour a few minutes before 11am.

"Everything go all right at the doctor's?" his supervisor asked.

"So far so good. He just wants to run a simple test. A precautionary thing. I'll have it done during the week."

Delaney started composing a letter of resignation to the chief of staff and the sport division head letting them know of his intention to leave the company in three weeks' time, Friday, September 5. There were plenty of eager young university graduates waiting in the wings for a newspaper job, although a few would likely think twice about it once they found it did not entail covering the AFL. Consume and Devour would not mind seeing Delaney go since any young journo hired to take his place would be on less money and receive a package containing fewer entitlements.

Less two hours later Delaney got a call on his mobile from the chief of staff. He walked away from his desk and got some privacy in the office of someone who was away on leave.

"You really want to leave us?" Mike Samuelson asked.

"I'm afraid so. I've received an offer I can't refuse."

"We won't stand in your way or make things difficult. You've been an important part of the staff and wish you only the best. Who are you going to work for"?

"*Turf News*," Delaney said. "I'll do some sub-editing, writing and help some of the kids with their copy."

"Sound like a good fit," Samuelson said.

"It is."

"I've talked things over with Sid Maddison and we can let you go in two weeks, which will give you a week off to get ready for the new job."

"Sounds good to me. Delaney said. "Thanks Mike, you've always been fair."

"Can you come into the city next week and fill out all the paperwork with HR? You'll get your long service leave, holiday and sick pay. It should be fairly routine."

"That I can do," Delaney said. "And thank Sid for me."

"I shall. I'll send you a note telling you when you can sign the paperwork."

"I'll look for it. Thanks again Mike."

So just like that, Delaney said goodbye to nearly twenty years of working at Consume and Devour.

He'd miss a couple of his mates he'd worked with and become good friends with but with his fifty-fourth birthday coming up at the beginning of next year, it was time for a change.

"Are you really fifty-three?" one of his colleagues asked the previous week.

"Sure am. And you?'

"Twenty-seven. I'm half your age."

"You've always been good with figures," Delaney sarcastically replied. "Think of life as a hill. When you hit 50, you're at the top of the hill. You, young man, can't even see the top yet. Well, I have not only seen it, but I have been on the top and now I am on the other side heading downhill and I'm picking up speed."

After lunch Delaney rang Bob Nicholls and officially accepted the job offer.

"Great news, Gary. "We'll have an office ready for you."

"My first day will be on Monday, September 8. That okay with you?"

"Sure is. That will give you just enough time to settle in before the spring carnival starts. It will be a busy couple of months, but you'll breeze through it.'

"I'm looking forward to it. If those international horses are as good as everyone says it should be a cracking carnival."

"On that Monday we'll go down to HR, fill out some paperwork and have you at your new desk by 10am. Don't worry about that week's Tuesday edition. It will be wrapped up by 3pm Monday. The Friday edition will be your first."

"Looking forward to it, Bob."

"Stay out of trouble over the next three weeks," Nicholls joked.

Delaney's last two weeks at Consume and Devour passed quickly. He didn't tell anyone about his impending departure except his best mate Steve. They had been pals for more than fifteen years and unlike most friendships in the workplace, they socialised outside work. When Delaney's marriage fell apart Steve invited him over for Christmas dinner where he got to see how a normal family behaved. They went to the races together, spent an occasional night at the cricket or football, and laughed and carried on like a couple of schoolkids on the Sundays when they had the office to themselves. They kicked a footy around and had a bat and a bowl in the long hallway, scattering a few items on several desks when a shot went astray. But by the time they left late in the afternoon all was back in place for the full team's arrival the next morning.

Their biggest laugh was unintentional and caused quite a ruckus at a picnic race meeting last summer. To save a few dollars on grog, Delaney and Steve brought a cool bag along and left it and its precious cargo at the rail past the finish line so they wouldn't have to lug it around.

They hadn't taken a beer from it in about an hour and a security guard took notice of the unattended bag. A few minutes later another guard appeared and then another. Ten minutes later two uniformed police officers showed up. Delaney and Steve were on the other side of the course looking at the horses in their stalls and having a chat with the strappers and trainers and were totally unaware of the commotion until a message from the track announcer boomed from the course's loudspeakers.

"Ladies and gentlemen, the running of the fourth race has been delayed as police tend to a suspicious bag left by the running rail. Please remain well clear of the area until police advise otherwise.

The ears of Steve and Delaney perked up simultaneously. "You don't think that's our bag, do you?" Steve asked.

"Well, we did leave it by the rail. There's nothing else in the bag but the beer, right? Nothing that would connect us to the bag?"

"None that I know of," Steve said. "It was a good idea I brought my own bag and not the one Consume and Devour gave everyone a few Christmases ago. That one still reeks from the potato salad I forgot to take out months ago."

"We can't go over there and claim the bag is ours," Delaney said. "We'll look like a couple of gooses and probably get tossed out on our arses."

So, they didn't do a thing except watch from a distance with everyone else as a police robot moved in to have a closer look at the bag.

Word had got out and on one of the TV screens by the TAB area a 'Breaking News' banner was now running under the cricket coverage. "Suspicious package found at picnic race meeting in in Victoria. Police not ruling out terrorism. More details as they become available and a complete wrap-up on the news at 6pm."

Delaney and Steve burst out laughing. "Terrorism? From six bottles of beer?"

Steve had brought his binoculars to the meeting and zoomed in as the police robot attempted to open his cool bag. He could barely keep a straight face as it cut through the bag and six bottles of beer fell out.

One copper walked over to the cool bag, picked up one of the bottles and opened it. He poured some of it into his hand, put a finger into the cool liquid, tasted it and then burst out laughing.

"It's just beer," he yelled to his colleagues. He took a big sip. "No use letting it go to waste."

Several minutes later there was an announcement from the race caller. "Ladies and gentlemen, the situation has been defused (a poor choice of words) and the horses for race four will be in the mounting yard shortly."

The meeting resumed and continued with no further delays or issues.

Delaney and Steve decided to leave after the sixth of seven scheduled races when a horse which had been beaten by fifty-eight lengths in its last start at Bairnsdale just two weeks ago got up and saluted and paid just $6.

"You can't bet on these things. Better to leave your money at home and load up on beer," Delaney said.

Steve nodded in agreement as they headed for the exits.

The lone hiccup in leaving Consume and Devour came at the human resources office in the city when Delaney went to sign the paperwork.

Delaney had done the figures on a calculator at home and there seemed to be a small discrepancy when he saw the numbers Consume and Devour gave him. He was being given about $1800 more than what he thought he was entitled to but kept the information under his hat.

"The numbers look good to me," he told Karl Farkas, the young fellow from HR. They each signed a handful of papers, shook hands and that was it.

"The money should be in your account by next Friday," Farkas said. "If it isn't, call me right away. Here's my card. All the best in your new job."

Delaney walked out of the building and hopped onto a waiting tram. *How good is this,* he thought. *Things are finally going my way.*

Delaney didn't want any fuss made at Consume and Devour on his last day. He spent much of the morning cleaning up his desk and deleting old files. Several important ones, including a contact list, he forwarded to his personal email account. He updated a detailed contact list later in the afternoon and printed one out for Steve and one for the person who would be sitting at his desk next week. He also emailed all his contacts telling them he was leaving Consume and Devour. Several responded with heart-warming notes. Delaney did not get one email or even a phone call from anyone in management wishing him well despite his close to twenty years on the job. He knew then that he had made the right decision to leave.

He told those he was close to in the office he was leaving and received a bunch of hearty handshakes from the blokes and hugs and kisses from several women when the clock approached 5pm. A few others, who he occasionally said good morning to, simply could not be fussed to even look up from their keyboards and utter a goodbye.

Delaney gathered his things, which fitted in one medium-sized box, and walked to the exit with Steve. "Well, you can't please all of the people all of the time," he said. Of course, the lift was still broken so they had to walk down three flights of stairs to freedom.

"I'll miss you mate, Sundays just won't be the same," Steve said.

The pair embraced in the only way grown men do, with a pat on the shoulder.

"I guess that's it. We'll meet up at Flemington on Cup Day," Delaney said.

"You can count on it."

And with that, Delaney turned left to walk to his car and Steve turned right to his. The end of an era.

When Delaney got to his car, he noticed a parking ticket on the windscreen.

"Son of a bitch," he shouted. "I haven't been here four hours. Bloody council. Thank you very little."

He was ready to blow a gasket. He took the ticket from under the windscreen wiper and was about to put it in his pocket when he gave it a closer look. It looked like a ticket, but it wasn't. He flipped the 'ticket' open and two movie tickets fell out. "Take Michelle for a night out." It was signed Steve.

"Best mate I have ever had," Delaney said as tears welled in his eyes. He tossed his box of belongings in the boot, hopped in the driver's seat and took a few minutes to compose himself before he turned the ignition key and headed home.

8

MANY MONTHS EARLIER, BEFORE HE MET MICHELLE, Delaney heard of a golf club he could finally afford to join; Cypress Golf Course in western Queensland where membership was just $5. Yes, $5. No terms and conditions applied although being up to date on one's vaccinations was recommended. He had to see it for himself. The course had three holes which were three of the worst imaginable; featuring dead grass, dirt and kangaroo shit.

The last person to lose a ball, just last month while playing the second hole, had never been seen again. But what a bargain!

Delaney had taken a week's holiday and flown into Brisbane on the nonstop screaming baby flight from Tullamarine. He saw the offending infant, wrapped snugly in his young mother's arms, as he waited to board the flight. *Just wait*, he predicted. *They'll be sitting right in front of me.*

Sure enough, the baby and her mother, along with Dad, dressed in his finest track pants, were seated just two rows in front of the sportswriter. The baby's screaming started almost immediately and did not let up once throughout the two-hour flight. Delaney tried earplugs, turned the volume up on the inflight entertainment system and then covered his ears with noise-cancelling headphones but nothing could drown out the high-pitched wailing.

Oh, to have a hearing aid which I could just turn off. I'll tell you this, Delaney vowed. *If I ever run an airline, babies and their parents will have designated seats at the back of the plane with a partition to help drown out the noise.*

Delaney literally ran off the plane to get away from the offending child and for a few minutes bathed in the relative peace of the domestic terminal. He made his way over to baggage claim to collect his bag and golf clubs, and then walked a few metres to the car rental desks and hired a spacious sports utility vehicle, one of the many foreign models which helped put Ford and Holden out of business. He adjusted the comfortable seat and mirrors, drove out of the parking lot and headed west. "Go west, young man," Horace Greeley once said. One could be sure he did not have his golf clubs with him.

Traffic thinned as Delaney passed Mt Glorious. And thinned even more until he was the last west-bound vehicle on the Warrego Highway. Nearly 600 kilometres and six hours after leaving Brissy he arrived at the tiny rural town of Cypress, population 175. There used to be another 100 or so people living in the town but once the sawmill closed its doors several years earlier, they left, most likely for the town of Mitchell, which was about 60k east. Cypress was also in the midst of a massive drought, so it didn't have much going for it.

Even on his meagre newspaper salary he felt like the richest man in town, and he was since the average income in Cypress was a little over $4100 a year. No, not $41,000. Four thousand, one hundred.

Besides the Cypress Club Hotel and the golf course, there was just a smattering of stores, a combination post office/library/bank and homes in various states of disrepair. One was a strong gust of wind away from becoming firewood.

It was at the Cypress Hotel, the only pub in town, where Delaney met Cypress's newest resident, Noah Moore, who the month before bought a house in the town for $40,000. *Forty thousand*, or stamp duty for a home in Melbourne. Moore said he fell in love with the area after visiting the pub while passing through. *Not a man who has loved before*, Delaney thought.

"Here on your own?" Delaney asked, fully knowing the answer as he nursed a cold beer.

"I am," Moore said.

Of course he was alone. Who would accompany someone out here? This place was so far out of the way that even the witness protection program wouldn't place someone here. Just as Delaney was about to ask him what he did or had done for a living, the bartender called Moore to the bar.

"Phone call mate. No, I don't know who it is, he just asked for you. You want a receptionist, go look in the yellow pages."

Moore walked to the bar, favouring his right leg, and picked up the horn. "Hello. Hello. You'll have to speak up. Hello. Is that you Frank?" A few seconds passed. "All right, see you then," Moore said. He handed the phone to the bartender who hung it up.

"Big night?" Delaney asked as Moore returned to their table.

"Just going to watch a bit of telly and have a bite with Frank," Moore answered.

Delaney was staggered. "There's television reception out here?"

"Frank's got Foxtel," Moore said. "We're going to watch *Jeopardy* and then the cricket."

Delaney nearly choked on a sip of beer. "Foxtel? Out here?"

"Yup. The premium package too," Moore said. "Ever watch that *Game of Thrones*?"

Delaney had to give up the premium package a few months ago to help ease the strain on his wallet and made do with the $26 basic package. At least it included Sky Racing where he could watch more of his money go down the gurgler three and four times an hour. Of course, it was nearly impossible to see the horses these days because of the graphics which took up nearly half the bloody screen. He complained to Sky several times, but nothing ever came of it.

Delaney had won his first ever bet, a $2 each way proposition on the 1975 Melbourne Cup when Think Big saluted for the second year in a row. But the winners were coming at less frequent intervals as the years progressed, even with a couple of tips from insiders thrown his way.

As he headed out of Brisbane earlier that afternoon, in what seemed to be a lifetime ago, he heard a preview of the midweek card at Doomben on the radio. Full fields and not one shortie in any of the eight races. "Tailor-made for me," Delaney said.

But now, sitting out in the middle of nowhere, with the nearest TAB 100ks away and no phone coverage, getting a bet down would require some doing. He'd stay here one or two nights, even sleep in the car if the hotel wasn't up to scratch.

He checked into the hotel, only after having a look at the accommodation, which was barely passable. He decided to stay two nights at $60 a night. "You should be paying me," he told the clerk, who looked to be anywhere between forty and a hundred. "Have you seen the rooms"?

The fellow did not even blink.

Delaney reached for his wallet.

"We don't take cards sir, only cash."

Delaney counted out $120 and gave it to the clerk. "Is there an ATM in town?"

"At the general store. It usually shuts around six. Barney likes to have dinner at home."

Delaney checked his watch. It was 5.45.

He dashed to the general store where he expected to find Barney with a serviette around his neck and a knife and fork in his hands. There were a couple of kids in there, the first people he had seen in town under the age of fifty.

"Mum said to get milk, not a bottle of Coke," the younger lad said.

"She can't tell one from the other anymore so what's the difference?" his older brother said. They took the bottle of Coke to the counter and reached for a loaf of bread from an old wooden shelf.

Barney got down from the step ladder he was using to stock canned goods and walked to the register. "That'll be $4.85 boys."

The older lad gave Barney a worn out five-dollar note and Barney handed them fifteen cents change.

"How's your mum doing"? he asked.

"Okay," he said.

"Tell her Ethel and I will bring over some leftovers later."

Delaney got $200 out of the ATM and was amazed not to see King George VI's picture on the notes.

Not knowing what would come out of the sink in his room he bought a couple of bottles of water just to be on the safe side.

He handed Barney a twenty-dollar note.

"Haven't seen you before. Just passing through?" Barney asked.

"Got here a couple of hours ago. Drove here from Brissy after flying in from Melbourne."

Barney adjusted his apron, stroked the grey stubble on his face and with a puzzled look, asked, "What in the hell for'? This ain't the kind of place people stop in, this is the kind of place people drive through."

"I heard about the town's golf course. I wanted to check it out for myself," Delaney said.

"Well that will take you all of ten minutes," Barney said. "Bring your clubs with ya and balls? We ain't got neither of them anymore."

"Yes, I brought them with me. I'm heading to the Sunshine Coast after I leave here for a few days of golf and R and R. A working holiday one could say."

"A holiday? The only holiday I get is on Christmas and even then, someone always rings me to open the store saying they forgot to buy something."

"Sorry to hear that mate. Maybe one year you and your wife can take a few days off and head to the city. Brisbane is pretty nice."

"Nah, Ethel doesn't like to go anywhere. She's more comfortable around people and places she knows."

"Fair enough. Say, Barney, who can I see about signing up for that yearly golf membership?"

"You're looking at him. Come by in the morning and I'll fix it up for you. I open the place at seven."

"See you around nine," Delaney said. "Have a good night."

Delaney heard a lone bell ring as he walked out the door.

Barney was a few steps behind. He turned the plastic open sign around so it read closed, shut out the lights and walked home, just a block off the main street where Ethel was waiting for him.

Delaney took a few steps and opened one of the bottles of water he had just bought. He took a long drink and wiped his brow. Six o'clock and it must have been about 35 degrees. He wondered how he was going to sleep in that room of his later without an air conditioner or a fan. Maybe the hotel had a fan somewhere it could lend him.

Delaney took his lone bag from his car and took it up to his room on the second floor, just above the pub where he guessed he would have dinner. His golf clubs were safe in the car.

The musty room had two windows in it. He opened one to let some fresh Cypress air in. The other just wouldn't budge. Now the first thing Delaney liked to do after flying and driving all day was take a shower. He put his thongs on, not wanting to put his bare feet on the bacteria-covered shower floor, and turned on the hot water. The handle came off in his hands. "I don't know why that doesn't surprise me," he said.

He turned on the cold water. The handle stayed on and warm water sprang from an old shower head. He got in and, using a bar of soap he brought from home, took a quick shower. He dried himself off with a large tissue which passed for a towel. Delaney held the towel up to his face and was able to see right through it.

He unpacked, hung up a few things and then tried the bed which surprisingly was not that bad, likely due to its lack of use. Delaney got dressed in a different pair of chinos and put on a fresh polo shirt. He walked downstairs to the bar where about ten people, all men, were sitting around drinking beers.

Delaney nodded to the group and took a seat. The news from Brisbane was on the closest TV but the sound was off. The same barman from before asked him if he wanted another beer.

"Sure do. Do you have a dinner menu?"

"There's not much; fish and chips, burgers, a chicken parma. Pick your poison."

Delaney decided a burger and chips would do the least amount of damage.

He got himself some cutlery and a serviette and took a seat at one of the tables.

The barman brought his meal over about twenty minutes later.

"You have any sauce around?"

"I'll bring it right over mate. Enjoy."

The burger was actually tasty, and the chips got a pass mark. He had another beer and paid the bill, $26 in all.

"There's not a spare fan around here I could borrow for the next two nights is there?" he asked the barman.

"I'll get old Daryl to leave one by your door. Got to keep our best customers happy," he said.

Delaney walked outside. It was still close to thirty degrees, but the sun was slowly going down. He hoped it would get down to twenty overnight so he'd be able to get some sleep.

Delaney had a walk around what passed for the town.

There was a petrol station, but it was closed. A feed store had one of those signs in the window with a picture of a clock pointing to 7am when it would reopen. And that was about it.

Delaney went back to his room and sure enough there was a small portable fan outside his door. He took it inside and was surprised that the room had cooled down a bit. He plugged the fan into the lone power point. It sprang to life, tossing a bit of dust from its filthy metal blades into the air. Delaney opened the *Courier Mail*, which he had bought in Brisbane, and with the fan pointed directly on him, had a read of the right-wing daily. He couldn't stomach it and tossed it in the bin. There was no mobile reception, not one bar, so he turned on the TV. Click, click, click. Nothing worth watching.

Delaney went down to his rental car and brought back his putter and a couple of golf balls. He used one of the two drinking glasses in the bathroom as a target and practised his putting for an hour or so before turning in for the night. It had been a long day and he had three holes of golf to play in the morning so he figured he would rest up.

9

THE STRONG QUEENSLAND SUN WAS BEATING DOWN once again in the morning. Delaney took a quick shower and with no provisions for breakfast in the room, not even a kettle or a package of instant coffee, went downstairs in search of a cuppa. The pub was closed so Delaney walked over to the petrol station. He made himself a coffee, again picked up the *Courier Mail*, as there was nothing else, and slowly walked over to the general store to get his Cypress Golf Course membership from Barney. There was no one else in the store so Delaney had a yack with Barney as he took his details and $5. Barney handed him his membership card, which didn't even have his name on it.

"Thanks Barney, see you later on."

Delaney walked to his car and drove the two kilometres to Cypress Golf Course.

The best value in Australia, a battered sign read above the entrance.

He pulled into what he took for a parking lot and got out of the car. He grabbed his bag, put on his hat and walked to the starter's shed. There was no need for golf shoes. There wasn't a green blade of grass for miles. Work boots were the appropriate footwear.

He knocked on the door of the shed and slowly opened it. It nearly came off the hinges. He didn't expect to find anyone here and there wasn't unless you counted the kangaroos.

Delaney walked to the tee of the first hole, placed his ball down and smacked a drive about 200 metres down the fairway. Two shots later he was on what passed for a green facing a three-metre putt for a four. He sank it but his ball barely went into the hole since it was full of dirt and dead leaves.

He hooked his second drive and made a six and then sauntered over to the third tee. He was on the green in three and two-putted for a five. He was at the top of the leader board with a fifteen for his effort. Since there was no one waiting behind him, he played the three holes again and had a fourteen for a two-round total of twenty-nine. He had made the cut. On moving day, he suffered a hiccup on the second hole and signed for a seventeen.

Delaney closed out the tournament with a spectacular thirteen and gave out a yell after sinking a six-metre putt on the third and final hole. He waved to the three kangaroos watching in the distance and told them his game had improved with a new swing coach and without the nagging advice of a caddie. He posed with the winner's trophy and the oversized winner's cheque for the waiting throng of media, answered a few questions, signed autographs and exchanged fist pumps with fans as he walked back to the clubhouse. "The drinks are on me," he hollered.

The Cypress Classic winner confidently walked back to his car, tossed his clubs back in the boot, took off his hat and wiped his brow. He started the car, saw that it was already 31 degrees at just 10.44 in the morning, and drove back to town. He pulled into the petrol station for a cold bottle of water. It went down smoother than an old man sinking into a warm bath. He was the only one at the petrol station save for the attendant who looked like a dead ringer for the clerk back at the hotel.

"You look just like the clerk back at the hotel; are you moonlighting?"

"That's my twin brother Daryl," said the fellow who was wearing a weathered T-shirt that said *Cypress Golf Club champion 1994*.

"I've just come back from the golf course," Delaney said. "Do you get out there and play?"

The clerk put his head down. "Not since the accident," he said before walking away.

"Accident? What happened?"

"Look mister, I'd rather not talk about it, okay?"

Not wanting to get the fellow stirred up, Delaney left it at that.

10

DELANEY WOKE EARLY THE NEXT MORNING, QUICKLY showered, grabbed his things and went downstairs to check out. There was no one at the desk or at the bar so he left his room key in the bar's mail slot, got in his rental car and headed east, bound for the Sunshine Coast. Traffic was light and he had plenty of petrol along with a couple of bottles of water.

Nearing the outskirts of Brissy he spotted several signs for home-grown fruit and vegetables. Tomatoes, potatoes, peaches, apples, lemons; the stands had everything. One sign written with a red marker on a piece of wood featured just one word—cherry—spelled out in capital letters.

The veteran sub-editor had a feeling whoever wrote the sign was not sure if the plural of cherry was cherries or cherrys so he or she wrote cherry. The road-side stands were a sign of more trusting times. Several were unmanned and simply had a container where customers dropped in the amount for whatever they purchased. Yes, the honour system was alive and well in the country. Meanwhile customers at Coles and Woolies are scanning apples as cheaper oranges and broccoli as lettuce at the self-serve checkouts to put a dollar more into their pockets and keep a dollar away from the multi-billion-dollar retailers.

Delaney enjoyed the fact that the same supermarkets which sacked staff in exchange for self-serve checkouts in a bid to cut costs were now being short-changed millions. Serves them right. He loved hearing the billionaire head of Harvey Norman, Gerry Harvey, complain that his chain was losing customers to online shopping, customers who were going online using the very same computers and laptops Harvey and co-founder Ian Norman had once sold them.

Delaney whizzed through Toowoomba and was making such good time that he decided to head straight for the Sunshine Coast instead of stopping overnight in Brisbane. He decided to stop in Caloundra and then push on to Noosa, the Melbourne of the north, in the morning. He had stayed in Caloundra once before, over Christmas several years back, which was a mistake. It was packed with kids and there wasn't a quiet piece of beach for miles. As he took the exit for Caloundra and made his way inland, Delaney passed the Sunshine Coast Turf Club. *Next meeting, Friday night,* was posted on its message board. He made a mental note and drove on.

It was nearly 6pm and there weren't many cars on the road.

He pulled into Caloundra. The shops on the main drag had all closed and there was not much activity. Every motel had its vacancy sign on. After the horror of the room in Cypress, he picked what looked to be the nicest and most modern of the lot, a four-star joint with Foxtel and a pool. He parked the car and walked into the reception area. There was no one there so he rang a bell on the desk. A few moments later a very tanned, middle-aged gentleman wearing white shorts and a bright red T-shirt came to the counter.

"Haven't got you in the middle of dinner, have I?"

"Happens all the time," the fellow said. "You get used to it."

"Just looking for a room for tonight. The best you have, please."

"How about room 22, down on the end. It's nice and quiet and $135 a night."

"Perfect," Delaney said. "Just for the one night."

Delaney filled out a registration card, paid by debit card and took the key.

"Enjoy the rest of your dinner."

"Thanks mate, you can check out at 11 tomorrow morning if you like; it's pretty quiet here in the middle of the week."

"I just may do that, thanks. Oh, and can you recommend a place for dinner?"

"Try the RSL. It's steak night tonight and there's a band too. My older brother is in it."

"Sounds good to me, thanks."

Delaney got into the rental car and drove to the end of the lot. He took his overnight bag, leaving the golf clubs, and turned the room key. He turned on a light by the door which like most motels and hotels barely lit up the room. But it was spacious and didn't have that musty smell of the place in Cypress. It had two double beds. He put his bag on the one closest to the door and lay down on the other.

"Ahhhhhh."

After about ten minutes he turned on the air conditioner and got up and took a shower. This time there was hot water and plenty of it.

He dressed and set off for the RSL which was just a few blocks away.

Delaney ordered a T-bone steak with extra chips and salad and a cold beer. The place was quite crowded for a midweek night. Fifteen-dollar dinner specials along with the lure of pokie machines and a live band was all any club needed to pull in a crowd, no matter what night it was.

As Delaney ate his meal, he watched the band set up. It looked as though there would be two guitarists, a drummer, a bass player and a keyboardist. A microphone stand was placed in front of each guitarist.

"What time does the band start playing?" Delaney asked the waitress who cleared his table.

"In about thirty minutes."

Delany figured he would hang around and listen to them. He walked over to the bar and ordered himself a pot. A poster of the band was plastered on a nearby wall. Its name was *The Defibrillators*.

Beneath a photo of the quintet was the wording 'Five guys in their 60s and 70s playing the hits of the '60s and '70s.'

The band was introduced by one of the waiters. "Let's give a warm Caloundra welcome to *The Defibrillators*."

It began its set with—what else—*Start Me Up* by the Stones. They were not half bad.

A dozen people or so, all over the age of fifty, got up and started dancing on the floor in front of the band and stayed there when the geezers launched into *Lola* by the Kinks.

He hung around for the rest of their set and then headed back to his motel room.

The next morning, as Delaney was packing his things, his phone rang. The call was from his chief of staff, Mike Samuelson. Delaney did not like to be bothered by people from work when he was on holiday but figured he'd better take the call.

"How's the holiday going?" Samuelson asked. "Played that $5 course yet?"

"Did that yesterday Mike. Was a heck of an experience."

"Look Gary, the reason I'm calling is that one of our reporters who was booked for this junket in the Whitsundays had to bail on us. His kid is crook and in hospital. You're already up there. Would you like to take his spot? It's all paid for. The resort has a nine-hole course and all the food and drink is free. When you get back all you need to do is write a yarn saying how great everything was. Are you in?"

Damn, Delaney thought. *I was looking forward to Noosa.*

"You say it's all paid for?"

"Yup, you just need to be at Brisbane Airport for a 2pm flight to Mackay. You'll be part of a group of about eight or nine."

"I'll do it if I can get a couple of paid days off when I get back."

"Consider it done," Samuelson said. "Go to the Qantas terminal in Brissy. It's all been arranged. The flight back is on Sunday morning. You'll have three days to do as you please."

Delaney checked out of his Caloundra motel around 10.30, passed the Sunshine Coast Racetrack where he would not be going to the races the next night, and instead of heading north, hung a left back towards Brisbane.

Since the morning rush was over traffic was not too bad.

He dropped off the rental car only to be told at the desk while paying his bill that he had not topped up the petrol tank.

"Can I do that now?"

"I'm sorry sir," the twenty-one-year-old sad sack behind the desk told him. "Once you hand the vehicle back to us the rental agreement is terminated. We'll put the cost of the petrol on your bill."

"And how much does *your* petrol cost?"

"Approximately $1.85 per litre."

Which was sixty cents more per litre than what the servos he passed on the way in were charging.

"That's robbery. You guys should all be wearing balaclavas."

"It's was all in the terms and conditions in your rental agreement."

"Have you ever read them?"

"No. But then again I don't need to."

"Great, well that's the last time you guys are getting my business."

Delaney figured the extra cost of the petrol would set him back about thirty dollars.

He signed the form, picked up his bag and golf clubs and walked to the shuttle bus to get a lift to the domestic terminal where he was supposed to meet his fellow group of freeloaders. It was not even noon so he was in no rush.

There were just two other people on the shuttle bus and both looked as though they had just lost their dogs. That's what happens to people when their holiday ends and they hear it is 14 degrees and raining back in Melbourne.

Fortunately, Delaney's holiday was continuing and from now on it was all gratis. He saw eight people milling about the Qantas check-in desk and except for one young woman, who he later found out was from the Queensland Tourism Bureau, and their chaperone, they looked miserable.

"Gary?" the bright and bouncy one asked. "I'm Amber from Tourism Queensland. So glad you could join us."

Amber was a peach. Delaney guessed she was around twenty-six or twenty-seven. She wore her blonde hair pulled back and was dressed for the Whitsundays. She had on shorts and sandals and a white collared shirt that had her name written over the left breast pocket.

"Let me introduce you to everyone," Amber said.

Delaney did not recognise a single face. Six were reporters and two were photographers and they were all from either Melbourne or Sydney. They had just met up for the first time not even fifteen minutes ago and none of them looked thrilled with the company they would be keeping over the next three days. The group was evenly split too; four men and four women. Delaney looked to be the oldest. The others appeared to be in their thirties or early forties. He later found out he was the only sports reporter and the only editor.

Two of the blokes had half of their heads closely cropped and sported beards and sleeve tattoos. Delaney named them Hipster No. 1 and Hipster No. 2. Another bloke had his head buried in his laptop while the last bloke looked as if he had spent many holidays at the buffet tables.

The four women were pleasant enough. He noticed right away that two wore wedding rings. All four were dressed in jeans and had their jackets over the arms.

Delaney was wearing his beige chinos and a blue polo shirt. Since he had been in Queensland for a few days his jacket was buried in his golf bag.

"Everyone looking forward for a few days in the sun and surf?" Delaney excitedly asked.

The mumbles he received in reply told him he would likely be spending his time on the golf course or at the bar—alone.

Well, at least Amber looks as if she wouldn't mind a bit of fun, Delaney thought. *I could be older than her father but a few cocktails could help narrow the age gap.*

Amber told him he had better check in.

All was in order. He got his boarding pass. The rest of the group picked up their belongings and headed for the gate. The flight was on time and boarding was set to begin in about forty-five minutes. Delaney excused himself but not before asking if anyone wanted a cup of coffee. All shook their heads no except for Amber, who surprisingly came along with him.

"I'm going to pick up a paper first. You would not believe the crap I have read the past two days."

He bought the *Sydney Morning Herald*. Another MP was in trouble over her travel expenses and Donald Trump had taken out another Republican primary.

"Do you read a paper every so often, Amber? You are after all baby-sitting a bunch of newspaper men and women for the next three days."

"I don't," Amber said. "My hands get too dirty from the newsprint."

Oh boy, Delaney thought.

"How do you keep up with what's going on?"

"From Facebook, obviously," she said as she tapped his arm.

"The media business is doomed," Delaney said to himself.

They walked over to a coffee kiosk some twenty metres away.

"What would you like, Amber?"

"A flat white."

"Two flat whites," Delaney told the barista. "Make one of them a large please."

"How many of these junkets do you look after?" Delaney asked, making chit-chat as the coffees were being prepared.

"Two or three a year," she answered.

"What do you think of this group?"

"Well, to be honest, until you showed up I thought it was going to be a real drag," she said with a smile.

"They do look as though they'd be more at home in a museum or library, but maybe they'll come around once we get to this island."

"We'll see. Hey, I saw you brought your golf clubs. Think we can play a round together?" she asked. "Play a round of golf that is, not play around. I mean you are, like, my dad's age."

Delaney's heart sank.

"But you are cute," she added.

"I think we have time to go get your eyes examined. I saw a Specsavers somewhere."

Amber laughed. "And you're funny too."

"Socrates," the barista called out. "Socrates."

Delaney approached the counter. "Yes, that's me," he said as he took the two coffees.

"Socrates?" Amber said.

"I like to see if they pick up on it. This one obviously did not."

"That is gold. I'll have to text that to my boyfriend."

Delaney nearly choked on his coffee at the mention of a boyfriend.

That right there is the difference between single men and women. A man would never mention the fact that he had a girlfriend or was involved with someone to a gal he had a chance to hook up with. Women however would bring it up pretty quickly either to (A) brag about it or (B) let the man know right off the bat that she was not interested in him.

"Hey, it's nothing. We have an open relationship. C'mon. Let's go join up with the group," the ever-enthusiastic group leader said.

The eight were waiting by the gate and even though Amber did her best to lift their spirits, they were not having a bar of it. The Victorians had been up early to make it to Tullamarine for their flight, but the Sydney-siders did not have an apparent excuse for their lack of enthusiasm.

Geez, if a three-day all expenses paid trip to a five-star resort in the Whitsundays can't get the group excited, what could? Delaney thought.

When they got permission to board, it was a prop plane they trudged onto. Delaney had never been aboard a plane with propellers. He imagined Amber asking if anyone in the group wanted to have a crack at turning the propellers to get them started.

The plane was cramped but the flight to Mackay would not be all that long. About eighty minutes, someone said. Delaney got an aisle seat. He tried to make some conversation with one of the tattooed blokes he was seated next to, but the fellow seemed to be more interested in playing with one of his cameras. Photographers were a different lot according to Delaney. Maybe they were wannabe reporters who were pissed off at being reduced to writing captions or maybe they yearned for the good old days of darkrooms where they were by themselves mixing chemicals to get the print they wanted instead of having an editor choose the photos that got published.

Delaney read the Sydney newspaper during the flight. Politicians from the left and right fighting amongst themselves instead of getting any meaningful legislation passed took up several pages in the front of the book and Australian cricket selectors arguing over whether to take an extra spinner on a tour of Sri Lanka dominated the back page. There were pages and pages of rugby league news and opinion pieces, and just a few snippets of AFL news despite the Swans having one of the best teams in the comp.

When they arrived in Mackay and waited to retrieve their luggage, Amber gathered the group together to go over the rest of the day's itinerary.

A van took them to their waterside hotel and a damn nice one at that. Delaney's level of accommodation was getting better with each place he checked into.

All the journos had separate rooms. And it was a good thing that they did because the days of Delaney sharing hotel rooms with fellow journos went out with the Fraser government. Now if someone like Amber wanted to share a room for the next three days ... But the likelihood of that happening was the same as John Howard admitting that going into Iraq was a mistake.

Two hours later the Mackay nine piled back onto the van for a reception/cocktail party at a local restaurant hosted by Mackay's mayor. He talked about his city's colourful history of mining, sugarcane and tourism and welcomed the visiting journos.

"What? He's not going to introduce us one by one? He'll never get my vote," Delaney whispered to one of the women in his group, trying to start up a conversation.

Debra Lerner of Wyong, NSW, looked at him as if he had just arrived on the afternoon flight from Neptune.

"What is wrong with you?" she asked.

"Nothing that my psychologist says can't be cured with daily visits over the next several months."

"Look, Gary," she replied, after looking at his name tag. "Don't take this the wrong way. But don't sit next to me during dinner."

Delaney put up his hands as if surrendering. "Tough crowd," he said as he stepped away, cradling his vodka and tonic.

Among those present at the reception were several of the city's bigwigs, obviously there for a free night out.

After the mayor's remarks everyone tucked into a meal featuring top-notch seafood and steak, along with several good bottles of wine. Delaney had one journo sitting on either side of him. They were intent on shovelling as many of the free prawns in their gobs as possible and washing them down with as much of the free wine as they could handle. Conversation was not on their menu. Even when it looked as though they were through, it turned out to be just a slight pause before the whole process began again. The steaks were disappearing from the platters just as fast as the waiter could bring them.

"Hey fellas," Delaney jokingly said. "How about saving some for the rest of us?"

"How about minding your own fucking business," the younger of the two said. At least that's what Delaney thought he heard through the guy's chewing.

Since Delaney had to spend the next two hours with the two as well as the others, he let the remark slide. He was however hoping for one of the large prawns to get lodged in the man's windpipe or lower intestine.

It started raining during dessert and bucketed down for the next twelve hours. Amber kibbitzed with the mayor and several councillors, telling them their city would be getting good exposure from the stories and pictures the assembled journalists would file when they returned home. The mayor looked at one of the journos who at that point was examining something he had pulled out of his ear. "I hope we get our money's worth," the mayor told Amber. "This idea of yours is costing us a small fortune. Did you see how much those fuckers ate? There's not a damn prawn left in town."

"You will," Amber said. "You will." She then planted a kiss on his cheek and flashed her tooth-whitening-kit smile.

She's good, Delaney thought. *Very good.*

After coffee, handshakes and goodbyes, Delaney and his weekend mates dodged the rain and numerous puddles running from the restaurant to the van.

There wasn't an umbrella to be found in the van but at least the front of the hotel was under cover. Half of the group went to their rooms and the other half went to the hotel bar. Amber was nowhere to be seen. She had obviously got a better offer back at the restaurant.

Delaney went back to his room. Under the door was the next day's itinerary.

He looked it over.

Breakfast at 8, checkout at 9, onto the van at 9.05 for a 9.45 arrival at Dusty's Dude Ranch for a round of horse riding. Horseback riding? "I'll bet on them but I sure as hell won't get on one of them," Delaney said.

Lunch was scheduled for 12.30pm at the ranch, followed by a forty-minute trip to the airport for the group's 3.30pm flight to Sunshine Island.

Delaney sat next to Amber on the way to the dude ranch. She had on a pair of dark sunglasses and was not too talkative, probably due to a hangover. One of the women at breakfast said she was dropped off at the hotel around 8.30am.

About ten minutes out of Mackay the landscape took on a different look. Sugarcane stalks were replaced by trees and bushes and the terrain became a bit hilly. Everything was still wet from the overnight downpour but would dry quickly once the sun came out. And it did, just as they got to Dusty's.

Delaney put his favourite hat on and squinted as he got out of the van. Debra of Wyong was the last off the van. She had misplaced her hat and finally found it under a seat as Dusty himself was finishing his welcome speech. Two middle-aged men stood alongside him in full riding gear.

"Any one of you ever ridden a horse before?" Dusty asked. Not one hand went up. "Well, we're gonna turn you city sissies into Queensland cowboys and cowgirls before lunchtime." Dusty whacked his ten-gallon hat on the side of his leg, placed it back on his head and told the group to follow Luke and Brendon down to the stables.

Luke and Brendon each looked like the Marlboro man. Delaney had no idea who was who and he was not about to ask. One of them was chewing gum and the other was twirling a large blade of grass in his mouth.

Everyone in the group was wearing jeans and laced-up shoes as asked.

They walked down a dirt trail to the stables where there were about twenty horses tied up at their stalls. They all seemed pretty docile. Not one was pawing at the dirt. The first thing everyone got was a helmet since the last thing Dusty's Dude Ranch needed was a lawsuit if someone fell off one of the horses and took a knock to the head. Nose plugs should have been mandatory as the stench of manure and urine was made even worse by the strong sun. Several in the group exchanged helmets until everyone had one sitting on their head which fitted.

"Tie them straps up too," Luke or Brendon barked. "Ya can pick your own horse if you want. The ones down this end have a little more pep," he said, pointing to his right.

Delaney slowly moved to the opposite end.

"Luke here will give you all a quick lesson. And you'd better pay attention."

In halting words, Luke, he of the chewing gum, told the group how to steer the horse by pulling on the left or right rein. "Pull back on the reins if you want them to stop. And if you want to get them to go a bit faster, give them a little kick on the side. But make sure you keep your feet in the stirrups at all times."

The tattooed duo were the first to mount up. The saddles were massive, not like the flimsy one Hugh Bowman sits on.

Tattoo No. 1 and Tattoo No. 2 didn't look all that uncomfortable sitting on their mounts, but they would never be mistaken for horsemen either.

The women in the group, including Debra and Amber, were put on two smaller horses.

"Hey old-timer," Brendon barked at Delaney. "We saved this one for you. Her name is Allie and she is twenty-two years old. Think you can manage?"

"Just to set the record straight, I'm prematurely grey," Delaney said.

Brendon gave Delaney a leg up onto the 550kg animal. It was the first time in his life he had been on a horse unless the mechanical ones outside KMart counted. This one though was going to move forwards, backwards and sideways and was not going to stop when someone pulled the plug or time ran out. Allie was a lovely chestnut and moved about as quickly as a seventy-five-year-old woman with a walking stick.

It was then that Dusty rode up on his horse like John Fucking Wayne.

"Everybody git in single file and follow me," he hollered. "We're going to take it nice and easy, up and down a few trails around the property to get you used to riding. Then later we'll pick up the pace."

Dusty led the way with Delaney and Allie bringing up the rear.

It took a few minutes for Delaney to get used to the horse's action. The others, only one of whom had even been on a horse before, began to put a bit more distance between themselves and the veteran reporter, whose arse already ached from all the bouncing around in the saddle.

"Hey old-timer," Dusty yelled. "Give her a kick to get her moving. We ain't got all day to wait for you to catch up."

Delaney held on tightly and gave Allie a slight tap on her left side. She responded with a lurch forwards which nearly knocked Delaney out of the saddle. "Easy Allie, easy girl." He pulled on the reins which slowed her down.

He caught up to the group, dodging tree branches hanging over a dirt trail which was beginning to narrow.

A creek ran alongside the trail and calmed his nerves a bit. The group climbed up a slight hill and made its way safely down the other side. Several horses were blowing a bit from the work but Allie, who had likely been on the trail hundreds of times, wouldn't have been able to blow out a candle.

Dusty then took the group to another trail which required the horses to canter a bit. Still bringing up the rear, Delaney was finally beginning to get comfortable. He looked at his watch. They had another half hour to go until a break for a smoko, or lunch. He'd make it but had no idea how a Damien Oliver or a Craig Williams got on a horse seven or eight times in an afternoon, weaving through traffic at forty five kays an hour all for a five percent share of the prize money. Being a jockey was without a doubt one of the most dangerous and nerve-racking jobs on the planet. It was the only one Delaney knew of where an ambulance was required to follow the workers as they did their jobs.

A clearing finally appeared, and Delaney recognised the spot from which the group started out. "Just a few more minutes Allie, just a few more minutes," he said calmly.

Either Luke or Brendon, he never would be able to figure out who was who, helped him dismount from the mare.

Allie was tied up along with all the other horses and given some water and a feed.

"That wasn't so bad now, was it?" Dusty asked everyone. The others were much keener in voicing their approval than Delaney whose aching arse needed a chair with a nice soft cushion.

"That was fun," Amber said as she took her helmet off and unfurled her long blonde locks. "I can't wait for the ride after lunch."

"There's another ride? Not for this cowboy. I've about had it."

"Don't be a spoilsport. Everyone else is going around again."

"Enjoy, enjoy."

The staff served up a tremendous lunch; steak with baked beans of course, and jacket potatoes followed by coffee. The Marlboro men and Dusty lit up cigars.

"That's enough down time," Dusty said. "Let's get back on them horses. We're gonna do some riding in the open country."

Everyone put their helmets back on except Delaney. Dusty slowly walked over to him and launched a wad of spit from his mouth that landed at Delaney's feet.

"You quittin'?"

"Well, quitting would not be the word I would use. Let's just say I am sitting this one out."

Dusty shook his head as he walked away to join the others.

Delaney spent the next hour getting a tour of the ranch from a woman named Barbara who he guessed was Dusty's wife. The ranch had several levels of accommodation for tourists, with the best of the lot being a hand-made cabin, featuring an outdoor shower. According to Barbara, the cabin and everything in it was all made by Dusty and some of the ranch hands. Delaney could barely hammer a nail in a wall, but these guys had made the tables, cupboards and the like from scratch. And best of all there was not a television or radio to be found. It was a great place to spend a few days roughing it and getting back to nature. The fantastic food would be a bonus. If Delaney and the other journos did the place justice in their write-ups, there'd soon be a bunch of Melbournians and Sydneysiders booking their holidays here.

Delaney's colleagues came back carrying on as though they just collected a massive quaddie. Even Debra of Wyong was exchanging high fives with the Tattoo No. 1 and Tattoo No. 2.

What in the wide wide world of sports happened on that trail? Delaney wondered.

Goodbyes were exchanged. Delaney saw Amber give Luke, or was it Brendon, a kiss on the cheek. The woman gave out more kisses than an old aunt at a bar mitzvah.

As Delaney was waiting to get in the van, Dusty gave him a look that could have gelded a colt on the spot. Nobody sat next to Delaney or even spoke to him on the fifty-minute drive to the airport. "Making friends wherever I go," he said softly.

11

THE JOURNOS GATHERED THEIR THINGS AT MACKAY airport and were asked to walk to the opposite end of the terminal from which they had arrived the previous afternoon. It was where chartered flights and small aircraft departed.

A small sign with the painted words *Island Airways* hung above an old desk where a teenager dressed as a pilot looked to be doing his homework.

Amber walked up to the lad and introduced herself. She pointed to the group and they exchanged paperwork. Delaney looked onto the tarmac where a twelve-seater was parked. A fellow who did not seem much older than the kid doing his schoolwork was giving it the onceover. Holding a clipboard, he checked the wings, flaps, tyres and then fuelled it up.

"We're flying in that?" Delaney asked no one in particular.

"Is that for us?" Debra of Wyong asked.

"It sure is," Amber said. "It is just a twelve-minute flight. Up and then down."

The lad masquerading as a pilot asked everyone to step on a scale before heading onto the tarmac. "We don't want to overload the old girl now, do we?"

Just how old is the girl? Is she a pensioner? Delaney wondered.

The luggage was to be weighed separately.

Much to the dismay of one of the female journos, the pilot called out everyone's weight which was recorded by the bloke who had fuelled up the plane.

"Another forty kilos and we would have overloaded her," he said.

"I don't like this," Debra of Wyong said.

"Now you know how I felt about that open country riding earlier," Delaney said. "It's a twelve-minute flight and we won't even be more than a few hundred metres up. Don't worry. If we happen to come down, I'm sure we'll be rescued before the sharks get us."

Debra of Wyong's knees buckled at the thought.

When everyone was safely buckled in their seats, the pilot introduced himself.

"I'm Dan Chambers and I'm in Year Twelve. Just kidding. I've been flying out to Sunshine Island for several years now. We're flying into a bit of a breeze this afternoon so the flight will be about sixteen or seventeen minutes. Enjoy the view."

And with those words the plane taxied onto the runway. Chambers waited for clearance and when he got it a minute later, he hit the throttle. They started to pick up speed and were airborne quite quickly. The coast faded from view. For such a small plane, the flight was relatively smooth. Five minutes or so later Delaney spotted the island to his right along with its small runway. The well-heeled vacationers came by plane, the others by boat. This weekend, Delaney and his colleagues were part of the well-heeled set.

The plane started its descent, and on its approach got so close to the water you could reach out and touch it. There was a bump and then another when the front wheel hit the runway. It was followed by a few sighs of relief.

Chambers taxied the plane to the far end of the runway where a van from the island's resort was waiting. The journos disembarked and for a gag Delaney got down on his knees, crossed himself and kissed the runway. No one laughed although Debra of Wyong looked as though she was about to throw up; from the flight, not the gag.

Chambers and his crewmate gathered the group's luggage and put it in the van.

Amber, who had obviously been here before, exchanged pleasantries with a man and woman from the resort who had come to greet the new arrivals.

"Hop in everyone," the woman said. "I'm Samantha. Everyone calls me Sam," she said facing the group. "Rob is behind the wheel. We'll look after you for the next few days and make sure you have a good time."

Rob stopped the van in front of the resort's reception area. Tattoo No. 1 and Tattoo No. 2 helped him unload the group's luggage.

There were palm trees everywhere and the place was immaculately landscaped. Delaney figured it was about twenty-eight or twenty-nine degrees. There was a bit of a breeze, but the air was not that humid. Perfect conditions. There were several pools within sight, one of which was quite crowded, and two tennis courts which were both unoccupied. A nine-hole golf course was situated to everyone's left. Luxury villas surrounded it. Delaney had earlier found out that the villas went for nearly $1000 a night which included all meals and drinks.

Rob went to park the van. It was the only vehicle on the island save for several golf carts which were reserved for the staff's use.

It was just after 4pm. Samantha walked everyone about a hundred metres to the edge of the beach. "Welcome to Sunshine Island," she said with a wide smile. Sam looked to be in her late thirties, with dark shoulder length hair. She was wearing shorts, which showed off her tanned legs, and the same white collared shirt which all staff seemed to be wearing. She was a stunner. "I'm the resort's general manager and Rob is second in charge. This is one of the nicer islands in the Whitsundays. Over to your left is Turtle Island and to its left is Henning Island. If you look to your right, you can spot Shore Island."

This is where Delaney piped up. "Are you shore?"

The group let out a collective groan except for Sam, who laughed and smiled at him.

"We run on solar power and have our own water treatment (sewage) plant. Supplies are shipped here a couple of times a week and you'll find that we have everything you'll need. Each of your rooms has a flat screen TV although with so much to do here not many people bother turning them on. You're free to use any of the snorkelling equipment, paddle boats and the like. Just be careful. There's a lifeguard on duty on the beach and we ask that you listen to him when going in the water."

Sam led the group back to their belongings and handed out the room keys. Everyone had their own room.

"Dinner is at seven but if you're feeling peckish the doors open at six."

Three days and two nights of paradise, Delaney thought. *Imagine living here.*

As if on cue a young lad in a golf cart came along. He collected everyone's bags and dropped them off at each of the guests' private rooms. As everyone scattered to their rooms, Delaney took a minute to admire the view, deciding what to do first. A swim? A few holes of golf?

Sam approached Delaney and extended her hand. "It's Gary, isn't it?"

"It sure is. And let me guess. You are … Sam?"

"That was funny what you said before about Shore Island. How would you like a private tour of your home for the next few days? Meet you back here in ten minutes?"

"Sounds good to me," Delaney said. "Can you point me in the direction to my room? It's number fourteen. I'd hate to waste valuable time looking for it."

Sam pointed to her left. "It's about fifty metres down the path on your right."

"Thanks Sam. Meet you back here in a few."

Once Sam turned to go back to reception, Delaney raced to his room. As promised his bags and golf clubs were waiting outside the door. He turned the key, opened the door and looked on in amazement. *So, this is how the rich live. Geez.*

Plush carpeting, two double beds, a couch, chairs, a table ... and that was just the balcony. Twin ceiling fans whirred above the massive room, cooling the warm tropical air. The bathroom had more towels than your average KMart. He could use one for each limb and still have a half dozen left over. There was a separate shower and bathtub, and the toilet would have easily met with George Costanza's approval. Delaney washed his face and brushed his teeth. He put on some deodorant, changed his shirt, adjusted his hat and went to meet Sam for his private tour.

Sam was waiting for him, wearing a pair of sunnies and a baseball cap with the Sunshine Island insignia on it. Her hair was in a ponytail and stuck out from the back of the cap.

"Do you like the room?" she asked.

"Like it? I'd like to take it home with me."

Sam led the way down to the beach, pointing out a small pond filled with small colourful fish. "When the tide goes out some of them get left behind until the tide comes back in," she explained.

The two walked down a dirt-covered, shady path for about fifteen minutes until they came to an old pier. "We've never used this pier but years ago this is where the other islanders tied up their boats. There's a sharp drop-off here so we don't even mention it to our guests, but it is a nice spot just to come to sit and relax."

"You couldn't find a spot nicer than this if you tried," Delaney said.

Small waves crashed against the pier while the sounds of birds were seemingly everywhere. The sun was beginning its descent in the west.

"So, what's your story, Mister Delaney? Have a wife back home?" Sam asked as she took a seat on the pier. Her long legs dangled over the edge but were still a metre above the water.

"Well, in name only. She and I are separated. We haven't lived together for quite some time, but we are still on good terms. There's no chance we'll get back together though. Too much water under the bridge. We are each dating," Delaney said as he sat down next to her.

"Seeing anyone special?" Sam asked.

"No, not really. I go out once in a while, but it usually never amounts to much."

"I'm sorry. You seem like a good catch from where I'm sitting."

"Thanks Sam. That's very nice of you to say."

"I wouldn't say it if I didn't mean it."

"And you? Surely a gorgeous woman like yourself can't be single."

"I'm not. I'm with Rob, the fellow who was with me at the airport. We kind of run this place."

"Wait a second," Delaney said. "You and Rob are living together, and you and I are sitting here like this?"

"We're not exclusive. There's a lot of temptation running a resort like this with new people checking in each day. We still love one another but are not in love with one another anymore if that makes sense."

It made perfect sense. Delaney and his ex were the same way.

"It may not be any of my business, but have you come down here with others beside me?"

"No," Sam answered.

"Why me?" Delaney asked.

"You made me laugh when you kissed the runway. The flight wasn't that bumpy, was it?"

"Not at all. I just like to laugh. I think of myself sometimes as more of an entertainer than a reporter."

"Have you ever been on stage?"

I've had a few gigs in Melbourne over the years but now I'm a bit too old to pursue it."

"You should give it another go. You make me laugh."

"If you were in the audience every night, I would."

Delaney thought about giving Sam a kiss but instead took hold of her right hand like a sheepish twelve-year-old. They sat together for a few minutes, taking in the fantastic scenery with neither saying a word.

Delaney nervously grabbed the underside of the pier with his right hand and suddenly felt a sharp pain in his index finger. He had cut himself on something underneath the pier, possibly a barnacle and the digit started to bleed quite badly.

Sam reacted like Chuck 'The Bayonne Bleeder' Wepner's cut man.

"What have you done?" she screamed. "Let me see."

"It's nothing, just a little cut."

Delaney wrapped his finger in the bottom of his shirt to stop the bleeding and within a couple of minutes it had stopped.

"We better start to head back," Sam said.

As she stood up, she stuck a hand in her pocket and took out a tissue. She wrapped it around Delaney's finger and kissed it.

"I'll give it a good wash when I get back to the room. It's nothing to be alarmed about, really."

They continued their walk.

"What sort of animals are on the island?" Delaney asked. "Besides the kangaroos?"

"There are a few koalas, wombats and small pythons that live in the trees. Occasionally they drop down and scare the heck out of people."

"Now you tell me?" Delaney said as he pulled his hat down and looked up.

He kept one eye on the trees and the other on the ground for the next thirty minutes. Eventually the two emerged from the bushes and trees on the far end of the golf course just as Rob drove by in a golf cart. He had been adjusting the sprinklers on the last few holes, spotted them and stopped.

Oh shit, Delaney thought. *This could get interesting.*

"Hey Rob, this is Gary. I was just showing him around the island."

"Pleasure to meet you Gary," Rob said extending his hand. "Quite a place, isn't it?"

"I thought so until Sam told me about the pythons."

"They won't hurt you mate, they're too small. If you see one just leave him alone. Eventually he'll go back in the trees."

Rob turned to Sam. "See you back at headquarters. There's a guest complaining about something in her room, so I better get back and see what the problem is."

"Okay hun. See you soon."

And just like that Rob got back in his golf cart and drove off.

"Seems like a nice enough bloke," Delaney said.

"He is," Sam said.

Neither said a word until they got back to the spot from which they'd set out more than ninety minutes ago.

"See you at dinner," Sam said. "And take care of that finger." She blew him a kiss and walked inside the main building.

Delaney walked back to him room not knowing what to make of the situation with Sam. Under the door was an envelope.

Delaney turned on the ceiling fans and opened it up.

There was a printed note inside.

You are cordially invited to attend a cocktail party/reception before dinner tonight at 6pm at the main bar located near the restaurant. It was signed Rob and Sam.

He looked at his watch. Six o'clock was less than thirty minutes away. Not enough time for a swim; better hit the shower.

After he towelled himself off, he put his horsey-smelling jeans in the shower and gave them a bit of a wash. He hung them on the balcony railing to dry. He found a Band-Aid in the bathroom cabinet and put it on his cut finger which hadn't bled since he left the pier. He had always been a quick healer.

Delaney put on the better of the two pair of shoes he'd brought along, tan chinos and a blue collared shirt. He looked in the mirror. "Not bad for an old-timer," he said. He closed the door behind him and walked to the main building. It was 6.10.

He walked into the bar and noticed everyone from his group, including Amber, was already there with drinks in their hands. It gave the appearance that he was being fashionably late or even unsociable which raised a few eyebrows.

"There you are," Amber said. "We thought maybe you weren't coming."

Amber had spent much more than half an hour getting ready. She had done her hair, put on a pair of tight-fitting jeans with heels and had even done her nails. They were a bright and shiny red. Her revealing top did not leave much to the imagination. She had it and was flaunting it. The bar was quite crowded, and she caught the eye of everyone in it.

"Would I miss this? Good company, free drinks. It's right up my alley," Delaney said.

"You scrub up nice," Amber said.

"Thanks, but when it comes to scrubbing up nice, you're on top of the podium."

"Ya think?" she asked as she did a one-eighty for Delaney to admire.

"Oh yes," Delaney answered.

"See you later. I'm going to catch up with the others." And just like that she was gone.

Delaney walked to the bar and ordered a vodka and tonic. Tattoo No. 1 and Tattoo No. 2 were each wearing a pair of skinny jeans and the regulation T-shirt to show off their artwork. Debra of Wyong was talking to the other women in the group. The other bloke from the group was nowhere to be seen.

Delaney got his drink, took a sip and heard his name being called.

It was Sam. If Amber looked good, Sam was absolutely stunning. She was carrying a glass of champagne and was wearing a light blue sundress with heels, had her hair down and just a bit of make-up on. He would soon find out why she was all dolled up.

She gave him a warm hug and a kiss on the cheek. Delaney returned the embrace. She smelled a hell of a lot better than the jeans he had left on the balcony. He sniffed. "What are you wearing," he asked.

"Practically nothing," she whispered in his ear.

"Sorry to interrupt, but Mr Chadwick would like to have a word with us," Rob said.

Delaney nearly dropped his drink when he saw it was Rob. He was holding a bottle of beer and had to have seen how chummy Delaney and his partner were getting.

"Excuse me," Sam said.

The two walked to the other side of the room where a big handsome fellow in a suit but no tie greeted them warmly. After a few minutes Rob called Delaney over to join them.

"Warren Chadwick, Gary Delaney."

"I'm originally from Melbourne. I've read some of your stories. It's an honour to meet you."

"No, it's a bigger honour for me," countered Delaney.

"Are you enjoying yourself so far?"

"Oh yes, what's not to like?"

"Remember to give us a nice write-up," Chadwick said, digging an elbow into Delaney's side. "We've poured a lot of money into this place."

Chadwick then spotted another fellow in a suit near the bar and excused himself. "Bill," he hollered as he walked off.

"One of the bigwigs?" Delaney asked Rob and Sam.

"He owns the place," Rob said. "He made a lot of money in Melbourne and moved his family up this way. When he heard about this place a few years ago he bought it. Rumour is he paid cash. Then he hired us to spruce the place up and run it."

"Well, he has to be happy with what you guys have done. The place looks great," Delaney said.

"And, we're nearly booked out for the weekend too," Sam added.

Delaney offered a toast. "To the good life."

The three clinked glasses.

"Excuse us for a second Sam," Rob said.

Rob and Delaney stepped away from Sam. Delaney had an idea of what was coming. He was wrong.

"Listen mate, Sam likes you and you seem like a nice bloke so if you and she want to get together later I don't have a problem with it, okay? I've been sleeping with Amber so it all evens out."

"Really, you and Amber? For how long?"

"About the last eighteen months. She came up here with some politicians on one of those fact-finding missions. And fact number one is she is fantastic in bed."

"And Sam doesn't mind?"

"Not at all. We have an open relationship. It wasn't always that way. We tell each other who we're sleeping with so there are no surprises. It works for us."

For once in his life Delaney was speechless.

"Well, if it works for you who am I to break up a good thing?"

Rob laughed, looked over at Sam and gave her the thumbs up.

"And if you excuse me, I have to get to the kitchen. With Chadwick and you members of the media here I want to make sure the chefs don't screw up dinner."

Delaney walked over to Sam.

"All okay?" she asked.

He smiled. "Could not be better."

12

GARY DELANEY WAS SIPPING ON HIS USUAL, STANDING close to Samantha and listening to a male guitarist and female keyboardist entertain a few hundred guests before dinner. They took turns singing. Delaney didn't recognise any of the tunes, but then again, his attention was focused on the lovely young woman beside him.

They looked at each other and smiled as the duo continued playing.

"I've got to go mingle with the other guests, and then I have paperwork to do," Sam said. "Enjoy dinner. I'll come to your room about nine, okay?"

"Sure. You're working. I understand. Nine o'clock it is."

Delaney moved closer to give Sam a kiss, but she pulled back.

"Not here, especially with Chadwick around. We'll have plenty of time for that later." She squeezed his hand and was off.

Delaney made his way to the restaurant.

A young staff member, likely a backpacker, greeted him and told him to sit wherever he liked and to help himself to the buffet. A waiter would come by for his drink order.

Many of the paying guests were wearing smart but casual attire. The men, mostly in their forties and fifties, were tanned and wearing blazers and slacks, while the women wore skirts or dresses. Several couples were holding hands across their table and looking at each other the way they had on their wedding day. They were on well-deserved holidays, free from the stress of children, jobs, the beeping of their phones and daily trips to Woolies, Coles and Bunnings.

If only more couples could afford it, Delaney thought. *I never could. Maybe a week at a place like this could have saved my marriage. Then again ...*

The journos stood out like greenies at a Tony Abbott fundraiser. Tattoo No. 1, or was it Tattoo No. 2, was wearing a Dead Kennedys T-shirt. Delaney felt like tossing the hipster out of the restaurant on his sorry arse. *You're a guest here for goodness sake. Act like one.*

The rest of the group was seated at a table towards the rear of the room. Debra from Wyong looked especially nice in a cute, light blue skirt, white top and heels. She had some class.

"Hello everyone. Mind if I join you?" Delaney asked as he pulled out an empty chair. "Quite a place eh? And have you got a look at the food?"

There were no objections, so Delaney took a seat.

"Everyone taken a vow of silence?" he asked.

Delaney waited for someone to speak up. One of the photographers mumbled hello and that was it.

Delaney excused himself, took what was left of his vodka and tonic and looked for another table. He recognised some of the resort's staff at one and asked if he could join them. None of the three blokes at the table objected so he took a seat.

"Not hitting it off with the others?" one of them asked.

"Not exactly. I've tried but ..."

"Don't worry about it. You're welcome to sit with us the rest of the weekend. We'll find some work for you too," the fellow said. He looked to be about twenty-five or twenty-six. He had a mop of dark hair and looked as though he had just finished posing for the latest edition of *Triathlon* magazine. He had probably slept with more women in the last year than Delaney had in his life.

The other two blokes at the table, who were about the same age, laughed. All three wore their resort issued polo shirts and navy-blue shorts.

"Where do I sign up? Seems like a great job," Delaney said.

"It is. I'm even thinking of staying a couple of months longer. Where else will I find a set-up like this?"

"Smart man," Delaney answered. "I'm going to help myself to the food."

Delaney looked at the massive buffet and couldn't decide where to start. Name it and it was there. Seafood, all sorts of salads, roast beef, baked chicken, broiled chicken, fried chicken, stuffed chicken, vegetables, a section of Asian food and another with Italian food. Plus, every piece of fruit imaginable and a dessert table.

I'd gain five kilos a week if I worked here, Delaney figured. *I don't know how they all stay so fit.*

Not wanting to discriminate, Delaney sampled a bit of everything with an emphasis on the roast beef at the carving station which was as lean and as rare as any he had ever seen. He washed everything down with a couple of soft drinks.

His substitute dinner mates finished before he did so Delaney had dessert by himself; a dish of vanilla ice-cream and fresh strawberries. *What would a meal like this cost back home? Eighty, ninety dollars?*

It was just after 8pm. On the way out of the dining room Delaney was asked by the young hostess how everything was.

"Fantastic, simply fantastic."

"Hope you saved some room for breakfast," she said.

"I am not going to think about breakfast until I've had a chance to digest dinner," he said.

"Have a good night," she said.

"I plan to."

Delaney ordered a drink at the bar and listened to the guitarist and keyboardist for a while before heading back to his bungalow. His date with Samantha was just thirty minutes away and he was getting a bit nervous, like an opener at the Boxing Day Test at the MCG. He had a pretty good idea of what might happen with Samantha, but wasn't taking anything for granted.

Delaney walked past the two deserted swimming pools. The lounge chairs were stacked up against a fence and the cream umbrellas tied up, ready for the next day's visitors. The bright green fronds of palm trees gently swayed in the soft evening breeze. He looked up at the sky. It was a clear night and there were stars everywhere. The sound of the ocean's waves hitting the shore was a perfect soundtrack.

He got back to his bungalow about 8.45. He poured himself a drink from the mini bar in a bid to relax but instead found himself pacing about like an expectant father.

A few minutes before nine there was a slight knock at the door.

Delaney slowly walked to the door, took a deep breath and opened it. Debra of Wyong was standing there with a bottle of champagne.

"Debra? I reckon you have the wrong bungalow. You're in number twenty-six, down the path on the left. I'll take you there."

"Now why would you want me to leave, Gary?"

Debra walked right in and looked around.

"Just like my place," she said.

Debra put the bottle of champagne by the fridge and took a seat on the couch, curling her legs beneath her.

"Get us a couple of glasses Gary, I'm thirsty."

"And a little tipsy too," Delaney said.

"I've had a couple of drinks. You'd be drinking too if you had to hang out with those arseholes we're with."

"I thought I was the number one arsehole on your list."

"Nah, we got off on the wrong foot Gary, that's all."

Any other time Delaney would have taken Debra of Wyong up on her offer. He looked at his watch. It was two minutes until nine.

"I'm sorry Debra but you really have to go. We'll talk tomorrow, okay?"

Debra stood up. "Tomorrow? What, you have plans? You don't think Amber is going to sleep with you, do you? She's young enough to be your daughter. I'm just the right age for you."

Just as she put her arms around Delaney's neck there was a knock on the door.

'Shit,' Delaney muttered to himself.

He turned towards Debra. "Come with me. Let's go on the balcony. It's too nice to be inside. I'm just going to the bathroom. Wait here."

Delaney ran to the front door and let Samantha in.

She too was carrying a bottle of champagne. *They must be giving the shit away*, Delaney thought.

"Thanks for coming," Delaney said.

"I wouldn't want to be anywhere else," Samantha said.

The two embraced. Samantha kissed him long and hard.

"Are my tonsils intact?" Delaney asked when they came up for air.

Samantha smiled.

"I'll be just a minute. I need to use the ladies."

As Samantha closed the bathroom door Delaney ran to the balcony.

"There you are. I thought you'd left me. Come sit with me," Debra of Wyong said.

"In a minute. Stupid me, I forgot the champagne."

Delaney ran back inside just as Samantha exited the bathroom.

"Ready for some champagne?" he said.

"Of course, let's have it outside."

Samantha slid back the balcony door and stepped outside before Delaney could stop her.

That's it. It's all over. I'll be bunking with the staff until we leave, Delaney thought.

He poured two glasses of champagne and went outside. But instead of hearing two women screaming at each other he found just Samantha. He looked around. Debra of Wyong was nowhere to be found.

"Looking for something, hun?" Samantha asked.

"Er, no. It's just that ..."

"Just what?"

"Nothing at all," Delaney said. He sat down next to Samantha and handed her a glass of champagne.

"To new friends," she said.

"And lovers," Delaney added.

Where the heck is Debra? Delaney wondered.

They made love twice that night and again in the morning. Delaney was surprised he was able to get it up three times in ten hours. Samantha was delighted.

"We could be looking at a new record," Delaney said.

"You couldn't have done it without me." Sam winked.

She was right, Delaney noted.

Sam was due at the front desk at eight.

"Gotta run," she said as she dressed. "See you later."

She left him with a big kiss which promised more of the same was planned for night two of his stay.

Samantha scampered back to her cottage, trying not to be noticed. She was wearing the same dress she wore at the reception/cocktail party and did not want the staff's tongues wagging.

Samantha took a few looks around before she opened the door to her cottage and took a deep breath as she closed it behind her. She then went into the bedroom to put on her work clothes and found Rob and Amber asleep in the bed she still shared most nights with him.

She knew Rob was having sex with other women and was okay with it, but this was the first time she had seen her partner with someone else.

She woke Rob, who was already late for work.

"Why did you bring her here for goodness sake? I sleep in this bed."

"Sorry hun. I knew you wouldn't be coming home last night. What time is it?"

"Time for you to never do this again in the bed I sleep in. Understand?"

"I do."

"And it's five past eight so get out of bed and get to the desk. And get her the fuck out of here," Sam screamed as she put her Sunshine

Island shirt on and hitched up her skirt. She grabbed her work keys and slammed the bedroom door shut.

Meanwhile Delaney showered and got dressed. He put on a pair of blue shorts and a white shirt. His bungalow had coffee and tea, and a wide selection of fruit but he decided to go to the restaurant for a proper breakfast. He went outside and checked the balcony to see if there was a sign of Debra of Wyong. There wasn't.

In the restaurant he spotted Debra and the rest of the group at the same table they occupied the previous night. Only Amber was absent. Delaney approached the table.

"Hello all, what do we have planned for today?" Delaney asked.

Nobody said a word.

Debra of Wyong put down her knife and fork and stood up. She looked Delaney in the eye and without saying a word socked him right in the jaw.

The unexpected blow staggered him and bloodied his mouth.

Debra of Wyong then sat down and went back to her pancakes and bacon. Delaney slowly walked away from the table rubbing his jaw.

"What the hell happened?" a girl with a British accent sitting at the staff table asked.

"Be damned if I know, but I sure as hell won't ever set a foot in Wyong again."

"Why who?"

"It's north of Sydney," he said. "How's the food this morning?"

"Great, not sure if you'll be able to chew any of it. I can ask the chef for a blender if you like."

"Very funny," Delaney answered. "I'll tell you this, she has a hell of a punch."

After Delaney tucked away as much as he could with his bruised jaw, he asked for some ice from one of the waiters. He gave Delaney a large glass filled with ice cubes. He took it back to his bungalow, dropped the ice cubes into a washcloth and laid it against his jaw to prevent any swelling. He washed down a couple of Panadol to dull the pain, made his way to the balcony and took a seat on the same couch he and Samantha shared the night before. The ice cubes melted in about twenty minutes, but his jaw felt much better. He went to the bathroom and looked in the mirror. There was hardly any swelling.

"Time to enjoy the facilities," he said.

Delaney swung his golf bag over his shoulder, put his hat on and walked to the nine-hole golf course which at this time of the morning was inhabited mostly by kangaroos.

He collected a hand buggy from the staffer manning the small pro shop and grabbed a score card.

The holes were longer than a par three course and were pretty straight forward; just a couple of dog legs with an array of bunkers protecting the greens.

Just as he was about to tee off, three guests approached the pro shop.

None had their own clubs but were quickly kitted up by the lad in charge.

"Hey mate," the lad called out to Delaney. "Would you mind playing with these three fellas to make it a foursome?"

"Sure," Delaney said.

The three blokes walked to the first tee and introduced themselves.

"Mark Renninson," the tallest of the three said as he shook Delaney's hand.

"Gary Delaney."

"Gary, this is Steve Gledhill and this is Jordan West."

Delaney shook hands with Gledhill and West.

The three were in their forties and looked to be quite well off. But then again who on the island wasn't? They all wore dark Nike shirts and white baseball caps and the same black Nike golf shoes. A pair of expensive sunnies was perched on each of their caps.

Delaney took them for bankers, barristers or real estate agents.

"A perfect day for golf," Renninson said. "Since you were here first why don't you do the honours, Gary?"

Renninson was well over six feet tall and trim with a full head of grey hair.

Delaney was hoping not to embarrass himself as he placed his ball on the first tee. It was quite a change from the course in Cypress where he had kangaroos for playing partners.

He took a couple of practice swings, stepped up to the tee and drove the ball straight down the middle of the fairway.

"Heck of a nice drive," Gledhill said as he stroked his beard.

The somewhat stocky West was up next. He took his time and sent a line drive down the left-hand side of the fairway. It landed about thirty metres behind Delaney's shot. Renninson then stepped to the tee. He was all arms and legs and hooked his shot. It landed just off the fairway after bouncing off a tree. Gledhill also hooked his shot and everyone lost sight of it.

Delaney's putter failed him on the first hole and on several others and by the time the foursome reached the last tee he and Renninson were each tied with scores of forty-one. Gledhill was four shots back and West five.

The four exchanged a few stories over the first eight holes.

"You know any of the pros?" Gledhill asked.

Delaney, who had a handicap of eighteen, was not a name dropper. But just to keep up with the others who talked about meeting the prime minister and partying with B Grade celebrities at the spring racing carnival, he told the others about the times he chatted one-on-one with Tiger Woods and Phil Mickelson after press conferences at the President's Cup several years ago.

"What's Tiger like?" Gledhill asked.

"Well, he is pretty quiet when the TV cameras aren't running. Mickelson is the opposite. He's a ripper bloke and will bet more money on one NFL game than I make in a year."

"Do you do any gambling?" Renninson asked Delaney.

"Just on the horses, a few dollars each way."

"Seeing how we are tied here at the last hole would you like to make things interesting?"

"How much?" Delaney answered.

"A hundred bucks I beat you. If we're still tied, we'll play the hole again."

The offer did not seem to surprise Gledhill and West. Delaney guessed they had lost a bit to Renninson over the years.

"You're on," Delaney said. "I'll hit first."

Full of confidence after his magnificent performance at Cypress a few days earlier, Delaney stepped to the tee on the par four ninth hole and hit his worst drive of the day, slicing it into the rough on the right-hand side of the fairway.

"Pressure get to you?" Renninson asked before sending his drive straight down the middle of the fairway.

Despite landing in the rough Delaney had a good lie and chose an eight iron. He took his time, choked up a bit on the club and hit one of the best shots of his life. The ball landed just in front of the green and rolled to within ten metres of the pin.

Renninson also found the green with his second shot and had the easier putt for par, being just about five metres away from the hole.

Being farthest from the hole Delaney putted first. He took his time lining up his shot. He needed to put some speed on the ball but not too much or else he would overshoot the hole. But he did just that and landed about three metres behind it.

Delaney chose to putt out and sank the shot to get his par, not bad considering where he was after his poor drive.

"Easiest hundred bucks I'll ever make," Renninson told Gledhill and West before lining up a fifteen-footer for the win.

He was on the sweet part of the green and the putt looked good as it slowly rolled to the hole. But the ball lipped the cup and rolled to the right. "Shit," Renninson yelled.

Ever so cocky he went to tap the ball in for a par with just one hand on his putter and missed.

"Tough luck," Delaney said.

Renninson opened his wallet, took out two fifty-dollar notes and begrudgingly handed them to Delaney. He grabbed his clubs and walked off the course before his mates even putted.

"He doesn't like to lose," Gledhill told Delaney.

"I'd hate to see what he's like when he wins," Delaney said. "I'm going to have a swim before lunch. Catch you guys later."

The win—in terms of money won—wound up being Delaney's biggest for over a year.

He spent the second of his two nights on the island with Samantha. She brought over some desserts from the dining room along with another bottle of champagne.

There were no interruptions this time. It was just the two of them.

They were less nervous than twenty-four hours ago so the sex—and there was a lot of it—was even better.

Delaney and Samantha stayed up most of the night talking. She got up before he did the next morning and left a note in his bag that she had written the previous day.

"Read this on the plane, the real plane, not the one piloted by the kid," was written on the front of the envelope.

She kissed him softly on the lips and left.

Sunday morning was a busy day with so many people checking out after breakfast and lunch. The guests bound for Melbourne usually left after breakfast while the majority of the Sydneysiders left on the boat back to Mackay after lunch or flew back on Island Airways.

Pilot Dan Chambers was going to be a busy man this day.

Delaney got up about 7.30 for the group's 9am flight back to the mainland.

He noticed the envelope Samantha left and kept it unopened as she requested. Delaney showered, dressed and had breakfast.

He passed by the reception desk after he had eaten, locked eyes with Samantha and motioned for her to come outside. She did. They ducked behind the building.

"Thank you for the most wonderful couple of days," Delaney said. "I'll miss you."

"I'll miss you too."

"If you're ever in Melbourne ..."

"You're the first person I'll come see."

She glanced at her watch. It was 8:25.

"You better get your things. Rob will drive the van to the landing strip in twenty minutes."

"Okay. Bye Samantha."

She stroked his face with her hand. "Bye Gary."

Delaney's group met near the main building fifteen minutes later. Rob helped everyone with their luggage, giving special attention to Amber, started the van and drove to the landing strip where the plane to take them back to Mackay was waiting for them.

Pilot Dan Chambers greeted everyone. They took the same seats they had two days ago on the flight in and buckled up. Chambers started the plane. It was parked at the end of the runway and on a perfect sunny morning Chambers gunned the throttle. The twelve-seater picked up speed and was airborne in about ten seconds. Delaney looked out the window for the entire twelve-minute flight and did not say a word.

When they landed back in Mackay, the group said goodbye and went their separate ways. Amber gave him a hug. "Hope you had a nice time," she said. "Samantha is gorgeous."

"I did. Thank you."

Delaney had a long day ahead of him. From Mackay to Brisbane and then on to Melbourne. He checked his bag and clubs through to Melbourne. He took his jacket with him—the planes were always chilly, and Melbourne was bound to be even chillier—and the letter Samantha had written.

He'd open it on the last part of his journey, from Brisbane to Melbourne.

There were a few hundred people waiting for the flight to Brisbane. Delaney took a seat as far away from the others in his group as possible.

He saw Debra of Wyong and gave her a wave. She gave him the finger.

13

ABOUT HALFWAY THROUGH HIS PRISON TERM, JOHNNY Pastrami was in the exercise yard one Saturday afternoon shooting baskets when he was approached by Louie Andressi, an accountant serving time for fraud. Andressi, was in his mid-forties and bore no resemblance to the tough guy his name suggested.

With his thick glasses, neatly trimmed hair and a face like a field mouse, all the accountant needed was a bowtie to complete the stereotypical image of a bean counter.

With his hands in his pockets, Andressi watched Pastrami for several minutes, grabbed a few long rebounds from his missed jump shots and sent the ball back to him with strong chest passes.

"Thanks mate," was all Pastrami said.

"Can I get a game?" Andressi meekly asked.

"You want to play me?" Pastrami laughed at the thought. Pastrami was a head taller than Andressi and had been on the court nearly every day over the last six months. Today was the first time he'd seen Andressi on the basketball or tennis courts.

"How much of a head start do you want?" Pastrami joked.

"Nothing. We start even."

"You think you can beat me?"

"I can give you a game if that's what you're wondering."

"Okay. You're on. A point a bucket. Twenty-one is game. Winner's ball. You can take the ball first."

Andressi took off his jacket, put his glasses in the inside pocket and laid the jacket on a nearby bench. He had a New York Knicks T-shirt on.

"Shit, I hope you go better than the Knicks are going. How long has it been since they played finals? Seven, eight years?"

"Five," Andressi said, receiving a bounce pass from Pastrami.

"How about a few warm-up shots before we begin?" Andressi asked.

"Sure, go ahead."

Andressi's first shot clinked off the front of the rim and rebounded directly to him. He fired up another shot which also missed. He chased down the loose ball, drove in for a lay-up and softly laid it off the backboard for a bucket.

"All right. I'm ready. Let's get started."

Pastrami guarded Andressi, watching his left since Andressi was right-handed.

Andressi dribbled to his right, stopped and let loose with a jump shot from about six metres away. It hit the back of the rim, then the front and went through the net. The accountant was up 1-0 and took possession.

His second shot, from even farther out went straight in, leaving Pastrami somewhat bewildered.

Andressi's third straight jump shot was also on the mark.

"You've played some ball, haven't you? Pastrami asked.

"Just a bit in school, but that was a long time ago."

Andressi's next attempt missed. The rebound landed straight in Pastrami's hands. He took the ball back to the free-throw line and then drove to the basket to get on the scoreboard.

Using his superior size, Pastrami muscled Andressi to the basket and added another lay-up to make it a 3-2 game.

The two began to work up a sweat on the warm cloudy afternoon and traded baskets before Andressi again made several long shots to nudge ahead 19-18. With possession he needed to make just two more baskets to win. He sank the first with another jump shot and with a win just another basket away, Pastrami moved in tight, not wanting to give Andressi a clear look at the basket.

Andressi took the ball and without dribbling faked going up for another jump shot. Pastrami took the bait and left his feet and Andressi drove around him and scored on a lay-up to win the game.

Pastrami, who did not like to lose at anything, was so mad at himself that he grabbed the ball and slammed it to the ground. He kicked the ball and then kicked the steel post holding up the basket, which he regretted immediately. The pole did not budge, and Pastrami's left ankle crumpled upon impact.

"Shit," he yelled as the pain coursed through his leg. He tried to put some weight on his foot, but it wouldn't hold it.

"Mate, can you get me some help? I think I've busted me ankle."

Andressi retrieved his jacket, reached for his glasses, put them on and turned to walk back inside to get the facility's nurse.

"Hey," Pastrami called out as he sat down on the court. "Thanks for the game, mate. You played well, real well."

"I enjoyed it," Andressi said as he turned back and leaned down to shake Pastrami's hand. "I was curious to see if I could still play a bit."

"Were you any good?"

"I was a starter on our state championship side when I was in Year Eleven."

Pastrami chuckled. Well, you sure had me fooled and that doesn't happen very often."

Pastrami struggled to take off his left sneaker while Andressi went to get the nurse. His ankle was already badly swollen.

Pastrami limped over to a nearby bench and waited for the nurse. Ernie Waite ran over a minute later carrying a first aid kit. "What happened, Johnny?" he asked as he examined his ankle.

"I kicked the bloody post after I lost a game to that guy who asked you to come out here."

"He beat you? That little pipsqueak?"

"Yeah, he did, and he'd likely beat your arse too so knock it off. How's the ankle?"

"You might have broken it. We'll have to get it X-rayed. We don't have an X-ray machine here, so we'll have to run you to hospital in Shepparton."

"Shepparton. How far is that?"

"About half an hour. Let me get some help to bring you inside. I don't want you to do any more damage to it by trying to walk on it. Stay put."

"Seriously Ernie, where am I going to go?"

Waite laughed and came back in two minutes with a big security guard. The two lifted him up and carried him inside like an injured footballer.

Waite got a bucket, filled it with ice and told Pastrami to put his foot in it.

"It will cut down the swelling. Take these Panadol too. It will help with the pain."

"Let me go see who can run you up to Shepparton."

Waite knocked on the door of Warden Stanley Blake and told him of Pastrami's injury.

"For crying out loud," Blake said. "Why in hell did he have to kick the damn pole?" He looked at the duty roster. "I'll get Hendricks and Jameson to run him up there. It's about time they did something besides sitting on their fat arses all day."

Sid Hendricks and Ron Jameson had each been on the job for more than twenty years. They were unarmed but would be able to hold their own if trouble broke out. They were chuffed to be asked to take a prisoner to Shepparton. It got them out of the prison for a few hours.

Hendricks brought one of the prison vehicles around, a four-door sedan, and he and Jameson helped Pastrami into the back seat. Fingers Tannenbaum had got wind something was up and was surprised to see his mate being put into the car.

"What's happened, Johnny?" he asked as Hendricks closed the back door.

"Looks like I broke me ankle playing basketball. I'm off to hospital. See you later, mate."

The three drove off. With Pastrami no threat to run off with his injured foot, Hendricks and Jameson both sat in the front seat although Hendricks did lock both back doors as a precaution. Hendricks drove and after twenty-five minutes of unbearable chit-chat they pulled up to the emergency room entrance at Shepparton Hospital.

Jameson got out first and retrieved a wheelchair from inside. He wheeled Pastrami into a near-empty room. A clock on the wall ticked over to 5pm. In another six hours the place would be overrun with drunks, druggies and accident victims.

With Pastrami's aching foot propped up, Jameson wheeled the chair to a window with a sign reading *admissions* over it. There was no one visible so he called out. "Hello? Hello?"

A middle-aged man with a stethoscope around his green smock finally appeared.

"How can I help you sir?"

"Mate, this man might have broken his ankle. Can a doctor have a look at it please?"

Jim Pearson came around the counter and looked first at Jameson and then at Hendricks who stood by the door. He recognised the uniforms they were wearing. "This man a prisoner from Murchison?" he asked.

"He is. How about having a look at the man's foot? He ain't gonna hurt you," Jameson said.

Pearson leaned over and gave Pastrami's foot a quick look.

"Hmmmm. I'll get an ice pack for it. In the meantime, there are forms to fill out."

"Forms? I'm fuckin dyin' here, doc," Pastrami said.

Pearson wheeled Pastrami to a spot in front of a wall that was covered with drawings by local school children. Jameson took a seat next to him. Pastrami had a look over each shoulder. "Even my leg looks better than these things," he said.

"That's not a nice thing to say," an old woman sitting nearby said haltingly. Pastrami figured she was close to eighty. She had an oxygen tank at her feet and a tube in each nostril. "Are you an art critic sir?" she asked.

"No. I'm in real estate."

"Well my great granddaughter did two of those drawings so please keep your opinions to yourself."

"Look lady," an angry Pastrami started to say.

"Yes?"

"I hope you get better soon."

"Thank you young man," the woman replied.

Pearson then appeared with an ice pack, a clipboard and a pen.

He wrapped the ice pack around Pastrami's swollen left ankle.

"Good timing doc. Speaking of docs, when am I going to see one?"

"Just as soon as she's finished with the patient she's working on. While we wait can you please fill out these forms? Would you like me to change the channel on the television for you?"

"Actually," Pastrami said, "you can turn the damn thing off."

Thirty minutes later Pastrami was wheeled into an examining area by a hospital worker.

Jameson and Hendricks stayed outside.

A young nurse took his blood pressure, temperature and asked if he was allergic to anything.

"Just long-range jump shots."

"Excuse me sir?" the dark-haired nurse said.

"I lost a game of hoops and kicked a pole in anger."

"I'm sorry," she said. "I don't follow the tennis."

Pastrami shook his head in disbelief.

"The doctor will be with you shortly sir," she said, taking the clipboard and completed forms from Pastrami.

"All people ever do around here is wait," he said to himself.

Cordoned off by a curtain, all Pastrami could do was listen to what was going on around him.

"You did all you could, doctor," a woman said.

"I guess you're right, but it doesn't make it any easier. Notify the morgue and his family. Who's next?"

"A man in examining room two with a possible broken ankle."

"Thanks, nurse. I'll tend to him."

Dr Ed Holzman pulled back the curtain and introduced himself to his next patient.

Pastrami liked the look of him, someone experienced.

The fifty-five-year-old grey-haired doctor, who preferred the excitement of an emergency room to a stuffy office, sat down next to Murchison prisoner number 3682521 and examined his ankle and foot.

"Are you able to put any weight on it at all, Mr Pastrami?"

"Not at all, doc."

Dr Holzman gently turned Pastrami's foot from side to side.

"Any pain there?" he asked.

"A bit."

"Looks to me as if you have a fractured ankle. I'm going to send you to X-ray just to be sure, okay?"

"Okay doc. Will it need to be in plaster?"

"If it is broken, yes. In six weeks or so you'll be fine, Mr Pastrami."

Holzman pushed back the curtain and motioned to the nurse who took Pastrami's vitals several minutes ago.

"Nurse Chambers will take you for those X-rays. One of my colleagues or I will have a look at them and determine what course of action needs to be taken."

After several X-rays were taken of Pastrami's left ankle and foot, he was wheeled back to his cubicle by the nurse who did not know a tennis ball from a horseshoe.

"I can give you something for the pain if you like," she said.

"I guess I could use something. It is hurting a bit."

"Be back in a tick."

The nurse returned with a couple of Panadeine Forte and a cup of water.

"Here you go. These should help."

"Thank you."

Pastrami tossed the pills in his mouth and washed them down.

"Sure hope these start to take effect soon."

"They will; give it about twenty minutes."

"I'm sorry, I did not catch your name earlier," he said.

"Kate Chambers," she said while checking his blood pressure.

"Your blood pressure and pulse rate are normal. We'll see what the doctor says about your foot. The orthopaedic surgeon is going over the X-rays. You're lucky. She's the best there is and was finished with her shift but agreed to hang back and take a look at the pictures."

"That may be the best thing that has happened to me today. Well, that, and meeting you."

Thirty-two-year-old Kate Chambers blushed. She was used to the unwanted attention of patients but there was something about this one that she liked. He was a bit rough around the edges but she liked the way he looked at her with his blue eyes. There was a tinge of excitement in them. And he wasn't a bad looking guy, probably seven or eight years older than she was with broad shoulders and a full head of dark hair. He was a lot better looking than those pencil-pushing geeks in administration who were always coming on to her. Since he wasn't in his prison issued garb and she hadn't seen the guards out front, Chambers had no way of knowing her patient was doing an eighteen-month stretch in confinement thirty minutes down the road.

"Why don't you go out with one of the doctors you work with?" her friends routinely asked.

Chambers did go out with a doctor in her first year on the job. They were nearly the same age and worked a lot of the same shifts. It was only after they slept together for the first time that he told her he was married with a young child. She immediately put an end to the six-week fling and vowed to never again go out with someone she worked with. Several months later the married doctor got offered a job in Brisbane and much to her relief took it. At his going away party Dr Unger said one word to her; goodbye.

"It's nice to meet you too Mr Pastrami. I've got other patients to attend to. Take care of your foot," she said.

As Kate Chambers left, the orthopaedic surgeon arrived holding Pastrami's X-rays.

"Hello Mr Pastrami, or should I say inmate Pastrami? I'm Dr. Fiona Madison," she said as she looked at his chart.

"Hi doctor. What do the pictures show?"

Dr Madison took a seat and as she did her short skirt rode up her thigh.

"Well it's not as bad as we originally thought. You have broken your ankle but there was no damage to the metatarsal bones. We will have to put your leg in plaster, and you will need to wear a moon boot for six weeks, and also use crutches."

Pastrami was so busy looking at Dr Madison's shapely legs that he barely took notice of what she said.

"What was that, doctor? Six weeks? And crutches?"

"Yes, you'll need to keep as much of your weight off your injured ankle as you can. One of the nurses will come by and put the plaster on your ankle, fit you for a boot and give you a pair of crutches. We'll have you back here in three weeks for another set of X-rays to see how you're healing. Do you have any other questions?"

He did but kept them to himself. "No doctor. I think you've covered everything."

And with that Dr Madison got up and walked away. She didn't close the curtain, so he leaned over and got a good look at her legs as she walked out of the ER.

"Enjoying the view?" Kate Chambers asked as she closed the curtain.

"The view?"

"Of Dr Madison."

"Well, to tell you the truth I was."

"Well you can put your tongue back in your mouth, loverboy. She was just about to leave for a social event, but Dr Holzman asked her to have a look at your X-rays. What do you think, she dresses like that while she's working? There'd be cardiac arrests all over the place."

"You would have the same effect, Kate."

"Thank you Mr Pastrami. What kind of a name is Pastrami anyway?"

"It's Italian. It was much longer once upon a time. When my folks arrived in Australia after the war, someone in the Immigration Department, who thought he was being funny, shortened it."

"Hmmmm. Makes sense."

Nurse Chambers prepared the plaster and then applied a bandage to Pastrami's lower leg and ankle which the plaster of Paris covered. The cast extended from just below the knee down to his ankle and dried rather quickly.

"Is it too hard?" she asked.

"I beg your pardon?" the patient said as he winked.

"The cast. Is it too hard wise guy? Can you wiggle your toes all right?"

Pastrami wiggled his toes for the nurse.

"All good there," she said. "I'll be right back. What size shoe do you wear?"

"An eleven."

Chambers returned a minute later with a moon boot and a pair of crutches.

"Let's try this boot on your good foot to see if it fits."

Pastrami stuck his foot into the boot.

"How does it feel, too tight? plenty of room?"

"There's plenty of room."

"When the plaster is completely dried, we'll put the boot on. Strap it up tightly every time you put it on. You can take it off when you're sitting down and when you go to sleep, but anytime you need to walk, even if it is just to the toilet, make sure you have it on."

"Okay."

"Now the crutches. Ever use a pair before?"

"Never."

"Stand up please," Nurse Chambers said.

She put one crutch under each of his arms and adjusted them a bit to get the right length.

"That should do it. Try walking with them. It's not too difficult to get the hang of it."

Pastrami lifted his injured left foot off the floor and pushed himself forward using the crutches. He turned around and walked back.

"How does it feel?"

"Not as good as I did when I woke up this morning, but I guess they'll do."

"That's it then. You can go home now. Here's a script for the pain and some plastic sleeves to put on the cast when you are showering. Try not to get the cast wet. I'll take you back to the admissions desk. In the chair please."

Pastrami groaned.

"It's hospital policy. In the chair please."

Nurse Chambers wheeled her patient back to the admissions desk.

Hendricks and Jameson approached the desk when Pastrami was wheeled in.

"Is he with you?" Chambers asked the guards.

"He is," Jameson said.

Chambers turned to Pastrami. "You're a prisoner?"

"Afraid so. But I'll be out soon."

The tone in Nurse Chambers' voice suddenly changed.

"Goodbye Mr Pastrami. Try and keep your weight off your injured foot."

"Do you have private health insurance sir?" Pearson asked looking at Pastrami.

"I'm sorry, what was that?"

"Do you have private health insurance? You left that part blank when you filled out your forms earlier."

"No I don't, just a waste of money."

"All right, how would you like to pay your bill?"

"My bill? What bill?"

"For your moon boot and crutches."

"You mean I have to pay for that?"

"Yes, you do."

"Jesus, doesn't Medicare pay for it?"

Pearson shook his head no. "Not in this case."

"It's a damn good thing I brought my wallet with me. How much for goodness sake?"

"Ninety dollars for the boot and sixty dollars for the crutches," Pearson said. "The cost for the doctors and plaster is covered by Medicare.

Pastrami shook his head and took three fifties from his wallet and handed them over.

In return he was given a receipt and a copy of the bill.

"Thank you Mr Pastrami. We'll see you in a few weeks for your follow-up. If there are any issues before then please see your GP."

"I'll do that, thanks mate."

Pastrami put the crutches under his arms and walked to the door of the ER flanked by Hendricks and Jameson. The ER was starting to fill up as it usually did after sundown on a Saturday night.

14

ON HIS FIRST SUNDAY OFF IN YEARS, JUST TWO DAYS after leaving Consume and Devour, Delaney received a text from one of his former colleagues at 11.34 am. "Okay. Played along with your joke long enough. What time do you start work today?"

He actually laughed out loud. He'd miss several of his colleagues but knew he had made the right decision to leave.

However, there were a couple of pranks he did not get a chance to pull and wished he had.

Once every couple of weeks a middle-aged woman came by to water the large plants in the office. The plants, believe it or not, were rentals and the woman was entrusted with watering them and carefully removing any dead foliage.

Consume and Devour trusted its employees to put out its newspapers and put things on its website but it did not trust anyone to water a fucking plant.

The plant waterer was quite a looker, even in her drab work clothes. She was slim with dark hair and had a cute pair of glasses which made her even more appealing. She carried a watering can, probably full of a nutrient laden liquid that Consume and Devour was paying extra for. Someone in management must have come across a story somewhere that plants in an office reduced stress and produced an environment in which workers thrived.

It was Steve who came up with the idea that he should dress up as a plant on watering day. Delaney would stand there in a large flower pot with his legs and arms wrapped in green paper. He'd hold his arms outward like branches and see what sort of reaction he'd get from the plant waterer. Steve would film it all. Candid Camera 2016 style.

The other prank involved one of the young account managers. They used to be called salesgirls. They sold ads and were primarily young women, hence the name. But today they were called account managers, like the way a garbage man is known as a sanitation engineer. Not that the account managers were peddling garbage. However, some of what was being written and passing for news in 2016 should have gone straight into a rubbish bin.

Back to the account manager. She was a tall glass of water, in her late twenties with long blonde hair and blue eyes that looked right through you. She mostly kept to herself. Lord only knew how she wound up at Consume and Devour and not on the cover of *Vogue*.

On her very neat desk was a framed photo of her and her boyfriend. He had his arm around her, and she had a very contented look, the *this is the one*, look. It had to be her boyfriend. She never wore a wedding ring, so it wasn't her husband. Brother? Now who keeps a framed photo of herself and her brother on her desk? Besides a nun.

So, Delaney had the thought that one Sunday afternoon, when there was no one around, he would tamper with the photo. The plan was to open the frame, cut the fellow's head out of the picture and replace it with his own and see just how long it took her to notice when she came in on Monday morning. Five minutes? Ten? Would she laugh? scream? March over to Delaney's desk and ask him to fix it immediately? Slap him? Ring HR? Delaney never got the chance to find out.

Delaney had a week before he began his new gig at *Turf News* and vowed to sleep in until at least 9am each morning. Michelle had a few days off during the week and they arranged several social outings.

A friend of Michelle's had been asking her for weeks to bring her new beau over for lunch, one of those, "I've heard so much about you, so nice to meet you," lunches.

Ellen Sherman and her husband lived on the Mornington Peninsula, about a ninety-minute drive. Since the warmest day of the week was going to be on Wednesday, and Michelle had the day off, lunch was locked in for 1pm.

It was a casual affair with two other couples, none of whom Delaney had ever meet. He felt like a first-time starter since everyone knew everyone else.

With not much traffic on the peninsula, for there rarely was any this time of year after passing Mornington, the trip down was uneventful until Delaney decided to pull into Woolies to get a bunch of flowers for the hosts. Michelle didn't think it was necessary, but Delaney wanted to make a good first impression. The parking lot was half empty and with a strong sun beaming down Delaney was able to find a spot in the shade of a gum tree.

Michelle decided to wait in the car. It would be a simple dash in and dash out.

Delaney found a nice mixed spring bouquet for fifteen dollars and with just two checkouts open waited in line. There were self-serve checkout machines available but they were there simply to take jobs away from school kids so Delaney avoided them as a form of protest.

Delaney looked at the two lines and what was in the trolleys of those waiting and chose the checkout to his left. An older woman was being served. She looked to be about seventy and slowly took the items from her basket and one by one gently placed them on the conveyor belt to be scanned by a woman even older than she was. *They're oranges, not hand grenades*, Delaney thought. *Toss them on there and be done with it.*

Behind the woman and in front of Delaney was a trolley filled nearly to the rim.

Two boys, one about four and the other about seven, stood by it. Their mother was nowhere to be seen. She had probably forgotten something and had run back to one of the aisles to get it.

The younger of the two reached for a chocolate bar on the display rack and started opening it. The older lad knocked it from his hands onto the floor. Typical horseplay between two brothers. Until the younger lad let out a piercing scream as if he had been wounded in combat. The screaming got louder and louder. Delaney locked eyes with the young lad, put his fingers to his lips and said, "Shhhhhh." The lad stopped screaming for a moment and then turned it up a notch. By now everyone in the checkout aisles was looking at the screaming kid. Several were covering their ears. The screaming sounded like an air raid siren.

It was then that Mum came running back holding a box of breakfast cereal.

"What's going on?" she asked.

"That man," the older kid said, pointing at Delaney, "told Bobby to shut up."

"Did you tell my son to shut up?" she yelled at Delaney. "Did you?"

"No. no. I merely did this," Delaney said, showing the mother, who looked to be in her early thirties, how he put his fingers to his lips and whispered "Shhhhhh."

"No stranger talks to my kid like that."

"But I didn't."

Delaney saw what looked to be the store manager coming his way, so he dropped the flowers, barged past the full trolley and the old lady and made a run for the car.

He jumped in, turned the key and was gone.

"What's going on," Michelle asked. "Did you rob the place?"

"Nothing, they didn't have anything appropriate. You don't bring roses to lunch."

In the rear-view mirror Delaney saw the store manager give up the chase. He was too far away for anyone to get a view of his number plate.

He made a left-hand turn out of the parking lot onto Nepean Highway headed for Sorrento.

Twenty minutes later thanks to the deft navigation skills of Michelle they pulled into the driveway of Ellen and Bryan's place.

There were several other cars there, much newer and expensive models than what they were driving. The house was a beauty; double storey with a view of the bay. Delaney was no real estate expert but figured the place was worth at least $1.5 million.

Ellen saw them drive up and shouted, "Let yourselves in," from the balcony. "We're all up here."

Delaney and Michelle walked up a flight of stairs and opened a sliding door to the balcony where everyone was seated around a large table and two bright blue umbrellas.

"We're here," Michelle said.

Ellen rushed over and gave her a big hug and a kiss on the cheek.

"So good to see you again," Ellen said.

Ellen was also in her fifties with dark shoulder length hair and a welcoming smile. She came out of the kitchen wearing an apron over a tan sundress and was holding a large salad spoon.

"And you must be Gary," Ellen said.

"I was when I woke up this morning."

Ellen laughed.

"Ever since Michelle told us about you, we have wanted to meet you."

She motioned to her husband Bryan.

Casually dressed in blue shorts, a white polo shirt and boat shoes, Bryan got up from the table and greeted Michelle with a kiss and Delaney with a handshake.

"Good to finally meet you," the retired engineer said. "Come and join everyone. Can I get you anything?"

"A beer would be nice," Delaney said as he took a seat around the table.

Several dips along with large cheese and fruit platters sat in the shade of the umbrellas on what was turning out to be a mild day.

Delaney also noticed—but did not say anything—a bee hive that was about just ten metres away. Ellen and Bryan were amateur beekeepers and that was not good news for the veteran sportswriter since he was allergic to bee stings. One summer when he was a kid he got stung by a wasp and went into anaphylactic shock. A country doctor saved his life with a timely shot of adrenaline. Delaney had to see an allergist once every couple of weeks for several years to get desensitised, but the series of shots worked. He always carried an antihistamine pill with him just in case. Money, keys, wallet, antihistamine pill.

He had got stung only once in the last forty-five years, on the hand, and it merely swelled up a bit after he swallowed an antihistamine pill. But he kept a keen eye on the hive just in case a few of its occupants were tempted by the nearby food.

Ellen walked Michelle over to the table after getting her a glass of red and introduced the newcomers.

Anna and John were sitting on the opposite side of the table along with Stephanie and Michael.

Delaney and Michelle shook the hands of Anna and John. Stephanie and Michael were a bit far away for handshakes, so nods were exchanged instead.

Michelle had met them all before. Anna was a schoolteacher and John a real estate agent. Stephanie worked at her local library and Michael was retired. Anna and John were the babies of the bunch; in their forties.

"Bryan tells us you're a sportswriter," John said to start the conversation. "That must be interesting work, especially this time of year with finals beginning."

"It is for some, but I don't cover the AFL, maybe a VFL match here and there. I'm mostly a desk man these days although I am starting a new job next week."

"Leaving the business?" Michael asked.

"Nah. I'll still be in the newspaper business but will be concentrating solely on horse racing. I'm going to work for *Turf News*."

"I have a look at that every once in a while," John the realtor said. "I owned a couple of horse a few years ago with a couple of mates."

"How'd they go?" Delaney asked.

"One ran in a couple of country cups but we never had a runner in the city. Still, it was good fun even though we never made a cent."

"It's a tough game," Delaney said. "Unless you can win something in town every so often or run a place there's no way an owner can make any money."

It had always been a dream of Delaney's to own a horse. But unless one forked out at least $100,000 for a decent animal at one of the yearling sales it was a losing proposition and Delaney was not fond of taking financial baths. So, he stood on the sidelines, enjoying the sport of kings as a very small-time punter and by writing the occasional story.

Ellen had been working overtime in the kitchen preparing the food and after a lull in the chatter on the balcony poked her head out from the kitchen to tell Bryan that the steaks and fish were ready for the barbecue. Bryan fired up the Weber and went to the kitchen. He returned with a massive dish of streaks and fish, gently laid it down on the side of the barbie and one by one tossed several of the well marinated steaks on the left-hand side of the barbie. The fish filled up the smaller right side.

Ellen and Bryan's guests were not the only ones taken with the sweet smell coming from the grill. A couple of bees started buzzing around the food. Bryan swatted them away several times as he tended to the steaks and fish. They were more of an annoyance than a danger.

"How does everyone like their steaks? Rare? Medium? Well?" Bryan asked.

There were two votes for rare and four for medium.

As the steaks sizzled Bryan kept a close eye on them. The first two off the grill went to Anna and Stephanie. A few minutes later the rest were put on a platter along with the fish and placed in the centre of the table.

"Dig in." Ellen said. And dig in they did. Hands flew in all directions and plates filled with the steaks and fish along with salads, vegetables and jacket potatoes.

Delaney took just enough to get started. He cut into a piece of steak, chewed it, savoured it and swallowed. "Fantastic, Bryan. Absolutely fantastic."

Everyone else piped in.

"Brilliant, Bryan."

"Best steak I ever had."

"What did you use to marinate them, Ellen?"

Just as Delaney was about to try the fish a wasp flew close by. He shooed it away with his free hand, but the wasp must have got pissed off at the gesture. It picked up speed and flew back towards Delaney like a crazed kamikaze pilot. It buzzed around his head once and then quickly stung him on the left cheek.

Delaney let out a bit of a scream and then then touched his face with his left hand.

"Sonofabitch. That thing stung me," he yelled.

"Let me see baby," Michelle said as she looked at his face.

The spot was already a bright red.

"Just put some ice on it. You'll be okay mate," the real estate man said.

"I don't know. Gary is allergic to bee stings," Michelle said.

"Allergic!" Ellen cried. "Can we do anything?"

Delaney reached into his pocket for the little pill case he carried around for such an emergency. He washed the antihistamine pill down with a slug of water.

"Go on everyone, finish your meals before they get cold," Delaney said. "I just took an antihistamine pill so everything should be okay."

But it wasn't.

The left side of Delaney's face quickly began to swell up until it looked as if he had a golf ball on his cheek.

Ellen brought an icepack out for him. "Come and lie down inside, Gary. This should help."

Delaney went inside and Michelle followed but not before putting another piece of steak in her mouth.

"This is bloody fantastic," she said to the others.

"I've never seen a reaction like that to anything," Stephanie the librarian said.

Her husband was checking Google on his phone too see what should be done.

"I reckon he needs to go to the hospital," Anna said.

Michelle concurred.

"Gary," she whispered to him as he lay on a couch in the living room. "We really need to get you to a hospital before it gets worse."

"Or this turns into a second head," he said.

Delaney got up and walked to the balcony with Michelle.

"Sorry everyone," he mumbled.

"We're going to the hospital to have it checked," Michelle told everyone.

"Let us know what happens, please," the librarian pleaded.

Delaney and Michelle walked down the balcony stairs to their car. Michelle got behind the wheel while Delaney sat slumped in the passenger seat with the melting ice pack on his cheek.

Harold Holt Hospital was the closest. Michelle put her foot down and they arrived in twenty minutes. She stopped at the emergency entrance to let her partner out and went to park the car.

Delaney walked in and looked around. For a midweek afternoon there was quite a crowd. One guy was on crutches, another was clutching a bloodied hand which was wrapped in what looked like a

T-shirt. An old-timer was breathing through an oxygen mask while to his left a young woman was holding her baby as her concerned husband paced the floor in front of them. Another fellow in a sleeveless undershirt and stained shorts was walking around in circles mumbling to himself.

Delaney approached the triage desk and a nurse asked him why he was here.

Delaney didn't have to say a word. He took the ice bag off his cheek which by now had ballooned even farther.

"Doctor," the nurse screamed. "I need you here now."

A middle-aged doctor of middle-eastern appearance wearing a thick pair of glasses approached the pair.

"What happened?" he asked.

"Wasp sting," Delaney mumbled. "I'm allergic."

"Quick, get him inside," the doctor told the nurse.

Michelle walked through the doors of the ER and saw her boyfriend being taken inside by a nurse.

"That's my boyfriend. Can I be with him?" she asked the doctor.

"Not right now. Wait here and we'll let you know what happens."

Inside the ER two doctors went to work on Delaney. His breathing was shallow and his pulse weak.

"He needs a shot of adrenaline, now," one of them said.

The older of the two doctors, who was in charge of the ER that afternoon, was quickly handed a needle. He sized up the dose and plunged it deep into Delaney's left arm.

The patient barely let out a whimper.

Some thirty seconds passed.

"His breathing is much better, and his pulse rate is returning to normal," said the younger doctor.

"Good, that's all he should need. Find a bed for him and monitor him. That swelling should start to decrease soon. He'll be out of here in an hour or two."

While two nurses took care of Delaney's needs, Michelle sat in the waiting room in dire need of a toothpick or dental floss to dislodge a magnificent piece of steak that had lodged in her upper right molar. When her name was called, she ran to the desk, nearly tripping over a pair of crutches which a patient had carelessly laid down at his feet.

"How is he? How is he? Is he okay?" she asked the middle-aged nurse.

I'm afraid he's expired miss," she said.

"From a wasp sting?" Michelle cried. She burst into tears. "Gary, Gary," she wailed.

"Oh, hold on. I'm sorry," the nurse said. "I was looking at the wrong file. My bad. Mr Delaney is going to be fine. The doctors gave him a shot of adrenaline and he's resting now. He'll be able to go home in a couple of hours."

"Your bad? You tell me my boyfriend has died and it's your bad?" screamed Michelle.

A security guard heard the ruckus and walked over to the admission desk and asked the nurse what the problem was.

"The problem is this woman told me my boyfriend died when he is very much alive," Michelle said.

"I made a mistake," the nurse said.

"We all make mistakes," the security guard said. "Why don't you take a seat and calm down."

Michelle gritted her teeth and walked away from the desk.

"Oh miss," the nurse said. "You'll have to fill out these forms please."

Michelle turned around and walked back to the desk. She took the forms, which were attached to a clipboard, and asked for a pen. She felt like putting it in the nurse's eye but took it along with the clipboard and found a seat at the far end of the room to cool off.

Name of patient was the first line that needed to be filled in. She printed the word Gary before the pen ran out of ink.

She tossed it away and dug into her bag for a pen. She always carried a pen in her bag, one with blue ink since that's what Delaney liked to write down the scratches and jockey changes with when they went to the races.

She filled out the forms, having to go into her wallet several times looking for Delaney's Medicare and private health insurance cards, and brought it to the same nurse at the counter.

"I'm sorry miss. You'll need to fill these forms out again," the nurse said.

"Why?"

"They need to be filled out in black ink only."

"Blue, black. What's the fucking difference?" Michelle screamed.

At that point the security guard, a large bear of a man with a shaved head with a nametag reading *Eldrick Monroe,* reappeared.

"What is it now?" he asked.

"She used the wrong colour ink to fill out the forms," the nurse said.

"What does it matter? Take the damn forms. They're filled out!" Michelle hollered.

"Miss. I am going to have to ask you to calm down," Mr Monroe said.

"I will not calm down, this is absolute bullshit. First, she tells me my boyfriend died and now I've used the wrong ink? What the fuck is wrong with you people?"

Eldrick Monroe then took out his hospital-issued taser gun and sent 1200 volts into Michelle's abdomen.

She collapsed to the ground and writhed around like a hooked barramundi on the deck of a Northern Territory fishing boat.

Hospital administrator Robert Shamsky heard the commotion from his ground floor office, ran over and saw Michelle lying on the ground.

"What in hell did you do?" he asked Eldrick Monroe.

"Tasered her sir, as I have been instructed to do in these sorts of situations."

"You don't taser middle-aged women. She was no threat to you. Give me that thing you halfwit and get the fuck out of my sight. She'll sue the shit out of us. And where the fuck is a doctor? I'm in an emergency room with a woman lying on the floor and there's not a doctor around?"

"They're all busy sir," the nurse at the counter said.

"Busy with what? Playing Pokemon? Get me a goddamn doctor now or you'll find yourself at a Centrelink office tomorrow, as a client!"

Michelle was wheeled into the ER by the doctor with the thick glasses. How he saw out of them let alone worked on patients was a mystery to everyone. But Dr Prakeesh was a superb doctor with a good bedside manner. Michelle was in excellent hands.

Dr Prakeesh took her vitals which were normal. Slowly she came around. Robert Shamsky, who was looking over the doctor's shoulder, took a deep breath as she did.

"What the hell happened?" Michelle asked to no one in particular.

"I'm afraid the security guard tasered you," Dr Prakeesh said.

"He did what? What the hell for?"

"To calm you down," Robert Shamsky said. "He got a little carried away."

"A little carried away?" Michelle asked as she rubbed the sore and red spot on her stomach where the taser struck. "Who are you? A doctor?"

"No miss, my name is Robert Shamsky. I am one of the hospital administrators. I am so glad you are feeling better and I want to relay the hospital's sincere apologies to you."

"Apologies? Just wait till you hear from my lawyers. You'll be giving me much more than an apology."

"Do you really think it is necessary to go to a lawyer?" Shamsky asked.

"Oh, it is very necessary. I could have died back there," Michelle added with a firm voice.

"The hospital is very sorry. Please miss. There is no need to see a lawyer," Shamsky said as he wiped his brow. "We won't charge you for parking today. We'll give you and your partner free colonoscopies."

"Will someone get him the fuck outta here?" Michelle asked.

Dr Prakeesh took Shamsky by the arm and escorted him out of the emergency room.

Shamsky was shaking. "Can you write me a script doc?" he asked Dr Prakeesh. "I'll lose my job over this. I was the one who said we needed to arm the security guards."

Delaney was lying down with his eyes closed, having a bit of a sleep when a nurse he hadn't seen before came around to check on him. Doris Clements had been on the job for thirty years and was nearing the end of her shift. It had been a long day and her feet ached despite her comfortable hospital-issued shoes. She gently woke the patient.

"How are we doing Mr Delaney? I see the swelling has gone down considerably."

"I'm feeling much better," he said as she took his blood pressure. "One-thirty over ninety. If the doctor agrees, you'll be free to go. Let's open the curtain for you."

Nurse Clements opened the white curtain and Delaney was shocked to see Michelle lying in the next bed.

"Michelle? What the? What happened to you?'

"They told me you were dead Gary, dead. Then they tasered me," she said, breaking into tears.

"They did what?"

"Tasered me, baby. I was out cold. I am going to sue the bastards."

"But why did they taser you? What did you do?"

"I got into an argument with a security guard over forms I had to fill out."

Delaney could not believe what he was hearing. He had known Michelle for a couple of months, and she had never even so much as raised her voice.

"I'm contacting my attorneys once we get out of here."

"You have an attorney?"

"Three. Dewey, Cheetum and Howe. By the time they are through with this place I'll be sitting in the sun on an island somewhere counting the money from the settlement."

For the first time in an hour Delaney laughed.

"What are you laughing at?"

"Dewey, Cheetum and Howe? That's brilliant. Sue them, honey. They can't taser you. You are not some criminal."

"That's right. Can we get the hell out of here?" Michelle asked.

"As soon as the doctors give us the okay."

Twenty minutes later Michelle and Delaney walked out of the emergency room and headed to the parking lot.

Robert Shamsky was following their progress and as soon as he heard they were discharged he gave chase.

He cornered them outside the ER.

"Please Miss," he said.

"It's Miss Garrett," Michelle told him.

"Miss Garrett, take my card and in a few days we can meet and talk this over. I am sure we can come to some sort of arrangement. We do not need to get lawyers involved. As a gesture of good will please take this twenty to cover the parking."

Michelle swiped the note from his hand.

"This," she said, waving the note in front of Shamsky's face, "is just the start."

"Let's go honey."

Delaney could not believe what he was seeing and hearing. His quiet, book-reading girlfriend had turned into a guest on the Jerry Springer show.

Michelle and Delaney locked arms and confidently walked to their car.

"Are you okay to drive?" she asked.

"I could ask the same of you."

Delaney opened the door for Michelle and gently placed her in the passenger seat. Her stomach still ached a bit.

Delaney got in and started the car.

He drove to the payment machine and stuck Shamsky's twenty-dollar note in it. The machine gave them their change, all of four dollars, and the gate lifted.

They drove off, one with a sore stomach and the other a swollen cheek.

"I hope my face is back to normal by Monday. I start the new job then," Delaney said.

Back at the hospital, Robert Shamsky, he of the wife and three kids and a $400,000 mortgage was wondering how much longer he would have his.

Delaney and Michelle were each feeling better the following morning. The antihistamines one of the emergency room doctors told him to take every four to six hours were doing their job. All that remained was a small red mark on his cheek. *Great,* he thought, *a fifty-four-year-old man with acne.* Michelle had the same sort of mark on her abdomen but the soreness she had from the day before had all but disappeared. With just four days left until he started his new job, Delaney was looking forward to a quiet few days; no doctors, no hospitals and no dramas.

Michelle had the day off as well. She was scheduled to be back at her desk on Friday where a mass of paperwork related to an upcoming exhibit awaited. It was tedious work, going through various checklists to make sure everything arrived intact, but it was nothing she hadn't done before. If something was damaged during the long trip from Europe or never arrived, it was Michelle's responsibility to get to the bottom of it. But that had happened just once in the past year, when a Picasso painting worth millions, failed to arrive in a shipment of over two-hundred and thirty pieces. National Gallery staff members spent hours looking for the missing masterpiece but were unable to locate it. Michelle finally tracked it down after numerous phone calls and emails. *Two Women With Five Breasts* had never made it onto the flight due to some bureaucratic mix-up in Paris. Crisis averted.

After comparing their battle scars from the previous day Delaney and Michelle had their usual breakfast; tea, coffee, toast and oatmeal. All was fine until Delaney saw a story in that morning's paper about an overseas researcher who supposedly found that dark toast could cause cancer. According to the researcher, when the starch in bread heats and burns it creates carcinogens which could develop into cancer. Delaney got up from the table, went over to the toaster and turned down the heating dial from four to two. Problem solved.

Increasing sunshine with light winds was the forecast with a high of twenty-one; a good day to get out and about. Pastor Chris rang mid-morning asking if he and Michelle wanted to meet up for lunch.

"I've got some things for you to have a look at," Pastor Chris said.

"Things?"

"Yup, things."

"Hmmmmm."

Delaney was intrigued. *Could it be a book of some sort, old racing programs, old newspapers?*

Pastor Chris and Delaney usually tried to find a café which was approximately halfway between their homes. Today they decided on a café on the main Bentleigh Shopping strip called Easy Over at 1pm.

Delaney spent the rest of the morning with a red pen circling mistakes in the former broadsheet, good practice for his upcoming job, while Michelle went to her art studio ten minutes away to touch up a couple of her paintings. She was getting ready for a show in a couple of weeks at a major gallery and a sale or two would be a major boost to her confidence. She was keen on a painting she had nearly finished of the Mordialloc foreshore on a hot summer's day. It featured several native bushes and young children standing around a drinking fountain, half bathed in sun and shade in the foreground, with the beach and pier in the distance.

Michelle was also curious about the items Pastor Chris was bringing along so she suggested she pick Gary up on her way back from the studio and they go to the café together.

They found a carpark on a side street, not an easy thing to do in Bentleigh around lunchtime. Pastor Chris must have been waiting for them because he pulled in and took the spot just behind them. Michelle had a bit of blue paint on her hands and on a strand of hair which received the unwanted touch up when she tucked it back behind her ear with one of her paint-covered fingers.

Delaney and Pastor Chris hugged and shook hands. The Pastor was the only one of his male friends he hugged. And it wasn't one of those awkward hugs, it was genuine. The Pastor then gave Michelle a hug and a kiss on her cheek. While still single, he was rapt for his good mate when he first told him about Michelle. He liked her right from the start, and she felt the same way about him. "She's good for you," Pastor Chris said.

Chris's warmth was heartfelt, and Michelle wanted him to be as happy as she and Delaney were. Being over fifty and living alone was not good for anyone. The Pastor wanted to meet someone. He knew plenty of women but was still looking for 'the one'.

Michelle meanwhile was doing some looking for him. There were several single women she knew of working at the National Gallery and a handful of the women at her art studio were also single. She planned on inviting one or two to her upcoming show and introducing them to Pastor Chris. If they clicked, great. If not? Well, at least she had tried.

Chris signalled for Delaney and Michelle to come to the boot of his car. He opened it. The 'things' he had were not books, but clothes; lots and lots of clothes.

"Going into the rag trade Chris?" Delaney asked.

"Ha. A mate of mine passed away a few months ago and I was one of those asked to clean out his apartment. All the furniture and white goods went to the Salvos. They even came around and picked everything up. His family didn't want any of his things and he was about your size. I thought you might like them."

A dead man's clothes? Oh boy, Delaney thought.

"Let's have a look at them," Delaney said.

Pastor Chris helped up a long-sleeved pink shirt. "It's a Van Heusen," he said.

"Do you have anything by Van Morrison?" Delaney asked. "I'll pass. Pink is not exactly my colour."

Pastor Chris then held up several other dress shirts. They were too loud for Delaney's taste with different coloured collars and cuffs.

A few polo shirts were not that bad. They were a little large for him but high-quality shirts, blues and beiges, so Delaney said he would take those.

Pastor Chris then pulled out several black suit jackets.

"Sorry Chris, they're just not what I would wear."

"All right," the Pastor said. "I was saving the best for last." He unfolded and held out a yellow jacket that Bing Crosby might have worn on a golf course or a yacht in the 1940s.

"Try it on pal," Chris said. Delaney looked at Michelle who motioned for him to go ahead.

Delaney took the lightweight jacket and put it on. It fitted perfectly. He felt like a canary and made a note to himself to stay away from coal mines.

"That's a great looking jacket," Chris said.

"I'll take this as well, thank you," Delaney said. He walked to the car, opened the back door and tossed the shirts and yellow jacket in.

"Lunch time," he said. He took Michelle's hand and the three walked a block to the Easy Over Café.

Delaney had a turkey sandwich as did Michelle while Pastor Chris went the more-healthy route, some sort of wrap with a fruit cup.

Ninety minutes later Chris put $15 down on the counter and left for a late afternoon appointment he had in the city. Neither Delaney or Michelle pressed him on what it was about.

Michelle and Delaney hung around for another fifteen minutes or so, finishing their coffees.

They paid the bill, a rather modest $46 for the three of them and walked outside.

Instead of the promised sunny skies the air had chilled and the wind had picked up. Michelle wanted to check out an art supply shop she had noticed on the way in. They both went back to the car to get their jackets. Only Delaney had not taken his since the forecast was for a sunny and warm afternoon.

There was only one option; the yellow jacket.

He put it on and despite feeling a bit uneasy he walked with Michelle to the art supply shop which was on the other side of Centre Road.

At the same time Mavis Rosenberg stepped out of the local chemist. The sixty-seven-year-old had just picked up a couple of prescriptions and two packages of Dr Scholls corn remover pads for her aching feet. She waited to cross the street and then saw a man wearing a yellow jacket holding a woman's hand walking on the footpath.

Despite the pain of her corns, she started to walk faster. "Ira, Ira," she yelled. "Stop, Ira. I know it's you."

Four years ago, Mavis Rosenberg had given Ira Nussbaum a yellow golf jacket as a birthday present. A week later Ira broke up with her after dinner at her home. When Mavis asked why he was ending their nearly ten-year relationship he said it had run its course.

"Run its course? That's rubbish. Tell me the truth Ira. After ten years I deserve to know the truth."

"The truth is," Ira Nussbaum said in a soft voice, "I don't want to grow old with you."

Ira Nussbaum then walked out of Mavis Rosenberg's home and her life.

Mavis Rosenberg began to walk faster, keeping a firm grip on her shopping bag and handbag. "Ira, Ira," she yelled.

She eventually drew even with Delaney and Michelle and stepped in front of them.

"Ira, you bastard," she said before taking a good look at the man in the yellow jacket. "You're not Ira," she screamed at Delaney. "What the hell are you doing wearing his jacket?"

Delaney was taken aback by the screaming woman, who was now trying to catch her breath after her hundred-metre dash down the street.

"His jacket?' Delaney asked before realising what she was going on about. "Oh, this jacket. A friend just gave it to me."

"But that's Ira's jacket. Look, I even had his initials embroidered on it. See? I. N. for Ira Nussbaum."

Michelle turned to the woman, took her arm and said in a soft voice, "I'm sorry miss, but Ira died several weeks ago. A friend of his gave away his things. That is why my partner is wearing the jacket."

"Ira's dead?" Mavis Rosenberg asked.

"Yes, I'm sorry," Michelle replied.

Mavis Rosenberg put down her shopping bag and let out a long sigh. "Serves him right."

She then walked away with a spring in her aching feet.

"What in heck was that about?" Delaney asked.

"Must have been one bad break-up," Michelle answered.

Delaney and Michelle continued their walk to the art supply store. Three doors down, they came across an op shop. Delaney walked in, took off the yellow jacket and donated it.

15

EXPECT DISAPPOINTMENT. NOT THE DISAPPOINTMENT one finds when fronting up to the deli counter at Woolies and seeing the customer in front of you walk off with the last slices of rare roast beef. Or the disappointment one gets when being put on hold for fifty-five minutes by one's mobile phone service, being told every five minutes that your call is 'very important to us' only to get disconnected when a human being finally gets to your call. Or the disappointment one feels when he finds out he is one of just two people in the office not invited for Christmas drinks with the boss; the other being home sick with the measles. Or the disappointment one gets upon realising that he missed the first episode of the new season of *John Oliver's Last Week Tonight* even though he had written three notes to himself, one of which was taped to the bloody TV.

Imagine Delaney's disappointment the night of the jacket episode when Michelle told him that she was going to go to her son's house for a few days to water his garden while he and his girlfriend were away for the weekend.

"Water his garden?"

"Yes."

"They're just going away for four days, right? Isn't there a neighbour who could do that or one of their many friends?"

"He doesn't trust them," Michelle said. "It's just for a few days. It will give me some time by myself and time to think too."

Ah, the old time to think line, Delaney thought. The timing wasn't exactly right with him set to begin his new job on Monday. He had enough on his mind as it was.

"When will you be back? Saturday? Sunday?"

"Sunday afternoon," Michelle said, giving her beau a soft kiss. "The few days away will be good for both of us."

Delaney could not ask her not to go. It was obviously something she had been thinking about. Her son's weekend trip out of town gave her the excuse she needed.

Delaney went to bed that night wondering what in the heck was going on. Everything seemed to be fine between them. They had been together for a while now and not once had they even raised their voices at each other. The day before she had cried her eyes out when she thought he was dead.

Delaney's suspicions grew even further that night, when, claiming she was tired, Michelle gave him a quick kiss, rolled to her side of the bed and turned off the lamp on her bedside table. Had she grown tired of their relationship? Was it a simple case of too much Delaney? He told himself that he would give her more space when she returned. It wasn't a case of someone else. Most of her workmates and fellow artists were women and she never even as much looked at another guy when they were out together. Plus, their sex life, three or four times a week, was fine.

The next morning, just after breakfast, Michelle packed a few things and took off for her son's inner-city home with the garden that needed daily watering. Just over an hour later Delaney got a text message saying she had arrived safely and would give him a ring that night.

On the peninsula, Robert Shamsky, he of the wife and three kids and $400,000 mortgage, was wondering how much longer it would be until he heard from Michelle Garrett's lawyer or the hospital's chief executive officer. The forty-two-year-old Shamsky was clearly worried about his job. All day Thursday he kept looking at his office phone, pleading for it not to ring while constantly checking his emails. There was nothing relating to the previous day's incident, so he felt a bit better as he took off his reading glasses and left work that afternoon headed to his heavily mortgaged home less than ten minutes away.

The four-bedroom home was a beauty on the beach side of Mt Eliza with a nice view of the bay. Shamsky and his wife, Stephanie, had saved for years for a down payment. Stephanie was two years younger and had recently returned to the workforce after spending close to a decade caring for their three children; Tom, Mark and Danielle. Danielle, who just turned four, had started kindergarten a few weeks ago which gave Stephanie a chance to get out of the house and make them a steady two-income family again.

Stephanie was a bookkeeper and had done a little bit of work at home for her old firm over the last few years. The money came in handy and the work was a welcome relief from the constant changing of nappies, cooking and laundry; at least a load a day. Apart from Stephanie, the washing machine was the hardest working member of the Shamsky household. Stephanie knew every word from the *Frozen* soundtrack backwards and forwards thanks to Danielle, who had watched the DVD at least 100 times. If Stephanie heard *Let it Go* one more time she told herself that she'd yank the DVD from the DVD player and smash it into 1000 pieces.

When she told her bosses she was ready to return to the workforce, first on a part-time basis until Danielle started primary school, they welcomed her back with open arms. She was given her own office and Jack Simms, the firm's president, personally introduced her to everyone on the staff. The staff at Simms and Harrelson had more than tripled since she was last in the building.

Stephanie was pleased to see several old faces including some who were at her going away party when she was eight months pregnant with child number one.

"She's hardly changed after three kids. She looks so good," Donna Pearlman said to Carol Haynes.

"Maybe she has a personal trainer," Carol said.

Now forty, Stephanie did look good. The weight she gained from her pregnancy with Danielle was the hardest to lose but lose it she did thanks to a combination of long walks and runs on the beach every morning. No matter how cold it was, or windy, even if it was raining, Stephanie was out there before her kids and husband woke up and in winter even before the sun came up. According to her Fitbit she was walking and running more than six kilometres each day. She didn't need an iPhone's music to accompany her. She preferred the sounds of the small waves crashing on the shore.

Stephanie looked at herself in the mirror on the morning she was due to return to work and was pleased. Except for a couple of stretch marks here and there, and who would ever see them besides her husband, she looked just as good as she did ten years ago, maybe even better. She was certainly fitter.

A day never went by without Robert Shamsky telling his wife how gorgeous she was. Stephanie was out of his league and he knew it, but they hit it off when they were introduced by a close mate of his at another mate's 30th birthday party. She was happy to talk with someone who wasn't trying to get into her pants and with someone who didn't feel the need to toss down half a dozen cans at a social gathering.

Towards the end of the night, the bespectacled, curly-haired, slim hospital clerk found the courage to ask for her number although if he hadn't, she would have asked for his. They spoke a couple of times during the week, exchanged cute text messages and the next weekend they had dinner together.

Four weeks later, on date number nine—he was counting—they slept together for the first time. He was a bit nervous. She was the best-looking woman and one of the nicest he had ever been with. Stephanie liked his gentleness. He wasn't like some of the others she had slept with over the past few years, guys who thought of her as nothing more than a sperm receptacle due to the porn they watched online.

Over the course of the next year Stephanie and Shamsky met each other's families, spent a few weekends away together and decided to get married. The first of their three children came nine months later. Both wanted a big family and they had one.

But on this Thursday night, Robert Shamsky, who worked himself up from clerk to administrator in a few short years, with a huge bump in pay to boot, was worried. He hadn't told Stephanie about the scene at the hospital the day before, but his wife of ten years knew something was up.

After the kids were in bed, Shamsky told his wife what happened the previous afternoon at the hospital's emergency room.

"It's not your fault," Stephanie said. "You didn't pull the trigger."

"I know, but I was the one who recommended arming the security guards."

"But how many serious altercations have there been since the guards were armed? Not even a handful. Before, there were a handful a week."

"You're right. But it's a worry. I'm just hoping nothing comes from it. The woman and her partner were very upset."

On Friday afternoon, just when he thought he was in the clear, Shamsky received a call from the hospital's CEO. Actually, it came from his assistant, who asked if Shamsky could report to the CEO's office at 3.30pm for a meeting. Shamsky's heart sank. *What if this is it? What if they march me out of here today? What am I going to do?*

He watched the clock on the wall of his office swing its hands to 2.30pm, then 2.45, then 3.00. By the time another fifteen minutes went by Shamsky's long-sleeved shirt was covered in sweat. At 3.20 Shamsky got up from his desk, put on his sports jacket, adjusted his tie, wiped his brow and walked to the lift. He pressed three and twelve seconds later was deposited on the third floor. He turned to his right, where the executive offices were, took a deep breath and walked into the CEO's reception area.

He told Don Koosman's executive assistant that he was there for a 3.30pm appointment.

"Take a seat Mr Shamsky," the assistant said. "Mr Koosman will be with you shortly."

Shamsky was too nervous to sit down. He looked at some of the art on the walls and was admiring an aboriginal painting when he heard Koosman's voice.

"Robert," he said extending his hand. "Nice to see you, come in, please."

Shamsky shook hands with Koosman and sat down in one of the two chairs facing Koosman's enormous desk.

The higher up the ladder, the bigger the desk, Shamsky noted.

There were numerous framed commendations on the wall behind Koosman, a diploma, and on his desk a picture of Koosman and his wife on the beach, each holding a tropical drink.

"Can I get you anything? A coffee? Water?"

"No need really, I'm okay."

"You know why you are here, don't you?' Koosman asked. He put his reading glasses on his desk and leaned forward in his chair. Koosman was in his early fifties, tanned, over six feet tall with grey hair that curled behind his ears. He looked every bit the retired sportsman he was. In his heyday he was an outstanding tennis player, winning a couple of Victorian titles but never was a part of the pro tour. He still looked as if he could go out there and take a set or two off anyone over the age of thirty-five.

"I still find it hard to believe that a security guard tasered that woman. There was no need for that sort of response," Shamsky said.

Koosman shook his head, agreeing with him. "Did you see the whole incident? I've just heard bits and pieces."

"I heard a commotion from my office. I had the door open at the time. I ran out to the emergency room and saw a woman lying in the floor after being tasered. I had a word with the security guard and the triage nurse at the window. Miss Garrett had been told that her partner, who was being treated in the ER for an allergic reaction to a wasp sting, had died so she was quite upset. And after that, after she filled in the usual forms, she was told by the same nurse that she had used the wrong coloured ink."

"The wrong coloured ink? You're joking, aren't you?" Koosman asked as he shook his head in disbelief.

"I wish I was. Miss Garrett filled out the forms in blue ink and the nurse told her that she had to use black ink to fill out the forms."

"What's the goddamned difference?" Koosman said, leaning back in his chair.

"That's what Miss Garrett said, only she said fucking difference," Shamsky said.

"I would have too."

"That's when the guard tasered her. I got to her just seconds after it happened."

"Jesus Christ," Koosman said. "This security guard, an Eldrick Monroe, you had a word with him?"

"I did, and the nurse."

"And when did Miss Garrett say she was going to call her attorneys?"

"As she and Mr Delaney were being discharged."

"Delaney, Delaney. Gary Delaney? The sportswriter?"

"Yes, that's him."

"Well I'll be," Koosman said. "That fellow wrote a few stories on me years ago, when I was playing pennant tennis.

"Robert," Koosman went on, as he leaned forward in his chair. "You're not to blame for any of this. Yes, it was your idea to arm the security guards, but the incidents of abuse in the ER since they got tasers are down, way down.

"The security guards are not employees of the hospital. They are employed by the security company the hospital hired. It has dealt with this Monroe fellow and if any lawsuit is going to be filed it will be filed against the security company, not us."

Shamsky had never in his life heard words any sweeter. "That's a relief."

"And the nurse, Janice Ramirez, has been placed on two weeks leave and been instructed to take anger management classes."

"Will she?"

"Well, when Gwen in HR told her she would have to take the classes, Ms Ramirez told Gwen to fuck off. I should sack her, but I don't want to see the rest of the staff rebel. If she apologises to Gwen and takes those classes, she can come back."

"Ramirez really told Gwen to fuck off?"

"That she did."

Koosman rose from his chair. "You just go back to what you've been doing, Robert. You're a valued part of the team. Take the rest of the afternoon off too."

Shamsky got up from his chair and shook Koosman's hand.

"Thank you," he said.

"Don't mention it. See you on Monday."

A very relieved Robert Shamsky left Koosman's office, wished his executive assistant a good afternoon and walked to the lift. He opened the door to his office, sat down at his desk and took a long drink of water from a large bottle on his desk. He sent a text to Stephanie, telling her that everything had been resolved and he was in the clear, shut down his computer, locked his office door and briskly walked to the employees' parking lot. He opened the door to his car, sat down and fired off another text to Stephanie. "Don't bother with dinner. We're all going out tonight." He drove to the parking lot gate and pressed his laminated pass against the gate's sensor. The gate rose and he drove home, sunnies in place, taking in the late afternoon sunshine.

16

INSTEAD OF WRAPPING HIS ARMS AROUND MICHELLE while the two of them watched Parker Schnable mine for gold in the Yukon on *Gold Rush Alaska*, one of the few TV shows they could stomach, Delaney spent his Thursday night getting stuck into some past editions of *Turf News*.

He wanted to become as familiar with the publication as he could before starting his new job. He noticed a few grammatical errors in several stories. They might not even be noticed by the average reader but to Delaney they stood out like a maiden in a Group 1 race. There were even a few misspellings in the form itself; a jockey's name here, a trainer's name there, Caulfield spelled as Caulfeld.

The paper's top columnist, Greg Grote, was the best in the business. People in the industry liked and respected him while his colleagues admired him. As good as he was, he never boasted and always went out of his way to help his colleagues when asked. Any advice or criticism, and the occasional plaudit, were always well-received.

Even when he was at Consume and Devour, Delaney always read Grote's columns. They were informative, well-researched and entertaining. Whether you agreed with his opinions or not, and many didn't, people always read him.

When his phone rang he was expecting the call to be from Michelle. Instead it was from Pastor Chris. Delaney made a note to himself to ring Michelle as soon as he got off the line with Chris. He told Chris that he was on his own for a few days while Michelle thought things out. Chris told him not to worry about it. Michelle would be back in a few days and all would be fine. Chris saw the way Michelle looked at Delaney. He wished a woman looked at him that way.

Chris had been with his share of women, but his last long-term relationship had been about eight years ago.

Now in his early fifties, he was finding it harder to meet someone he wanted to be with long term despite being one of the most personable people Delaney knew. Chris remembered when he used to meet the parents of the girls he was dating. Now he was meeting the kids of the women he went out with.

Chris was bright, witty and above all, caring. If someone needed a hand moving house, Chris was there. If someone was alone in hospital, Chris made sure he visited. If someone needed to talk, Chris was there to listen. If he had read a book and thought it would interest a mate, he'd bring it over and say keep it. And, he was still a good-looking rooster. As a counsellor, Chris often took on clients others frowned upon; those with drug and alcohol problems and those with domestic violence and anger issues. He was making a difference in a world where most were in their jobs only to enrich themselves.

He was home preparing dinner one recent night and was flipping through his local paper which still carried ads for adult services in its classifieds section. One ad caught his eye. It read; *Little bit older, little bit bolder, not over the hill, still able to thrill.* Chris let out a big laugh. There was a phone number listed followed by the words *Call me now.*

His curiosity got the better of him. He picked up his phone and after a few hesitant minutes punched in the number. It was ringing but there was no answer. Just as he was about to put down the phone, he heard a woman say, "Hello, this is Emily." Chris was momentarily lost for words. "Hello," she said again. "Come on, I know you're there, I can hear you breathing."

Chris laughed.

"Don't be shy, honey, you're not the first man to ring me, get cold feet and hang up."

"Well, I saw your ad and thought it was quite clever. I was wondering who the person was behind the ad."

"What's your name and what would you like to know?"

"I'm Chris and first I'd like to know how old you are?"

"I turned fifty last year but don't look it if that is what you really want to know. I'm about 5-6, very busty, and yes they are real, have dark hair and green eyes."

"You sound nice."

"I am, honey. Do you want to make an appointment to see me?"

"Hmmm. How much is an appointment?"

"If I come to you, $275 for an hour. If you come to see me, in South Yarra, it is $245 an hour."

There was silence from Chris's end of the line.

"Well, do you want to make a date or not? I've got time open later tonight."

"I'm sorry, you do sound really nice and it has been a while, but I am going to pass. I'm more interested in what you do and why. You see, I'm a psychologist."

"There have been a few in your profession who have asked me the same question. I tell them the same thing. The money is great, I get to meet interesting people and I like to fuck. That answer your question?"

"You sure are direct. I'm sorry to have wasted your time. Thanks for the chat."

"All right, but you do have my number if you get lonely. I guarantee you an hour with me is an hour you will never forget."

With that sort of confidence, Chris had a feeling she was right.

He had never paid for sex in his life and he wasn't about to start now. But he did tear Emily's ad out of the paper and put it on his desk for future reference.

Chris then rang Delaney. "How'd you like to go to a party on Saturday night?" he asked. "A mate of mine is having a bunch of people over to his place in Hampton."

"Tell me more."

"Food, drink, good people. No sense sitting home and stewing over Michelle. You know she loves you. Come along, it will do you a world of good."

"Okay. I'll be there. What time?"

"Around seven will do if you want to get a decent feed. Stan always has great food at his parties. If you get there any later all the good stuff will be gone."

"Have I met Stan?"

"Don't think you have. He owns an electronics firm and keeps a low profile. You'll like him, he's a Melbourne supporter and loves his racing. He's owned a few horses along the journey and his wife is absolutely lovely."

Delaney took down the address and told Chris he'd meet him there.

Michelle was waiting for his call when Delaney rang her moments later.

"Hi baby. Glad you made it down there safely. Everything going okay?"

"Yes, have watered the garden and had dinner."

"Anything special?"

"Well, you wouldn't believe it but there's this Chinese place a couple of blocks away and they have the best lemon chicken."

"You're kidding, you know that Chinese place here, near the station? I finally went in there and ordered the same thing. Took it home and added some rice."

"How was it?"

"Not too bad, but probably not as good as what you ate. Bring some back if you can. We'll dissect it under a microscope and see if we can figure out the ingredients in the recipe."

Michelle laughed. "I miss you, baby."

"I miss you too sweetheart."

"What are you going to do for the rest of the night?"

"I was just going over some copies of *Turf News* to get better prepared for Monday."

"Good idea."

"And you?"

"I'm going to read a bit and then turn in early. The kids fixed up the spare bedroom for me. It looks really nice and it doesn't face the street so it should be somewhat quiet."

"Sounds nice. This is the first night since we moved in together that we're spending apart. I have a feeling it is going to be very lonely in bed tonight."

"It will be for me too," Michelle said. "I'll be home in a few days baby, don't worry. Sleep well. I love you Gary,"

"I love you too Michelle, goodnight."

Delaney felt much better after hearing Michelle tell him she loved him. Pastor Chris was right. What was he worried about?

Delaney later flicked on the TV. But with over 100 channels to choose from he could not find one single thing to watch. In frustration, he threw the remote down on the couch.

'I'll have an early night," he said.

Delaney took his usual handful of nightly pills, washed his face, flossed (one has to floss), brushed his teeth and went to bed. It took Delaney an hour just to get used to Michelle's absence. Another hour later he finally fell asleep.

In the city, Michelle's mind was also racing. *Maybe I shouldn't have come. What if Gary thinks I want a break, a real break?*

Delaney played the part of house husband on Friday morning. He did the laundry—two loads—and hung them up outside in the warm sun. He changed the sheets, vacuumed, did all the dishes and cleaned the toilet.

The place was spotless. He then went back inside and took the pruning shears to some branches that were hanging over a fence he shared with a neighbour. He knocked on the door of his closest neighbour and asked if he could put the cuttings in his green bin. Delaney had called the council months ago asking for a green bin, but one never arrived. After the neighbour gave his okay, Delaney filled it up about a third of the way. He proudly looked at his handiwork and checked the clock on the wall, only 11.32.

He got dressed and walked down to the shops to kill a bit of time before lunch. He stopped at several op shops to have a gander at the books but came away empty-handed. In the second op shop he visited he noticed a familiar woman among the volunteers. He used to see her every so often at the train station. He was sure they had exchanged names once before but for the life of him Delaney could not remember hers. She approached him and was relieved when she told him she could not remember his name either. She did remember that he was a newspaper man.

"I may have a story for you," Susan said.

"Even if it isn't sport-related I could pass it along to one of the news reporters."

"Come this way," Susan said. A slim woman in her mid-fifties with short dark hair, Susan was wearing a blue apron. She led Delaney through the shop and out the back door to an outdoor area where there were several large flower pots and two yellow charity bins where people could drop items of clothing and shoes. To the left was a vegetable garden that Susan had started from scratch. There was a small lemon tree, several tomato plants, beans and other veggies Delaney couldn't identify.

"Notice anything unusual?" she asked.

"Not yet."

"Look closer, look at the flower pots and then the lemon tree," she said.

He did and that was when he noticed that the flower pots were chained to a fence and the lemon tree was chained to a wall.

"Chains?" he asked.

"People are coming here at night and stealing the flower pots and plants. They even took the first lemon tree I planted."

"You have got to be kidding me. They are stealing from an op shop? What in God's name is going on when people are stealing from a charity?"

"Think there's enough for a story?" she asked.

"I do. Let me get a photo of you next to the lemon tree. I'll show it to the news editor and see what she thinks."

Delaney took a few photos with his phone. He showed them to Susan who gave her okay. Later in the day Delaney emailed the photos with a few lines of what was going on at the op shop to the news editor at his former paper. He heard back from her quickly and she said she would get a reporter on to the story and send a photographer to the shop to take some better-quality photos.

Before he left the shop, Delaney asked Susan if she would be interested in meeting a single friend of his.

"If I was available I might but I am seeing someone and we're quite happy. Thanks for asking though."

He asked for her phone number—to pass along to the news editor—and she gave it to him.

"I promise the only person you'll hear from is either the editor or a reporter."

"Thank you, Gary. You've always been a gentleman. I have a question for you."

"Okay."

"When we used to see each other at the train station, how come you never asked me out for a coffee? I would have said yes."

"Really? I thought about it but didn't think you would say yes."

"Next time you find yourself in that sort of a situation, ask."

She kissed Delaney on the cheek and went to help a customer.

"I guess I should have asked," Delaney said to himself. A wasted opportunity? Perhaps. He shrugged his shoulders and walked back into the early spring sunshine.

When Delaney talked to Michelle that evening, he told her about the party in Hampton.

"Chris said you can come along if you like."

"That's okay baby, you go and have a good time. I'm going to catch up with a friend of mine in Carlton for dinner. I'll be home on Sunday."

A friend? Should I ask her which friend? Nah. That will just reek of jealousy, Delaney thought.

"I'm really looking forward to having you back home baby. You have a good night out tomorrow and I'll ring you on Sunday. Be safe."

"I will. See you on Sunday, probably about lunchtime."

Delaney spent Saturday reading the former broadsheet and watching the races on the telly from Caulfield at home. The good horses were starting their spring campaigns, so the card was a bit better than average. He decided not to have a bet. With Michelle having taken the car into the city, Delaney took a cab to the party in Hampton.

He arrived on the crowded street just after seven and was let in by the night's host, Stan Griffiths. It was just as well he took a cab. He would have had to park three or four blocks away if he had driven. There were cars parked everywhere, and high-end models too.

"Gary Delaney," the sportswriter said, sticking his hand out.

Stan was in his mid to late fifties, tall with close cropped hair and a bit of a beard. He wore slacks, a dark T-shirt and a sports jacket so Delaney did not feel overdressed. He had on beige chinos, a blue dress shirt and a black sports jacket.

"Nice to meet you," Stan said shaking his hand. "Chris said you were coming. Come in, a lot of people are here already. There's plenty of food and drink. Help yourself. I'll introduce you to my wife when I find her."

Stan's home was straight out of a home-living magazine. A large open living area led to a tidy backyard. The food and drink were inside. People were milling about, both inside and out, most with a plate in one hand and a drink nearby. Soft jazz was playing at just the right volume so people could converse without having to shout.

Delaney saw Pastor Chris at the buffet table and said hello.

"You got here just at the right time. The good stuff has just landed," Chris said as he piled chicken and what looked to be potato salad onto his plate.

"There's a heck of a crowd here, especially for this time of night," Delaney said.

"When Stan throws a party, people know to come early. Have you had a look at the talent here? Amazing, simply amazing."

Delaney had a look around. There must have been at least fifty people in the living room and backyard. And Chris was spot on. The women were stunning. But Delaney had a stunner of his own coming home the next afternoon so all he did was look. He had a good feed first and then with Chris leading the way, he started to mingle.

"Are any of these women single?" Delaney asked.

"Most are married but there are several available women here," Chris said as he sipped a red wine.

"Any catch your eye?"

"A couple. They're all pretty fit, aren't they?"

"Fit is one way to describe them," Delaney said.

"Elliott," Chris called out to a stocky bloke holding a bottle of beer. "This is my mate Gary Delaney, the sportswriter."

"Nice to meet you," Delaney said, putting his vodka and tonic in his left hand as he shook Elliott's hand.

"A sportswriter, eh? What do you cover? the footy?"

"I have in the past but starting on Monday my focus is going to be on racing."

"Like to have a punt, do you?"

"Just a couple of dollars each way. What sort of work do you do?"

"Stockbroker."

"Like a punt yourself?"

"I do but it's a lot more than a few dollars each way." Elliott laughed.

Chris laughed along with him.

Delaney took the joke at his expense in stride. He was used to blowhards like Elliott Agee, those who bragged about the hundreds of thousands they spent at yearling sales or their MCG memberships.

"Elliott has made quite a bit of money for several people here tonight," Chris added.

"Is that so? What's hot right now?"

"You mean besides that hot blonde in the corner?" Elliott laughed at his own joke. People usually laughed with him. The man looked like he just stepped out of a Myer catalogue.

"You married, Elliott?"

"What are you, keen on me? Get me another drink and maybe I'll go home with you."

Oh boy, Delaney thought. *How can I get away from him?*

"Mining is still where it's at, isn't it Elliott?" Chris asked.

"Has been and always will be. In fact, I can let you in on something that not many people know."

"Go on," Delaney said, his ears perking up.

"There's a small company about to sign a big deal in Mongolia. The government there has just given the all clear for another gold mine to open and this company's stock is going to soar."

"Mongolia?" Delaney asked.

"Yup. There's a lot of gold and copper there. This new gold mine is going to be about 110k north of Ulaanbaatar, the country's capital."

"Ulan who?"

"Ulaanbaatar," Elliot repeated.

"And this mining company? How is its track record?"

"Pretty small scale. It's doing okay now but when this new mine opens a lot of people are going to be very wealthy. I reckon the new mine should start producing gold within six months, if not sooner."

Hmmm, Delaney thought. "Are you in, Chris?"

"I am, put up $20,000."

"That's a lot of money," Delaney replied.

"It is but the last company Elliott told me to invest in doubled in value within a year. I reckon this mining company has the potential for even bigger returns."

"What's the minimum investment, Elliott?"

"Its shares are selling for about two dollars. I'd say $5000 would be a good start."

"What's the name of this lot?" Delaney asked.

"Motherlode Mining Group," Elliott said

"I'll do some research on it and get back to you. Do you have a card?"

Elliott reached into his wallet and handed Delaney one of his cards. "If you're interested, get in touch with me by Monday. If you're not there are plenty of others who will jump at the chance."

"Hey hun," Elliott called out to a dark-haired, woman standing a few metres away chatting to a group of what Delaney took to be her girlfriends. "Can you get me another one of these please?" Elliott said pointing to his empty beer bottle.

Within a minute the bronzed, dark-haired beauty appeared with another bottle and took his empty one.

She was a head taller than Elliott and took hold of his free arm.

"My husband's not trying to part you and your money, is he?" she asked.

"Nothing of the sort honey. Just telling Mr Delaney here about a fantastic opportunity."

"Well, if I were you Mr Delaney, I would jump at the chance. See all this jewellery I am wearing? It's all courtesy of Elliott's penchant for picking winners."

The two walked off.

"He sure picked a winner in her," Delaney told Pastor Chris, who nodded affirmatively.

"You going to invest?" Chris asked.

"Only after I do some research on Motherlode Mining Group."

"Fair enough," Chris said. "Just let him know by Monday."

"I will."

Chris caught his mate looking across the room.

"What are you looking at?"

"When I tell you, casually look over at the group standing by the bookcase. There's a woman in a blue dress who keeps looking at you."

"Really?"

"Look over now."

Chris nonchalantly glanced over at the group and had a glance at the woman.

"Wow, she is gorgeous. Should I go over and introduce myself?"

"What have you got to lose? If she's wearing a wedding ring keep it brief, if not ..."

"You're right. I should go over there and at least say hello."

Christopher Simmons composed himself, took a deep breath and walked over to the woman in the blue dress.

He was so nervous that he barely got the word hello out of his mouth. "Quite a party, isn't it?"

"Hello," she said. "Yes, Stan really knows how to throw a party. Are you a friend of his?"

"I am," Chris said, glancing at the fingers on her left hand. There was no wedding ring. "We go back quite a few years. I'm Chris," he said, "Christopher Simmons."

"Allison Roberts," she said extending her hand. "My friends call me Ally."

"Very nice to meet you Ally."

"Moving a little fast to the friendship stage, aren't we?" she asked with a smile that showed a magnificent set of teeth.

"One can never have too many friends," Chris said.

"So, Chris, what sort of work do you do?" Ally said looking directly into his eyes. She was a few centimetres shorter than Chris even in a pair of heels. She put all her weight on one foot and then the other as she took a sip of white wine.

"I'm a counsellor and I also coach footy. And you?"

"I'm a primary school teacher."

"How about that?" Chris said.

"What sort of counselling do you do?"

"I deal with kids mostly, kids who are having problems in school and at home. That's where most of the problems start, at home. I try and steer them over the rough patches and help them decide what they want to do with their life once they finish with Year 12."

"That's a lot of responsibility," Ally answered.

"It is, but I love what I do. To turn a kid's life around gives me a lot of enjoyment."

"I get that same sort of enjoyment working with second and third graders. They pick up so much in a year. It is remarkable."

"Do you have any children of your own," Chris asked.

"No, but I have twenty-five kids from 8.30 to 3pm five days a week. That's enough, I think."

"I don't have any kids either. And I am not married."

"That was going to be my next question. So how is it that an attractive man like yourself isn't married?"

"This will sound like a cliché, but I guess I have never found the right woman."

"And a gorgeous woman like yourself? How is it that you're not married?"

"Like you, I have never found the right woman."

"Woman? Are you gay?"

"No. I was just teasing."

"Not that there is anything wrong with that," Chris said.

"No, nothing at all, but I prefer men."

"Noted."

"What kind of women do you like, Chris?"

"Someone who is fit, down to earth, someone who likes a laugh and socialising. She doesn't have to like sport, but I'd like her to be interested in what is going on in the world and keen to want to help."

"Well, I am big believer in helping the less fortunate. And, just to let you know, I am a paid-up Carlton supporter."

"Hmmm, that could be a sticking point. I barrack for Richmond. However, you do look good in blue."

"Why thank you Chris."

Ally was a woman who would look good in any colour, Chris thought. Cute was not the right word to describe her. Adorable? Possibly. She had a pair of sparkling dark eyes, was showing a bit of cleavage and had firm tan legs, the legs of a walker or runner.

"Looking at something?" she asked, catching Chris looking at her breasts.

"Sorry," Chris said. *Well, I blew this. Why did I have to look?* he asked himself.

"It's okay. I don't mind you looking. But when you're with me, don't go looking at others. Deal?"

"Deal," Chris replied as they shook hands.

"Hey look, a couple of seats. Let's grab them," Ally said taking Chris by the hand. "I'm tired of standing in these heels."

Chris caught Delaney's eye as he made his way to one of several couches in the living area.

Delaney gave his mate a big thumbs up and didn't get a chance to speak to him the rest of the night. He'd ring Chris for a full report the next afternoon.

With no one to talk to, Delaney took out his phone and Googled Motherlode Mining Group.

Motherlode was a small company based in Perth. It was a relative newcomer to the mining game but carried no debt and had a collection of well-heeled investors. Its website made no mention of any mining in Mongolia. Delaney had the $1800 that he was overpaid by Consume and Devour and some savings and decided to take a shot. He'd have a stab at the market for a change instead of the horses.

He went to find Elliott. He located the life of the party in the backyard. Elliott was with a small group. He tapped Elliott on the shoulder.

"Delaney, what's up? enjoying yourself?"

"Sure am. Listen mate, I'm been doing some thinking and want in on the Motherlode Mining Group."

"That's a wise decision," my friend. "How much should I put you down for?"

"An even $10,000."

"Outstanding," Elliott said. He handed Delaney his iPhone and told him to type in his number and details.

"Someone from the office will get in touch with you early next week to go over all the details, okay?"

"Okay."

The two shook hands.

"You have made a wise decision my friend, a very wise decision. There's just one thing."

"Being?" Delaney replied.

"If you ever go to Mongolia don't drink the airag."

"What is airag?"

"An alcoholic concoction made from fermented horse milk. It's bloody awful, but the locals love it."

"Noted," Delaney said.

Chris wound up following Ally back to her place, a two-bedroom unit in East Bentleigh, not even ten minutes away from the party. She parked in her designated spot—number six—while Chris found a spot on the street.

"You're not a murderer, are you?" Ally joked as she turned the key to her front door.

"Nah, I picture myself as an embezzler; taking from the rich to give to the poor."

"I'm not rich."

"Well, in the case maybe I should get going."

Ally laughed as she turned on the lights.

A good-sized fish tank sat in the carpeted lounge room. There were roughly thirty brightly coloured fish dashing about the green plants, rocks and shells. A mini scuba diver was on the right side of the tank along with a treasure chest. The tank's pumps barely made a sound.

"It's very relaxing," Ally said.

"It is. I had one years ago but it was nothing compared to this."

"Shall I make us some coffee?" Ally asked.

"That would be better than a drink. I'm just about over the limit."

"I have a muffin left. We can share it if you like."

"That would be nice," Chris said as he plunked himself down on the sofa. He took a quick look at what was on her coffee table; the former broadsheet turned tabloid, the latest John Grisham novel which had a bookmark placed about halfway through it, a Coles circular and a couple of cooking magazines.

There was a nice plant over in the corner and a large Samsung TV perched on a black entertainment unit. A Foxtel box occupied one shelf and a DVD player the next. He sneaked a peek at her DVD collection; *Veep, Curb your Enthusiasm, Castaway*, the box sets of *Seinfeld, Breaking Bad, Mad Men.*

Outstanding, Chris thought. *She has taste.*

While the kettle was boiling Ally took off her heels and joined him on the couch.

"What do you think?"

"Very nice place. One bedroom or two?"

"Two, I use one as an office/computer room. And there's a bit of a backyard too."

"I'm impressed."

"What's your place like?" Ally asked.

One bedroom with a yard. No fish tank. It's all I need, I guess."

Ally bolted upright as the kettle boiled and scampered into the kitchen.

"How do you like your coffee?"

"White please, two sugars."

Ally brought out the coffees and placed them on the coffee table after making space by clearing away the magazines. She went back and got the muffin; blueberry, which she split in half.

"Cheers," she said lifting her mug.

Chris tapped her mug with his. "Cheers."

They talked and laughed for nearly two hours before Chris, not wanting to do anything stupid which could ruin such a promising start, decided to call it a night.

"Hey, we haven't exchanged numbers," Ally said.

Ally punched her number into Chris's phone while Chris tapped his number into hers.

"I have had such a good time, thanks for inviting me over," Chris said as Ally walked him to the door.

"Me too, just don't turn out to be a jerk," Ally said with a smile.

"I won't. That's a promise."

Chris leaned down and gave Ally a soft kiss on the mouth.

"I'll call you tomorrow," he said.

Pastor Chris walked in the near darkness to his car, pressed the remote to open it and sat down. It wasn't that late, so he decided to call Delaney to tell him about his night.

The phone rang but it was not Delaney who answered.

"Can't stand being away from me for even a minute, can you?"

"Huh?"

"You said you would call tomorrow but you're about forty-seven minutes early," Ally said.

Oh shit, Pastor Chris thought. *What is she going to think about me now?*

"Hi, Ally. Sorry. I meant to call my mate Delaney but dialled your number by mistake. This is embarrassing."

"I think it's cute. Talk tomorrow, good night."

Chris leaned back in his seat. "Good night," he said but she had already hung up.

He'd ring Delaney in the morning. He turned the key and headed home.

Delaney spent his third night alone doing just what he had the first two, tossing and turning. He missed Michelle but didn't want her to know how much so he cut back the length of the welcome home banner he was working on from three metres to two.

After having a read of the Sunday paper—just a handful of mistakes, including a missing caption on page two—Delaney fixed himself a turkey sandwich for lunch, flicked on racing.com for the first couple of races from Geelong and waited for Michelle to come home.

On the other side of town, house sitter Michelle gave the overwatered plants one last drink, cleaned up the kitchen, packed her things and headed home.

As she drove along Punt Road, which was surprisingly quiet, and made her way to Nepean Highway, which was surprisingly busy, Michelle's mind was racing. The few days by herself made her wonder if the decision to move in with someone so quickly after her marriage fell apart was a mistake. It had been just ten months after a twenty-four-year marriage.

"Would it be better if I got my own place and spent a few nights a week at Gary's?" she asked herself. "How would he take it?"

It would be tougher financially with two rents to pay plus separate electric and internet bills, but it could be done. Michelle wasn't unhappy but wondered if she could be happier. But with Delaney starting his new job the next day she decided not to bring it up when she got home. He didn't need any more on his plate. It could wait.

Over dinner, steaks and burgers on the barbecue which Delaney prepared, and salads courtesy of Woolies, Delaney told Michelle about the party he and Chris had been to and his decision to invest in Motherlode Mining Group.

Michelle was sceptical. "Ten thousand dollars? In Mongolia? Sounds a bit risky."

"Everything carries a risk," countered Delaney. "But this guy ..."

"What's his name?"

"Elliott Agee. He seems to know what he is doing. Even Chris is putting some money up."

"I'd look into it a little bit more," Michelle said between bites of her medium rare T-bone.

"I will baby. Oh, and how about this? Chris met a woman at the party. He can't stop talking about her. He wants us to have dinner with them next weekend."

"We could do that; what's she like?"

"Very pretty, not that I noticed. She's a school teacher, single, in her mid-thirties I'd guess, with no kids. Chris is positively smitten. And from what I hear she is very keen on him too."

"Wow, you go away for a few days and there's news everywhere. Maybe they could go to Mongolia for their honeymoon."

Delaney laughed. "I better warn them about drinking the airag."

"The what?"

"Airag. The locals drink it. It's made from fermented horse milk."

"I'll pass on the airag but you can top up my glass please."

Delaney reached for the bottle of white wine he bought that afternoon and topped up Michelle's glass. He looked at her and smiled. "I am so glad you're home."

"Me too baby, me too," Michelle said.

17

AS THE DAYS TO HIS AND FRANKIE "FINGERS" TANNEN-
baum's release drew closer and with his ankle fully healed, Johnny
Pastrami was back on the basketball court, albeit running and jumping
a bit gingerly to avoid any flare-up.

Pastrami had served eighteen months and Tannenbaum sixteen.
Several months earlier, the pickpocket had lifted a monthly wall calendar
from Stanley Blake's office while the warden was on one of his frequent
afternoon trips to the toilet. After using a bottle of white-out—also taken
from the warden's office—to erase the dates of birthdays and his wedding
anniversary that were crudely scribbled down, Tannenbaum circled the
date of Monday, September 6 in red ink; his scheduled release date.

Pastrami was the first to be given his walking papers. He gathered his
things from the cottage he shared with Tannenbaum and four others
early on the morning of August 2, leaving the well-worn moon boot and
crutches in one of the cottage's closets.

He had a light breakfast and reported to Blake's office at 8am.

"You've served your time," Blake said, handing over Pastrami's official
release papers in a sealed envelope. "Stay out of trouble, okay? A judge won't
be sending you to a country club like this again if you continue to offend."

"I've learned my lesson Mr Blake. You won't be seeing me again, and
nor will any other warden. I've lost eighteen months of my life."

The pair shook hands.

"Hendricks," the warden called out, "Escort Mr Pastrami to the
front gate."

The two walked down the path to freedom, past the mess hall and
the two dozen or so cottages housing the rest of the inmates, and the
basketball and tennis courts. The air was cold and the skies grey, but

Pastrami was beaming. Not only was he leaving, but one of his many girlfriends was coming to give him a lift back to Melbourne.

"Who you got waiting for you?" Hendricks asked.

"A gal I know," Pastrami said with a wink.

"I've never seen a guy have so many different women come here for conjugal visits. You got a salami in your pants, Pastrami?"

"Could be."

Starting back in high school, Pastrami had heard that line thousands of times.

A grey Mercedes was waiting at the end of the long driveway, parked near a small sign reading *Murchison Correctional Facility*. A shapely brunette opened the door of the car, got out and waved.

"Geez, get a look at her. What a knockout," Hendricks said, his eyes about to pop out of their sockets.

"Settle down mate," Pastrami said, giving Hendricks a few taps on the shoulder. "She's my sister."

"Oh, sorry mate."

Hendricks and Pastrami shook hands. "Look after my mate Tannenbaum, will ya? He gets out of here in a month."

Pastrami walked the thirty or forty metres to where his sister was waiting. They warmly embraced and as they did so, Pastrami whispered in her ear. "I'm going to give you a long pash just near your lips. Play along with it, okay?"

"Sure, Johnny."

Hendricks watched the pair lock lips. "Close family," he said, adjusting his cap.

"You're looking well, Johnny, a little thinner, and you're walking okay. How's the ankle coming along?" Judy Saunders asked.

"It healed well. It's nearly 100 percent. The doctors and nurses in Shepparton did a good job. Appreciate you coming up here so early to come and get me. It'll be the last time. Nothing shady again for me."

"I hope not Johnny. We wuz all worried about you, especially your nephews. They kept asking 'where's Uncle Johnny?'"

"What'd you tell them?'

"That you were away on business; overseas, taking care of a few investments."

Pastrami smiled. "And Bill? He's treating you well?"

"Sure is. He's a good man, Johnny."

To say Judy Saunders was in a rush to get married after leaving university so she could ditch the surname Pastrami was an understatement. She had been teased all through middle school and high school. A couple of times big brother Johnny was called in to issue a stern warning to the troublemakers.

She met Bill Saunders in her second year at uni and they married a year after they graduated when he snared a good job with Melbourne City Council in the communications department. By the time they both turned thirty, they were a family of four.

"He didn't mind you coming up here to get me?"

"Not at all. In fact, he even took the morning off to get the kids off to school."

"You picked yourself a winner," said the man who knew a few things about finding winners.

"It would be nice to see you settle down."

"In due time sis, in due time."

After a few minutes of silence Pastrami asked how things were with his apartment.

"Everything has been taken care of. I had a cleaner over once a month and yesterday I stocked your fridge with all your favourites. And there's two tubs of that vanilla ice-cream you like so much in the freezer."

"I've missed that. How much do I owe you for everything?"

"Owe me? Not a cent. We made a fortune betting on Prince of Penzance in the cup last year."

"I did too. So much that I am through with the real estate business. I'll check in with Bobby Robertson in a couple of days and get my financials all sorted out."

"You're going legit?"

"I didn't say that," Pastrami said, turning to his little sister with a big smile.

Judy Saunders kept her eyes on the road, slowing down as they passed through Nagambie, the birthplace of undefeated champion Black Caviar.

"They put up a statue of the horse here. I've never seen it. Let's get ourselves a coffee and have a look," Pastrami said.

"I'd love a coffee," she replied.

After becoming reacquainted with his apartment, Pastrami rang his mate Bobby Robertson. Pastrami had entrusted Robertson to look after his cash while he was in the Alabama slammer.

"I'm fine Bobby, thanks for asking, but let's get to the heart of the matter. Where's the dough and when can I expect it to be delivered?"

"Well, here's the thing Johnny. Your money is in safe hands, just not mine, and you won't be able to access most of it for another two months."

"And why is that Bobby?"

"Cause it's in the bank."

"The bank?"

"Yeah. Let me explain. I know a guy at one of the big four banks who owed me a favour, a large favour. He took all the cash—no questions asked—and put it in several term deposits—all in your name. They've been earning 2.75 per cent interest and mature in another 60 days."

"Shit, I had a couple of heart palpitations when you said the word bank Bobby. But you've done well pal, you've done well."

"Thanks mate. I've got about 30 grand of yours in cash to tide you over until the term deposits mature."

"Good. I always like to have some walking around money. Come by my place tomorrow afternoon. Bring the cash and all the paperwork from the bank. Yeah, same place mate. Tenth floor."

Tannenbaum had nearly five more weeks of his sentence to serve. He did not care too much for the fellow who took Pastrami's spot in the cottage. John Seiling was a family court judge with over thirty years on the bench. He was close to retirement but was caught taking bribes in exchange for imposing more favourable conditions for several well-to-do mates when the terms of their divorces were decided. Not happy with the bucketloads of untraceable cash he received, he was also known for making sure several very attractive women got what they wanted—whether they were entitled to it or not—through evening meetings at some of Melbourne's best hotels.

Seiling bragged about it constantly despite being sent away for three years, a fine of $250,000 and disbarment.

"Hey judge, no disrespect, but enough already, okay? I've got four more weeks here and I don't want to listen to your bullshit any longer," Tannenbaum said one evening when Seiling was going on and on about the 10 hottest women he had banged. "If I want a top 10 list I'll watch Letterman on YouTube."

"I find you in contempt of court," Seiling said, trying to be funny.

"Yeah, whatever. Just put a sock in your mouth, all right?"

Seiling nodded.

Despite sharing the same cabin and the same bathroom for the next month, the pair never said another word to each other.

18

FOR THE FIRST TIME IN NEARLY TWENTY YEARS, GARY Delaney was facing his first day at a new office.

They're never easy as all eyes are on the newcomer.

"He's older than I thought he would be."

"I hope he doesn't come in with a raft of changes."

"What if he's worse than the prick he's replacing?"

After skipping breakfast, he was too nervous to eat, Delaney left home early and caught the 7.45 train into the city. Michelle left for her job at the National Gallery thirty minutes later. Despite the intermittent morning rain, he was at the Turf News office door at 8.35.

Without a swipe pass to get in—whatever happened to the office key?—he rang the bell outside. Lisa the receptionist let him in and after an exchange of good mornings led him to his desk.

It was in the corner of the large room right next to a window which had a tremendous view of the MCG. With a good pair of binoculars, he'd be able to watch the footy or cricket.

"Wendy Seaver, she's one of our editorial assistants, will be over shortly to give you your passwords to get into the system and an office card to get in," Lisa said. "The kitchen is right over there. Help yourself to the coffee and tea. Someone is always bringing in biscuits or cake so if you see something on the table help yourself. If you need anything, just ask."

"I'll do that. Thanks Lisa."

Delaney took off his jacket and hung it over his chair. He opened his umbrella to let it dry, placed his briefcase and paper on the large desk and took a seat. He adjusted the height of the leather chair until it was just right.

There was a large filing cabinet to his left and the phone was posit-ioned on the left-hand side of the desk just as he liked it.

As he was taking stock of the filing cabinet drawers, which were empty except for an old phone book and a stapler, he heard a knock on his desk. He looked up to see a blonde woman standing in front of him. She was casually dressed and carrying a folder of paperwork meant for new employees.

"You must be Wendy," Delaney said as he rose from his chair.

"And you must be Gary."

"Indeed I am."

"Like the desk?"

"I do and the view is pretty nice too," he said pointing to the MCG. *Geez if I hadn't pointed to the MCG she would have thought I was talking about her. Sexual harassment within the first ten minutes of a new job. Ouch.*

Wendy, who Delaney guessed was in her mid-forties, handed him his office card and then showed him how to log into the system. He typed in his first initial and his last name, and with Wendy looking away from the screen, punched in his password, *quaddie.* He hadn't hit one for quite some time. Perhaps the change of jobs would help his luck.

Wendy also gave him the office phone number and his extension. In less time than it took to cover the two-mile distance of the Melbourne Cup, Delaney was right to go.

"Thanks Wendy. So far so good."

"If you need any help," she said, "just ask. My desk is on the other side of the office."

Delaney opened a couple of word documents and saved them in his main folder. All was okay there.

He was curious to find out the speed of the office internet and punched the words *NY Times* into Google. It loaded with surprising quickness.

The main *Turf News* folder had a couple of feature stories in it. He'd have a look at them later.

Wendy and her team were responsible for putting the form guide together and all the stats. It was mind-numbing work at times but was the paper's bread and butter. The comments after each horse's past performances, such as *raced three-wide off a hot pace and held on well in better grade last time out*, were considered by many to be the best in the business. Punters, big and small, relied on them.

As 9am neared, the rest of the team began to trickle in, spaced out like a steeplechase field at Warrnambool.

Robert Nicholls, the fellow who hired Delaney three weeks ago, was first through the door and made his way over to Delaney's corner of the room.

"Good to see you again Gary," he said. "Settling in all right?"

"So far so good," Delaney said as he quickly stood up to shake Nicholls' hand. "Wendy has teed everything up. I'm ready to roll."

"I don't know what we would do without her. She's the one who keeps everything running smoothly. We're going to have a staff meeting in about thirty minutes where I'll officially introduce you to everyone. Until then get yourself a cup of coffee and relax."

"Will do."

"And just one other thing. In the meeting call me Bob, not Mr Nicholls. We run a pretty informal ship around here and it works well."

At 9.30 Delaney walked into the conference room. Nicholls and Wendy were already seated, coffee cups in front of them. Delaney put down his notebook and took a seat.

The reporters filed in one after another. Two of the younger ones put their mobile phones on the table in what Delaney thought was a gesture to prove their importance.

A young woman followed and judging by the reception she received from her fellow journos it was evident that she had told them all at one time or another that she did not date colleagues and would not take any shit from anyone. In a business where more and more trainers, jockeys and owners were women, Jodi Clendenon was just what *Turf News* needed. Delaney had read some of her recent yarns over the past couple of weeks and found her feature pieces to be good reads; entertaining and informative. All they needed was a bit of tightening.

The paper's two photographers, Daryl Jones and Ken Ryan, were out at jobs; Daryl at the Cranbourne trials and Ken at Caulfield for a yarn on a young trainer that Jodi was working on.

Nicholls opened proceedings with the usual, "hope you all had a good weekend and enjoyed the racing." He then got down to business.

"Today we welcome Gary Delaney to the staff."

All eyes turned to the newcomer who nodded.

"He'll take over the role that was held by Matthew Gentry. He'll go over all your copy and hand out assignments if need be. You each have your own beats and that won't change. As Gary settles in, he'll do some writing as well. Check in with him daily as you did with Gentry so there is no doubling up and try and file your stories as soon as you can so Gary can go over them. Otherwise it is business as usual although we could tweak things a little as the spring carnival kicks into gear."

Nicholls went around the table, introducing the reporters to his new sub-editor.

There were Jodi, Adam Swoboda who sported a light beard as most young men did these days, the pair with the phones—Graeme Bell and Alexander Watson—ace columnist Greg Grote, and Roger Hodges, who was the oldest of the bunch, excluding Nicholls and Delaney.

All got up and shook Delaney's hand except Bell and Watson who were too busy checking their phones. Delaney would be sending them to the next night meeting at Tynong North, the new track which replaced the old Pakenham circuit. It was a good ninety-minute drive out of town.

When the meeting broke Delaney went back to his desk and had a look at the weekly schedule. Echuca on Tuesday, Sandown on Wednesday, Moe on Thursday, Cranbourne on Friday and Flemington on Saturday.

All were staffed so Delaney got to work on a piece on a long-time clerk of the course based in the southeast. He had talked to Bernie Charles a few weeks ago at his place on the peninsula but never got around to writing the story. He retrieved the notes from his personal email account and copied and pasted them to a new word document. There were plenty of photos of him in the *Turf News* archives but none that stood out, so Delaney gave the veteran horseman a ring to ask if he was available to for a photo shoot. He said he was free on Thursday which was perfect.

Delaney made a good start on the yarn, writing about 500 words, and took a few minutes to ring Elliott Agee's office to officially purchase his stock in Motherlode Mining Group. Agee's assistant, Laura Groggin, took all his details and confirmed that he would be buying 5000 shares at two dollars a share which was what Motherlode Mining Group was trading for at the start of the day. There was also a commission of $120. Delaney gave the okay for a one-time direct debit of $10,120 from his savings account. He hadn't laid out that kind of money in ages but had a good feeling about his first-time venture into the market.

Groggin told Delaney he would receive all the paperwork from the transaction in the post by the end of the week and wished him good luck.

On Tuesday Motherlode Mining Group's stock had rose to $2.04 and by the end of the week was up to $2.12. "Looks like Agee was spot on," Delaney said as he glanced at the financial pages at his desk.

By the end of the month the stock was up to $3.00 and following news that a new gold deposit showed promise, Motherlode Mining Group skyrocketed to $4.00 a share.

Pastor Chris, whom he had seen just twice since he started dating the lovely Ally Roberts, rang Delaney the afternoon the stock hit $4.00. He said he had heard some news online about a possible coup in Mongolia.

Delaney told Chris he had heard the same news except that the coup plotters did not want to shut down any of the mines since it brought in a substantial amount of money via a hefty mining tax. The troublemakers didn't know the first thing about mining, and Motherlode Mining Group along with several other miners employed a large group of civilians who would be left jobless and very angry with any shutdown. In the worst-case scenario, Delaney figured the miners would bribe a few highly-placed plotters to keep their operation running.

However, the word *coup* set off alarm bells for Pastor Chris. He unloaded his stock and doubled his $5000 investment. Delaney saw no reason to abandon ship. Motherlode Mining Group's new mine was booming and talk of a coup was dying off as the government cracked down on demonstrators.

The stock shot up to $4.60. Life was good, maybe not for the demonstrators in Mongolia, but good for a certain sub-editor in Melbourne. Work was going better than he expected and Delaney had more than doubled his initial investment.

It was at that time that he was approached by his colleague Adam Swoboda.

The bearded one had noticed the financial pages on Delaney's desk and asked him how his investments were going.

"There's just the one, in a mining company and it's going quite well," Delaney said. "You want in?"

"Nah. I'll stick with the horses. But I do know of a syndicate that has sold nineteen shares in a stayer from the UK. There's one spot left for $15,000 and the head of the syndicate asked me if I knew anyone who would be interested."

"Why don't you take it?" Delaney asked.

"I would but I have some more pressing issues. My partner and I are having a baby soon and we need to save every dollar we have."

"Congratulations. That's great news. Your first?"

"Yes, and I'm bit nervous. Do you have any kids?"

"Not one. I never thought I would be able to handle the 24/7 responsibility of being a parent."

"I sure hope I can."

"You will. Now tell me more about this stayer."

"The owners brought him over here last year as a four-year-old. He's a chestnut gelding, a beautiful looking horse, and they had high hopes for him. They were looking at him as a legitimate Caulfield Cup horse. But believe it or not he came down with travel sickness and never had a start. It took him about six months to fully recover. But he's fully healthy now and from what I hear is going very well. He has his first trial at Cranbourne next week."

"Who's training him?" Delaney asked.

" Jack McCarron at Caulfield."

"Well if the horse is fit and is being trained by McCarron why can't the owners sell that last spot?"

"Nobody wants to put up the money until they see him in an official trial. He hasn't run in nearly a year."

"Makes sense. What's the horse's name and how is his pedigree?"

"Too Hard Wrong Spot." He's out of the smart UK stallion Morning Fog."

"Too Hard Wrong Spot?" Delaney asked. "It sounds like a porn movie."

"Supposedly his owners and trainer in the UK had a difference of opinion about his ability. The owners wanted the horse to make his debut in a stakes race at Newmarket but the trainer, Hershel Kranepool, said the race was too hard for a first-time starter. 'It's the wrong spot,' he kept telling them. 'It's the wrong spot. He needs something easier, at least for now.'

"One of the owners picked up on the phrase and they had its name changed."

"What was his original name?" Delaney asked.

"Ya Gotta Believe."

"Either one would have worked for me."

"In his first run," Swoboda continued, "he came from the back of the pack and closed to be a strong third over 1500m. He ran the same way in his second start two weeks later over 1600m and placed second. His times were good and the horses who finished in front of them were good quality animals. He broke through for his first win a month later over 1800m in the same style and the owners were rapt. They wanted to keep running him but Kranepool had his doubts. He wanted to spell the horse and have him fresh and stronger for his four-year-old campaign. It was then that some representatives from Australian syndicates started coming around the stables."

"Were they offering decent money?" Delaney asked.

"Close to $250,000 for a horse that was bought for 25,000 pounds."

"Wow. Let me guess, Kranepool wanted to keep the horse and the owners took the money."

"Spot on. They did well on their original investment and after some haggling with Big John McGraw from City Winners Syndication, the horse changed hands."

"You boys are learning fast," McGraw told the former owners after sealing the deal. "You know what we are looking for and are taking us to the cleaners."

Big John McGraw walked away with the paperwork while one of his minders led the horse to his new home at a nearby stable at Newmarket. "I think we have ourselves a genuine cups horse here," McGraw told Ronnie Taylor, his partner at City Winners, later in the morning by phone. All those owners could see was the money. The trainer, Kranepool, knew he was losing one of the best if not the best horse in his stable.

"Now he's ours and if he is as good as we think he is it will be money well spent," McGraw said.

Taylor agreed. "We'll give the horse a nice spell and then send him to McCarron. He'll get the best out of him."

Too Hard Wrong Spot took some time adjusting to his new surroundings at Newmarket. Trainer Reggie Gaspar, who was looking after the horse until he flew out of the UK, had his hands full. The animal had a bit of a temper. He bit one stable hand, sent another to hospital with a well-placed kick to the ribs and was a genuine pain in the arse. The only person who could calm him down was Danielle Frisella, his twenty-one-year-old strapper.

Gaspar, who would not go anywhere near the horse after the incidents with his stable hands, put Frisella in charge of the beast.

She fed him, hosed him down and talked to him while they walked to a nearby paddock where he picked at the lush grass. Frisella would stroke the horse's neck when they returned and give him a carrot or two if he behaved, which he always did around her.

It was Gaspar who brought Too Hard Wrong Spot's antics to Big John McGraw's attention.

McGraw was a large man in his mid-forties who did not like to hear bad news. Always well-dressed and well-prepared for the cool English mornings, McGraw had a weakness for food, women and horses, not necessarily in that order. But he loved money more than the other three combined. The money brought him a seemingly endless supply of young, gorgeous women who did not mind sleeping with a 125 kilogram, six-foot, forty-five-year-old man with more hair on his chest and shoulders than George 'The Animal' Steele. Getting dolled up and being seen in the marquees at the spring racing carnival with B Grade celebrities and footballers was worth the trade-off, even though McGraw liked to have his girls dress up as jockeys when they rode him. "Use the whip, honey. That's what it's there for," he'd yell at them.

"The horse is a nut job?" McGraw asked Gaspar.

"Only when Frisella is not around."

"Jesus Christ. He wasn't like that when he was with Kranepool. What the hell is wrong with him? We've shelled out nearly a quarter of a million dollars. How the fuck is he supposed to get on a plane and travel twenty-eight hours?"

"My guess is that he misses Kranepool. He was with Kranepool since he was a yearling."

"And he's perfectly fine with this Frisella woman?

"Yes, she's the only one here that he responds to."

"Well, she doesn't know it yet, but she's going to Melbourne in a few weeks."

"That might take some doing."

"Why is that?" barked McGraw, a man who was used to getting what he wanted.

"Frisella's mum is ill and she's taking care of her. Her father passed away a few years ago. Her older brother lives in Manchester and couldn't give a rat's arse about the family."

"What's wrong with her mum?"

"Cancer. She recently had surgery and depends on Danielle for nearly everything."

McGraw took his hat off and scratched the sparse grey hair on his noggin. "Tell Miss Frisella I'd like to see her."

"She's left for the day."

"When the hell will she be back?"

"Early in the morning. She leaves about ten for a few hours and then comes back to look after Too Hard Wrong Spot and some others.

"I'll be here at nine tomorrow. Tell her not to go anywhere until I get here, okay?"

"I'll tell her. How are you going to convince her to go to Melbourne?"

"I'll make her an offer she can't refuse," McGraw said as he walked to his car with his hat in his hand.

The next morning McGraw drove up to Gaspar's stables. It had rained during the night and large puddles of water were everywhere. McGraw dodged the puddles and several piles of horse shit and walked to Gaspar's office. The sky was clearing but McGraw was in a dark mood. He usually was when he had to unexpectedly part with money.

He knocked and opened the door. Gaspar was sitting at his desk and was on the phone. He ran a busy operation with over fifty horses in work and owners were always calling him, checking up on their horses. Since they paid the bills, Gaspar had to take the calls.

He nodded when he saw McGraw. He put one hand over his phone. "Be with you in a minute."

McGraw looked around. There were two whiteboards with horses' names on them and next to the names the work the horse had done in the morning. 'Three furlongs, 37.35' was scribbled next to the name of Kiner's Corner.

'Six furlongs, 1.14 flat' was written next to the name of Ryan's Express.

McGraw looked for his horse's name and found it on the bottom of the larger board. The words *stay the hell away from him,* were written. McGraw let out a huge laugh which drew the attention of several people in the office.

Gaspar walked over. "Danielle is at Too Hard Wrong Spot's box right now," he told McGraw.

"Let's go."

The pair passed the boxes of several other of Gaspar's horses. They were as calm as could be after their morning workouts. Gaspar rubbed the necks of several of them.

"Ya got any good ones?" McGraw asked.

The two walked about fifty metres. Gaspar stopped at the box of a muscular black colt.

"This one here—Solitaire—could be anything. He's a sprinter and won easily first time out."

"He's a beauty."

"We just have to keep him sound. He's had some foot issues."

About fifty metres away Gaspar and McGraw spotted Danielle Frisella. She was walking Too Hard Wrong Spot who seemed to be enjoying himself.

"How's he doing this afternoon?" Gaspar asked.

"Just fine, Mr Gaspar. He ate up and could race today if he had to."

"Danielle, this is John McGraw. He's the head of the syndicate which owns Too Hard Wrong Spot."

Danielle Frisella extended her hand. "Pleased to meet you Mr McGraw."

"Likewise. Gaspar tells me that you're the only one who can tame this animal. Is that true?"

"Well, we get along well. He just needs a little TLC."

So do I, McGraw thought. The head of City Winners Syndication was immediately taken with the tall twenty-one-year-old, green-eyed strapper. She had her dark hair pulled back from her angular face and was wearing a snug jacket over a sweater, tight jeans and dirt-covered boots.

"We're shipping the horse to Melbourne in a few weeks and I'd like you to accompany the horse down there and stay with him throughout the spring carnival. You'll be well compensated, Miss Frisella."

The offer took Danielle by surprise. Travel with the horse to Melbourne was one thing, but to stay there? The only time she had been out of the UK was three years ago when she treated herself to a weekend in Paris with her high school friends. She ended up with a tattoo of a butterfly on her lower back after a night of partying.

"I don't know, Mr McGraw. Mr Gaspar might have told you that I look after my mother. I can't leave her by herself."

McGraw had come prepared and had an answer for everything.

"I'll get a housekeeper to stay with your mum when you're away. She'll prepare her meals and do anything else that is required. The two of you can choose whoever you like. And we'll give you a mobile phone in Melbourne and pay for it so you can ring your mum anytime you want."

"That's a very generous offer, Mr McGraw. We've all heard so much about the Melbourne spring racing carnival. To be a part of it would be very exciting."

"We'll give you $1000 a week plus put you up in a hotel. Talk it over with your mum and get back to me. I'm here until the end of the week. The horse flies out two weeks from today. It's the chance of a lifetime, Miss Frisella. You're the only one we know of who gets along with the horse."

At that point Too Hard Wrong Spot shook his head up and down and whinnied.

"Looks like he agrees," McGraw said.

Danielle Frisella had another couple of hours of work at Gaspar's stables before she could go home. She gave Too Hard Wrong Spot's coat a good brush and put him back in his box. For now, he was a happy camper. She was checking in on Solitaire when Gaspar came by.

"Take the rest of the afternoon off and go home and tell your mum the news."

"Thank you, Mr Gaspar." She gave Solitaire a pat around the ears, gave Gaspar a hug and walked to her car a few hundred metres away. She checked her phone for any texts or calls—nothing on both counts—started up her eleven-year-old white Ford Fiesta, one of the oldest cars in the employees' parking lot, and headed home.

Danielle and her mum Victoria lived in Fulbourn, about a fifteen to twenty-minute drive from Gaspar's Newmarket stables. Their home—two bedrooms with a bath, garage and a nice backyard—was nothing special but it was paid for. Mr Frisella, a highly thought of claims adjuster, hated the word debt and had paid off the mortgage on the house six months before he suddenly passed away at the age of just fifty-four. Danielle was eighteen and nearly finished with Year 12.

Danielle's older brother came home for the funeral, left in his just-buried father's car and had not been back since. A cafe owner, he rarely even called to check up on his mother's declining health. When Danielle last rang him to ask him why, he said he was too busy. She hung up on him. That was eight months ago and the last time the two spoke.

Victoria Frisella was forced to stop working soon after her husband's death when she contracted breast cancer. Danielle put her uni plans on hold to take care of her. She was there for her when she went through the pain of chemotherapy and never complained about the many hours spent taking her mum to and from hospital and to various doctors. "You're a gem," Victoria repeatedly told her daughter.

When Victoria's medical and prescription medication bills started to mount, Danielle put her hand up and went looking for work. She had enjoyed being around horses ever since she was a kid and as a member of a local pony club had won numerous ribbons and trophies for her horsemanship. When she heard of some job openings at Newmarket, she hastily put together a resume and applied. An office job was not for her. She preferred being outside even at 4am when the only things awake were horses and the people who cared for them.

The first person to respond to her emails and phone calls was Reggie Gaspar. He rang her directly and told her to come around to the stables two days later. Gaspar was surprised to see Danielle show up at 6am and was impressed by her kind manner with his horses. Gaspar was from the 'treat an animal nicely school' to get him to do what one wanted and knew right from the start that Danielle would be a good addition to his staff.

She put bandages on several horses before they headed out for their morning gallops, cooled them down when they returned, mucked out stalls and prepared their feed and water. She had a knack with troublesome horses. They almost immediately calmed down when she was around them and were much happier animals off the track which resulted in better performances on it.

Gaspar saw enough from her two-day trial period and offered her a permanent job. Over the next ten months Danielle became a valued member of his staff.

She even strapped several of the harder-to-handle horses on race day and was often rewarded with a sling from owners who were thrilled to finally see their horses finish at the front of the pack and not the rear. One owner gave her 200 pounds when his four-year-old filly finally saluted after a long run of outs.

Her good looks drew some unwanted attention from several owners, jockeys and even from some of Gaspar's staff, but she brushed it all aside. At the end of her first week Gaspar told her to tell him if anyone got out of line and he would handle things.

"I have a daughter your age at uni and don't even want to think about the sort of stuff she must hear and deal with," he explained.

"You get used to it I suppose, although some of the things I have heard over the years have been pretty rude. Being pretty does have its drawbacks. Anyway, what is your daughter studying?"

"She's an economics major."

"She didn't want to work with horses?"

"She did when she was younger but got to hate the early morning starts. It's not for everyone."

"You get used to it," Danielle said. "Even in winter when you're chipping ice from the water buckets."

Danielle wasn't sure how her mum would react when she told her about the opportunity to go to Australia.

Victoria Frisella had been in remission until six weeks ago when the cancer, which her surgeons thought they had got all of, made an unwelcome return. She had lost one breast and now faced the loss of the other. She was looking at another mastectomy and another round of chemo as her fifty-third birthday neared.

"I'll lose all my hair again. It's a good thing I kept those wigs," she jokingly told her daughter.

Danielle parked her car in the driveway of her home on the cool September afternoon and found her mother seated at the dining room table finishing off her lunch. She planned to do some gardening in the afternoon if the sun came out and warmed things up.

"I have news, Mum," Danielle said, taking a seat at the table.

"Oh, have you met someone?"

"No. Not that kind of news. The owner of that hard-to-control horse I told you about wants me to go to Australia to look after him."

"Australia?"

"I know it's a long way, but Mr McGraw, the horse's owner, will arrange for someone to look after you while I'm gone. He'll pay for everything. They'll cook for you, clean the house and take you to all your doctor's appointments. And he's going to pay me $1000 a week while I'm in Melbourne, put me up in a hotel and give me a phone so I can ring you every day. What do you think?"

"It's all so sudden. When would you leave?"

"In two weeks. But I won't go if you don't want me to."

"Will Mr Gaspar be going as well?"

"No. He'll have a new trainer in Melbourne."

"That's a shame. I really like him. He'd look after you. But you should go, honey. It will be good for you to get away from here for a while."

"Really?"

"Yes. Tell Mr McGraw you'll be going to Australia."

Danielle bent down to give her mum a hug and a kiss. "Thank you so much, Mum, thank you so much."

"Just one thing. Can I pick the person who will be looking after me while you're away?"

"Of course you can. Who do you have in mind?"

"Carol Weiss from across the street, your friend Bridget's mum."

"Do you think she'd do it? She'd be wonderful."

"I'll ask her this afternoon. Her position was made redundant a few weeks ago so she has the time and I'm guessing she can use the money."

"I'll let Mr Gaspar know tomorrow and he'll get in touch with Mr McGraw about hiring Carol. He'll pay Carol in cash, too."

"Just take care of yourself in Melbourne. It's a lot bigger than Fulbourn."

"I will, Mum, I will."

19

AFTER A TWO-WEEK STAY IN QUARANTINE, WHERE Too Hard Wrong Spot was only allowed to have contact with horses also flying to Australia, the horse was loaded onto a float at Newmarket bound for Heathrow. Danielle Frisella and another stable hand, Duffy Cardwell, were with him. Gaspar drove the float himself, not wanting to take any chances when the horse was officially handed over to McGraw and the team from City Winners Syndication.

McGraw was waiting for his horse and was delighted to see Danielle lead a very relaxed Too Hard Wrong Spot off the float. She walked the horse around for a few minutes and then led him into a container. He was then hoisted onto a specially-designed transport plane where a groom provided by the horse transport company was waiting for him.

Too Hard Wrong Spot was throwing his head about and peering through the open grill of his box as if searching for Danielle.

There were half a dozen other horses on the flight, a few of which were genuine Melbourne Cup chances. The rest, like Too Hard Wrong Spot, would have to qualify for the Caulfield and Melbourne Cups via a series of lead-up races that were held at Geelong, Bendigo, Caulfield and Moonee Valley.

The plane was divided in two with the horses on the bottom and their handlers on top. Some horses tolerated the long trip better than others. Danielle kept talking to Too Hard Wrong Spot on the twenty-four-hour-plus journey to keep him from getting agitated. It seemed to work.

The horse ate and drank, although not as much as if he was in his box at home. He lost about eight kilograms on the trip, which was normal. When they finally arrived at Tullamarine mid-morning, Danielle was lucky to have gotten four or five hours of sleep.

Once the plane taxied to a stop, Too Hard Wrong Spot and his equine companions, all of whom were covered in colourful blankets, were this time hoisted out of the plane and allowed to stretch their legs on the tarmac before being led onto a float which was bound for a quarantine facility at Werribee racetrack, about an hour west of Melbourne. A batch of photographers and several film crews recorded the scenes. Danielle could not believe the turnout.

Danielle and Too Hard Wrong Spot were greeted by Ronnie Taylor of City Winners Syndication and the driver of their float, Rod McAndrew.

"How'd he handle the trip?" Taylor asked.

"Like a champion. Could not have gone any better," Danielle replied.

"And how are you feeling?"

"Tired, Mr Taylor. Very tired."

"Not to worry, once we get the horse to Werribee and he's settled in, McAndrew here will take you to your hotel which is not too far from the quarantine centre."

"Thanks Mr Taylor. I could sleep for a week."

McAndrew gathered Danielle's luggage; two suitcases and a carry-on bag, and tossed them into the float's cab

Unlike Danielle, Too Hard Wrong Spot was not going anywhere. Under rules set down by Racing Victoria, the horse had to stay at Werribee for at least fourteen days before he would be allowed to leave the centre for training or racing. Horses usually adjusted well to Werribee where they had access to the racetrack, day yards, sand rolls and internal walking paths. There was also twenty-four-hour security at the complex guarding the millions of dollars of horseflesh.

Trainer Jack McCarron was waiting for Too Hard Wrong Spot at Werribee to get his first look at the horse. Danielle led him off the float after the forty-minute drive from the airport and McCarron asked her to walk him over to one of the day yards near his stall so the horse could have a pick of the grass.

McCarron introduced himself to the young strapper he had heard so much about.

"Word is you're the only one who can handle this horse. You'll have to tell me what he likes and dislikes so we can get the best out of him on the racetrack. Gaspar told me that within a few days he should go for a nice long gallop."

"He's not that hard to handle Mr McCarron, really. He's a big baby. Treat him nice and talk to him and he'll do his best. He doesn't like to be forced into doing things. He's not a bad worker in the mornings either. It takes him awhile to get going but once he does, he goes well."

McCarron gave the newest arrival to his stable a hello by rubbing his face and head. "That's a good boy. We've got big plans for you over the next couple of months," he said.

McCarron removed the travelling bandages from the horse's legs and ran his sure and experienced hands over them. There was not a hint of heat in any leg and they looked strong. He re-wrapped the legs and looked the animal over. His winter coat was coming out and it gleamed in the Werribee sunshine. He was muscular; big and athletic and looked perfectly suited for the 2400m Caulfield Cup which was five weeks away. All he had to do was qualify for the $3 million-plus race.

"He looks much better in person than he does on video," McCarron said. "Looks like McGraw and Taylor bought themselves a winner."

"He's a good horse Mr McCarron," Danielle said. "He's never had a problem fitness-wise and as you know he is lightly raced."

"Well, he's about to do plenty of racing, Miss Frisella. We're looking at two starts before the cup unless he wins first time out and qualifies. And after a few days' rest we'll get him on the track here and see how he handles it.

"Can you lead him over to his stall? My assistant Janice will look after him the rest of the day. McAndrew will take you to your hotel and you can stop at a supermarket on the way to pick up anything you need."

"Thanks, Mr McCarron."

"Hey, enough of this Mr McCarron talk. Just call me Jack, okay? We're not as formal as they are at Newmarket around here."

Less than two days after his arrival, Too Hard Wrong Spot started to labour a bit with his breathing. Danielle alerted McCarron at his Caulfield base and a vet was at his stall within ten minutes.

As Danielle held the horse, Dr Jim Otis gave the horse a full check-up. After listening to his breathing and taking a sample of his lungs by an endoscope, and some blood, Dr. Otis was almost certain that Too Hard Wrong Spot had come down with pleuropneumonia, the technical term for travel sickness, a respiratory disease of the lung tissue and pleural cavity.

If the tests came back positive Too Hard Wrong Spot would miss the entire spring carnival. There'd be no chance for City Winners Syndication to recover the $50,000 shipping cost on the racetrack, at least not this year.

Dr Otis rang McCarron with the bad news.

McCarron in turn rang McGraw, who was about to tuck into his breakfast. He had a feeling how McGraw would react.

"He's got what? Travel sickness? What the fuck is that? The girl was supposed to look after him."

"She did look after him," McCarron said. "The horse was in perfect shape when he got off the plane thanks to Danielle. It's just one of those things. The horse is highly stressed to begin with and that didn't help matters."

"When will be able to race the friggin' horse?" McGraw asked.

"Well, if the samples that Dr Otis took come back positive, he'll miss the entire spring and summer. We'll resume his training in the autumn and hope to get him a run or two then."

"Holy underwear. He'll miss the spring and summer? Are you fucking kidding me?"

"I'm not, Mr McGraw."

"And you'll be charging me, what, $150 a day to look after the nag?"

"One hundred and ten plus GST and any vet and farrier bills."

"Vet bills? Fuck me. I'll ring Taylor and the others. Let me know if there's any change in the horse's condition. And tell the girl she can go back home. There's no need to keep her here now."

"She just got here, Mr McGraw, and with a horse as valuable as yours is it is better for the horse to be around someone he knows."

"All right," McGraw said. "Between her, the vets and someone looking after her mum in England this is costing me a fucking fortune."

"You'll get it all back," McCarron promised. "The horse is a winner. Once we get him on the track the money will come. Just be patient."

"I'm about to become a fucking patient. I can feel my goddamn blood pressure rising as we speak. Call me when you have more news, okay?"

"I'll do that Mr McGraw," McCarron said but McGraw had already hung up.

McGraw picked up his plate of bacon, eggs and pancakes—breakfast after all is the most important meal of the day—and threw it against the kitchen wall. The noise brought his overnight houseguest, Ophelia Nutz, running into the kitchen.

"What's the matter, honey?" she asked.

"My horse has travel sickness."

"I get the same thing when I travel," a very naked Miss Nutz said.

"Oh yeah? Well how about you travel the fuck out of here and leave me alone."

Miss Nutz ran from the kitchen in tears. She got dressed in the bedroom. It didn't take very long since the twenty-two-year-old wasn't fond of wearing underwear.

"Can you give me money for a cab?" she asked on her way out.

"Take the tram," McGraw barked.

"But I don't have a myki card."

"A what?"

"A myki card."

"How much is that going to cost me?"

"Twenty dollars."

McGraw found his wallet and put a $20 bill in Miss Nutz's hand.

"Thank you," she said, kissing him on the cheek. "See you tonight?"

"I guess so. I'll need a night out to forget about that goddamn horse."

Back at *Turf News*, nearly a year after Too Hard Wrong Spot's bout with travel sickness, Swoboda was telling Delaney that Too Hard Wrong Spot was training the house down in the morning.

"He hasn't had a start yet but he's getting close. He has a trial at Cranbourne next week. If you want to go have a look at him at McCarron's stable let me know and I'll set something up for you."

"Is the girl still with him?"

"Nah. She went back home. Rumour is she's been promoted to assistant trainer of Gaspar's stables. The horse has settled down a bit as a five-year-old. McCarron's assistant Janice looks after him. He likes women."

"Who doesn't?"

Delaney told Swoboda he'd pop in to Caulfield on Friday morning to have a look at the horse.

Since Delaney wasn't needed for the Tuesday edition of *Turf News*, he put his focus on Friday's paper. All the copy was handed in before deadline which is every sub-editor's dream. And it was pretty good too. The reporters wanted to get off to a good start with him and they did.

There were a couple of good feature pieces in the queue which Delaney tweaked just a bit. The accompanying photos were top notch. Only one yarn, on a jockey who had recently acquired her training licence, had to be cut to fit the space allocated to it.

Delaney also found that laying the paper out—physically putting the stories, photos, headlines and captions on a page—was much easier with the publishing system *Turf News* used.

The one used by Consume and Devour was a nightmare. There were constant operating issues and every week there were more updates to deal with. If it was a car it would constantly be in a garage being worked on by a mechanic.

There was a massive ten-day race card at Caulfield on Saturday featuring the Group 3 Naturalism Stakes over 2000m. A big field of sixteen was entered with many big names stretching their legs in preparation for the riches of the spring carnival which was less than a month away from starting.

The reporters put their selections in for each race on late Thursday afternoon. It was an almost impossible task to pick a winner—unless a superstar like Winx was running—since the picks were made almost forty-eight hours before the races. If it rained and the track was soft or heavy, the picks would be nearly worthless. But the forecast was a good one. After a few millimetres of rain on Thursday clear skies were predicted for Friday and Saturday. If a reporter was able to pick three winners on the ten-race card two days beforehand it was considered a good effort.

Delaney signed off on all the editorial pages just after 6pm on Thursday night. The form guide would be ready for him to have a look at just after 7pm.

With coat and briefcase in hand, Bob Nicholls stopped by Delaney's desk.

"How's your first edition looking, Gary?" he asked.

"I'd say pretty good. The staff is making me look good."

"Might be a case of them saving their best for their new boss. Let's see what they hand in over the next couple of weeks. You may have a different opinion then."

"You could be right. But from what I've seen so far they seem like a good group."

"Listen, you'll be here till after seven tonight so don't come in until lunchtime tomorrow."

"Thanks, see you then."

Just as Delaney was about to run to one of the food courts along Southbank to get himself some dinner, Wendy Seaver rang.

"You haven't put in your selections for Caulfield on Saturday," she said. "There's an empty space sitting there."

"You want my picks? Can't you get them from one of the kids?"

"They're gone for the day. Just your top four for each race okay? Email them to me as soon as you can please."

"Okay, give me a few minutes."

Delaney put his handicapper's hat on and with his stomach rumbling picked a mix of short-priced favourites and a few horses around the $6-$7 mark. Twenty minutes later he emailed them through. With a half hour until the form guide was ready to be looked at, Delaney hustled downstairs and got himself some honey chicken and rice from one of the many Asian food outlets. Rather than listen to the din in the food hall he took his dinner upstairs. He grabbed one of his diet cokes from the fridge—he refused to pay $3.50 for a can so he took one from a ten pack that he bought at Woolies on the way in for $7.

He planted himself at his desk and ate slowly, looking at the MCG in the distance instead of his computer screen.

Just as he was about to polish off his dinner, his office phone rang.

"I'm printing off the form guide now and will bring it to you in a couple of minutes," Wendy said.

Two minutes later Wendy appeared with the pages.

With his red pen in hand, Delaney went to work.

The first two pages were error-free, but he noticed a few typos on the third page and another on the fourth. A caption on the sixth page had the names of the jockey and trainer the wrong way around. He circled the miscue and pushed on until all sixteen pages were done. Nearly forty-five minutes later he brought the pages to Wendy's desk. She made the changes, pressed a few keys and the pages were electronically sent on their way to the printer.

"You're happy with your first paper?" Wendy asked.

"I think so. Just hope I didn't miss anything."

"I'm sure it's fine. You're free to go. My assistant Sally and I will mop things up and stick around just in case there are any problems on the other end."

"Thanks Wendy. It has been a long day. See you tomorrow."

Delaney went back to his desk, turned off his computer, grabbed his coat and his half-read paper from the morning, and walked out the door to the lift.

It was 8pm, dark and the wind was blowing off the Yarra. He zipped his coat, walked the five minutes to Flinders Street Station, touched on with his myki card and made his way to platform eight. The travel gods were on his side. The next Frankston-bound train was in three minutes.

20

SINCE DELANEY DIDN'T HAVE TO BE AT THE OFFICE until lunchtime on Friday, he rang Swoboda just after 8am and told him he'd pop by McCarron's stables just behind the Caulfield backstretch on the way into town.

Swoboda told Delaney he'd get back to him in a few minutes. Not even sixty seconds later Swoboda rang back telling him McCarron had already left to run some errands.

"I spoke to Janice, McCarron's assistant, and she said she would be happy to show you around if you got there around nine. Too Hard Wrong Spot worked four furlongs in forty-eight and change this morning. He's ready for his trial."

Delaney drove to Caulfield, missing most of the morning rush, and parked his car on Booran Road.

The door on the main office of *Jack McCarron Racing* was open. Delaney knocked and poked his head in. "Hi. I'm looking for Janice, Mr McCarron's assistant," he said to a woman whose head was buried in a stack of paperwork.

"You're looking at her," the slim, dark-haired 40-year-old said. "Janice Roselli," she added, taking off her reading glasses and getting up from her chair. "You must be Gary Delaney, pleased to meet you."

The pair shook hands.

Roselli's dirty jeans were a lot cleaner when she started her shift at 4am. She was wearing a polar fleece vest which had the *Jack McCarron Racing* logo sewn onto the upper left-hand corner.

"You wanted to have a look at Too Hard Wrong Spot, right?"

"I sure do. I've been told he has some ability, but his temperament is another story."

"You'll see that he's settled down a lot since this time last year."

Janice Roselli put her *Jack McCarron Racing* cap on and led Delaney to Too Hard Wrong Spot's stall.

The now five-year-old, with only three starts in his career, was quietly standing in his stall, one of about fifty on the premises, calmly taking in all that was going on around him. Horses were returning from their workouts, being hosed down and walked by several members of McCarron's staff of forty. They were the ones who looked after the seventy-five horses in McCarron's stable each day.

"This is the horse who was too hard to handle?" Delaney asked incredulously.

"This is the one. I told you he has calmed down a lot in the past year."

"What brought about the change?"

"Well, he is a year older and he seems quite happy in his surroundings. He just likes to do things his way and prefers the company of women. That's all there is to it."

"And you think he has better than average ability? I hear he's working well."

"Jack is very high on him. He's trialling at Cranbourne on Monday and if he runs well, we're looking at running him in the Herbert Power on Guineas Day at Caulfield."

"Can you let him out of his stall so I can have a look at him? I'm not going to kick the tyres, but I'd like to see him before I plunk down $15,000."

Janice Roselli opened the stall, attached a lead to the animal and walked him out.

"Hmmmmm," Delaney muttered as he examined the horse. "He's an impressive animal. Very muscular and he's not carrying an ounce of fat on him. Jack must be doing a lot of work with him."

"He is. We want him ready for the Herbert Power. The owners are quite keen on running him in the Caulfield Cup after what happened last year. He's paid up for it."

"Have you had the pleasure of meeting John McGraw?"

"Twice, he's quite a character."

"How long did it take before he propositioned you?"

"About five minutes. I told him to take a long walk off a short pier."

"From what I hear he is a man who gets what he wants."

"There aren't many certainties around a racetrack but this one you can take to the windows. He's not getting near me and he better watch his arse cause my husband was not too happy when I told him about it."

"Is your husband in the racing business?"

"He breaks in yearlings for Jack."

"I'd hate to think of how he would break in McGraw."

"Into a few pieces is what I'm guessing."

Delaney laughed. "I've seen enough of the horse, Janice, thanks."

"So, are you in?" she asked as she put Too Hard Wrong Spot back in his stall.

"I am. I'll write you a cheque back at the office."

He took a few photos of the horse to show Michelle later that night.

Delaney made out the cheque to City Winners Syndication. His hand shook a bit when he wrote down the amount.

He handed it to Janice Roselli.

"Congratulations, Mr Delaney. You now own one-twentieth of the horse.

Delaney beamed. He had a share in his first racehorse.

"And I am guessing that $15,000 would have been $30,000 or not be available at all after the trial. McGraw wants to recoup as much of the money he paid for the horse as he can if he turns out to be a dud," Roselli said.

A little concerned, Delaney asked for her opinion of the horse.

"He's not a dud, that's for sure. Come see for yourself on Monday morning at Cranbourne. He's entered in the fifth trial. It goes off about

10.15. It's over 1000m. Way too short for him but he'll be finishing better than any of the others."

"I'll be there," Delaney said. "Will you?"

"Yup. McGraw wants me with the horse every step of the way."

Delaney took a good look around the stables before he left. Two brick structures faced each other, leaving plenty of room for horses to be moved and walked. The stable dog, a mixed mutt named Macca, followed Carla, one of the young stablehands, who was wheeling a fresh batch of bedding to a stall near the horse washing area. He moseyed on over and asked her about the chestnut she was cradling while the horse's bedding was being laid.

"We call this one Forest. He's not the quickest but he's so nice to be around."

"Do you hug all the horses you care for like that? I'm told that they respond better to a woman's touch."

"Horses like Forest I hug all the time. But some of them, like the stallions, you don't get near. The guys are stronger, they look after them," Carla said.

One of the youngest people employed by McCarron, Carla had just turned twenty. She was dressed in her usual work attire of jeans, work boots and a thick hoodie which helped keep the morning chill at bay. On winter mornings she wore a sleeveless down vest over the hoodie.

The racing business is not for those who enjoy sleeping in. Carla and the other staff members were at work by 4am. Many leave mid-morning and come back for a few hours in the afternoon to give the horses in their care a walk. Sunday hours begin at 6am. It helped that she lived just a couple of kilometres away in North Caulfield. The oldest of three children, she rode her bike to and from McCarron's stables every day, leaving each morning at 3.45. Apart from the odd delivery truck or a taxi, she was the only person on the road. Carla had every second weekend off and often acted as a strapper at race meetings which could take her anywhere from Caulfield to Echuca to Geelong. The night meetings at Moonee Valley, Cranbourne and Pakenham put a bit of extra strain on McCarron's staff but those who worked at night often had the next morning off.

"Are you on the road this afternoon?" Delaney asked.

"I am. We have two horses running at Seymour. Luckily, both are in the first couple of races, so I'll be back by about 5pm. When they run in the last couple of races we run into all kinds of traffic coming back here and usually it's after 7 by the time we get back. Then we need to walk them, feed them and help settle them down for the night."

"You must love your job with those kinds of hours."

"I do. These horses are my babies. Win or lose I love them to death."

Delaney smiled. "Good luck later on," he said.

Delaney rang Michelle at her office when he got back to the car.

"It's all very exciting baby. And you'll have your name in the racebook too," she said.

The last time Delaney had his name in a racebook was a few years ago when a few mates pooled their funds and had the fifth race at a mid-week meeting at Sandown named the Happy 50th Delaney Handicap.

"The horse is trialling on Monday morning at Cranbourne. I'll go out there and see how he does."

"It will be very exciting. I've got to get going, sweetheart. Friday morning meeting time. See you at home later. I'll cook dinner."

"Okay baby. See you around six."

Delaney had not only coughed up $15,000 for his share but was also now responsible for 1/20th of the training, feed and vet bills—about $200 a month. On the plus side he would get 1/20th of any purse money Too Hard Wrong Spot won.

The Herbert Power was worth $400,000 with $260,000 going to the winner. After the trainer took his cut of ten per cent and the jockey five, the syndicate would split $221,000 if the horse won. Delaney's share of the winnings would be about $11,000.

If he trialled well Too Hard Wrong Spot was going to make his Australian debut at Caulfield in the Herbert Power over 2400m. Ordinarily McCarron would have liked Too Hard to have a good, tough run under his belt to kick off his cups campaign. But McGraw put a stop to that plan. He wanted to cash some big bets and felt that a lead-up run prior to the Herbert Power would drive down the horse's odds.

Since McGraw paid the bills, McCarron had no choice but to go along with the idea. He had been giving Too Hard Wrong Spot strong, testing gallops to build up his stamina. The horse was dead fit and McCarron was sure Too Hard Wrong Spot would be able to run a strong 2400m in the Herbert Power if he came away from his trial in good order.

Delaney parked his car in the main Caulfield parking lot and took the train into the city.

The first edition under Delaney's guidance was on the newsstands and the staff seemed pleased with it. He hoped the readers concurred.

Nicholls gave it a big thumbs up. "Love the layout Gary," he said at Delaney's desk. "Good yarns, good pics. Not so sure about those selections of yours though," he added with a laugh.

"I'd be happy if one of them gets up," Delaney said.

Just three hours after he wrote the cheque for $15,000, Delaney got a call from Pastor Chris on his mobile.

"Have you seen the papers, pal?"

"I just glanced through them. What's up?"

"Are you sitting down?

"Should I be?"

"There's been some sort of coup in Mongolia."

"A coup? Is the military involved?"

"Looks like it. I just read an update on the *Wall Street Journal's* website."

Chris's phone fell silent.

"Gary? Are you there, Gary?"

"I'm here. Shit. Why didn't I pull out when you did? I could lose it all."

"Look, it's not a fait accompli."

"Fait accompli? Have you been studying at Harvard?"

Chris laughed. "I read that somewhere."

"Is the mine still running? Has Motherlode Mining Group put out any sort of statement?"

"I don't know mate. What I do know is that you don't want to be in Ulaanbaatar, the country's capitol. There are troops on the streets."

"Shit. Let me see if I can get a hold of Agee. I'll ring you later, Chris."

Delaney rang Agee but predictably there was no answer. He left a short message asking him to ring back. He didn't. Delaney had no luck at Agee's office either. Agee's assistant, Laura Groggin, was not answering the phone, but why would she? There'd be plenty of others wanting to know what the hell was going on north of Ulaanbaatar.

Delaney found some more information later in the afternoon on the *New York Times* website.

Some fellow named Ganzorig Grabbit was leading the coup. There was a file photo of him in green military fatigues accompanying the story.

A heck of a name, considering he and his thugs were at this moment likely taking everything they could get their hands on in and around the capital. The country's democratically elected president, Batbayar Ganbaatar, was rumoured to be locked in the presidential summer palace's main bathroom with his family.

The rumour was true. There was only one seat and it was a beauty, made of 24-carat gold, which the president commandeered.

"All of you, please shaddup and let me think, will you?" he yelled at his wife, a woman who was cleaning the toilet when he barged in, who happened to be his mistress, and his three spoiled kids, the eldest of whom was posting photos on Facebook.

"What the hell are you doing? Have you lost your mind? Now they'll know where we are. Give me that thing."

He grabbed his eldest daughter's iPhone out of her hands and threw it against the wall.

Mrs Ganbaatarr barely looked up. She was too busy checking her make-up in the room's massive mirror.

Does she think a film crew is waiting outside? And then they wonder why men take mistresses, Ganbaatar thought.

With his security team out of commission, the president figured his only way out might be to flush himself down the toilet.

He walked over to his youngest daughter, Altan, and got on his knees to talk to the six-year-old. Altan was holding her favourite toy, something the Disney people left after they screened *Finding Dory* at the palace a few months ago. Ganbaatarr managed to get a hand job from his mistress during the screening while his family was seated barely ten metres away. He thought he would never be able to get it up after having to listen to the voice of Ellen Degeneres for ninety minutes.

"Sweetheart," he said to Altan. "Daddy needs you to do something for him. Could you do what I ask?"

"What is it, Daddy?"

"I want you to see if there are any bad men out there. If you don't see anyone go to your room and press the red button under your desk. Can you do that sweetheart?"

"Yes, Daddy."

"That's my girl," President Ganbaatarr said as he kissed his daughter's forehead.

"If you see anyone out there, come right back, okay? And be very quiet."

"Like a mouse, Daddy?"

"Like a mouse, precious. And remember, push the red button under the desk in your room. When you do that get under the desk and stay there, okay?"

"Okay Daddy."

President Ganbaatarr turned out the lights around his wife's mirror and told everyone to be quiet.

He slowly opened the door, heard nothing but some faint noise downstairs, and whispered to Altan, "Go ahead sweetheart."

Five seconds passed, then ten. Ganbaatarr listened by the door. Thirty seconds passed. "She made it," he said to himself. "She'll get the Presidential Medal of Honour for this. I'll see to it."

Ganzorig Grabbit and his men were so interested in the food and drink inside the kitchen's massive stainless-steel refrigerator they hadn't even bothered to go upstairs. They had never seen such an array of food in their lives and picked the shelves of the fridge clean. They washed the food down with imported beer, wine and soft drinks.

"What the hell is this? Coke Zero? What the fuck has happened to regular Coke? I can't drink this shit," Grabbit's second in command said.

For dessert Grabbit and his men gorged themselves on a chocolate cake Ganbaatarr's mistress had made to accompany that night's dinner.

"Hey," Grabbitt yelled to his men who had thrown their used dishes and bottles on the dining room and kitchen floors. "We're revolutionaries, not animals. Clean this mess up. Now!"

The red button young Altan Ganbaatarr pressed was connected to the presidential palace's roof. It slid open when she pressed it and a fully functional helicopter emerged, fuelled up and ready to go.

President Ganbaatarr told his two eldest children, the housekeeper/mistress and then his wife to follow him out the door on his command and quietly head to Altan's room. He ripped the 24-carat gold toilet seat from its hinges. The more he looked at it, the more he noticed that it resembled the winning trophy given to a soccer team in Australia, or was it Austria?

"Before you did that you might have asked if any of us needed to go," his wife Tuli said.

"Do you need to tinkle darling? Follow me and be quiet for goodness sake."

"Can't I get some things out of my wardrobe?" Tuli Ganbaatarr asked.

"Only if you want to be left behind."

"But what about my new handbags?"

"Your handbags? We'll be lucky if we make it out of here with our lives. But if you want to get them be my guest," he said winking at his housekeeper/mistress. "I sure as hell won't stop you."

"Dad, I'm scared," his elder daughter said.

"We all are, sweetheart. But do as I say, and we'll make it out of here."

The bathroom door opened slowly, and crouching like a group of Russian square dancers, the group made it safely to Altan's room. The president took Altan's desk chair and pushed it firmly up against the door handle. No match for a Kalashnikov assault rifle but it might give them a few valuable seconds.

Altan came out from behind her desk and hugged her mother and father.

"Fantastic job sweetheart, fantastic," Ganbaatarr told his youngest as he hugged her.

The president took down a *Finding Dory* poster from the wall, pressed the button behind it, and put the poster back in its place.

As he pressed the button a panel on the ceiling opened and a rope ladder dropped down.

"Who are you? James Bond?" his twelve-year-old son Arslan asked.

"Today I am.

"C'mon everyone, quickly. Altan, you go first. When you get to the top move out of the way so the next person has some room, okay?"

"Yes Daddy."

Altan climbed up the rope and was followed in quick succession by Arslan, Sasha, Tuli Ganbaatarr and the housekeeper/mistress,

Chabi. The president was the last up the rope. He got a nice look of the housekeeper/mistress's familiar arse as he scampered to the roof.

He lifted the rope ladder and gently placed it on the roof. He then pressed a button and watched the ceiling panel slide back into place. *Perfect. So glad I thought ahead. I'm not going to wind up like Hussein or Gaddafi.*

Inside the helicopter were bulletproof vests and a Kalashnikov rifle. He told the kids and women to put the vests on and climb in.

"Arslan. You're riding up front with me."

"This is so cool, Dad."

"It might not be when they start shooting at us."

Ganbaatarr closed all the doors, climbed into the pilot's seat and switched the chopper on.

"You can fly this?" Arslan asked.

"It's been a few years, but we'll get out of here. Buckle up everyone," he yelled as the blades and rotor roared to life.

"Arslan, you have to cover us if the rebels come up after us, okay?"

"Cover us? With what?"

"This," Ganbaatarr said as he put a loaded Kalashnikov into his hands. "It's just like you see in the movies, son. If you need to shoot take the safety off, point the gun out the window, pull the trigger and fire away."

Arslan took the rife, turned his New York Mets baseball cap around and balanced the assault rifle on the door frame. "I can do it Dad. Don't you worry."

Downstairs, Ganzorig Grabbit thought he heard a helicopter. "Shut up everyone."

It was a helicopter. "They're getting away. You guys check the lawn," he yelled to a group of six on his left. "We'll go to the roof."

"Hang on," President Ganbaatarr yelled as the chopper lifted off the roof into the late afternoon sunshine.

Grabbit and his men ran up the stairs. They broke into the first room they saw, the president and first lady's bedroom, and ran to the windows. The chopper banked to the left and picked up speed and altitude.

The rebels on the ground opened fire but were unable to get a good look at the chopper which was flying right into the sun's harsh rays.

Seeing the soldiers on the ground, Arslan took the safety off and let rip. The recoil nearly knocked him from his seat. But once he got used to it, he kept firing. The rebels were forced to take cover. Grabbit and his men in the presidential bedroom did the same.

President Ganbaatarr turned on the radio and searched for the frequency his vice president was supposed to be on in case of an emergency. There was nothing but static. Shit. North Korea was to the East. Russia to the north and China to the south. His best chance was to continue west to Razakhastan. He had hosted its president earlier in the year and given him the keys to the city. It was his time for him to reciprocate.

"Shit," Ganbaatarr screamed loud enough for everyone to hear over the noise of the chopper.

"What is it, Dad?" Arslan asked.

"I forgot the fucking toilet seat."

21

LESS THAN TWO HOURS LATER, AFTER NEARLY GETTING shot down by Razakhastani troops, Ganbaatarr received permission directly over the radio from Razakhastan president Damir Ibragimov to land on Razakhastani soil. He had less than a quarter of a tank of fuel left. After making a soft landing, Ganbaatarr and his family were greeted by heavily armed troops and immediately relieved of their Kalashnikov. They were led away in a convoy of dark sedans while the helicopter was lifted by a crane, placed on a huge flatbed truck and driven to an army base.

"Ibragimov better keep his word to offer us asylum," he said to his family and mistress on the ride to the capital.

They were taken to a five-star hotel and nearly thrown out when Ganbaatarr's credit card was declined.

"What do you mean declined? I've got 200 million euros in the fucking bank," he yelled at the young clerk manning the counter.

"Your account has been frozen," the clerk said as he pissed himself.

"Put me in the goddamn suite. Ibragimov will get it all sorted."

"Who?" the terrified clerk said.

"Your fucking president. Don't you know who your president is?"

"I do sir. One of our men will take you to the suite and get you anything you like."

Back in Melbourne, Delaney learned that Mongolia was under martial law. All foreign assets had been seized, including Motherlode Mining Group. His $10,000 investment was all but history, which Agee confirmed later that evening.

"Look, it could be worse Delaney. Everyone working at the mine has been taken into custody. Motherlode Mining Group's management was rounded up as well. There looking at a few months in prison before they're given a trial, if they're given a trial."

"What are they going to be charged with?" Delaney asked.

"Who the hell knows? But whatever they're convicted of—and they will be convicted—they're looking at time in jail. You'll be able to go home tonight Gary."

"You're right Agee. But I am out $10,000 and just a few hours ago I bought a share in a horse for $15,000 because I was $10,000 ahead."

"A horse? That's even riskier than buying into a mine in Asia. Who's training it?"

"Jack McCarron."

"Well at least with him you have a chance of making some money. I'll talk to you when I have some more information. I'm going to console Miss Groggin."

"How much is she in the hole for?"

"More than you. I told her to get out last week, but she didn't."

"Well, at least I'll have company at bankruptcy court," Delaney said as he hung up.

The long-time sports writer/sub-editor went to the toilet to splash some cold water on his face. He turned the handle on the door, but it wouldn't open. He tried again. Bupkus.

He looked down and saw a security pad on the door. "What the?"

He turned around, went back into the *Turf News* office and approached Lisa at reception.

"Excuse me, Lisa. Do you know what is going on with the toilet? There's a lock on the door."

"Sorry, Gary. I was supposed to let you know. It was installed this morning."

"Why?"

"There's been some vandalism in the men's and women's toilets, so the building owner made the decision to lock them. A security pad is easier than giving out keys."

"Who the hell would be vandalising the toilets?"

"Looks like kids and addicts who are getting past security downstairs."

"Drug addicts? In Southbank? What the hell is going on in this city?" he said, shaking his head.

"I wish I knew," replied Lisa. She wrote the number 5017 on a post-it sticker and handed it to him.

"That's the code. Punch it in, hit okay and the door will open."

"Thanks Lisa. I'll give it a go."

Delaney walked back to the men's toilet. He punched in the numbers 5017 and the door opened.

"Great, another bloody password to know. What a day," he said as he washed his face and cleaned his glasses.

Delaney had a quiet one on Saturday. He and Michelle planned to visit a couple of op shops before they went out for lunch.

The two shops were of opposite sides of the street. They walked into Vinnies first. Delaney headed for the large collection of books and Michelle had a look at the knick-knacks and handbags.

As Delaney was giving the books a look, a very large man walked over and did the same. The fellow was about forty and was dressed in a T-shirt and faded jeans. A moment later Delaney was hit by a smell that nearly put him on his knees for a standing eight-count.

The offensive odour seamlessly replaced the usual op shop smell which is closely related to the smell which hits you when you visit an elderly relative and set foot inside their apartment. "Mum, do we have to visit Aunt Alma? I can't breathe in there!"

Finally, the man's odour became too much, and Delaney gave in. He walked away and headed straight for the door and some fresh air.

Michelle walked out of the shop a few moments later.

"I think I've had my fill of op shops today." she said.

After lunch at a local cafe, Delaney watched a few races from Caulfield. Not one of his top selections in *Turf News* won, but a few placed so it was not a total loss. Swoboda was the one with the hot hand. Five of his top picks won, returning a combined $37.50 based on ten one-dollar investments.

"Hope he was smart enough to back some of them."

Michelle suggested visiting some art galleries on the peninsula on Sunday. It was just what Delaney needed to keep his mind off his troubles. Landscapes and seascapes were a nice diversion from gold mining and racing even if he couldn't afford to buy a blank canvas.

22

AWAY FROM THE TRACK ADAM SWOBODA WAS HAVING problems of his own. His wife, Patricia, who was eight months pregnant with either their first child or a basketball, had brought a kitten into their home a year earlier and it was really starting to get on Swoboda's nerves.

A friend of Patricia's who lived nearby had a cat who in turn had a litter of six. The McDougals kept one of the kittens and had managed to palm off four of the remaining five to friends and family. Only one was left. Patricia took one look at the six-week-old female kitten when she visited Trish McDougal one Saturday afternoon for a coffee and took it home.

Thirty-two-year-old Adam Swoboda was a dog person. He had a beagle as a kid and while at uni he and his roommates had rescued an old golden retriever from the pound. The dog was eleven-years-old and was brought to the pound by a couple who was moving to northern New South Wales. The problem for Gus, which is what they later named the animal, was that eleven-year-old dogs, even golden retrievers, are about as popular as root canals. Gus, it turned out, had just one week left before he was due to be put down. Enter the uni lads who had heard about Gus's plight through a mutual friend. Half asleep, the quartet rocked up to the pound one Saturday morning and took the dog home.

He was a welcome addition to the share house which had a good-sized backyard. Gus was taken for walks every day, was fed well and inadvertently got as high as a kite one night when Swoboda and his mates lit up a couple of joints while U2's *Rattle and Hum* played in the background. He got an awful case of diarrhoea one afternoon when he drank water off the kitchen floor, water which had leaked from a twenty-year-old refrigerator bought at a garage sale. The boys regularly took Gus to local footy matches on

Saturday afternoons where he liked to run around the field after the game. Swoboda once tried to sneak him into a mid-week meet at Mornington as a seeing-eye dog. He put a harness on Gus, wore dark glasses and used a walking stick while slowly making his way to the front gate. The pair were denied entry by a sharp-eyed security guard who had seen Swoboda drive his battered Commodore into the track's parking lot.

Two years later, when the boys were in their last year at uni, Gus gradually became unsteady on his feet and started to lose control of his bowels. Swoboda and his best mate, Randy Waller, took Gus to the vet, who after several tests, told them Gus had cancer. After talking it over, the four mates made the decision to spare Gus any more pain and to put the old boy down.

Swoboda and Waller carried Gus to the car late one Friday afternoon for a return trip to the same vet. Waller couldn't bear to watch so Swoboda tightly held Gus while the vet administered the life-ending injection. He tearfully said his goodbyes as the drugs flowed through Gus's veins. The aspiring journo needed nearly thirty minutes to compose himself in the animal hospital's carpark before he was able to drive back to the share house. Waller, who was as close to Gus as Swoboda was, was so overcome with grief he was inconsolable for a week. Dogs will do that to you.

Swoboda had a chance to get a dog when he moved into his own place soon after starting at *Turf News* but decided against it. He was often out on work assignments and knew it would be unfair to leave a dog alone for such long periods of time.

At first, the kitten Patricia Swoboda brought home was cute and fun to play with. But once the cat grew and started to scamper about at all hours of the night and rip things to shreds, Adam Swoboda became more and more unhappy. But what could he do? Patricia loved the cat and couldn't wait to show it to the latest addition to their family, whose due date was in twenty-nine days.

He was in a bind.

He was also at war with his health care fund which due to some computer foul-up kept taking $263.75 out of his account once a week instead of once a month.

He tried calling. "Thank you for your call. It is very important to us. Press 1 to make a claim. Press 2 to join Aussie Health. Press 3 to change your policy. Press 4 to ..." On and on it went.

"Stay on the line to speak with one of our special consultants who may or not speak English. Your estimated waiting time is thirty-seven minutes."

Swoboda was about to lose it. He put the call on speaker and listened to some electronic garbage pretending to be music. He took the phone into the kitchen when he made a coffee, he took it to the bathroom when he needed to take a shit. Finally, a human being came on the line.

"This call may be monitored for coaching purposes. Do you agree to being recorded?"

"Yes. Yes."

"How may I help you sir?" a young woman from the Philippines asked.

Swoboda had his health care card and banking details in hand. Just as he was about to tell her about the direct debits, the line went dead.

"Are you fucking kidding me?" he screamed.

Patricia was not too fond of her husband's sometimes salty language. Several times she had recently said, "please don't talk like that in front of the baby," as she patted her expanding tummy. But on this Saturday morning he did not have to worry. Patricia had left with the cat, probably over to the McDougals' place, for a cat reunion.

Swoboda looked at his watch. Ten minutes to eleven.

Aussie Health's offices were open on Saturday until noon so he decided to go to the local mall and speak to someone in person and see if they could straighten out his account. How bloody hard could it be? One account, one monthly deduction.

Swoboda found a parking spot without too much difficulty and walked inside the massive centre which was teeming with shoppers. Aussie Health's office was on the second of the three floors. He stopped at his bank's ATM and withdrew $100. He looked at his balance on the receipt. "Son of a bitch," he screamed when he noticed that another $263.75 had been taken out of his account. An older woman carrying a Target shopping bag looked at him and shook her head.

"Sorry," he sheepishly said.

Swoboda stormed into Aussie Health's storefront and took a seat. Fortunately, there was no one waiting. Three people were being served at counters marked one, two and three. Healthcare specialist number four must have been in the toilet. He looked at the three specialists. One of them looked to be about twenty-one. The other two, both women, were a little older and likely to be more experienced. Swoboda was hoping to be served by one of them.

Five minutes went by, then ten.

Finally, the old-timer being taken care of at counter two put his cap on, got up, put some papers into a large white envelope he brought in with him and slowly shuffled out.

The woman at counter two made eye contact with Swoboda and motioned for him to take a seat.

"Good morning Roberta," he said to the woman after noticing her name tag. "I sure hope you can end this nightmare I am going through."

Roberta took his health fund card and swiped it.

"Let's see what we have here," she said as his information popped up on her computer screen.

Roberta was in her forties, with fashionable glasses, blonde hair cut short and a large wedding ring. It was hard not to notice it as she worked the mouse and adjusted her glasses with her ringed hand.

"You've had three direct debits for the same amount this month," Roberta said. "There's something wrong here."

"There sure is. And make it four. There was another $263.75 taken out of my account between yesterday and today. I was just at the ATM. What's wrong? If this is not fixed today, I am cancelling my account and taking my business elsewhere."

"That won't be necessary, Mr Swoboda. I'll fix this."

"Please do."

Roberta kept typing away. Two minutes passed, then three.

"Mr Swoboda, I'll have to speak to my manager to get authorisation to make the refunds due to you. But I have put a stop on any extra direct debits. There will be only the one for $263.75 on the first of every month."

"Okay," Swoboda said. "I'll wait."

The *Turf News* reporter gazed at the posters hanging on the walls which featured a mix of young and old people. They all had one thing in common. They were smiling. Swoboda was not.

Finally, Roberta emerged with her manager. She was in full business attire even on a Saturday and had a very serious but pleasant look on her face. Swoboda guessed she was close to fifty.

"I am so sorry for the problems you are having Mr Swoboda." Dorothy Goldstein said. "We have refunded the two direct debits but the one for $263.75 deducted today was not taken out by Aussie Health."

"What do you mean it wasn't taken out by Aussie Health? It's for the same amount," Swoboda said.

"I guarantee you, Mr Swoboda, the money taken out today was not taken out by us."

"But it is for the same amount."

"I realise that Mr Swoboda, but it was not deducted by us."

"We'll see about that. I'll be back on Monday with a bank statement," he told the two women.

Swoboda got up from his chair, took his card and ATM receipt and stuffed them into his wallet.

"Look, I'm sorry I've lost my temper and I apologise. I've been getting the run around and it is very frustrating."

"I do understand," Dorothy Goldstein said. "We've fixed the problem with the direct debit and refunded the two that were made erroneously. That money should be in your account now. Please come back Monday with your bank statement so we can get to the bottom of the third."

"I'll do that. Thank you, ladies."

Swoboda walked out.

"Are you sure that last direct debit wasn't taken out by us?" Roberta asked her manager.

"I'd stake my job on it," Dorothy Goldstein said.

Swoboda made his way back to his car and realised he had forgotten to take his tape recorder with him, the one tool of the trade even more valuable than a reporter's notebook. The recorder on his phone did not work properly so he went back home to get it. He'd miss the first few races on the card, which he would later catch the replays of, but he'd get to Caulfield with plenty of time before the feature races of the afternoon which he was assigned to write up.

Patricia's car was in the driveway. Mother, cat and unborn child safely home from the cat reunion.

"Hun, are you here?"

Swoboda checked the kitchen, living area, bedroom, bathroom and the nursery. No sign of Patricia or the cat who went by the name of Sugar.

He slid open the back door and found Patricia sitting on the wooden bench they bought together last Christmas. She was cradling Sugar.

"Hi baby. Have a good time with Trish?"

"I didn't go there," she said. "I was at the vet."

"The vet? What's wrong with the cat?"

"Her name is Sugar."

"Okay, what is wrong with Sugar?"

"You haven't noticed, but she hasn't been well. She hasn't eaten for two days and this morning she threw up. There was blood in it. I rang the vet and they had an appointment, so I went over there."

"Why didn't you tell me?"

"I didn't want to wake you. I know you have a big day today. Hey, it's after twelve, aren't you supposed to be at Caulfield?"

"I am but I went to Aussie Health at the mall to clear up the mess with our account."

"Were you able to?"

"Almost. There was another direct debit taken out of our account yesterday or today. They said it was not taken out by them. I'll go to the bank on Monday and get a statement and sort it out once and for all.

"What did the vet say is wrong with Sugar?"

"She's not sure. She examined her and didn't seem to think it was anything serious. She's running a fever so the doctor took some blood and will have the results on Monday. She also gave Sugar a shot to help with any inflammation she may have."

"So how much did it all cost?"

"Is that all you can think about? How much it costs? Don't you care about Sugar? What if it's something serious?"

"She probably has a virus of some sort. In a day or two it will clear and she'll be fine."

"And the cost, Mrs Swoboda?"

"Two hundred and something dollars. The bill and receipt is on the kitchen table."

Adam Swoboda went inside and had a look at it. And then looked at it again.

Consultation, injection, blood work plus GST totalling $263.75.

Adam went back outside.

"How did you pay for this?" he asked his wife, who had seemingly calmed down a bit.

"With our bank card, what else?"

"Oh boy."

"What do you mean, *oh boy?*"

"Well, the amount of the vet bill is the exact same amount we pay each month for our private health insurance."

"You're kidding."

"Nope. It's $263.75. I accused Aussie Health of taking out another $263.75 from out account when in fact it was the vet bill that was taken out. I owe the women there an apology."

"What did you say to them? You didn't curse, did you?"

"No baby, nothing like that. I told them I would close our account and go elsewhere if things weren't sorted out by Monday. The manager assured me that Aussie Health did not take out the $263.75 and she was right. I'll go down there on Monday and apologise."

"I think you'd better."

"I will. But I need to run. I have got to get to Caulfield. I'll take the train since there'll be no place to park there."

"Want me to run you to the station?"

"Not necessary, baby. It's Saturday. There'll be plenty of parking spots at the station. I'll ring you later to see how Sugar is doing. And if she has started eating and is better, we'll go out to dinner tonight."

"Okay sweetheart," Patricia Swoboda told her husband.

Adam Swoboda kissed his wife goodbye, gave Sugar a pat around the ears, picked up his tape recorder that was in the kitchen and drove to the station. A train was just about to pull into the station as he arrived. He parked the car, locked it and ran to the platform where he touched on with his myki card. He took a seat and checked the pockets of his jacket. "Shit," he said, not loudly enough to be heard by anyone else in the carriage. "I left the bloody tape recorder in the car, and my notebook too."

23

FRANKIE 'FINGERS' TANNENBAUM BARELY SLEPT A wink the night before his release. Sixteen long months had been reduced to just hours. He tossed and turned for most of the night, his mind awash with thoughts of what he would do on his first day of freedom. A good Italian meal was at the top of the list. Going to bed and getting up when he chose was a close second.

Warden Stanley Blake handed him his release papers and the personal items he had with him on his arrival more than a year ago, including his mobile phone.

Tony 'Breadsticks' Battaglia lived up to his word, even sending his personal driver to pick up his former numbers man.

Vinny Carmona, a man who looked as though he had not missed too many meals in his fifty-two years, was behind the wheel of a sparkling silver Mercedes which had been washed the day before. He greeted Tannenbaum with a hug even though the two had never met and tossed the freed man's bag into the boot.

Tannenbaum got into the back seat. "Nothing personal, but I'm going to try and catch some sleep."

Before turning onto the highway back to Melbourne, Carmona pulled into a petrol station and reached into his pocket for an envelope which he handed to Tannenbaum. "Mr Battaglia said I should give you this right away."

"Thanks," Tannenbaum said as he opened and peered inside the envelope. There was $10,000 in cash along with a yellow post-it sticker which had two words written on it in blue ink; "Thanks, Tony."

"Mr Battaglia says I'm supposed to drop you off at this apartment in one of them new buildings in Carlton."

"And all my things from my old apartment?"

"Mr Battaglia took care of it. Everything is in a storage unit. You tell me when you want the stuff delivered and I'll bring it over."

"Tomorrow afternoon okay with you?"

"Yup. I'm free, tomorrow afternoon it is."

"Hey, do me a favour, mate. Plug this phone in and charge it for me, will ya?"

"Sure thing Mr Tannenbaum."

While Tannenbaum stretched out in the comfortable back seat, Johnny Pastrami was having a coffee at the kitchen table of his tenth floor Southbank apartment. It was high enough to give him a good view of the ever-expanding city but low enough so his fear of heights didn't kick in.

The morning papers were strewn out over the round wooden table along with several racing stories from overseas newspapers he had printed out. This was Pastrami's time of the year, the lead-up to the spring racing carnival. He was up to date on the European horses who would be coming to Melbourne for the Caulfield Cup, Cox Plate and Melbourne Cup, having watched many of their races in Europe, often staying up to two and three in the morning to catch them live on Foxtel. He recorded them as well, making notes as he watched the races time and time again. He kept his own speed figures and had a file on each of the nearly two dozen European horses and the more than fifty Australian contenders for the spring's top three races.

Pastrami sent Tannenbaum a text message congratulating him on getting out which Fingers saw when he woke two hours later. His neck was a bit stiff from his awkward sleeping position, but he quickly got the kinks out by twisting his head from side to side several times.

"We'll catch up in a few days. I need to get settled in first," Tannenbaum texted back to Pastrami.

"I understand, mate. Maybe Flemington on Saturday if you're up to it," was the reply.

Tannenbaum was impressed with his new digs. It had a nice-sized balcony which caught the morning sun, a large bedroom, a study and a kitchen with all new appliances. The fridge looked like something out of *The Jetsons*. A washing machine and dryer were tucked into a small alcove near the bathroom.

The apartment came with a bed, couch, kitchen table and matching chairs. Since his stuff would be arriving the next day. Tannenbaum walked the couple of blocks to Woolies to pick up some linen.

The aroma of coffee from the first cafe he passed lured him in and he had his first good latte in nearly a year and a half. He sat outside and watched the parade of people walking past. Young and old, men and women, mums pushing prams. He gave a dog a pet around the ears. It was not only the first dog he had touched since he was carted off to prison, it was the first dog he had seen.

"It's so good to be a free man again," he said to no one in particular.

At Woolies he grabbed two towels, sheets and pillowcases and a blanket. He bought queen-sized sheets since he hadn't checked what size the bed was. *Better for the sheets to be too big than too small*, he thought. He stocked up on the essentials; bread, milk, butter, coffee, jam and Uncle Toby's Oats for his breakfast the next day, paid for with a crisp new hundred dollar note and headed home, carrying the haul in two plastic bags.

An only child, there was no need to check in with any siblings, nieces or nephews. His parents had passed away within two months of each other five years ago. He had an uncle and a couple of aunts along with a handful of cousins who all lived in the Melbourne area. He wrote to them from prison, a real handwritten letter, not an email. He could't recall why he had their addresses in his wallet but with nothing but free time on his hands he told them of his circumstances and that he would not be attending any family functions for a while.

He wrote four separate letters and did not get one reply. When Rita Potvin ended contact with him after her one and only visit to Murchison, he truly felt alone. Since he had cut his ties with Battaglia and his associates, his friendship with Johnny was a lifesaver.

The next day, as agreed, Carmona brought his things over just before noon. He was accompanied by two brawny young men. Tannenbaum greeted them downstairs and told them not to bother with the bed, fridge and couch. "Give them to Vinnies if you want or someone who might need them."

It took all of five minutes for them to deposit Tannenbaum's belongings in the lounge. There were several boxes with his cutlery, dishes, pots and pans, books, DVDs, CDs, clothes and his laptop. His slacks and shirts were in garment bags. *A nice touch*, Tannenbaum thought. He renewed acquaintances with his favourite recliner which he put right in front of his forty-inch TV. He plugged it in and after sixteen months of inactivity it lit up like a string of Christmas lights. Since the apartment was wired for Foxtel, he plugged the black box in, connected the cables—always a crap shoot—and sat down in his recliner. It worked. *Like old times*, Tannenbaum thought.

With no girl, no job and eager to put his hands back to good use, Fingers gave Pastrami a ring the next morning.

"Still going out to Flemington on Saturday?"

"Good to hear your voice, mate. Sure am. This has been the longest I've been away from the racetrack since I was a teenager. I've looked over the form and there look to be a couple of good things to build our bankrolls back up."

"Outstanding."

"You settling in all right? It took me a few weeks to adjust."

"So far, so good. I'm in a new apartment in Carlton that's paid up for a year—utilities included—so there's no money worries."

"Glad they kept their word. Rest up the next few days. I'll meet you in the bookmakers' ring at noon. I'll put a couple of bets on and then we'll head up to the members, have some lunch and a couple of beers."

"Noon it is. See you on Saturday."

Pastrami had watched numerous replays of the horses scheduled to run on Saturday and was keen on a horse in the third race over 1800m; Polyp in the Duodenum.

The four-year-old had run into nothing but dead ends in his last start at Caulfield over the same distance and finished sixth. Meeting the same quality of opponents, and on the bigger Flemington track, Pastrami could not believe the opening quote of $14. He put a grand on him with an online bookmaker and decided to plonk another two grand on him at the price of $12 with an on-track bookmaker he often did business with.

"Johnny, where you been?" Ben Watergate bellowed when he looked up and saw Pastrami. "Word is you were away on a forced vacation."

"Something like that. You gonna take my bets?"

"Sure, who do you like?"

"In the third give me two thousand to win and two thousand to place on number 8, Polyp in the Duodenum.

The juicy place odds of $3.80 would get him his money back—and more—if the horse failed to win.

Watergate's computer printed out two tickets and Pastrami handed over $4000 in one-hundred-dollar notes to the bookmaker.

Watergate immediately wound in the odds on Polyp in the Duodenum to $7 and $2.80.

Tannenbaum spotted his mark on the train from Southern Cross Station to Flemington. The gent appeared to be in his mid-fifties and had his members pass attached to his expensive suit jacket. He was with a gorgeous woman, who likely had spent two hours getting dolled up earlier in the morning for a big afternoon of sipping champagne with her girlfriends over an expensive lunch. In her heels the brunette was a head taller than her husband even without the fascinator perched on top of her head. Her members pass dangled off her handbag and swayed in the soft breeze.

As the large crowd walked to the gates Tannenbaum strolled up behind them. In the blink of an eye he ever so gently nudged the handbag from the woman's grasp. It fell to the pavement. Her husband reached down to pick it up, and in a nanosecond, without even breaking stride, Tannenbaum lifted the man's wallet, put it in his suit jacket pocket and blended in with the rest of the crowd walking to the main entrance.

"Try and be more careful dear," the man said to his wife as he gave the bag back to her. The two scanned their passes and took a left, Tannenbaum scanned his and walked to the betting ring to meet Pastrami. The gentleman who had his wallet stolen would not even realise it was gone until he either reached for his bank card to pay for lunch or made a wager. Many men now carried their bankroll in their front pockets but based on experience Tannenbaum knew that most men over fifty still stashed their cash in their wallets and placed them in their rear left pockets.

Tannenbaum went into the first men's toilet he came across, went into a stall and closed the door. Bingo. There was $320 cash in the man's wallet and several bank cards. He removed the cash and cards, put them in his jacket pocket and flushed the toilet. Tannenbaum wiped the wallet clean—he was after all fingerprinted when he was arrested—and casually tossed it into the bin by the sink.

Tannenbaum did have a heart when it came to thievery. In the past he dumped any pilfered wallets into the nearest post box so the owner didn't have to go through the hassle of getting a new driver's licence. On the average Tannenbaum picked two pockets a week. He got the idea as a teenager after seeing Chico Marx attempt to pick a fellow's pocket in the 1930s film *Monkey Business*. Chico put his hand in a man's pocket, trying to steal his passport, and was caught red-handed. He was told to keep his hands to himself. Tannenbaum's hands were a bit quicker than Chico's so he had never been caught in the act.

Tannenbaum practised on his friends until he became quite good at it. At first, he used a good-looking woman as his partner. She would bump into a man and while he was distracted Tannenbaum went to work.

He split the profits evenly with his accomplice. Later, when he was more accomplished from spending hours doing sleight-of-hand magic at home, he ditched his partner and worked solo. He also found that the magic tricks impressed women. He'd do a couple of card tricks at parties and before he knew it a crowd had gathered around him.

"How did you do that?" one of the girls would ask.

"It's a gift," he would say. Then Tannenbaum would reach into his jacket pocket and pull out a black lace bra. "I think this is yours."

The woman in question always checked her own bra just to make sure the one Tannenbaum held in his hands wasn't hers.

24

TOO HARD WRONG SPOT WAS ACCOMPANIED TO CRAN-bourne by Jack McCarron, Janice Roselli and stable strapper Don Byers, who drove the stable's transport truck featuring the *McCarron Racing* logo on both sides. Roselli kept the horse calm during the seventy-minute ride from Caulfield to the Cranbourne Training Complex in Melbourne's southeast while McCarron sat in the front passenger seat.

If they hadn't been going against the flow of the morning traffic the trip would have been even longer.

"How the heck do people put up with this traffic five days a week?" Byers asked McCarron as he motioned to the city-bound bumper-to-bumper traffic. He did not get a reply. McCarron had been up since 3am and was busy inspecting the inside of his eyelids.

Accompanying Too Hard Wrong Spot to the trials were three other horses; two unraced fillies and a colt who had not raced for six months. Since the four horses were due to trial fairly close to one another timewise, McCarron was hoping to be back on the road by 1.30pm.

It was 8.45am when Byers swiped a card that opened the gate to the complex. Normally McCarron would skip the trials, but he wanted to see Too Hard Wrong Spot run in person and see if he had the class to run in either the $400,000 Group 2 Herbert Power Stakes at Caulfield over 2400m or the Cranbourne Cup, which was worth $300,000, was 400m shorter and run the day after the Herbert Power.

The temperature was 19 degrees when they departed, and skies were partly cloudy. A stiff breeze was blowing out of the south east. The track was a soft 5 which would likely be upgraded to a good 4 as the day progressed. Except for the breeze, conditions were perfect and with twenty-five trials scheduled it was going to be a busy morning and afternoon at the biggest training complex in Australia.

The training track was adjacent to the main track which several years ago was transformed into a night venue with the addition of a state-of-the-art lighting system.

The surface of the training track was just as good as the main track, if not better, and for that reason was very popular with trainers who came from all over the area to work and trial their horses.

Byers parked the truck close to the tie-up stalls assigned to the McCarron horses and he, McCarron and Roselli unloaded them. All four walked down the ramp without an issue and were taken to their stalls.

Once the four were secure, McCarron walked a hundred metres or so to the scales payment office, exchanging hellos with several of his fellow trainers and a few exercise riders and jockeys.

"How many you trialling today Jack?" Group 1 winning trainer Robbie Kelley asked. "Family okay?"

"Family is fine Robbie," McCarron said as he adjusted his baseball cap.

"I see you brought that import here this morning. Word going around says he's a pretty smart one."

"We'll find out soon," McCarron said. "To tell you the truth I'm not sure what to expect from him."

McCarron collected the saddle cloths for each of his horses and told the clerk who would be riding them. Jockey Wendy White, who rode for McCarron at many provincial meetings, was to ride Too Hard Wrong Spot. She was a veteran rider with good, strong hands and had a calming effect on the horses she rode. Because of Too Hard Wrong Spot's problems in the past, McCarron felt she was a perfect fit for the horse. McCarron took the saddle cloths back to the tie-up stalls and saddled Too Hard Wrong Spot himself. The horse was wearing saddle cloth three and had six opponents in the 1000m trial after two horses were scratched earlier in the morning.

His trial was seventy-five minutes away.

With all the bad news coming out of Mongolia, Pastor Chris was keen to accompany Delaney out to Cranbourne for the trial; primarily to see how his mate was holding up after his $10,000 vanished overnight, and to have a look at Delaney's latest investment in the flesh.

After saying goodbye to Allison Roberts, with whom he was basically living with after knowing her for just a couple of weeks, Chris motored up Nepean Highway and managed to dodge the seemingly never-ending school-bound traffic. The plan was for him to leave his car at Delaney's place and have Delaney drive to Cranbourne, but Chris beeped his horn when he arrived and told Delaney to hop in.

"Hold on a second, we've got to drop Michelle off at the station first. She's inside gathering her things and locking up."

"Things going well between you two?" Chris asked.

"Very well. And you with Allison?"

"Fantastic, mate. I stayed at her place last night."

"Things getting serious, eh?" Delaney asked, giving his mate a nudge in the ribs.

"It's crazy. Just a few weeks ago I had nobody and now it's like being married. And the thing is I'm loving it."

"Are you sure you're not loving, it?" Delaney asked with an emphasis on the word *it*.

"Loving it all my friend, loving it all."

"You're in a pretty good mood for eight on a Monday morning," Michelle told Chris as she made her way to the kerb.

"Things are looking up, Michelle. Hey, what's wrong with this picture? We're off to the racetrack and you're on your way to the office. Are you sure you can't come along?"

"Not on a Monday, Chris. But I'll be at Caulfield on Saturday if the horse runs well today."

Michelle squeezed into the back seat of the pastor's Kia, her thermos of tea in one hand and her briefcase in the other as Delaney fetched his copy of the former broadsheet turned tabloid which this morning was teetering on the top of his neighbour's fence.

"How the hell did it wind up there?" he asked himself.

Dodging schoolkids on their bicycles, Chris deftly manoeuvred his two-year-old car the three blocks to the station.

Michelle scampered out of the backseat at a traffic light, kissed Delaney goodbye and wished him luck.

It was clear sailing for Chris and Delaney after they navigated the notorious Balcombe Road roundabout and got on Nepean Highway. Twenty minutes later they turned left at Carrum, the home of numerous *No Skyrail* posters, and onto Thompsons Road. Cranbourne was just 15kms away.

New housing estates, and the shopping centres to serve them, blanketed both sides of the road. Not even ten years ago it had all been farmland filled with horses and cattle as far as the eye could see. They had been replaced with new homes and two cars in each driveway and since there was virtually no public transport out this way, all had to use the one road which was a single lane in each direction for much of the way.

"If this is progress," Delaney said as they sat in a line of 100 cars backed up at a roundabout, "count me out."

"I concur. I'd love to move out of this city, but this is where the jobs are," Chris said.

"And Allison."

"She's the best reason for staying," Chris said.

Ten minutes later Chris turned right onto Grant Street and then hung a left into the Cranbourne Racecourse complex. They passed the main track and as they neared the training track came upon a steel gate which was blocking the entrance. Chris pulled over and waited for the horse float behind them to make its way to the gate. The driver touched a card on a pad, the gate opened, and Chris followed the float into the huge parking lot.

"I sure hope security is better at Parliament House," Chris quipped.

Horse floats and trucks were everywhere. Many still had their ramps in the down position waiting for their occupants to return. It was all one-way traffic since the first trial had not yet been run. The smell of manure was in the air.

Since it was the first time at the training track for each, it took a while for Delaney and Chris to get their bearings. Tie-up stalls were everywhere. Delaney later noticed the numbers on the stalls reached well into the 400s. More were nearing completion, part of a massive multi-million upgrade of the complex. Several local trainers had recently started housing their horses at the complex full time, sparing them the time and expense of hauling their horses to and from their stables.

Just under 200 horses were expected on course to contest the twenty-five trials.

Wondering where the starting gate was, Chris and Delaney headed down a dirt road. They spotted it and kept on going until they came to a clearing where they got out. Chris found a bush to relieve himself—one coffee too many—while Delaney walked 100 metres or so to the starting gate where seven barrier attendants were milling around.

A new batch of horses was being trotted to the starting gate every fifteen minutes to be sent on their way by the starter over distances ranging from 800 to 1500 metres.

A drone, one of racing's newest innovations, hovered 100 metres overhead. It was able to capture audio in addition to its clear video so the jockeys, exercise riders and barrier attendants had to be careful of what they said. One ill-timed remark could land them in trouble with the stewards.

If successful, the drone would be a big improvement on the helicopters used by Channel 7 on big race days, first by eliminating the noise which was an unnecessary pain in the arse for racegoers and second by getting rid of the big expense of hiring a helicopter, pilot and putting a cameraman on board.

As the horses for the first trial neared the starting gate, Delaney noticed two well-known jockeys leading their mounts to the gate. Another rider put his phone back in his pocket after checking his messages. A jockey riding with his phone? Only at the trials. A jockey's use of his or her phone on race days is strictly prohibited yet here was a rider actually checking his phone while on horseback.

The seven horses, including two Group 1 winners, loaded quickly. The starter pressed the button, the gates flew back and off they went. The drone went with them, following their every step over the 800-metre distance.

"That drone might have footage of you taking a leak," Delaney kidded Chris as they made their way back to the car. "I can see it now ...

"'Police are looking for a man who exposed himself at the Cranbourne racing trials this morning. Judging from the footage he does not appear to be well-armed but police are warning anyone who sees this man not to approach him and to call Crime Stoppers.'"

Parking in the main lot, Chris and Delaney got a copy of the entries for the trials and asked the clerk where Jack McCarron's stalls were. He looked over a long list. "They're in stalls 220 to 223."

In the background an official was announcing that it was time for horses for Trial 2 to make their way onto the track and to the starting gate.

The gathering spot was the Canteen.

The small building was adjacent to the office and was where trainers, owners and riders milled about and chatted over their coffees, breakfast and later in the day, lunch. Racing pictures covered the walls. A notice for a track rider needed was taped onto the front door. A female strapper, one of a handful of women in the room, tucked into a fruit salad.

Delaney noticed several Cranbourne-based trainers having a chat and a laugh. They held onto their entry sheets as if they were live quaddie tickets. Each trial was shown live on two television screens and as the gates opened the noise level dropped so everyone could hear the track announcer's call. The starting gate and finish line were so far away that only a good pair of military binoculars would be able to pick up the action. The screens gave the trainers a good view of each trial. They'd get the dirt from the riders once they came back to the stalls.

There was a sprinkling of women amongst the jockeys and exercise riders. Unlike race day when they all wore the same white pants with their names stencilled on them, today they were all in jeans, making it almost impossible to put names to the weathered and tanned faces. Delaney recognised several familiar faces as did Chris.

The riders walking to and from the many stalls had their protective vests on but not their colourful silks which showed off their Popeye-like arms. They'd be mortal locks in any arm-wrestling contest. A friendly bunch, most said hello when they locked eyes with Delaney and Chris, who as far as they could tell, were the only non-industry people onsite.

Delaney and Chris waited for several horses for Trial 2 to walk past before they headed over to McCarron's stalls. One horse in particular, an unraced three-year-old, was a bit fractious. The strong wind was whipping up dust and dirt around the entrance onto the course proper and the colt did not like it one bit. He reared up once and needed to be calmed by a clerk of the course. He finished a well-beaten last.

"You should have done some of your watering over here Chris," Delaney joked.

Delaney and Chris found McCarron's stalls without much trouble and said hello. Big John McGraw was there with a different woman. The guy had more women than McCarron had horses and they all had one thing in common—large breasts and short skirts. In a place where jeans were worn by ninety-nine percent of the people present, McGraw's latest bit of stuff stood out like a yacht amongst a bunch of dinghies. Delaney momentarily forgot what he was there for.

"So," Delaney said. "Let's have a look at those breasts—er ... horse of ours."

Too Hard Wrong Spot was in the far-left stall with nothing to his right or left. He stood quietly as Chris, Delaney, McGraw and his gal pal Sonja looked him over.

"He's doing well, Janice?" Delaney asked.

"Doing very well, Gary. We're expecting a big run from him today," Janice said as she brushed the horse's mane.

With less than an hour before his trial, McCarron came over to saddle Too Hard Wrong Spot.

Wendy White soon came by. McCarron introduced his owners to the jockey. They exchanged handshakes and small talk. McCarron then took her aside and told her to let the horse settle.

"He needs a strong hit out so don't be afraid to get stuck into him in the last couple of hundred metres. Give him a few slaps with the whip so he knows you mean business."

"Will do Mr McCarron. And the others?"

"The opposite. Nice and easy. The fillies could be anything. The one you're on has shown some speed at home. The colt really needs a run. He's been away from the races for a long time."

"Well boys, this is it," McCarron told Delaney, McGraw and Chris. "He'll really have to hit the line hard for us to run him in the Herbert Power or the Cranny Cup. See you at the Canteen."

Delaney gave Too Hard Wrong Spot a pat on his head.

"You're all I've got left pal," he said to the horse. "Do you know where Mongolia is? Of course you do. And you heard what happened there, right? Now go out there and show us what you can do, show me that I haven't thrown away another $15,000."

The words weren't exactly inspiring, but they were all Delaney could think of.

"Go out there and show us what you can do? I've heard more encouraging words at an Auskick match," Chris quipped.

Fifty minutes later the words, *horses for Trial 5 on the track, horses for Trial 5 on the track*, boomed from the complex's speakers.

White was given a leg up by Roselli and got herself comfortable. She checked her goggles, put her whip in her left hand and slowly guided Too Hard Wrong Spot from the stalls to the track. Delaney, Chris, McGraw and Sonja followed. The horse was not bothered at all by the blowing dirt and sand and cantered off into the distance on the way to the starting gate. Three of his rivals were already on the track. The other three were a little late in making their way onto the track leading to another call of, *horses for Trial 5 on the track please.*

At the Canteen, McCarron was seated at a front table sipping a coffee and chatting with two other trainers. Delaney and Chris stood at the back with McGraw and Sonja. They had an unimpeded view of the two screens. The horses were milling behind the barriers and all seven appeared to have their minds on the business at hand. Not one had broken into a sweat.

Delaney watched as Too Hard Wrong Spot was led into the starting gate. The others quickly followed as the red light on top of the gate started flashing. The starter pressed the button and the seven were sent on their way. The small field broke in a good line except for Too Hard Wrong Spot who broke a length and a half behind the field.

Not good, Delaney thought.

Wendy White let her mount settle into stride and moved him two spots off the rail behind the leaders, who were practically walking over the first 400 metres. The field was bunched as it made its way around the far turn. Too Hard Wrong Spot was still last with just over 400 metres to go and was travelling nicely just four lengths behind the two leaders.

"Take him to the outside Wendy, take him to the outside," Delaney said.

Sonja piped up as well. "Which one is ours, honey?" she asked McGraw, who did not answer.

On straightening, White angled Too Hard Wrong Spot to the centre of the track and began a steady run at the leaders. One horse dropped back off the pace, but the other co-leader, Marble Rye, wearing saddle cloth 6, was being strongly urged to the line by her rider. Too Hard Wrong Spot passed half of the field as though they were standing still and with one tap of the whip and very little urging got to within a half-length of Marble Rye at the finish.

The time was a very good 59.11. Too Hard Wrong Spot had run the last 600m in about thirty-four seconds. Delaney and Chris exchanged high fives. McCarron nodded in approval and scribbled some words in a small notebook.

The happy group walked back to the stalls to wait for horse and rider.

"Very impressive," said Roselli, who'd listened to the call along with Byers. "Something tells me we're going to see each other again at Caulfield on Saturday."

A few minutes later White brought Too Hard Wrong Spot back to the stalls. She got off the horse, removed the saddle and gave him a pat on the head.

Roselli lifted a bucket up to Too Hard Wrong Spot who took a few large gulps of cold water.

McCarron was out of earshot, talking with White.

"He did it all by himself," White said. "I barely touched him. You've got yourself a real good horse there Jack."

McCarron was pleased but had seen this sort of scenario played out hundreds of times, a horse who runs like Phar Lap in the morning and turns into a picnic horse in the afternoon. He'd hold off judgement until he saw how he performed at Caulfield.

"He looked good, fellas," McCarron told Delaney, Chris and McGraw. "But let's not get carried away. We'll see how he pulls up. If he pulls up well and eats up we'll enter him in the Herbert Power on Saturday."

"He's hardly even blowing," McGraw said. "He'll run on Saturday. I'll tell Taylor the good news."

Delaney shook hands with McCarron and left feeling pretty good about his investment.

"Geez, he looked good," Chris said.

"Sure did," Delaney said. "Let's get out of here. I've got to get to work, for goodness sake, as do you."

Roselli led Too Hard Wrong Spot to the cool down area where he was given a hosing down and a walk. The horse acted as if he hadn't even had a run.

"He's a stayer this one and a good one too provided he behaves," Roselli said to herself.

On the way out, Delaney and Chris encountered the same problem as they had going in; the gate at the entrance. They waited in the wings a few minutes until a silver four-wheel-drive pulled up to the gate. The driver tapped his card on a pad and the gate opened. It started to close just as the car excited forcing Chris to put his foot down to beat the gate. They made it with about a metre to spare.

"Nice driving, Indiana," Delaney remarked.

25

AFTER HIS PROMISING TRIAL, TOO HARD WRONG SPOT was entered by City Winners Syndication in the $400,000 Group 2 Herbert Power Stakes at Caulfield over 2400m on Saturday, just five days away. The race, an important lead-up to the upcoming Caulfield and Melbourne Cups, was short of entries so Too Hard Wrong Spot, the winner of just one race in his career, was guaranteed a start. Big John McGraw also entered Too Hard Wrong Spot in the Cranbourne Cup, a day after the Herbert Power just in case the Caulfield track was too firm or something went wrong in the lead-up to the Group 2 race.

McGraw and fellow syndicate man Ronnie Taylor decided to run the horse in the Herbert Power to get their horse used to the tight Caulfield circuit. McCarron concurred. However, he was not as enthusiastic as McGraw and Taylor when it came to the Caulfield Cup. He felt they were getting way too ahead of themselves. "They pay the bills, but ..."

All going well, McGraw and Taylor wanted to run their horse in the $3 million Caulfield Cup a week after the Herbert Power. The winner of the Herbert Power automatically got a start in the cup. Those finishing just behind the winner would be strongly considered by Racing Victoria's head handicapper.

McGraw did several radio, TV and print interviews in the days leading up to the Herbert Power which was part of Caulfield Guineas Day, one of the biggest days on the Caulfield calendar. Before the interviews, he put several bets down on Too Hard Wrong Spot. Once punters became aware of the horse's ability, he was bound to shorten in the markets.

Too Hard Wrong Spot was $41 with the TAB to win and $12 to place. McGraw bet several thousand dollars on the horse to place and put $100 on the nose just in case he managed to get up. He also put several thousand dollars on the horse to place in the Caulfield Cup at the juicy odds of $18. That bet was a futures bet, meaning that if the horse did not run he would not get his money back.

The field for the Herbert Power had come up a bit short of overseas talent this year and with several speedy types in the race the pace was going to be hot, giving a closer like Too Hard Wrong Spot a genuine chance. A dozen horses were entered for the race which was scheduled for early in the afternoon. It was a good opening act for the feature race of the day, the Caulfield Guineas which had attracted a very good field including boom colt Triumph who was unbeaten in five career starts.

Delaney was a bit on the nervous side in the four days leading up to the Herbert Power. The other members of City Winners Syndication were used to the attention coming up to a big race. They had previously had horses in the Caulfield and Melbourne Cups.

Delaney was a maiden at the caper and needed the horse to run a place to get something back from his purchase since the sudden closure of Motherlode Mining Group.

There was nothing but bad news coming out of Mongolia. Even though the mine employed hundreds of locals, built a school and hospital and paid its fair share of taxes, it was closed and would stay closed until those now in power gave the all clear for it to open. Millions of dollars would probably have to change hands for that to happen. While Delaney felt bad about his $10,000 loss, he felt worse for the people who worked at the mine and now had no income at all.

26

MONGOLIAN PRESIDENT BATBAYAR GANBAATARR WAS still in hiding at the five-star hotel in Razakhastan which was costing him 2500 euros a night. Even worse, he had been able to shtupp his mistress just once since they arrived. His calls for a meeting with the Razakhastani president went unanswered and he had a feeling he and his family were on their way to exile somewhere in South America.

"I'll have to learn Spanish and eat that spicy food," he said over dinner one night. "I hate paella."

On the bright side, Ganbaatarr's bank account had been unfrozen by Razakhastan president Damir Ibragimov but it came at a price— 50 million euros.

"For administrative fees and transport costs," Ibragimov told Ganbaatarr in a rare phone call between the two leaders. Ganbaatarr kept his cool, knowing he still had approximately 150 million euros left, but nearly lost it when he was told that his mistress would not be accompanying his family to the Central American country of Costa Rica.

"C'mon Damir. Give me a break. You can't expect me to sleep with my wife every night. Between her and her handbags there's barely enough room in our bed for me."

"That's a shame Batbayar. I feel for you. I really do, but that mistress of yours, what's her name? Chabi? She makes the best fucking chocolate cake I have ever had in my life. She's taking care of me now. And I do mean taking care of me if you know what I am saying."

"You're fucking her?"

"Fucking is such an awful word to use when talking about such a beautiful young woman Batbayar. I'm shtupping her brains out."

Ganbaatarr closed his eyes while he listened to Ibragimov laugh loudly through the phone line.

"Anyways my friend, I've made the necessary arrangements with the Costa Rican authorities. You'll live like a king down there. It's fucking beautiful; no snow and ice, just blue water, sunshine and women. You'll meet another Chabi. Plus, the exchange rate is fucking terrific. Those euros of yours will be like gold fucking bars."

"Costa Rica Damir? Costa Rica? I don't even know where the fuck that is."

"Google it my friend. I could always change those arrangements and send you to Peru."

"No. No. Costa Rica sounds wonderful. Thank you, Mr President."

"A car will pick you up at 10am to take you and your family to the airport. Have a safe trip."

The words "call ended" appeared on the screen of Ganbaatarr's iphone. He hurled his phone at a living room chair in his suite.

"What a crumb," he said. "What a crumb."

Ganbaatarr would have blown a gasket if he had known his former mistress was on her knees in Ibragimov's office during their phone call.

"What is this shtupping you speak of Mr President?" Chabi asked when the call ended.

"Get up from there and I'll show you," Ibragimov said. "But first, go get me a piece of that chocolate cake of yours. It's fucking fantastic."

Ganbaatarr called for his three children and wife, telling them to come into the living area for an urgent family meeting.

"Where's your mother?" he asked the three kids when they came into the room.

"She said she was going shopping daddy," his youngest daughter, Altan, said.

"Shopping? For more freaking handbags?"

Ganbaatarr took a minute to compose himself and told the kids that they were leaving Razakhastan in the morning.

"I want everyone packed and ready to go by 9am sharp."

"Where are we going daddy?" Altan asked.

"Someplace far away from the snow and ice honey. Costa Rica it is called. It has some of the nicest beaches in the world. You'll love it there." Ganbaatarr said.

"Do you think mom will like it?" his son Arslan asked.

"Of course, she will son. We all will."

What he really wanted to say to his son's query was "who gives a shit"?

27

DELANEY RECEIVED A FEW CALLS FROM SEVERAL racing journos after the barrier draw was held, wanting to know the circumstances in his purchase of the last share of Too Hard Wrong Spot. Being on the other end of the conversation, answering questions instead of asking them, was new. He told the journos, spread across print, radio, TV and online outlets, the colourful story and mentioned the bath he took in his first foray into the stock market.

He was hoping for a better result on Saturday in his first venture as a racehorse owner.

Too Hard Wrong Spot drew barrier nine in the twelve-horse field which was not a worry. Since the horse liked to come from off the pace, jockey Damien Smithton, a regular rider for trainer McCarron, would take the horse back at the start, put him to sleep down the backstretch and call on him to start his run approaching the far turn.

None of Delaney's colleagues at *Turf News* picked his horse to win the Herbert Power, instead going with logical favourite Lake Havasu, who had run a very good second from just off the pace in the Underwood Stakes three weeks earlier.

Speedsters The Wheels are in Motion, No Puppet and Big Ball of Oil would assure a good fast pace. Delaney was most worried about I Get No Respect, a five-year-old French-bred mare who had made up a lot of ground in the Underwood and was primed to run a strong race over her favourite 2400m distance.

Greg Grote wrote a good piece on Too Hard Wrong Spot's long journey back to the races. It ran alongside a strong photo of McCarron, Smithton and McGraw taken at Caulfield on Thursday morning. McGraw wanted his female companion in the photo while the *Turf*

News photographer wasn't too crazy about the idea. To placate McGraw, he took a few shots with her and a few without. He deleted the shots with the girl as soon as he got back to his car.

The only mention of Delaney's part ownership of the horse in *Turf News* appeared in the Form Guide where his name was listed last in the list of owners as G. Delaney. He got a buzz out of seeing that, much the way he did out of seeing his first byline in print over thirty years ago.

When Delaney left the office late on Friday afternoon, Swoboda gave him a pat on the back and wished him well for the next day.

"It's all thanks to you, Adam. I would never be in this spot if it wasn't for you, and to tell you the truth, it's damn exciting."

"I'll see you at the track tomorrow," said Swoboda, who as usual was scratching his beard. "Just wanted to let you know I might be a bit late. I'm having a little domestic problem."

The reporter in Delaney caused him to pause and ask Swoboda what was going on.

"Well, my wife has this cat and ..."

Sensing a long story, Delaney took a seat.

"The fucker runs and jumps all over the place, knocks things off shelves in the middle of the night. It sleeps during the day and then when it's time for lights out, her lights come on. The litter box is disgusting," Swoboda continued. "The other morning there were turds in the toilet. I told Patricia she forgot to flush, and she told me not to worry, that it was just cat shit. Cat shit? Where I shit? I nearly vomited mate. And the vet bills. There was another one for $275 last week," Swoboda continued.

When Swoboda finally got the anger out of his system, Delaney offered the young lad a bit of advice.

"A mate of mine went through the same problem with his girlfriend Adam. Her cat recently had a vet bill of $1320 which he paid. Thirteen hundred and twenty dollars. But sometimes you just have to bite the bullet and accept it."

Swoboda nodded.

"Isn't Patricia expecting?"

"In four weeks. I still can't believe I am going to be a dad."

"Here's what you need to do Adam. Get a cat door put in, immediately. Even if you are in a rental it is worth every cent. If you need to install a new door when you leave, so be it.

"My mate got a cat door installed for her girlfriend's cat and it took care of her night-time jaunts around the house and the cat shit all in one go. They don't even have a litter box anymore. The cat does everything outside and basically just sleeps when she is in the house. She comes and goes when she wants. The only downside is …"

"Uh oh," Swoboda interrupted.

"Is that every so often the cat brings a mouse into the house. And once she left a bird near the cat door."

"Were they dead?"

"Yup. He put on a pair of gloves, used a dustpan to sweep them up, put everything into a bag, including the dustpan, and dumped them right into the bin."

"Hmmm. I can live with that. Thanks Gary. You're a bloody lifesaver. On Sunday I'll go to Bunnings, get a cat door and install it. Maybe Patricia will forget all about the cat once the baby arrives."

"Doubtful mate, doubtful."

28

A LITTLE RAIN ON FRIDAY NIGHT WAS WELCOMED BY Too Hard Wrong Spot's connections. Like most European horses who preferred a bit of give in the ground, Too Hard Wrong Spot would have no excuses with the jar out of the Caulfield track.

The sun broke through the clouds on Saturday morning as Delaney and Michelle walked to Mentone station for the twenty-five-minute trip to Caulfield. They were armed with their copies of *Turf News* and the form guide from the previous day's broadsheet turned tabloid. Delaney also had a glance at Consume and Devour's form guide just to see what the paper's pundits thought of his horse. Not much. Only two of the six handicappers even mentioned Too Hard Wrong Spot and they each put him fourth in the twelve-horse field.

Plenty of racegoers, decked out in their finest, were already on the train when it arrived in Mentone. Delaney was wearing his best suit, one of the two he owned, the one without the stain on the lapel, while Michelle was simply dazzling in the turquoise dress she picked up at Myer earlier in the week. She'd practised walking in her heels over the past two days to get used to them and pronounced herself fit to take her place among the glitterati.

As part owners they were given members tickets. Delaney attached his to his jacket while Michelle fastened hers to her newest handbag.

The promise of a nice day and the Caulfield Guineas brought a bumper crowd to the track. Well-dressed men, most sporting beards, and women, most without any sort of stubble but plenty of visible tattoos, got off the train and had to stand in long lines to purchase tickets while Delaney and Michelle simply scanned their tickets at the gate and walked right in.

Delaney figured 25,000 people would turn up for Caulfield's second biggest day of the year. Marquees were up and champagne was being poured by picnickers on the front lawn and the well-heeled in the members' dining rooms.

Long-time track announcer Glen Kays was giving the scratches and changes for the card over the track's PA system as Delaney and Michelle arrived. "There are no changes in the fourth race, the Herbert Power," Delaney heard as he and Michelle walked to one of the members' bars for a refreshment.

Delaney was so nervous he didn't even have a bet on the first three races. The first went to the well-backed favourite while a $10 chance and a $6 chance took out races two and three. Before the third race of the afternoon Delaney and his better half went to the tie-up stalls at the back of the course to have a look at Too Hard Wrong Spot.

The horse was relaxed but Big John McGraw wasn't. He kept peppering McCarron with questions and orders as Janice Roselli took protective bandages off Too Hard Wrong Spot's legs. It wasn't long before McCarron saddled the horse.

"Make sure the hoop doesn't make his run too late," McGraw shouted. "Tell him to stay away from the inside rail, it looks off, don't you think?"

"Smithton knows how to ride the horse," McCarron told Mr McGraw. "There's nothing to worry about. We might even get our photos taken if everything goes according to plan."

McGraw, who was trying to impress his latest lady friend, Tiffany Larue, backed off.

"C'mon honey. Let's go and get a drink."

"Just let me give the horse a pat on the head for luck," answered Miss Larue, who was thisclose to falling out of her dress.

Delaney shook hands with McGraw while Michelle and Miss Larue exchanged brief hellos.

"Pretty damn exciting, ain't it Gary?"

"Sure is. The horse looks in great nick. McCarron and Janice have done a bloody good job with him."

"We'll see you later in the mounting yard."

Delaney took Michelle's hand and walked to a buffet set up for the owners behind the grandstand.

"Did you see the dress that girl wasn't wearing?" Michelle asked.

"I'm sorry, I didn't notice," Delaney said with a smile.

"She's young enough to be McGraw's daughter for goodness sake."

"That won't stop him from, ummmmm."

"From what?"

"From having an intimate evening or maybe an interlude in the toilets."

"Have you ever done it in a toilet?" Michelle asked.

"Nope."

"What if a girl like Miss Larue wanted to?"

"I'd tell her to finish her homework before dinner."

"Good answer."

The two took their place in line at the buffet. The prawns were so popular they had to be restocked twice while they filled their plates.

"If I had known the food was this good, I would have become an owner years ago. All we get in the press room are sandwiches and meat pies," Delaney said.

With their stomachs full after a long stop at the dessert table, Delaney and Michelle walked inside, passing a host of bookmakers, many of whom had Too Hard Wrong Spot at $19. He was paying $16.60 and $5.80 on the tote some twenty-two minutes before race time. The horse would have been triple that if not for the run at Cranbourne.

Delaney put down $20 each way on his horse. Michelle took a pineapple out of her purse and bet all of it on Too Hard Wrong Spot to run a place. "Confident?" Delaney asked.

"Either that or very silly," she said.

Pastrami and Tanenbaum were at the track as well as interested observers. After hours and hours of form work, Pastrami had settled on the French-bred mare I Get No Respect as his Melbourne Cup horse. In early betting the horse was 31-1. But those odds came down to 21-1 after Pastrami placed a fixed odds $20,000 win bet and a $10,000 place bet with the TAB earlier in the week.

Tannenbaum, whose bankroll was on the skinny side when compared to his mate's, put a grand on the same horse; $500 to win and another $500 to place. It was the largest amount of money Tannenbaum had wagered in his life. The pay-offs would be much bigger now than on race day but there was a catch. If for whatever reason their horse did not start in the Melbourne Cup their money was lost. There were no refunds on futures bets. Refunds were only made on bets after entries were taken and the horse listed as a confirmed starter.

Pastrami had $1000 to place on I Get No Respect in the Herbert Power. He figured the horse needed the run in her first race since being spelled. Her workouts had been sharp, but the pressure of race day would be an entirely new ballgame.

They watched the day's races from the enclosed grandstand, having a few beers along the way to avoid the large crowds.

As one would expect on Caulfield Guineas Day, the mounting yard was packed. Delaney had been there many times before as a member of the working press but today was his first time as an owner. He and Michelle were introduced to several other members of the syndicate and were making small talk as the horses entered the mounting yard. The owners of the twelve horses squeezed their way down to the front to get a better look at their investments. Delaney had a look at the massive TV screen in the infield and saw that punters were warming to his horse. He was down to $14 at fixed odds and $12.80 on the tote.

Too Hard Wrong Spot was wearing saddle cloth number 5 and was the picture of health as Janice Roselli led him into the mounting yard. There were fifteen minutes until race time.

"I'm going to have another bet on the horse," Delaney told Michelle. "He looks good and relaxed, just as he was at Cranbourne."

Delaney weaved his way through the crowds to the TAB window and put $20 on his horse to place at the fixed odds of $3.40.

He returned to the mounting yard just as the jockeys came out of the tunnel. Smithton was dressed in the syndicate's red and white colours. His cap was red which would make him easy to pick out during the running of the race.

McCarron had a word with Smithton and then gave him a leg up. The horses paraded around the yard once more with their jockeys aboard and then made their way onto the track.

Too Hard Wrong Spot had never been in front of a crowd this large in his young life. The large crowd stirred as the horses stepped onto the track. Too Hard Wrong Spot picked his head up and seemed a bit annoyed by the loud crowd down along the outer fence. Smithton angled him towards the inside rail to get away from the noise which calmed him down as the pair cantered past the starting gate situated at the top of the stretch.

Once the race got underway a tractor would move the starting gate into the infield and out of harm's way well before the horses arrived at the top of the stretch. If for some reason the tractor failed to get the job done, a back-up was situated nearby. Only once had Delaney seen a tractor falter. It was somewhere up in the bush a few years ago and without another on course, the track announcer yelled at the top of his lungs for the jockeys to stop riding. The barrier attendants ran to the far turn frantically flapping their arms in a bid to get the jockeys to pull up their horses. They all managed to do so. The race was declared a non-race and all money wagered was refunded. It was the play of the day of every sports broadcast in the country later that afternoon and night and embarrassing for all concerned which was why most clubs fired up their tractor prior to races over longer distances which in most cases called for the horses to make a complete circuit of the track.

Smithton gave Too Hard Wrong Spot a good warm-up and felt good about his chances as the field approached the starting gate. There were three minutes until race time.

Delaney rang Chris.

"It's crazy down here," he said over the noise over the crowd. "And he's being backed too. Shit I hope he runs a place."

"Allison and I are watching, mate. We even saw the two of you on the telly. Good luck, talk to you tonight."

At the Newmarket Training Grounds in the UK, Danielle Frisella was also tuned in to see how Too Hard Wrong Spot went in his first start since leaving the UK 15 months ago. It was just after 5am but Frisella had already been at work for an hour and a half. She could not believe how much her former charge had grown when she spotted him in the mounting yard.

"He looks like a real race horse," she said to an empty office.

Frisella had risen to second in charge of trainer Reggie Gaspar's operation, her mum was in remission after successful cancer surgery and she was dating the stable foreman of a top trainer who also based his horses at the world-class Newmarket facility.

With less than two minutes before the start, the voice of Glen Kays filled the air. "The horses are being loaded into the gate for the Herbert Power. The winner gets a berth in next Saturday's $3 million-dollar Caulfield Cup."

Lake Havasu was the lukewarm $3.40 favourite on the tote with I Get No Respect a $3.80 choice. Likely pace setter Wheels Are In Motion was at $4.80.

Delaney and Michelle had their eyes peeled to the starting gate at the top of the stretch along with everyone else. Too Hard Wrong Spot was one of the last to load and without a nudge from any of the barrier attendants walked into the gate.

"The field is set, and they are racing in the Herbert Power," Kays said above the roar of the crowd.

Just as he did at Cranbourne, Too Hard Wrong Spot broke a length and a half behind the field. Delaney groaned. Smithton steered the horse to the inside rail and was about six lengths behind the pack as the field of twelve passed the crowded stands for the first time.

As expected, Wheels Are In Motion was in front after the first 400m which was travelled in 23.56, quick but not that quick on the good 3 surface. He was being pressured on the outside by Big Boil Of Oil with closer I Get No Respect much closer to the pace than usual back in third. Longshot Black and White Cookie was on his outside fourth with race favourite Lake Havasu well positioned in fifth as the field made its way down the backstretch.

No Puppet was next as its jockey decided to take a sit instead of getting involved in a suicidal speed duel up front. The first 800m was run in 47.63, a fast and honest pace.

Smithton had Too Hard Wrong Spot ninth along the rail some eight lengths off the leaders and was being hemmed in by $51 chance In Conclusion.

"He's not too far back, is he?" Michelle asked.

"Don't think so but we don't want to get trapped along the rail and have no place to go," Delaney replied.

With 800 metres left to race as the field made it was way down the railway side of the course, Smithton made his move as In Conclusion weakened and fell back. He moved Too Hard Wrong Spot to the outside where he had clear sailing and set his sights on the leaders, who were now six lengths in front.

Wheels Are In Motion still led by a bit more than a length despite running the first 1200m in 1:10.56. Approaching the turn Lake Havasu peeled off the rail giving Smithton a perfect cart into the race.

"Wheels Are In Motion leads but here comes Lake Havasu as the field heads for home," Kays bellowed from his perch atop the grandstand.

The big crowd was getting into it. Their eyes shifted from the big screen to the action now right in front of them.

"Lake Havasu hits the front with 200 metres left to run and here comes Too Hard Wrong Spot along with No Puppet and I Get No Respect.

Delaney was screaming, "Come on Too Hard."

Michelle was jumping up and down clutching her place ticket.

Too Hard Wrong Spot moved into third spot with 100 metres left to run and was gaining on the two horses in front of him when he ducked to the inside, most likely from the loud noise of the crowd.

Smithton quickly got Too Hard Wrong Spot back in stride, but his chance of winning was lost.

Lake Havasu crossed the line first, a length in front of I Get No Respect. Too Hard Wrong Spot was two lengths farther back in third with No Puppet fourth. The final time flashing on the infield board was 2:27.31, a heck of a good time, just two seconds off the race record.

The rider of No Puppet, Stan Simmons, was of the mind to lodge an objection against Too Hard Wrong Spot for interference but thought better of the idea once he saw the replay of the stretch run. There was nothing in it. The result stood.

Too Hard Wrong Spot returned $3.60 to place. Michelle got back $180 which paid for her dress.

"Can you cash my ticket?" Michelle asked her partner.

"You want me to go the window and get your money? One of the thrills of winning is handing a clerk a scrap of paper and receiving cash for it. Go on honey, I'll watch you."

Michelle waited a few moments for the three people in front of her to collect their winnings. She handed over the ticket and received a $100 note, a $50 note, a $20 note and a tenner. She was absolutely bubbling as she stashed the money in her purse. Delaney took a photo of the momentous occasion, the biggest win of her life. Before the two of them teamed up Michelle had been to the races just once and could not even remember if she had a bet. Now she knew how to read the form guide, was hanging out in the members' section, going to stables and was $130 ahead.

Delaney got back a bit less while City Winners Syndication received about $28,000 after McCarron and Smithton took their respective cuts of ten and five percent. Delaney's share of the winnings was roughly $1400.

However, all the money earned by the Syndicate in the Herbert Power was being put towards the nomination fee to run in the Caulfield Cup. With $3 million dollars up for grabs, Delaney's original outlay of $15,000 was beginning to look like a good investment.

Delaney and Michelle walked back to the tie-up stalls after the race to await Too Hard Wrong Spot's return. Roselli had hosed him down and was walking him to cool him off. McCarron was at the stalls, having a look at another of his horses, Articles of Impeachment, who was a $10 chance in the Guineas.

"Happy with the run of Too Hard, Jack?" Delaney asked.

"If he broke from the gate better and not ducked in deep in the stretch he might have won. We'll fit him with a pair of earmuffs and work with him from the gate over the next few days to get him ready for the Caulfield Cup," McCarron said.

"Do you think he's ready for a Caulfield Cup?"

"Ordinarily no. But McGraw and Taylor want to run him and if he's fit he'll run. By the looks of things there won't be a full field of eighteen so he should get into the field off his run today. He showed that he could handle the distance and he'll be weighted well. I'd say he has a decent chance."

"Amazing," Delaney said. "Two weeks ago I wasn't even involved with the horse and now I'm the part owner of a horse running in the Caulfield Cup."

"It's a hell of a game, isn't it?"

"It is when you're on top. Thanks for everything Jack. Talk during the week."

"Just don't get too carried away. He's had just the one race in Australia and this is the Caulfield Cup, not a mid-week handicap in Bendigo.

29

"WE'VE GOT TROUBLE," PASTRAMI TOLD TANNENBAUM after the race. "We've got thousands of dollars of bets on I Get No Respect and this Too Hard Wrong Spot could ruin everything. He was flying before he ducked in. He could be anything."

"What do you think we should do?"

"Wait. Let's first see how the McCarron horse goes in the Caulfield Cup. But I'll tell you this, if that horse runs well in the Caulfield Cup I'll make sure he isn't in the gates come the first Tuesday of November. I've worked too hard and have too much money on the French horse to get beaten by that thing."

Pastrami was so pissed off that he left before the Caulfield Guineas. "I'll talk to you soon mate," Pastrami said as he rose out of his seat. He stopped by the windows first to collect on the place bet he had on I Get No Respect. He won $900 from his only wager of the day and then decided to do a little homework back at the tie-up stalls.

From a distance he looked on as the McCarron team cooled down Too Hard Wrong Spot. Working alongside McCarron were two women. One was walking the horse around while a younger woman was filling up a water bucket. The younger woman gave Too Hard Wrong Spot a cuddle and a kiss on his nose when he was brought back into the stall.

Pastrami took a good hard look at her. *If I have to, she's the one I'll target*, he thought. He tucked his program into his back pocket, walked to the exits, turned right and made a beeline to the nearby train station and went home.

Delaney and Michelle hung around Caulfield for the Guineas where Triumph was run down in the shadow of the post by Sydney galloper

Slippery Pete, who paid $18.60 on the tote. Judging from the rush of people leaving the track after the race, it was not a popular result. Delaney was not about to take the $1.75 on offer for Triumph and did not have a bet. As they walked to the exit Delaney couldn't help but notice that the crowds were bigger at the bars than at the betting windows. Several young lovelies, having had a bit too much bubbly, were wobbling about in their high heels, taking selfies, checking their make-up and making sure their spray-on tans were holding up.

Groups of men were packed around tables guzzling cans, looking at TV monitors posting odds of the next from Morphettville in Adelaide in a bid to recoup their losses from the Guineas.

Bookmakers were busy setting the odds for the next at Caulfield on their electronic boards. Gone were the days of a scribbled number with the kind of bet made and amount wagered on a bookie's ticket. Everything was now computerised.

With Fashions on the Field handing out thousands of dollars of prizemoney during the races and bands and DJs playing afterwards, it was a very different game from the days when Ming Dynasty, Tristarc and Let's Elope were lighting up the Caulfield turf. But Delaney had a stunning woman on his arm, money in his pockets and was part owner of a horse running in the Caulfield Cup.

As he and Michelle left the track there were still people coming in for the last couple of races. Ordinarily Delaney would give them his race book, but today's book had his name in it so he stuck it in his jacket pocket and kept walking.

Plenty of taxis were waiting for the departing racegoers and Delaney gathered that while many would be thrilled with the fares, they would not be too happy with what they would have to clean up later. There were not too many happy faces on the 4.35 train to Frankston. The people, it seemed, were just as miserable on a Saturday clutching their Myer and Target bags as they were on a weekday when they were heading home after a long day at the office. But Delaney was positively giddy. He asked Michelle if she would mind if he asked Chris and Allison if they were free for dinner.

"We'll go home first, freshen up and go out and celebrate. Up for it?"

"Sure am. I've met Allison just once and it was just for a moment. I'd like to see the two of them together."

"Great."

He took out his phone and rang Pastor Chris. The phone rang and rang and rang before Chris finally answered. "Haven't caught you at a bad time have I buddy?"

"It's not the best time, but what's up?"

Delaney heard Allison giggling in the background. At least he hoped it was Allison.

"How would you and Allison like to have dinner with Michelle and me tonight?

"Sounds good, let me ask Ally."

After a few seconds of silence Chris got back on the line.

"All good mate. Where we headed?"

"That Chinese place in Bentleigh okay? Our treat."

"Perfect, but we'll split the bill. I had $100 on your horse to place. It's the biggest bet I ever made in my life. I got a little worried when he started wobbling about like a drunken sailor in the stretch. What was that all about?"

"McCarron says he got spooked from the crowd noise. He's going to put a pair of earmuffs on the horse in the Caulfield Cup?"

Chris laughed. "Earmuffs? And a scarf? You've got to love it."

"See you around seven," Delaney said. "I'll call and make a reservation."

30

ALWAYS WONDERING WHAT OTHERS IN THE RACING industry and racing media were up to, Gary Delaney regularly checked newspapers, websites, television and radio shows.

Unfortunately, it was all pretty vanilla since the suits running things couldn't come up with a fresh idea even if they were forced to muck out a stall. If given the all clear Delaney planned to make some subtle changes to *Turf News* in the months ahead to give it a fresher feel and make it easier to read; new fonts for headlines and captions, along with the addition of a letters or talkback section and more international racing news from Europe and the US.

The only program on radio or television that he found even remotely entertaining was *Get On*, an hour-long show which aired once a week on racing.com (Channel 78). It contained humour, good natured banter between the panellists and selections for Saturday's metropolitan racing in Victoria and Sydney and Group 1 races throughout Australia.

He sampled Sky's *Thoroughbred Weekly* on Sunday mornings where a former Sydney-based jockey tried to inject some life into the proceedings. But the program was so heavily tilted towards Sydney racing that a major stakes race in Victoria got the same amount of airtime as the second race at Randwick. They seemed to place more importance on the brand new $13 million Everest Stakes, which wasn't even a Group 1 race yet, than the Melbourne Cup and its 150 plus years of history.

While he was doing some shopping at Woolies on a recent Friday morning, when he wasn't due the office until a bit later, Delaney stopped at the customer service desk at the front of the store where the day's newspapers were lined up. He looked at the headlines on Consume and Devour's national masthead. *PM holds lead in latest poll, New coal mine gets green light*, and then started flipping through Consume and Devour's daily Melbourne paper. Nothing but pictures of models, celebrities, puppies and kittens. Anything to take the public's mind off the myriad of problems that were quickly turning Melbourne into one of the world's most unliveable cities.

Delaney looked at several more pages before he was confronted by a cashier.

"Are you going to buy the paper?" the woman asked.

"Not sure, just looking through it," Delaney replied.

"Well," she said, taking the paper out of Delaney's hands and putting it back with the others, "You can't read the paper unless you buy it."

"You're kidding, aren't you?"

"No, I am not. You licked your finger and then put it on the page."

"And you're not going to throw it in the bin? Someone could get infected from a micro-sized piece of dried saliva," Delaney said as he walked out the door and waited for Michelle, who had run back to get cat food.

When she came out of the store, Delaney told her what had happened and asked her if she would go back in, have a look at the paper and see if the same thing happened to her.

Michelle went back in, took a copy of the daily, laid it out on the counter and started thumbing through it from front to back. She got to page five, page seven and all the way up to the editorial pages without incident.

She then quickly turned and walked out of the store.

"Did that woman tell you to leave?'

"Nope."

"Then why did you?"

"I got to Allen Nutt's column."

31

THE WEEK LEADING UP TO THE CAULFIELD CUP IS A massive one for owners, trainers, jockeys, journalists and track officials, especially the track superintendent in charge of presenting the best possible surface on race day. Does he water the track or wait for the forecast rain? If the track is too hard on race day, he risks the wrath of trainers, jockeys, owners and punters. If it is too wet, a different batch of trainers, jockeys, owners and punters voice their complaints. He needs to get it just right and this week, Rick Badderley's best mates were those at the weather bureau and the radar loop on its website.

Badderley, a forty-six-year-old with fifteen years on the job, usually got things right. But three years earlier he watered the track since the forecast for the twenty-four hours leading up to the cup was for sunny skies. Not one forecaster mentioned the word rain. But on the morning of the cup, appearing out of nowhere like a despised mother-in-law, dark skies approached from the west and dumped ten millimetres of rain on the track in less than forty minutes. Suburbs ten minutes away in every direction did not even get a drop. The track went from a good 4 to a heavy 8.

Local trainers threatened to scratch their horses from the cup, saying the track was a bog. Several said on twitter that Badderley should be fired. Many punters were not as kind. On the other hand, trainers and connections of the six European horses entered in the $3 million-dollar handicap were ecstatic. Their horses preferred the heavy going and with the sting out of the track were likely to improve by several lengths. Bookmakers immediately tightened the odds on the European horses and lengthened the odds of the local horses.

Badderley, who did not like to be in the public eye, was in the middle of a shit storm. He was tracked down by a reporter from Channel 7, the host broadcaster, and explained the situation to viewers. "It was just bad luck. The rain came out of nowhere."

The reporter agreed as did the Channel 7 commentators.

His bosses were not as amiable. They summoned him to a meeting after the last race in the committee room. If the amount of money wagered by punters on the day was down and the outcry from trainers, owners and big punters continued, someone would have to take the blame. Badderley was all but certain his days as track superintendent at Caulfield were over.

The sun did come out in the afternoon and dried the track a bit but it was officially listed as a soft 7 come race time. Badderley was toasted by the connections of French stayer Croissant, who took out the cup by a short half head in a blanket finish.

"We'd especially like to thank the track superintendent for watering the track last night," winning owner Francois Beliveau said at the post-race party. The buoyant forty-five-year-old owner of a string of massage parlours across Europe raised his glass of Dom Perignon. "To Rick Badderley," he said. "We couldn't have won this without you," he said, lifting the Caulfield Cup.

"To Rick Badderley," his group hollered in response.

With the track posting record betting numbers on the day and its third highest on-track attendance even with the wet lawn in front of the grandstand, the calls to sack Badderley died down.

"It was a freak storm," the committee chair said at the early evening meeting in the lavish committee room. "No one could have seen it coming. And with one of their own winning the race, we're bound to get some more European horses next year."

A very relieved Badderley kept his job.

With the footy season over, racing dominated the front and back pages of Melbourne's newspapers. Network camera crews were at the Werribee Quarantine Centre every morning for reports on the foreign contingent of horses which this year numbered ten.

The Caulfield Cup barrier draw was held late Tuesday morning at the Black Caviar bar at Caulfield. It was covered live on television and radio. A full field of eighteen, with no emergencies, was entered.

Too Hard Wrong Spot was given 53.5 kilograms by the handicapper while the high weight, Lake Havasu, would have to carry 57kg.

The morning of the draw, Jack McCarron and Janice Roselli worked with Too Hard Wrong Spot on his starting gate issues. With Damien Smithton in the saddle, Roselli walked Too Hard Wrong Spot into a small starting gate on Caulfield's training track. He was flanked by a horse on either side. The starter pressed the button and again Too Hard Wrong Spot missed the start. Not by much, but just enough to cost him a race.

The riders brought the horses back to the barriers after they had run just a couple of hundred metres. McCarron had a brief chat with Smithton and asked Janice to bring a barrier blanket over to the starting gate.

McCarron figured that Too Hard Wrong Spot was a bit nervous in the cramped space of the stall and that the actual feel of the barriers was putting him off. A barrier blanket draped over his back, just behind the saddle, would help relax him. It attached to hooks on the gate itself and stayed there when the gates flew back.

McCarron put a barrier blanket on Too Hard Wrong Spot and Roselli once again led him in the starting gate. The blanket was attached to the gate while the two other horses took their places. The all clear was given, the gates flew back, and Too Hard Wrong Spot jumped with the others. A big smile came over McCarron's face. Problem solved. He would notify the stewards immediately of the change in equipment. *The son of a gun actually has a chance*, he thought.

Big John McGraw represented City Winners Syndication at the all-important barrier draw. Gary Delaney watched the proceedings at *Turf News*'s office.

In racing, the horse carrying the most weight in the field wears saddle cloth 1 and the horse lumping the least amount is given the number which corresponds to the total number of the horses in the race. In the Caulfield Cup, which featured eighteen starters, low weight, Kramerica, with fifty-two kilograms, was assigned saddle cloth 18.

The barriers were chosen at random. For the Caulfield Cup, eighteen miniature Caulfield Cups were placed on a large table.

Connections of each horse, also chosen at random, would then come up to the stage and select a cup. The barrier number was printed on the bottom.

Compere Jordan Ricketson welcomed connections and the live TV and radio audience to the draw. Head steward Jerry Bailey, not to be confused with the hall of fame American jockey of the same name, drew the first number from a barrel.

"Horse number twelve, Firecracker."

The horse's co-owner, Buddy Cronk, the former AFL star, bounded onto the stage. He shook hands with Ricketson, who asked him if he was more nervous now or before several of the grand finals he played in and won.

"Never been so nervous in me life, mate."

Cronk reached to his left, picked up a miniature cup and turned it over. Barrier 5. There was scattered applause in the room. Cronk drew a sigh of relief.

"Well done, mate," Ricketson said.

Ten minutes later there were only four horses left to be called and Too Hard Wrong Spot was one of them.

Barriers 6, 11, 14 and 18 remained.

Jerry Bailey reached into the hopper and pulled out one of the four remaining balls. "Horse number 16, Too Hard Wrong Spot."

McGraw stood up. But instead of walking up to the stage he sent his latest companion, Tiffany, to pick one of the four remaining cups.

A couple of wolf whistles were heard as the want-to-be model, dressed in a tight red mini skirt with matching heels and top, sashayed to the stage.

For the first time in his long career, compere Ricketson was at a loss for words.

"I don't believe I know you. Are you one of the owners?" Richardson asked.

"Oh no, I'm here with Big John," she squeaked as the crowd laughed.

"Ahhh, yes. John McGraw of City Winners Syndication. Are you his good luck charm?"

"I suppose so."

"And your name is?

"Tiffany."

"Have a last name?"

"Not that I'm aware of," she chirped to howls of laughter.

"Well Miss Tiffany, choose one of the four cups left on the table."

Tiffany adjusted her big breasts, which were clearly too big for her top, thought for a second and reached for the cup towards the back of the table. Her breasts all but fell out of her top. The chief steward was aghast. He later fined McGraw $1000 for bringing the sport into disrepute even though the video of Miss Tiffany had 10 million hits on YouTube before the end of the day and pictures of her were splashed in every newspaper in Australia the next morning.

Miss Tiffany held the cup up so all could see the all-important number. It was 14.

Not great but not that bad since Too Hard Wrong Spot was going to be taken back at the start no matter which barrier he broke from.

"Did I do good?" Miss Tiffany asked McGraw when she returned to her seat.

"You did just fine hun," he said with every eye in the house on them.

"That concludes the barrier draw for this year's Caulfield Cup," said Ricketson, who was as red as the sash on an Essendon football jumper.

He adjusted his ear piece. "What's that?" he said into a live microphone. "We still have three more horses? Shit. But did you see the tits on her?"

Bailey made a mental note to fine Ricketson and later that afternoon issued a new dress policy for all televised barrier draws.

"Excuse me ladies and gentlemen. I apologise," Ricketson said, as McGraw laughed his head off. "I got a little distracted. Let's continue."

The barrier draw concluded without any further incidents.

"Thank you all for coming; we'll see you on Saturday," Richardson said

As the live broadcast ended every photographer rushed over to McGraw and Miss Tiffany and started snapping away at Australia's newest household name.

At *Turf News*, Delaney and the rest of the staff could not stop laughing.

"Have you seen her before?" Swoboda asked Delaney.

"Nope. McGraw must have a closet full of girls like that. Every time I see him, he's with another one."

"He'd be wise to stick with this one," Swoboda said. "The whole country knows who she is now and him too. Along with your horse."

"Maybe it will all die down by Saturday."

"I doubt it. She'll bob up on *The Project* tonight and the morning shows tomorrow. Just watch. And I bet Channel 9 pays her a fortune to be on that new show of theirs, *Shtupp Island*."

"You're doing the yarn on the barrier draw for online or one of the others?" Delaney asked when the laughter died down.

"I was going to do it."

"Well, we can't ignore the star of the show. Mention it, but keep my name out of it, okay?"

"Will do."

The rest of the week was uneventful. All eighteen cup horses passed their veterinary exams on the morning of the big race and were declared fit to run. Punters had been flocking to Too Hard Wrong Spot all week due to Miss Tiffany's show at the barrier draw. He was going to go off at much shorter odds than the double-digit odds of a week earlier.

Conditions for cup day were perfect. Sunny skies, a light breeze and temperatures in the mid-twenties greeted the nearly 40,000 people who poured into the track.

Several leading pundits started talking up Too Hard Wrong Spot's chances when his gear changes became public.

Even Delaney got caught up in the excitement. He made Too Hard Wrong Spot his top choice in a bumper edition of *Turf News* and got a bit of a buzz when he saw several racegoers clutching their copies of the paper and overheard them talking about his horse when he and Michelle got off the train at Caulfield and walked to the main entrance.

As it had for decades, the team from Channel 7 was covering the spring carnival. Many men watching at home turned to 7 instead of Channel 78 just to get a few peeks at the network's racing analyst, Anastacia Sharimani. It was a warm day in Melbourne, so she was wearing a sleeveless light blue dress and matching low heels topped off with a fascinator in her perfectly styled brown hair.

"I love you, Anastacia," a couple of blokes carrying cans of VB yelled as she was giving her pick of the yard. She looked up and flashed that million-dollar smile of hers, never once losing her train of thought. Once her segment finished, she walked over to the mounting yard rail.

"Hey loverboys. Who do you like, besides me?" she asked. The two twenty-somethings, decked out in their finest suits, were so tongue-tied they couldn't get a word out between them.

They weren't the first to lose their power of speech in front of the gorgeous 27-year-old who primarily worked in the UK.

Network cameraman, Jake Kramden, who had dreamed all week of getting the assignment to follow Sharimani around, had been waiting all day to ask her what she was doing after the network's cup coverage.

"I got all of that. The guys in the truck loved it," he told Sharimani, who was nearly as tall as he is.

Kramden liked his chances with the stunning Sharimani. A good-looking bloke in his mid-thirties who spent more time in front of the mirror than his girlfriend, he had his finest hipster apparel on; skinny black jeans, a vest, shirt and loud tie topped off with a splash of cologne endorsed by a Brazilian soccer star all in a bid to get Sharimani's attention.

"Kramden, right?" Sharimani asked.

"Yes."

"What is that shit you are wearing? It smells worse than the manure I just stepped in."

A month later, Kramden was still unable to get an erection.

Thirty minutes before the running of the Caulfield Cup, Channel 7 went to a piece taped earlier in the afternoon on City Winners Syndication and their suddenly live cup chance Too Hard Wrong Spot who was $8 with the bookies and a bit less on the tote.

Big John McGraw was being interviewed by veteran racing man Neal Quick and relating the story on how he came over from the UK with his own personal strapper, his bout with travel sickness, his year away from the races and his superb run in the Herbert Power Stakes the week before.

Pictured in the background was Janice Roselli with Too Hard Wrong Spot, who had just been walked over from McCarron's stable to the Caulfield stalls behind the grandstand.

The camera then swung around to the group of the horse's owners.

"I understand you were the last one to buy into the horse and that was just a couple of weeks ago," Quick said to Gary Delaney.

"Best decision of my life," the journo said. "My partner and I," he said motioning to Michelle who stood next to him, "are having the time of our lives. My first horse and we're in a Caulfield Cup. It's unbelievable."

Twenty minutes later the large Caulfield Cup field turned for home. Mystic City took a two-length lead at the top of the stretch, and after fighting off the challenges of Lake Havasu and Where's My Coffee, looked home with 150 metres to go.

But Too Hard Wrong Spot was rapidly gaining ground on the far outside. Under Smithton's strong urging Too Hard Wrong Spot drew level with fifty metres to go. Charlie Jackson was doing all he could to keep Mystic City's head in front, but Too Hard Wrong Spot gained the upper hand and stuck his neck out on the line to win.

Smithton pumped his fist as he crossed the line. McCarron was momentarily lost for words but not the members of City Winners Syndication who were jumping up and down, yelling and screaming and slapping each other on the backs. Miss Tiffany's breasts came out of her dress during the celebrations and in the excitement Big John McGraw leaned over and kissed them both on national television. Channel 7 was later fined $100,000 for the wardrobe malfunction since it occurred before 8.30pm and impressionable children could have been watching.

Bookmakers immediately installed Too Hard Wrong Spot as the $7 Melbourne Cup favourite even though the five-year-old had just two career wins from six starts.

French mare I Get No Respect flew home to grab fourth place, giving every indication that she would relish the added distance of the Melbourne Cup.

While the connections of Too Hard Wrong Spot were getting their photos taken, being handed the Caulfield Cup and talking to members of the press. Delaney found Swoboda in the chaos and gave him a big bear hug. "This is all thanks to you, Adam. Don't know how I can ever repay you. Thank you."

Swoboda had a few ideas but kept them to himself.

The celebrations continued well into the night. Delaney figured his five percent share of the winner's purse was worth about $60,000.

32

DELANEY GOT A CALL FROM BIG JOHN McGRAW LATE on Sunday morning.

"I'm ringing all the owners, mate. I was at the stables this morning and McCarron told me the horse didn't leave anything in his feed bin and has pulled up fine. He's a go for the Melbourne Cup. We'll have to wait another day and see if he gets a penalty for winning at Caulfield, but it looks as though he won't carry more than 52.5 kg at headquarters."

"Great news, John. It's all happening so fast. It's unbelievable."

"That's the way it is in this business Delaney. You've got to take advantage of the opportunities when they present themselves. You never know what could happen. It might be Too Hard Wrong Spot's only chance at a Melbourne Cup. With the 52.5kg on him he should get the two miles."

"I guess that's my main worry," Delaney said. "Will Smithton be able to make the weight?"

"He should, but if he can't there are plenty of good hoops out there who would kill to be on a Caulfield Cup winner in the big one.

"Turn on the news later mate. There were camera crews down there this morning. Tiffany was more popular than the bloody horse."

Delaney laughed. "You backed a winner there."

"The mileage City Winners Syndication is getting out of this is unbelievable. People are ringing me and Taylor asking if we have more horses for sale. We'll be able to go to the yearling sales on the Gold Coast in January with plenty of money to spend."

"Keep me posted on how our cup horse is going."

"I will. See ya, mate."

Delaney was greeted with a standing ovation when he arrived at the *Turf News* offices on Monday morning.

Lisa the receptionist gave him a kiss on the cheek and there were plenty of pats on the back and handshakes from the reporters.

His in-box was filled with notes of congratulations. Bob Nicholls was especially pleased.

"You can't buy this kind of publicity," he said. Everything I'm reading mentions you and your connection with *Turf News*. It's gold Gary, gold."

"Being on the other side of things is amazing, Bob. Now I know how the owners of all those winners I've interviewed over the years feel."

"You think he's got a chance on the first Tuesday in November?"

"The only query I have is whether or not he can get the two miles. But he is in with a feather. We'll have to see how the foreign horses do. There's the Geelong Cup on Wednesday and the Moonee Valley Gold Cup on Cox Plate Day."

"Wendy and her team are putting together the form guide for the Geelong meet this morning. It's a good card," Nicholls said.

Delaney informed Nicholls that Swoboda and Jodi Clendenon were doing the previews as they spoke. "She's at Werribee checking on a couple of the foreign runners. I'll see if the photos from this morning have been put in the system and then we'll be ready to go."

"Gary, you've been here a month and all I'm hearing from the staff is good things. That you're fair. There's none of the bickering going on the way there was before. And, every edition has been ticked off well before deadline. If we're late going to press it costs us money. Keep it up."

Nicholls clapped his hands once and walked to his office. He left his door open, always a sign he was in a good mood.

Too Hard Wrong Spot was now a certain starter in the Melbourne Cup and after another stirring Cox Plate on Saturday, won by the Irish import I'll Have Another, attention turned to headquarters for the four-day Melbourne Cup Carnival. As the Flemington gardeners were doing their best to have the racecourse's roses in pristine condition for Victorian Derby Day, Johnny Pastrami went to work on his plan to keep Too Hard Wrong Spot out of the cup. He had to stop the horse from running in the race that stops a nation so the French mare he had thousands on had a better chance of saluting.

And he had to move before Derby Day when all Melbourne Cup horses were placed under twenty-four-hour guard at their respective stables.

Any stranger around the stables would arouse suspicion so Pastrami drove over to Caulfield on Thursday morning and parked the car he had stolen earlier in the day a few blocks away from McCarron's stables and walked to Kambrook Road. He put on his sunnies, planted a Los Angeles Dodgers baseball cap on his head and with the beginnings of a scraggly beard from not having shaved all week, waited for Carla Clydesdale to pass by on her bicycle after she finished her morning shift. Pastrami also had a fake sleeve of tattoos covering his left arm and another small tattoo on his neck.

Ten minutes passed before he spotted McCarron's stable worker pedalling slowly towards him. He stood up from the car he was leaning on and stood directly in Clydesdale's path. She came to a sudden stop.

"Hey, what are you doing mate? Get out of the way."

"Carla Clydesdale?" Pastrami calmly asked, putting his hands on the bike's handlebars.

"Yeah."

"I need to talk to you for a moment."

"What do you want and who are you?"

"This will just take a second and then you can go."

With Clydesdale unable to move her bike forwards or back she had no choice but to listen.

Cars whizzed passed them as Pastrami spoke.

"You need to listen and listen carefully. Too Hard Wrong Spot cannot run in the Melbourne Cup."

"Of course, he's running. What are you talking about?"

"You are going to keep him from running by slipping him something on the morning of the race."

"Slip him something? Are you crazy?"

"Carla. How's your little sister Catherine? She missed school today with a cold, didn't she?"

"How do you know that?"

"That's not important. But if you don't do what I ask, she is going to get a lot sicker. Do you understand?"

Carla felt a chill run through her. "You'd hurt an eleven-year-old girl?"

"If I have to, yes."

"What do I have to do?" Carla asked, her voice cracking.

Pastrami pulled a small packet out of his front pants pocket and put it in Carla's right hand. "It's simple. On the morning of the cup, you slip these two pills, both of them, into Too Hard Wrong Spot's feed."

"What will they do to him? They won't kill him, will they?"

"No, no. They're sedatives. He'll sleep like a baby and will have to be scratched from the cup. He'll be up and about come dinner time. The horse will be fine."

"I can't do that."

"You'll have to."

"And if I don't?"

"Well, Pastrami said, leaning in to Clydesdale, now just centimetres from her face, "your sister Catherine will find herself in need of some urgent medical care of her own."

Clydesdale did not say a word.

Pastrami broke the silence.

"You are not to tell anyone about this conversation, understand?"

Clydesdale nodded.

"Do we have a deal?"

"We do."

"Remember, you drop those pills into his feed on cup morning."

"Okay," she said.

"Don't be foolish, Carla. Do what I tell you and everything will be fine."

Pastrami walked several blocks away from the opposite direction Clydesdale was travelling. He looked over his shoulder once and saw Clydesdale walking her bike down Kambrook Road. Pastrami put on a pair of gloves he retrieved from his back pocket, got into the stolen car and drove off. He parked it at Malvern train station and left the keys in the ignition, just the way he had found it.

Carla Clydesdale was shaking as she walked her bicycle home.

She found her younger sister in the lounge room in her pyjamas watching TV.

Carla sat down next to her and gave her a big hug.

"Don't get too close, you don't want to catch my cold," Catherine said, pushing her big sister away.

"You feeling okay?"

"A bit better. Mum says I should be able to go to school tomorrow as long as I don't get the shits again."

"Where on earth did you hear that expression?"

"You said that a few months ago."

"I did?"

"Yup."

Carla gave her younger sister a kiss on the cheek and got up off the couch.

"You did save some toilet paper for the rest of us, didn't you?"

"It was bad, but it wasn't that bad," Catherine said, laughing.

Carla laughed along with her and then went to her room to change out of her work clothes.

She wore her robe to the bathroom, hung it on a hook on the back of the door and looked at herself in the mirror. "What am I going to do?" she asked her.

The warm water of the shower washed away her tears.

Pastrami stuffed the Dodgers baseball cap and the polo shirt he was wearing in a trash can on his way home. He arrived home around noon wearing a dark blue collared shirt he had stashed in the stolen car. He washed the fake tattoos off his arm and neck, shaved and showered.

If Clydesdale did tell anyone about what happened, the law would be looking for a guy with tattoos, a beard, a beige polo shirt and a baseball cap.

"It's all taken care of," Pastrami said when he phoned Tannenbaum later in the day.

"What'd ya do?"

"Let's just say I made someone an offer they couldn't refuse and leave it at that."

"Nobody's going to get hurt? Are they?"

"No one, mate. I don't operate that way, you know that."

"I do. See you at Flemington on Derby Day?"

"You bet. It's the best race meeting of the year. I'm going to spend the next two days doing my homework."

"Find us a couple of winners."

"That I will. I'll ring you on Saturday morning."

Carla was back at McCarron's stables in the afternoon. A little shaken, she went over to Too Hard Wrong Spot's stall.

"How's he doing, Janice?"

"He couldn't be better. We have a real chance on Tuesday."

Carla gave the five-year-old horse a good brush and hugged him.

"I won't do anything to hurt you boy and neither will anyone else," she whispered in his ear. "You go out there on Tuesday and win."

However, Carla was worried about her little sister. Would the stranger with the tattoos follow through on his threat to hurt her if Too Hard Wrong Spot ran in the cup? Should she should tell Janice or Jack McCarron? Call the police? She needed to talk about it with someone and decided to give the newspaperman and part owner who came around the stalls earlier in the day a call. He'd know what to do. She knew his name but could not remember which paper he worked for. So she did what hundreds of millions of people do each and every day, she looked for it on Google.

She took out her phone, punched in the name Gary Delaney, scrolled down and found what she was looking for; *Turf News*. She found a quiet spot where no one would be able to listen in on the call and dialled the *Turf News* office. A young woman answered the phone.

"Could I speak with Gary Delaney please?"

"Sure, I'll connect you. Hold the line."

"Good afternoon, Gary speaking."

There was silence on the other end of the line.

"Hello? Anyone there? C'mon, don't be shy, speak up."

"Mr Delaney?"

"Yes, this is Gary. Who's this?"

Carla was shaking as she spoke. "This is Carla Clydesdale from Jack McCarron's stable."

"Hi Carla, everything all right with our horse?"

"Oh yes, he's fine but I'm worried."

"What's wrong, Carla? Has something happened?"

"A few hours ago, some guy stopped me while I was on my bike going home and told me if Too Hard Wrong Spot ran in the cup he would hurt my sister."

"Hurt your sister? Have you ever seen him before?" Delaney asked.

"No. He was real rough looking, covered in tattoos with a beard. He gave me a packet with two pills in it and told me to put it in Too Hard Wrong Spot's feed on Tuesday morning."

This was a new one for the newspaperman. There had been threats in racing before, heck, someone even took a few shots at the great Phar Lap on the Saturday before the Melbourne Cup in 1930 to keep him from running.

"Carla, there's no reason to be worried. It was probably a punter who has a lot of money bet on someone else and doesn't want our horse to run. He was just trying to scare you."

"Are you sure?"

"I'm sure, Carla. Throw those pills away."

"He said they were sedatives and Too Hard would be unable to race."

"Carla, throw the pills away. Flush them down the toilet. Racing Victoria will have extra security on every horse beginning on Saturday. If this guy approaches you after the cup, and I seriously doubt that will happen, tell him you did not have the security clearance to go near the horse. Only McCarron, Janice and Byers had that level of clearance, okay? Nobody is going to hurt you or your sister. I promise."

"You do?"

"Yes Carla. Try not to worry, okay?"

"Okay."

"Have you told anyone else about this?"

"No. Not anyone. I'm so scared."

"It's okay. You just go about your usual business. Nothing is going to happen to you or your sister. I'd bet every dollar I have on that."

"Thank you for putting my mind at ease, Mr Delaney."

"You're welcome, Carla. I'll see you on Tuesday. All right?"

"Yes. And you know what? I really think the horse can win."

"I do too. We are going to have a great day."

Delaney gave Carla Clydesdale his mobile number just in case anything did happen between now and race day which he figured was a 100-1 shot. He had himself a heck of a story but had no choice but to sit on it. If word ever did get out, the fellow who threatened Carla and her sister would be back, whether Too Hard Wrong Spot won or not.

Delaney leaned back in his chair and tossed a pen onto his desk.

There are a lot of characters in this game. If they can pop up at a Melbourne Cup imagine what goes on at the country tracks.

It was not a thought he wanted to entertain.

Derby Day was a stinker weatherwise. It was cool and overcast and rained intermittently which kept the crowd down to less than 100,000. Johnny Pastrami met Tannenbaum in the betting ring.

The last spot in the Melbourne Cup went to the winner of the Lexus Stakes. It was the third race on the card and Pastrami was keen on the local gelding Cleans the Gut.

It was a 6-1 shot and since the track was downgraded to a soft 5 and Cleans the Gut had no wet track form, Pastrami eased back on his bet and put $1000 each way on the gelding. Tannenbaum had a $250 each way bet on the same animal and when it won by a couple of lengths they celebrated with a good meal and a few cold ones at one of Flemington's better restaurants.

All eyes then turned to the Victoria Derby. With so many live chances and the soft track to deal with, Pastrami was not willing to back anyone to win. He put two grand on Sydney speedster Fortune Smiles to place at

8-1. The horse went straight to the front and held a length lead heading into the stretch. He began to tire with 200 metres left to run and the field caught up to him, but the gallant three-year-old held on to finish third, just a nostril in front of the fourth-placed finisher to give Pastrami and Tannenbaum yet another win.

"We own this carnival," Pastrami crowed as he and Tannenbaum exchanged high fives.

SEVERAL HOURS AFTER CLEANS THE GUT CLAIMED the last spot in the Melbourne Cup field of twenty-four, and in time for the final field and form guide to be included in the Sunday editions of the nation's newspapers, the all-important barrier draw for the $6.2 million race that stops the nation was held in the VRC committee room.

Not wanting a repeat of the scenes with Miss Tiffany at the Caulfield Cup barrier draw, only owners and trainers were allowed into the committee room. A couple of big security men at the door made sure of it, checking the passes of everyone attempting to walk through the front door.

Compere Jordan Ricketson kicked off proceedings at 6.30pm by announcing the entire field to a nation-wide television and radio audience. The connections of each horse in the great race had to stump up close to $50,000 to cover the entry fees, a mere bag of shells to the sheiks who bankrolled the massive world-wide Godolphin operation, but a lot of money for everyone else.

The winner would take home $3.6 million of the $6.2 million purse. The prize money extended down to the tenth-paced finisher whose connections would pocket $125,000.

There were twenty-four miniature Melbourne Cups laid out on a table. Once again head steward Jerry Bailey drew the number and name of a horse at random from a barrel. Its connections stepped onto the stage to pick a cup from the table which had a barrier number printed on the bottom.

Too Hard Wrong Spot was one of the lightweights in the field and was assigned saddle cloth number 20.

After half the field was set, Bailey called out, "Horse number 20, Too Hard Wrong Spot".

Big John McGraw walked up to the stage and heard a few boos from the crowd of owners, trainers and media who were hoping to get another look at Miss Tiffany.

"Sounds like there are a few disappointed people out there," Ricketson told McGraw as he stepped onto the stage. "Where's your better half tonight?"

"She's at one of the members' bars. Not sure how much luck she's gonna bring us from there."

"Did she give you any advice?"

"Yeah, but nothing I can share with you now," McGraw answered to scattered laughter.

The head of City Winners Syndication reached over the table, his large belly straining against his dark suit jacket, and picked the cup to his far left. He turned it over and smiled when he saw the number 12.

"Too Hard Wrong Spot, a $7 chance with the bookmakers, draws barrier number twelve," Ricketson said. "You've got to be pleased with that, John."

"The whole team is. It's just where we want to be."

At a Southbank Restaurant, where they were watching the barrier draw on a TV perched above the bar, Johnny Pastrami and Frankie 'Fingers' Tannenbaum exchanged high fives as one of I Get No Respect's owners turned over a miniature Melbourne Cup, revealing the number 9 on the bottom which drew sustained applause from the committee room crowd.

"It's the perfect barrier. We can either go forward and sit right off the pace or go back and make one long run," Pastrami said.

The horse's jockey, Andre La Plume, had never ridden at Flemington before, but had been on him in the Caufield Cup. His manager had secured a couple of rides for him earlier on the cup day program so he would be able to familiarise himself with the large circuit. La Plume would be arriving in Melbourne on Monday morning after having ridden at the Breeders Cup meeting in California over the weekend.

Pastrami had no doubt about La Plume's ability. He was more worried about jet lag. But those who had ridden in the Breeders' Cup races and then backed up in the cup had never voiced a complaint; few do when they're travelling in business class.

Delaney watched the barrier draw from the office. *Turf News* would be on newsstands the next morning with its biggest edition of the year. The form guide featured a colour insert with a brief review of every start each cup horse had over its career. There were more than twenty lines for some and just five for Too Hard Wrong Spot. Up front there were features from columnist Grote and the rest of the team, and a synopsis of each horse in the great race with bullet points on why each could win and why it couldn't.

Swoboda and Clendenon wrote them and Delaney was interested to see what was written about his horse.

Why he can win: Caulfield Cup winner, training brilliantly, light weight, top trainer and jockey.

Why he can't win: Lightly raced, untested at distance, third run in four weeks.

He still liked the horse's chances even though none of the *Turf News* selectors picked him to win. All the late money was going on I Get No Respect, who was a close third in last year's Prix de l'Arc de Triomphe and had the pedigree of a two-miler. The French mare was sitting at $6.50 which many punters thought was a bargain.

The paper was taking shape nicely. Delaney was proofreading the yarns from that afternoon, including a two-page spread on the Victoria Derby, and placing them on their assigned pages. He wrote the headlines and captions and when Swoboda's Melbourne Cup barrier draw yarn arrived via email, loaded with quotes from connections of the more fancied runners, not even thirty minutes after the draw was concluded, Delaney placed it onto the page which featured a breakout box of the entire field, complete with jockeys, trainers and the latest odds.

Too Hard Wrong Spot hadn't budged from his $9 quote but several of the foreign horses had tightened in the betting following their favourable draws.

Delaney printed the final few pages to run his eye over them and after making several minor changes, signed them off and relayed the information to Wendy Seaver. She was putting the final touches on the form guide. Ten minutes later she brought it over to Delaney. Despite the rush job, he couldn't find a single mistake as he turned each page. He returned the pages to Wendy and gave the okay to send the paper to the printers. With a touch of a few buttons, the Melbourne Cup edition of *Turf News* was on its way to the printers, twenty-two minutes before the 9pm deadline.

Delaney got back to his desk, leaned back in his chair, looked out over the twinkling lights of the city and took a deep breath.

Michelle arrived at Mentone station to pick him up just as Delaney's train pulled in. It was 9.40pm. With so much of Mentone's population over the age of fifty, the streets surrounding the station were practically deserted.

Michelle greeted Delaney with a long kiss. "How'd it all go? You look beat."

"It went surprisingly well. Not one hiccup. I just hope I didn't miss anything."

"I'm sure it will be fine. Don't worry about it."

Delaney had a late dinner—leftover chicken casserole—which tasted even better than it did the night before.

As he was eating Michelle left the dining room table. "Be right back," she said. "I have a surprise for you."

"I do like surprises."

Michelle returned and cleared her throat to get Delaney's attention.

She was wearing a light blue off-the-shoulder dress with heels and had a white jacket flung over her right shoulder. She twirled around, giving Delaney a good view of her long legs and cleavage.

"Wow," Delaney said. "Are you dessert?"

"It's my Melbourne Cup outfit; what do you think?"

"I reckon even if Too Hard Wrong Spot runs last, I'll walk out of Flemington a winner. You look fantastic."

Michelle took Delaney's hand and led him to the bedroom. "It's more fun taking it off than putting it on," she said with a wink.

With the next print edition of *Turf News* not out until Thursday, Delaney had Sunday and Monday off. The kids in the office threw cup updates on the *Turf News* website several times an hour and tweeted until they could tweet no more. All twenty-four horses were fit and passed to run and in a very even field, the connections of at least a dozen horses had a good chance of drinking champagne from the cup on Tuesday night.

Michelle and Delaney were among the thousands in the CBD on Monday for the annual parade down Swanston Street. They were not seen in Melbourne's many live music venues on cup eve, preferring a quiet one at home.

Delaney heard from Pastor Chris in the afternoon. He reported that he and Ally were going to the cup and would try and catch up with him and Michelle in the mounting yard prior to the race.

"Nervous, buddy?"

"A little bit. I reckon that with a bit of luck he can be in the top five."

"Should I bet on him?"

"I'm just going to back him to place. The prize money is ridiculous so even if he runs tenth the syndicate will recoup its entry fees and still make money."

"Imagine making money for running tenth. Too bad nobody's looking out for us punters. It's $75 just to get in the joint tomorrow and you don't even get a seat," Chris bellyached.

"I know mate, it is getting out of hand. If they keep raising the entry prices people will just decide to stay home and watch on the telly. We'll catch you tomorrow."

34

PASTRAMI WOKE UP EARLY ON CUP DAY AND TURNED on the radio waiting to hear the day's scratches from Flemington. Track announcer Glen Kays was on a panel of experts going over the cup field and the rest of the day's card. The weather was perfect with the track rated a soft 5 which would almost certainly be upgraded to a good 4 by the middle of the day. The day's scratches came through at 7am. There were several scratches in some of the earlier races on the card. Pastrami turned up the radio's volume when the announcer got to Race 7. "In Race 7, the Melbourne Cup over 3200 metres, there are no changes."

"Damn," Pastrami said.

He sank back in his chair and gave the situation some thought. 'Maybe the pills the girl put into the horse's feed haven't take effect yet. Or maybe she got cold feet and couldn't go through with it. It's early yet. Let's give it a few more hours and see what happens.'

At eight o'clock, the full field of twenty-four was still intact. It was the same at 9am and 10am.

'I wonder if she went to Jack McCarron and told him or went to the cops. In either case there's no way they could tie me to the plot.'

Pastrami got to Flemington around noon. He checked his phone on the way over for any cup news, but there wasn't any. It seemed all twenty-four horses were going to take their places in the great race.

Ninety percent of those going to Flemington take the train and get there early to get a good spot on the lawn.

With their members' tickets there was no need for Delaney and Michelle to rush. They arrived around noon, well after the first race of the day had been run.

Michelle, who was at her first Melbourne Cup, was blown away by the massive crowd, the colour and characters. Guys were dressed in loud suits, others in jockey silks and a few were decked out in wedding dresses for their Bucks Night celebrations. Women, young and old, were carrying on as if it was VE day. Every spare hand was wrapped around a wine glass or a can.

"I've been to Royal Ascot, the Prix de l'Arc de Triomphe, and the Kentucky Derby and I have never seen anything like this," UK trainer Clive Anderson said on cup day a year ago. "There were over 100,000 people here on Saturday for the Derby, another 100,000 here today. It is just unbelievable. Everywhere you go people want to talk about racing. I'll tell everyone back home that they have got to get down here at least once."

Anderson failed to mention the 75,000 who show up on the Thursday for Oaks Day and the 80,000 who routinely turn out for Stakes Day on the Saturday which closes out the carnival.

City Winners Syndication had a table in the members' area.

"Lunch and drinks are on me," Big John McGraw shouted over the din of the crowd. Of course, the syndicate, of which Delaney was a member, was footing the bill, but there was no need to bring up that minor detail. Miss Tiffany was seated next to Big John and seemed to be wearing a bra, a lacey black one, as a top. She had a jacket on the back of her chair which she would have needed to get past track officials who are very fussy of what is worn in the members' area.

"Is she wearing just a bra?" Delaney whispered to Michelle.

"Seems like it. Go on, enjoy the view," she said, nudging him in the ribs.

McGraw later asked everyone at the table, about twenty-five in all, to "raise a glass to your Melbourne Cup winner Too Hard Wrong Spot."

The whole crew then headed over to the mounting yard to wait for the pre-race festivities.

Delaney and Michelle walked over to the tie-up stalls to have a look at Too Hard Wrong Spot. There were people everywhere, but trainer McCarron made sure they gave his cup horse plenty of space. The last thing he wanted was to see Too Hard Wrong Spot get riled up before he even got to the mounting yard. Janice Roselli was in the stall with him and gave Delaney and Michelle a wave when she spotted them.

"I'm glad it's a cool day otherwise he might be sweating up," McCarron said as he shook Delaney's hand. "He knows something is up. That being said, I believe he's going to run well."

"He's still about $8," Delaney said checking his phone for the latest odds. "Are you going to have a bet on him?"

"No need mate. I get a piece of the pie if he finishes in the top ten and I'd be shocked if he doesn't."

A Channel 7 camera crew then appeared out of nowhere to get a final word from McCarron.

He told them the same thing he told the horse's part owner. "I'd be shocked if he doesn't run in the top ten."

"Should we have a bet on our horse?" Michelle asked Delaney.

"We've got to."

With forty-six minutes remaining until the start of the great race, Delaney stood in line for a few minutes at a TAB window and put $25 each way in Too Hard Wrong Spot. Michelle went the more conservative route, putting $40 to place on the horse who was paying $8.20 and $3.40 on the tote. He was the fourth choice in the race. After word got out on the big bets placed on I Get No Respect, the French mare was a $5 choice the morning of the race and was backed even further into favouritism at $4.80. Cleans the Gut was second choice at $5.20. The German horse Don't Mention the War was a steady $7.50 to win. The $90 that Delaney and Michelle put through the betting window was part of the approximately $150 million wagered on the race.

The French stayer Too Tight Too Loose, named in honour of the great post-impressionist painter Toulouse Lautrec, was getting plenty of late support at the windows, tightening from $21 to $16. Delaney had a feeling that comedians and those who fancied themselves as joke tellers were behind the plunge. The old joke about Toulouse Lautrec and his tailor—the tailor asking the painter how his pants fitted with the words 'Too Tight Toulouse?' had been making the rounds since the horse showed up in Melbourne a month ago.

After the jockeys were separately introduced to the crowd of over 100,000, the twenty-four horses, accompanied by their strappers, and in the case of the overseas horses also by their trainers, made their way to the mounting yard in the order of their saddlecloths.

The coats of all twenty-four horses were shining in the mid-afternoon sunshine. Janice Roselli kept a firm hold on Too Hard Wrong Spot who was sweating just a bit around the flanks. Despite having his earmuffs on, the horse looked a little nervous parading in front of the massive crowd. But several other horses were also sweating, including Don't Mention the War, who reared up twice, and the French stayer Bolt From the Blue.

The runner-up of the television series *The Voice*, Dustin Beaver, sang the national anthem. To be fair the young bloke didn't do a bad job.

"Guess they couldn't get the winner," Delaney quipped to Michelle.

"She must have got a better offer, probably at the opening of a new Smiggle store," Michelle said.

Delaney looked over at the tote board. There were no late-minute betting plunges. It was a wide-open betting race according to the punters.

There was a roar from the crowd when the call for riders up went out.

Dressed in the syndicate's usual red and white colours, jockey Damien Smithton walked over to Roselli and Too Hard Wrong Spot. Jack McCarron gave him a leg up and one last bit of advice. "Stay out of trouble and don't make your move too soon."

Smithton, who was riding in his ninth Melbourne Cup, nodded and got settled.

The horses were parading around the mounting yard when suddenly and without warning, an official photographer, who looked a lot like Frankie "Fingers" Tannenbaum, tripped and fell over his tripod. One of his cameras flew out of his hands and landed at the feet of Too Hard Wrong Spot. The lightly-raced horse reared up and tossed Smithton onto the grass. Bolt From the Blue, who was parading behind him also reared up and tossed his rider.

Both jockeys were okay and the strappers of the two spooked horses were able to calm both down. Smithton and Guy Lapperiere were not allowed back on their mounts until Dr Hugo Z. Hackenbush, one of the track veterinarians, examined both horses. They were both passed fit to run.

Pastrami, who was looking through his binoculars from his reserved seat in the Hill Stand, leapt to his feet when Too Hard Wrong Spot tossed Smithton. "Scratch the fucking horse, scratch him," he said as the vet gave him the once over. "Shit," he barked when Smithton remounted.

Carrying his gear, Tannenbaum left the mounting yard in a hurry. He deposited the two cameras he bought dirt cheap at a pawn shop earlier in the week in the nearest bin, ripped his official vest off and placed it under his shirt. He left the tripod in the press room next to two others and scooted to the Hill Stand where Pastrami was seated.

"I tried," Tannenbaum said.

"You nearly pulled it off, but it looks like we'll have to win this outright," Pastrami softly told his mate.

"Ladies and gentlemen," track announcer Glen Kays said to the throng of 105,000. "Both Too Hard Wrong Spot and Bolt From the Blue have been examined by the track vet and will run in the Melbourne Cup."

The crowd, which by this point had consumed over 80,000 glasses of champagne and tens of thousands of cans, roared.

"She can win. I'm confident," Tannenbaum said. "I'm not the only one who thinks so. The mare is going to go off as favourite."

The field of twenty-four was steered to the safety of the track and settled down by their jockeys and handlers. As connections calmed themselves, the horses were warmed up and finally made their way to the starting gate which stood at the halfway point of the straight six chute at the top of the stretch. The start was three minutes away.

Behind the gate, Smithton jumped off his mount and carefully looked down at his horse's right front hoof. "Shit," he said. "He's thrown a bloody shoe."

Smithton motioned to one of the barrier attendants and he immediately came over with the vet and a track official.

"We'll need the farrier," Dr. Hackenbush said. "It's just routine."

On the massive screen in the infield near the finish line the crowd saw Smithton dismount from Too Hard Wrong Spot.

Big John McGraw raised his binoculars and pointed them towards the starting gate some 800m away.

"Shit," he yelled.

"What is it?" Ron Taylor asked.

"It looks like Too Hard Wrong Spot has thrown a shoe."

Track announcer Glen Kays confirmed his suspicions.

"Ladies and gentlemen, horse number 20, Too Hard Wrong Spot has thrown a shoe on the way to the barriers and is being reshod."

All eyes were on veteran farrier Herman Namath as he got to work on Too Hard Wrong Spot.

"What a sensation," Channel 7 head commentator Bruce McGinley said. "First the incident in the mounting yard and now this. But we'll be underway shortly," he assured the three million plus viewers tuning in.

The sweat was pouring off Namath as he put a new shoe on Too Hard Wrong Spot with a Channel 7 camera trained on him. He hammered it into place and filed it down. The job took less than three minutes. He took his bag and tools and walked off the course with an arm raised to the applause of the crowd.

As the other horses started being loaded into the starting gate, Too Hard Wrong Spot was taken by a barrier attendant and walked around as Dr Hackenbush looked him over. He gave the thumbs up sign to the starter.

"Too Hard Wrong Spot has been cleared to run," Kays announced. "He'll be one of the last to load."

Eighteen horses were in the gate and despite the delay and goings-on, they all were on their best behaviour. Bolt From the Blue was led into his spot in the gate leaving just one horse—Too Hard Wrong Spot—to load.

However, Too Hard Wrong Spot, with Smithton back aboard, would not budge when his reins were taken by a barrier attendant.

"C'mon boy," Smithton said to his mount, giving him a tap in the sides with his boots.

The horse stood his ground. Pastrami rose from his seat, his binoculars trained on Too Hard Wrong Spot.

The attendants again tried to lead him into the gate, but Too Hard Wrong Spot baulked.

Smithton again dismounted and watched as the attendants joined arms behind Too Hard Wrong Spot and tried to move all 550 kilograms of him into the gate. Nothing.

"Son of a bitch!" McGraw yelled as he peered through his binoculars. "He won't go in the gate."

With the rest of the field getting fidgety in the starting gate, the attendants were down to their last shot. They put a blindfold over Too Hard Wrong Spot and tried once again to get him to move but the horse stood his ground.

Smithton climbed back aboard Too Hard Wrong Spot, stroked the horse's neck and tried to get him to budge but he was seemingly nailed to the spot where he was standing, five metres behind the starting gate.

Steward Vic Stemkowski consulted with Dr Hackenbush and gave the order for the horse to be scratched.

Perched above the stands, a phone rang next to Glen Kays. "Hello, broadcast. Yes, yes. He's out."

A few seconds passed. "Ladies and gentlemen, we have a late scratching in the Melbourne Cup. On vet's advice, take out horse number 20 Too Hard Wrong Spot. All money wagered on horse number 20 will be refunded."

The crowd let out an audible groan. McGraw threw his binoculars to the ground in disgust. Delaney was numb.

"What's happening?" Michelle asked.

"He's not running. He wouldn't go into the bloody gate."

Pastrami jumped out of his seat and pumped the air with his fist. "Can you believe this? Can you fucking believe this?" he shouted.

Carla Clydesdale was a bundle of nerves after throwing the two pills given to by her by the man with the tattoos into the garbage earlier in the morning. She hadn't been able to eat the last three days and had shed more tears than Hillary Clinton on election night. She was on her guard at the tie-up stalls where she was looking after one of McCarron's horses, Brown Sugar, a beautifully bred colt running in the race after the cup.

Clydesdale was expecting a visit from the creep who accosted her five days ago and was thankful that Don Byers, another one of McCarron's strappers, was nearby. He was bigger than the guy with the tatts and would be able to hold his own if things got out of hand.

She broke down and cried when she heard the announcement of Too Hard Wrong Spot's scratching over the PA system. "He's not running, he's not running. Catherine is going to be okay, Catherine is going to be okay," she wailed.

Byers came over from the adjacent stall, put his arm around her and consoled her. "It's not the end of the world," he said.

"No, it isn't," she said as a smile slowly came over her face.

Smithton took the saddle off Too Hard Wrong Spot as one of the clerks of the course came over to lead the horse out of harm's way. With his head not facing the starting gate, Too Hard Wrong Spot was more than happy to walk down the chute where the 1200, 1100 and 1000m races started from.

As soon as Too Hard Wrong Spot was safely positioned well away from the starting gate, the red light on top of the gate was turned on.

"And they're racing in the Melbourne Cup," Kays announced.

Three minutes and twenty-six seconds later, under a perfect ride by the wide awake La Plume, I Get No Respect found clear running room at the 300m mark and stormed out of a pack of horses to win the Melbourne Cup by two widening lengths. Bolter Fashionably Late was second with longshot Napping On the Job third. The trifecta paid nearly $2500.

Pastrami was numb. He had gotten it right and won the biggest bet of his life, pocketing well over $780,000. The TAB gave him a cheque for $700,000 two days later. He took the other $80,000 in cash. Tannenbaum also had more money than he knew what to do with. He owed it all to the man he called "the best handicapper in Melbourne".

Delaney and Michelle got refunds on their bets and headed for the tie-up stalls to check on Too Hard Wrong Spot. Delaney's phone rang. It was Pastor Chris.

"What the hell happened out there?"

"We're trying to make some sense of it now. I'll ring you later."

At the tie-up rails, Jack McCarron and Janice Roselli were going over Too Hard Wrong Spot from head to tail trying to figure out what went wrong some thirty minutes earlier.

"He looks okay to me. Maybe getting reshod spooked him. I'm not sure," McCarron said.

Roselli carefully looked at the horse's right front foot. There was nothing wrong with it, but she would have the stable's farrier have a look in the morning just to make sure.

McCarron looked up as he saw Delaney and Michelle approach the stall.

"How's the horse doing, Jack?" Delaney asked.

"He looks fine. We're not sure what happened. He might have got a fright from being reshod. Only he knows for sure and he isn't saying a word," McCarron said as he gave the horse a pat on the neck.

"Have you ever seen anything like this happen before?"

"Never, and I've been in this game for thirty years. But that's racing. Two weeks ago we were on top of the world. At least we get the entry fees back."

Carla Clydesdale, strapping McCarron's horse in Race 8, Satisfaction, walked the colt out from his tie-up stall three down from Too Hard Wrong Spot's. She caught Delaney's eye and waved, giving him the thumbs up sign.

Delaney returned the gesture.

Eleven days later Too Hard Wrong Spot moved into the starting gate at Sandown in Melbourne's south east as quickly as a teenager being called in for dinner for the $300,000 Zipping Classic over 2400m. He broke with the field of eleven and with his customary late rush took out the Group 2 race by a length. He paid $4.20 on the tote as the second choice in the race.

The $160,000 winner's share of the purse which went to City Winners Syndication hardly compared with the $3.6 million which went to the connections of Melbourne Cup winner I Get No Respect but was more than most race horses bank in a year. Delaney's share of the winnings from the Zipping Classic was approximately $7,500.

After the race McCarron announced that the horse would be spelled and pointed to the Autumn Carnival in Sydney.

They'd have another go at the Melbourne Cup in a year's time.

35

AFTER THE FIFTY-HOUR WEEKS OF THE SPRING RACING carnival and the ups and downs with Too Hard Wrong Spot, Gary Delaney needed a holiday. However, since he had just started at *Turf News*, he wasn't entitled to one until the first of February.

That wasn't all bad since that marked the end of school holidays and with it the end of the crowds and higher prices.

Since Melbourne can experience its hottest days in February, Delaney and his better half decided to head to the cooler climes of Tasmania.

They booked two return seats on the Spirit of Tasmania along with their car which set them back nearly $800.

They set sail on a Monday morning from Station Street pier. The ship was scheduled to leave for Devonport at 9am. Last call for boarding was at 8.15 and with rain forecast for the morning and a forty-five-minute drive ahead of them, Delaney and Michelle decided to leave their Mentone breadbox no later than 6.30am.

They set two alarms, the second one for five minutes after the first, to make sure they got out of bed. It was still dark when they woke. At the Swoboda household, Sugar the cat was asleep; a dead mouse by her side.

The travellers finished packing their bags, had a quick breakfast and in pouring rain made their way down Beach Road which was surprisingly busy. They were surrounded by utes carrying their cargo of tradies to their 7am jobs. One ute had several planks of wood precariously hanging from it. A bit of frayed rope held them in place. One bump would be enough to dislodge the planks and send them careening into oncoming traffic. Delaney weaved his way through traffic, the car's wipers working furiously to clear the windscreen of the morning deluge and managed to pass the offending vehicle. Traffic increased when they reached St Kilda.

Stopped at a red light, the travellers were surprised to see graffiti covering nearly the entire back wall of Luna Park.

"What is happening to this city?" they wondered aloud.

As the car's clock ticked passed 7am, Ross and John returned to the airwaves of *3AW* following the news and another commercial for *The Drain Man*. Delaney and Michelle still had time on their side. As they got closer to Station St Pier, they got their first glimpse of Spirit of Tasmania 2, its distinctive red and white markings cutting through the early morning darkness.

The travellers got in a massive line and inched forward. "It's a good thing we left when we did," Michelle said.

Men and women dressed in bright orange raingear waving Star Wars-like light sabres directed the cars, camper vans, motor homes and motorcycles to their correct lanes for security checks. Occupants were then asked to show their tickets, photo IDs and after getting the all clear, drove their vehicles through a maze of turns before finally reaching the ramp which led them onto the ship itself.

"I wonder if we'll get a piece of cheese for making it through," Delaney cracked.

The travellers were directed to their parking spot by another light sabre-carrying worker who was lucky enough to be out of the rain. They got what they needed from the car for the nine-hour-plus voyage—book, laptop, the morning paper, snacks—and made their way from deck 6 to deck 7, the first of three passenger decks.

Delaney and Michelle found themselves a couple of seats—there was no need to book a cabin for a daytime crossing—and made themselves comfortable. Delaney checked his watch. It was 8.15am. Forty-five minutes till they got on their way and two hours and fifteen minutes till the start of Super Bowl L1 between the New England Patriots and Atlanta Falcons. Much to Delaney's delight the ship had several televisions and they were tuned to Channel 7 which was broadcasting the game. He took one look at Kochie and the rest of the *Sunrise* crew, nearly threw up, and vowed to return to the television not a minute before the 10.30 kick-off.

Delaney was not that big of a gridiron fan due to its constant stopping and starting, endless penalties, official reviews and the obnoxious showboating of the players themselves, who after knocking players out with vicious tackles and often illegal hits, stood over and taunted them. The most destructive hits and disgusting taunts were rewarded with places in ESPN's SportsCenter package of highlights. The NFL had always used Roman numerals for its showpiece game, but Super Bowl LI did not have the same pizzazz as Super Bowl XLVIII.

Delaney had put $25 on the favoured Patriots to cover the three-point spread and also parlayed it with the time needed to complete the *Star Spangled Banner*, the national anthem of the US. He picked over three minutes and forty-five seconds and was rewarded when the trio *Crap Fondue* went over the four-minute mark.

But Delaney's mood soured when the Falcons burst out to a 21-3 lead at halftime. Pretty boy New England quarterback Tom Brady, he of the supermodel wife and $100 million-dollar contract, was having an awful afternoon. He had won four previous Super Bowls with the Patriots and win number five was looking extremely unlikely,

The much-hyped halftime entertainment with pop star Sadie Goo Goo Gai Pan was in Delaney's humble opinion better with the sound off. Lowered from the ceiling of *KFC-PizzaHut-Doritos-Pepsi Max Stadium* clad in a one-piece outfit available at an S & M store near you, she "sang" a couple of tunes while a troop of male and female dancers gyrated behind her.

It was then that Delaney took notice of an older fellow strolling over to the TV. The old-timer, who was wearing three sweaters, a hat and gloves to ward off the frigid temperature inside the Spirit, was transfixed to the screen and had the same look on his face that the audience had at the beginning of the number *Springtime For Hitler* in the film *The Producers*. For a man brought up on the music of Bing Crosby and Perry Como and the words of Banjo Patterson, he had a look of shock, disbelief and astonishment on his face, which was turning blue from the cold.

About an hour after they had left Melbourne, Delaney, who was bundled up himself, saw three crew members walk by.

"Excuse me," he said. "It's quite cold in here. Would it be possible to turn down the air conditioning?"

"Sir," the tallest of the three said, "the air conditioning is set at twenty-two degrees. Nobody else has complained."

"Is that twenty-two degrees Fahrenheit? Look around. Everyone is freezing."

"May I suggest moving further away from the door?"

"That's not going to help. It's warmer outside than inside. Just turn it down a bit please."

The three crewmen turned and walked off.

"You know, we're living in a society," Delaney yelled, channelling George Constanza.

The old fellow slowly shuffled off when the Falcons made it a 28-3 game in the third quarter.

"The Patriots are not going to come back from here," he said to no one in particular. "They're finished."

Another geriatric, sitting under the screen with his eyes closed, concurred with just one word. "Gone."

Delaney was so disgusted with the 25-point deficit that he gave up and went with Michelle to get some lunch. Michelle had been keeping herself occupied with a work by Pulitzer Prize winning author Richard Ford.

After a surprisingly good feed, and it should have been at $24.50 a pop, Delaney returned to the game while Michelle returned to her book.

Lo and behold, the Patriots had rallied and were just a touchdown and two-point conversion from forcing the first overtime game in Super Bowl history.

"Never count out Mr. Brady," Delaney said to no one in particular. As the Patriots drove closer to the Atlanta goal line, the crowd around the TV increased. Even if they did not fully understand the game, people realised that something special was taking place.

The Patriots scored and then tacked on the two-point conversion to force overtime.

The fellow asleep beneath the screen had missed one of the greatest comebacks in sports history. Delaney pumped his fist when the Patriots won the coin toss and let loose with a loud "Yes!" when they scored the game-winning touchdown moments later. His winnings covered the cost of lunch.

Delaney looked at his watch as the crowd dispersed. Nearly four hours remained until the ship arrived in Devonport. He told Michelle about the miraculous victory and his windfall which was greeted with total indifference. She was lost in the book. Delaney knew how good it was since he had recommended it to her.

Delaney took a seat in his comfortable chair, closed his eyes and within a few minutes was asleep, a victim of the 5.15am alarm.

Now two-thirds into Ford's epic. Michelle roused Delaney just as the ship entered Devonport harbour. The sun was shining and there were kids fishing from the rocks on the eastern side of the Mersey River.

"We're here," she said.

"How long have I been asleep?"

"About three and a half hours."

Delaney could not remember the last time he had slept for three and a half hours in the afternoon or gone that long without needing to urinate. Another milestone recorded.

Dispose or declare on disembarking, read a large sign that the occupants of the nearly 500 or so vehicles inching their way to the terminal exit could not miss.

Delaney had a royal gala apple from Melbourne safely tucked away in Michelle's handbag. He had been saving it for an afternoon snack, but his unplanned nap had thrown a monkey wrench into the plan.

Tasmania had strict biosecurity regulations about what can be brought into the state and judging by the sniffer dogs and patrols up ahead, was serious about it.

Delaney got the offending apple out of Michelle's handbag and handed it over to an officer when they reached the exit. They were not going to begin their eight-day stay in Tasmania as criminals like those who arrived 200 years earlier. The female officer chucked the offending piece of fruit into a large yellow bin and gave them the all clear to proceed.

After securing the last deluxe cabin at the local caravan park, Delaney and Michelle went out for dinner and supplies—in that order. On the short drive from the ship to the caravan park, which was always their preferred mode of accommodation due to the kitchen facilities and front porch, the two Tasmanian newcomers spotted a large road-side sign outside a restaurant spruiking $15 chicken parmas.

Not being one to pass up a bargain, Delaney convinced Michelle they should go there.

It was 7.45pm when they walked into the establishment. The place was packed and there was still a line of people waiting to order dinner. A very good sign they thought.

There seemed to be just one table available. It was nudged up against the front window overlooking the road. They took a seat and were looking over the menu when a young member of the restaurant staff approached.

"Excuse me, sir. This table is reserved. You can't sit here."

Delaney and Michelle had failed to spot a reserved sign on the table number. It read, "Reserved 7pm."

Delaney looked at his watch. It was 7.47pm.

"The table was reserved for 7pm," Delaney said. "That was forty-seven minutes ago. I don't think the party is going to show."

"Nevertheless sir, you are going to have to find another table."

"Okay then, find one for us."

The staffer led them to table 36 which had been recently vacated. The only problem was that it was adjacent to a kids' playground. Bringing the kiddies along was apparently one of the ways pokie venues got new customers. Nothing better than getting the sounds of a pokie machine into a two-year-old's still developing mind. One of those future customers, who was about fifteen years shy of gaming age, was at this point smearing his ice-cream sundae over a young girl's white dress. Instead of screaming, the girl picked at the ice-cream, nuts and syrup and placed them in her mouth. She appeared to ask the offender if he had any more.

Too late to find another venue, Delaney and Michelle sat down, had a look at the menu and got up to place their order. Delaney ordered the meals, Michelle got the drinks. Delaney ordered the $15 parma for himself and the pan-fried Atlantic Salmon with garlic mash and vegetables for Michelle.

Delaney's beer was served in a massive schooner. Michelle's wine glass was overflowing.

Fifteen minutes later dinner arrived. The pan-fried Atlantic Salmon, mash and vegetables filled an entire dinner plate.

Delaney's parma was a bit on the small side. Okay, it wasn't small, it was virtually non-existent and so overcooked that the cheese covering it had curled up and died.

"What is this, a $15 joke? I'd rather have the beer served in a shot glass and a decent-sized parma."

Three bites later the parma and small batch of chips was gone. Michelle, meanwhile, was savouring every bite of her massive perfectly-cooked meal.

When Michelle had finished, an older staff member, who seemed to be one of those in charge, came to their table to clear the dishes.

"How did you like your meal?" he asked Delaney.

Since he was asked, Delaney told him.

"To be honest, it was a little on the small side. I know it was only $15 but c'mon. Did I get the last one? the runt of the litter?"

"I assure you sir you did not," he said, removing the dishes.

"How about giving me another one on the house so I can feel like I've had something to eat?"

"I'm afraid we cannot do that sir."

Delaney looked the fellow in the eye. "Sure you can."

The fellow didn't say a word and walked off with the dirty dishes.

"C'mon hun, let's get out of here," Delaney told his better half.

The veteran newspaperman walked to the door and was followed by Michelle, who grabbed a toothpick from a jar on the cashier's counter and removed a piece of salmon which had been lodged in her upper left molar.

After more than a week of Tasmanian sightseeing, which included stops in the high country of Scottsdale, Cradle Mountain, the small seaside village of St Helen's and the Museum of Old and New Art (MONA) in Hobart, it was time for Delaney and his better half to drive back to Devonport and rendezvous with the Spirit of Tasmania for their return trip home. They were armed with sweaters and scarves for the cold journey back.

Before leaving Hobart, the travellers stopped at a busy Caltex station to fill up the near empty Nissan's fuel tank for the three-and-a-half-hour drive. Michelle was driving and pulled up at one of the bowsers.

Delaney got out of the car and pumped $62.45 worth of fuel into the 2016 white Nissan.

He walked inside to pay and did not see Michelle move the car away from the bowsers so that the car behind her could exit.

Delaney bought a bottle of water, paid for it all by card, nodded to a large security guard and took his receipt.

He walked through the doors toward the bowsers, putting his bank card back in his wallet and the receipt in his front pocket. His head was down as he walked to where he left Michelle.

He opened the front passenger door of the white vehicle, sat down and was greeted by the loud scream of a middle-aged blonde woman, who was in the driver's seat. It was not Michelle.

"I'm sorry, I've got into the wrong car," he said.

"I'm being carjacked," she screamed at the top of her lungs. "Somebody, help me. Help, help."

"No. no. No carjacking. I thought this was my car."

The woman's loud screams carried from the car's open windows straight to the ears of Larry Plunkett, the store security guard.

Plunkett, who spent a large portion of his day helping himself to the petrol station's display of candy bars, sprang into action from his near sugar-induced coma. He adjusted his cap and pushed his 150kg frame through the doors and into the warm outside air.

He saw a man in the passenger seat of a white Ford and a screaming woman behind the wheel.

"Help me. He's going to rape me," she screamed.

"Rape you? What are you, nuts?" Delaney opened the passenger door and got out of the vehicle only to run straight into Plunkett, who was armed with a taser in his right hand and a Mars bar in his left.

"There's been a misunderstanding," Delaney said. "I got into the wrong car. My wife is in the car ahead, really."

Plunkett quickly sized up the situation. His training consisted of a three-hour class that he slept through and endless hours of Channel 7's *Highway Patrol*.

"Get down on the ground sir," Plunkett ordered.

"It's all a misunderstanding," Delaney argued.

Plunkett pointed his taser at Delaney. "Sir, for the last time get down on the ground and spread your arms and legs."

Delaney stayed upright. "Let me explain, officer," he said, moving closer to Plunkett.

Feeling threatened, Plunkett fired his taser straight into Delaney's belly. The darts struck the journalist and delivered 1200 volts to his midsection. He immediately crumpled to the dark pavement, his arms and legs flailing like one of those giant inflatable men you see anchored outside a car dealership.

Michelle, who was checking her phone to see if impeachment proceedings had been brought against US President Donald Trump, saw the commotion in her rear-view mirror and ran over to her better half who was sprawled on the pavement.

"Stay where you are ma'am," Plunkett said. "This man's in custody."

"In custody? For what?"

"Attempted rape and carjacking."

"Rape? Of who? Are you out of your bloody mind?" she yelled.

"The suspect attempted to rape the woman driving this car," Plunkett said, pointing to a white Ford.

Michelle looked at the woman. She was on the other side of fifty, overweight with messy hair and was wearing an oversized T-shirt and a pair or trakkie daks.

Michelle laughed. "Gary has better taste than that. He wouldn't go near a woman like that, let alone try to rape her."

"Hey, what's that supposed to mean?" the woman accusing Delaney of rape said as she got out of her car.

"That's enough from everybody," Plunkett yelled, waving his taser to show that he was in charge.

The sound of police sirens in the distance were getting closer.

Delaney raised his head. "Can I have some water please?" he asked no one in particular.

Plunkett picked up an unopened bottle of water from the pavement and examined it.

"Did you pay for this?" he asked Delaney.

"Yes."

"I don't think you did. We'll add theft to the list. Theft, attempted rape and attempted carjacking. You're in a shitload of trouble mister."

Delaney shook his head in disbelief.

"Sometimes, things happen," he said slowly. "And they always seem to happen to me."

36

NINE MONTHS LATER

With their jobs secure, Delaney and Michelle had moved into a larger
unit, with an actual backyard, closer to the city. After their trip to Tassie,
where they barely left each other's side, Michelle had gotten over any
doubts she had of their relationship. She was in it for the long haul.
Unbeknownst to Michelle, Delaney was pricing engagement rings to
make their relationship official.

As the spring carnival moved to Flemington for the four-day cup
carnival, Too Hard Wrong Spot was an outright favourite to win the
Melbourne Cup after claiming the Underwood Stakes and running
third in a roughly run Caulfield Cup.

For the first time in the cup's 158-year history, the winner of the
previous year's Prix de l'Arc de Triomphe had made the trip down under.
Scissors, a five-year-old mare trained by Reggie Gaspar, was accompanied
to Melbourne by his assistant, Danielle Frisella, who just a few months
earlier had received her trainer's licence. The plan was for Scissors to go
straight to the cup without a lead-up race, a tactic which had worked in
the past for other European horses.

Adam Swoboda and his wife Patricia became parents. Patricia
Swoboda was so taken with her new daughter that she forgot all about
her cat. With Patricia's blessing, Adam put an ad on Gumtree for a
lovable, adorable and FREE two-year-old cat. Two days later a young
mum and her six-year-old daughter showed up at their home to have
a look at Sugar. It was a case of love at first sight. Adam collected the
cat's things and carried them to June Gerrard's car. "We didn't want
a kitten. They're too much trouble," June Gerrard said. Daughter

Hailey cradled Sugar in her arms as they drove off. As soon as the car carrying Sugar was out of sight, Adam Swoboda started removing the cat door.

Also becoming parents were Big John McGraw and Tiffany Larue. McGraw had to be revived by paramedics when Tiffany told him over breakfast one summer morning that she was pregnant with twins. "And I ain't getting no abortion. I'm keeping them," Tiffany told him when he came to. McGraw cried for the next 48 hours. "Whoever heard of a fuckin' condom breaking? It's a 1000-1 shot," he told City Winners Syndication partner Ronnie Taylor.

Pastor Chris moved in with Allison Roberts just eight weeks after they had met. Eight weeks later she asked him to move out. "I'm with little kids eight hours a day, five days a week," she told him for the tenth time. "If you want a child, I suggest you have one with someone else."

Heartbroken, Chris moved into his brother's house. A year later he was still there. "I'll be okay mate," he told Delaney. "The job is going well and the footy is a good distraction. I just need a little more time before I jump back into the game."

Despite having more money than they knew what to do with, Johnny Pastrami and Frankie "Fingers" Tannenbaum continued to go to the races on Saturday afternoons and the occasional Friday night meet at Moonee Valley. Frankie's pick pocketing days were over as were Pastrami's real estate scams. They had lunch—or dinner—a few beers and threw a few hundred dollars each at the bookies. They rarely, if ever, lost.

Pastrami spent his winters in Noosa where plenty of cashed up women from Melbourne and Sydney were eager to spend an afternoon with a handsome 38-year-old man instead of their older, inattentive, impotent husbands. "Please, you don't have to pay me," he told several women who left him, on average, $300 a visit. He reluctantly took the cash, calling it his "fuck you" money.

"Fingers" also sought warmer climes during the winter. He rented an 18-foot yacht in Airlie Beach and cruised the Whitsunday Islands. A man with a yacht, even a rented one, is never at a loss for female companionship. The following winter he bought a small beach house on Airlie Beach. The real estate agent who sold it to him, a small-town country gal named Jacquie Sutton, moved in with him. In October, he and Jacquie flew to Melbourne for the spring carnival. "Fingers" had done his homework and backed several winners at long odds which easily paid for their flights, accommodation, meals and Jacquie's shopping trips.

Over dinner one night at Pastrami's apartment, with Sutton and one of Pastrami's Melbourne lovelies in attendance, Pastrami presented "Fingers" with a crown, robe and sceptre, and proclaimed his mate 'King of the Spring Carnival'. Pastrami opened an obscenely-priced bottle of champagne and led the toasts. "Long Live the King," he shouted. Ten hours later the King and his Queen woke up with the Kosciuszko of hangovers. He was wearing the robe and she, just the crown.

Deposed Mongolian President Batbayar Ganbaatar celebrated his first year in Costa Rica by taking a bath in calamine lotion. Every mosquito in the Central American country had bitten him at least once in the past 12 months. "Just put me in a fucking bubble for goodness sake. I can't take any more of the itching and scratching," he begged his wife Tuli.

"Oh, did you say something dear?" Tuli said on her way out.

"Are you going to the market?" Ganbaatar calmly asked.

"I could be."

"Do me a favour please. Pick me up another case of calamine lotion at the chemist and half a dozen boxes of Claratyne."

"And what's in it for me."

"Anything you want, name it."

"Well, for starters, how about you stop bonking our housekeeper? Even the kids know."

"They do?"

"Yes."

Ganbaatar pictured the housekeeper in her nurse's outfit checking his pecker for mosquito bites.

Damn, I'm going to miss that, he thought.

"Okay, no more. I promise."

"That's one promise you better keep Batbayar. I've done a little research on Costa Rican law over the past few weeks. Since we are citizens, I get half of everything you have if we divorce. And I do mean everything. Understand?"

"Shit, for once, she's got me by the balls," Ganbaatar said to himself.

"I understand Tuli."

"Now don't fall asleep in the tub and drown. That would be a real tragedy, wouldn't it?"

As Tuli walked out of the main bathroom, Ganbaatar heard the click of her heels on the floorboards and then the front door slam shut.

"Fuck. She's serious this time. Starting tonight, I'm going to have to sleep with one eye open," the deposed president said.

Acknowledgements

Special thanks to Kerry Russell, a constant inspiration and outstanding editor; my wife, who wishes to remain anonymous; mates Simon McEvoy, Brad Beitzel, David Turner, Chris Tatman, Rebecca David and Professor Quincy Adams Wagstaff; consultant Sally Odgers; Forty South Publishing's Lucinda Sharp and Kent Whitmore; Allan Jamieson of the Fellowship of Australian Writers Tasmania (NW); Parkdale (Vic) Library, where much of *Too Hard Wrong Spot* was written, and to my mum, dad and brother, Alan, who would have enjoyed the read and the references to the 1969-1973 NY Mets, Knicks and Jets (characters' names).